Three-times Golden He[...] learned to pack her suit[...] learned to read. Born to [...] lived in the United States, Puerto Rico, Portugal and Brazil. In addition to travelling, Tina loves to cuddle with her pug, Alex, spend time with her family, and hit the trails on her horse. Learn more about Tina from her website, or 'friend' her on Facebook.

Marion Lennox has written over one hundred romance novels and is published in over one hundred countries and thirty languages. Her international awards include the prestigious RITA® award (twice!) and the *RT Book Reviews* Career Achievement Award for 'a body of work which makes us laugh and teaches us about love'. Marion adores her family, her kayak, her dog, and lying on the beach with a book someone else has written. Heaven!

Also by Tina Beckett

The Surgeon She Could Never Forget
Resisting the Brooding Heart Surgeon
A Daddy for the Midwife's Twins?

California Nurses miniseries

The Nurse's One-Night Baby

Also by Marion Lennox

Dr Finlay's Courageous Bride
Healed by Their Dolphin Island Baby
Baby Shock for the Millionaire Doc

Paramedics and Pups miniseries

Her Off-Limits Single Dad

Discover more at millsandboon.co.uk.

TEMPTING THE OFF-LIMITS NURSE

TINA BECKETT

THE DOCTOR'S BILLION-DOLLAR BRIDE

MARION LENNOX

MILLS & BOON

First published in Great Britain 2024
by Mills & Boon, an imprint of HarperCollins*Publishers* Ltd,
1 London Bridge Street, London, SE1 9GF

www.harpercollins.co.uk

HarperCollins*Publishers* Macken House, 39/40 Mayor Street Upper,
Dublin 1, D01 C9W8, Ireland

Tempting the Off-Limits Nurse © 2024 Tina Beckett

The Doctor's Billion-Dollar Bride © 2024 Marion Lennox

ISBN: 978-0-263-32155-5

04/24

This book contains FSC™ certified paper
and other controlled sources to ensure responsible forest management.

For more information visit www.harpercollins.co.uk/green.

Printed and Bound in the UK using 100% Renewable Electricity
at CPI Group (UK) Ltd, Croydon, CR0 4YY

TEMPTING THE
OFF-LIMITS NURSE

TINA BECKETT

MILLS & BOON

To my family

PROLOGUE

SHE SHUFFLED BACKWARD, trying to coax her baby brother, who was almost ready to start walking, to come to her. All eyes were on whether or not he would succeed.

He burbled in laughter as one foot went forward, and he tottered for a second but remained on his feet.

"Keep going, Elia! He's doing it."

Buoyed by her mom's words, she took two more steps back, then three, as her brother continued to lurch toward her, big pauses between each step. She motioned to him. *"Venha aqui, Tomás!"*

He took another step. *Yes!*

Something caught at her foot, and she found herself staggering backward. She tried to catch herself but failed. She fell, still laughing in glee at her brother's accomplishment and that she was the one who'd succeeded in helping him where others had failed: to take his first steps.

She landed with a jolt that knocked the wind from her. An instant went by, and what had been shrieks of joy morphed into screams of agony as pain seared up one of her legs and her back.

Hands snatched her up and away from the heat, but the horrible stinging sensation continued and a weird scent filled the air. Vaguely she could hear her mother yelling for her father as she rocked Elia back and forth in her arms.

Her mind was numb, but she felt more hands grab her, hauling her away from her mom and racing away with her. A few seconds later, she was plunged into the icy stream behind their house and the burning stopped. She shut her eyes for a second in relief, only to open them and meet the gaze of her father. But there was no smile on his face. No words of encouragement. Only worry. And something else. Something worse.

It was at that second that her gaze went back to where she'd been helping her brother learn to walk and noticed the small bonfire they'd made to celebrate his first birthday was being put out by her *tio* and several other of her relatives with buckets of water from the stream. Her mother still sat on the log staring over at them in horror. It was then that Elia realized what had happened, just as her dad lifted her from the cooling water. She'd fallen into the firepit.

The burning began all over again, taking her thoughts captive as it engulfed her right leg and lower back. She moaned, clutching her dad's shirt before crying in earnest as the scorching sensation grew and grew and grew until nothing else existed.

She heard the word *hospital*, and then her dad was running with her in his arms, faster than she'd ever seen him run. Someone else drove their car as he held her in his arms the whole trip, his soothing words containing a shaky note that she'd never heard before.

He was big and strong. Stronger than anyone she knew. But now as he hunched over her, her *papá* just seemed...afraid.

CHAPTER ONE

J<small>AKOB</small> C<small>ALLIN</small> <small>LEANED</small> over the bed of his patient, a teenager who'd been involved in an accident involving fireworks, and tried to decipher what the boy was saying. The reconstruction process on his jaw would be a long and arduous one. And the burns on his face would require some painful debriding and, very likely, skin grafting. The meds had eased some of the pain, but that combined with shock meant that he was trying to talk when he should be lying quiet. But he would have plenty of quiet days when his lower jaw was immobilized after surgery, leaving him to speak between clenched teeth.

"I want go rom…"

"Your room? You're already in your room."

The boy's eyes shut, and he shook his head, his right hand going up to his face. "Rom…" he tried again. "Go rom."

Jake took the boy's hand and pressed it back onto the mattress, trying his damnedest to work out what he was getting so upset about. Maybe about his looks?

"We'll do all we can to make sure that your face is restored—"

"He's not worried about his face right now. He's worried about not getting to go to prom next week with his girlfriend, who is right outside this room."

The soft female voice came from over his shoulder, making him glance back. The slight accent caught him off guard, even more than her irritation, which was thinly veiled. Very thinly veiled, judging from the way her brows were pulled together in a sharp V.

He looked back at his patient who was now nodding his head.

So that's what he was trying to say. How had she…?

And what was she so irritated about?

Although he should be used to that by now. His ex's growing frustration every time he'd said "let's give it some time" when she'd wanted to start a family had soon sounded the death knell to their relationship. Frustration had soon given way to manipulation and then anger.

"Right now, you need to concentrate on healing, Matt, okay? Do you want me to go out and talk to your girlfriend?" He hesitated. "What is her name?"

"Gracie. Her name is Gracie," came the voice from behind him. Again.

This time he didn't look. But surprisingly, and despite the impatience he'd seen in her expression, her face was already imprinted on his brain. With hair the color of his daddy's mahogany cigar box—the one Jake kept on his desk as a remembrance—the swirls and curves of those shiny locks had led his gaze straight to her face. Which was…beautiful. Even when she was angry. Or maybe *because* she was angry.

He kept his eyes on his patient. "Do you want me

to talk to Gracie? Or maybe you'd like to see her for a few seconds."

This time the kid shook his head with a vehemence that told Jake everything he needed to know. He'd seen that look before on any number of his patients who didn't want their loved ones to see them like they were. Most didn't even want to look at themselves in the mirror in the beginning. Jake always did his best to change that.

"Okay. I get it. I'm sure she'll understand, though. Do you want me to talk to her?" he asked again.

The boy gave a hard nod, but his eyes stared at the ceiling, not coming back to meet his.

Matt wasn't sure the girlfriend would understand. Jake wasn't sure, either. But hell. He hoped she would.

He swiveled on his stool to face the nurse who'd, in effect, scolded him. He was right about what she looked like. With delicate brows and cheekbones that seemed a mile high, she was a plastic surgeon's idea of perfection. Only Jake didn't deal in perfection. Not anymore. He simply did everything in his power to help his patients get back to living their lives in a way that caused them as little physical or emotional distress as possible.

Since this woman seemed to have definite ideas about what he should do, he arched a brow at her and inclined his head toward the other side of the room. He got up from his stool and moved to the area he'd indicated, halfway surprised when he turned and saw that she'd followed him.

"So do you want to go out and talk to Gracie, or do you think I'm capable of that, at least?"

Color rushed into her face, and he realized he'd embarrassed her. It wasn't his intent. He'd been trying to make a joke at his own expense. But then again, he didn't have much luck with that, either, when it came to talking to women, it seemed. At least not judging from the way his ex-girlfriend—a model—had chosen to break things off, moving out of their apartment when he'd been away at a conference. Looking back, he could see how poor of a match he and Samantha had been. He'd finally realized he'd been taken in by a pretty face—someone more interested in the status symbol of dating a doctor and what that could give her than she'd been in him as a person. He was pretty sure the having children angle had been her way of manipulating him into staying when it looked like their relationship was beginning to fracture. She'd obviously never expected him to say no to the request.

Whatever the reasons, he never wanted to go through a messy breakup like that again.

"I'm sorry if I…" The nurse's words trailed away, that same slight accent coming through that had caught his attention before. He was around people of all nationalities so he should be used to accents. But this one was a little different from what he was accustomed to, he just wasn't sure how.

"No. I'm sorry. We seem to have gotten off on the wrong foot. You're new here at the hospital?"

She hesitated. "Sort of. I've been here for two weeks, but in the scheme of things, you could say I'm new. To the hospital, anyway, although I've lived in Texas ever since I was his age." She indicated their patient on the bed.

"Sorry not to have welcomed you to Westlake Memorial before now, then. Have you been in this department the whole two weeks?"

If so, he wasn't sure how their paths had not crossed yet.

"Yes. We've worked together on a couple of other patients."

Hell, he was slipping. He normally prided himself on noticing the little things and chatting with the nurses he worked with. But evidently not this time. "In that case, I'm sorry again." He glanced at the badge hanging from her lanyard. "Eliana Pessoa?"

She corrected the pronunciation of her last name, although this time she smiled. And those high cheekbones carved out hollows beneath them that made his mouth go dry.

Get it together, Callin.

"So what do you suggest we tell Gracie?"

"The truth. But I wouldn't make any promises you can't keep about his appearance."

"I don't do that, since every patient's body reacts differently to surgery."

There was a pause. "Yes, it does."

Something about the way she said that made him glance at her a little closer. Maybe a little too close, since she looked behind her before taking a step back. "Well, I need to check on a couple of other patients. Are you sure you don't want me to talk to Gracie?"

"I've been doing this a while and haven't had too many

complaints, so I think I can do it." He smiled to soften the words.

"Okay, then. I'll see you later."

With that, she walked toward the door, a hitch in her step that was as faint as her accent, and something that he probably wouldn't have caught if he hadn't been staring at her.

Before she walked out, she looked at the patient. "I'll check on you in a bit, Matt. Try to get some rest."

The boy somehow managed to give her a thumbs-up sign, which made her smile again before she swept out of the room.

What had just happened here?

He wasn't sure, but it seemed he'd just met a nurse who advocated for her patients as strongly as he prided himself on doing. Not that Westlake wasn't full of nurses who did everything possible to help the patients under their care. There was just an empathy…an understanding to her manner that caught his attention.

Or was it her looks?

Was he really that shallow? Hell, he hoped not, although Samantha had caught his attention for the exact same reason. And he didn't like it.

So he was going to do his best to tread lightly around Eliana Pessoa. Because another thing Jake prided himself on was learning from his mistakes. No matter how painful that process might be.

Elia was glad to be out of there. She wasn't sure why, but being around Dr. Callin made her jittery in a way that made her grumpy. She was pretty sure some of that had come through when she'd addressed him, but it was either that or let him get under her skin, where she wasn't sure she could shake him off.

The fact that he couldn't even remember working with her those other times shouldn't make her feel invisible. There were enough nurses coming in and out of rooms that it was probably hard to keep them all straight. And from what she understood, he was a plastic surgeon who had shifted over to specializing in burns and reconstruction from traumatic injuries. Like Matt's, though the teen's burns were almost as significant as his shattered jaw. That was one thing she hadn't had to deal with as a child when she was in a burn unit in her home country of Portugal and undergoing surgery after surgery. Despite all of that effort, her right leg looked and behaved quite a bit differently from her left one. But at least it was still there. Things could have been so much worse.

She lowered herself into a chair in the hospital's Mocha Café and took her first sip of coffee. Hot and sweet, the espresso didn't have quite the bite the ones that her mom made for her at home had, but it was still good. Or maybe she'd just become Americanized.

Stretching her leg out in front of her, she tried to relieve a little of the neuralgia that being on her feet all day caused while, at the same time, keeping a slight bend in her knee so as not to aggravate the contracture that the scarring from her burns had caused. She couldn't straighten it all the way, and her last doctor had told her that after all this time, things were pretty much set in stone unless they went in and did some cutting and regrafting. There was no guarantee that it would help, since her body didn't deal kindly with scar tissue—a result of genetics.

She took another sip of her coffee, relishing the heat that washed down her throat and hit her stomach. Resting her chin on the palm of her free hand, she took another sip, letting her eyes close.

She was bone tired. She still had two hours left of her shift, but her nursing supervisor had taken one look at her as she came out of Matt's room and had told her to take a break. Elia hadn't argued. She hadn't wanted to watch Dr. Callin go over to talk to Matt's girlfriend.

Maybe she shouldn't have specialized in burns in nursing school. But it was where she felt like she could do the most good. She'd gone through some of what her patients were experiencing, although maybe not to the degree that Matt would, since the reminders of her injuries were hidden from view. So many of their patients didn't have that luxury. Some were even fighting for their lives.

She sensed more than felt someone's presence and opened her eyes to find Jakob Callin had entered the room and glanced her way.

Deus! Just what she needed…for him to find her practically asleep. Although she hadn't been really. For Elia, "resting her eyes" wasn't a euphemism for sleeping. It really did help to shut out the world for a few moments and quiet her soul.

He changed his trajectory and headed toward her. She braced herself, bending her right knee until her legs were together under the table. She didn't know why she was wary of him noticing something like that, but she was. When she was dressed she could pretend she wasn't different. And she wasn't, in so many ways, but even after all these years she still got self-conscious about it, which was why she rarely ever wore a swimsuit or shorts, even in the middle of a Dallas summer, when the heat could take your breath away.

When she'd arrived in the States, there had already been so much different about her besides her leg: her grasp of English, being the new kid in a school where friendships were already formed, wearing yoga pants instead of gym shorts to PE classes. So there was a tiny part of her that felt that people were looking for any sign of weakness, even if they weren't. It made her strive to excel in everything she did, including her job.

Dr. Callin arrived at her table and glanced down at her. "Just wanted to say I'm sorry for not properly welcoming you to the team. Sheryll confirmed you've been here for two weeks already. That's not like me."

Had he not believed her?

"It's okay. Really." Another thing Elia tended to do was stay in the background where she was less likely to be noticed. So it was pretty unlike her to go up and challenge someone who was in authority over her. But Matt's case had touched her heart, for some reason. Maybe because she was willing his girlfriend to stick it out with him. To not care that he might look a little different— once all of the surgeries were over and done with—from the guy she'd first been attracted to.

While Elia had never actually had a man drop her once they found out about her scarring, she had caught them avoiding touching those areas, probably in deference to her feelings. And one of the men she'd dated had actually kept the covers pulled up over their legs whenever they'd made love. All it did was make her even more self-conscious. She'd stopped seeing him soon afterward.

Well, it didn't matter, because she wasn't dating Dr. Callin.

"It's not okay. Do you have time for me to join you for a few minutes? Sheryll said she's already given you the rundown on the department, but I'd like to get your thoughts on a few things."

So maybe she was going to be lambasted for challenging him in public. Although she didn't really see it that way. She'd merely been helping him understand what the patient was saying. The way she'd wished people had been able to understand her when she'd first arrived at her new home in Austin. Matt was going to have to learn to talk all over again once his jaw was reconstructed, especially if his tongue had been affected by the explosion.

"Um…sure." If she said no, he was going to wonder why. And she was going to have to work with him. No matter that he made her insides tuck and roll for some reason.

With thick hair—already peppered with some gray— that was swept up and over his forehead, bright blue eyes and some scruff on his jaw, the man was an imposing figure. He looked strong and sure and in control. And for someone like Elia, who in her twenty-six years had gone through life events where she felt completely out of control, he was intimidating, even though he probably didn't mean to be.

"Great. I'll be right back. Do you want anything while I'm up getting my coffee?"

"No, I'm good, but thank you."

When her dad, who was an engineer, had been approached to work for a company in the States, he'd traveled back and forth from Portugal to Austin for close to a year before her mom had said enough was enough and that if he liked his job that much, they would relocate so they could all be together. And so began the second big upheaval in her life. First her leg. Then leaving behind her friends and everything she knew.

But she didn't regret the move. She missed her relatives in Castelo Branco, but she went back to visit her home country every couple of years, usually jigging her holiday time so it coincided with her parents' when they flew to Portugal.

She watched Dr. Callin as he walked and ordered coffee, which was handed to him in a big American-sized mug rather than the much smaller demitasse her own espresso had come in. She drained the rest of it, grimacing when the now lukewarm liquid hit her tongue.

When she'd decided she wanted to work in a hospital with a burn unit, the huge hospital in Dallas was the obvious choice. Her mom had been afraid her career would make her relive the trauma of being burned over and over, but surprisingly it didn't. It made her feel stronger, if anything, like she was turning something terrible into something useful by helping people who found themselves in a position like the one she'd been in throughout her childhood. And strangely, it sometimes helped when people found out she really did know what it felt like to undergo some of those not-so-fun procedures.

He was headed back to her table, so she took a deep breath and braced herself for a barrage of questions about why she'd chosen the field, etc.

He slid into the chair across from her, and the click of his cup as he set it down on the table seemed extraordinarily loud, even though it hadn't been. And the silence that followed seemed horribly, terribly empty. She racked her brain to think of something to say.

"So how long have you been at Westlake?"

His cup stopped midway to his lips as if surprised by her question. "I've been here ever since I started med school."

Of course, that made sense. Westlake Memorial was a big teaching hospital. She'd actually been surprised to be hired on by them, since they probably could handpick their staff just from the students who came through their doors. But she'd been top of her class, too, even though the school she'd gone to wasn't quite as prestigious as the one attached to Westlake.

He took a sip of his own coffee. "And Sheryll tells me you're originally from Austin?"

That made her smile. She knew she still had an accent so there was no way that he thought she was born and raised in Austin. "Not originally, no. I was born in Portugal, but my dad got a job in Austin, so we moved to the States when I was just starting high school."

"And you didn't want to go back after you graduated?"

The question surprised her. "My closest family members are here, although I go back to Portugal to visit when I can."

He nodded and didn't say anything for a minute. Suddenly she regretted slugging back the rest of her coffee. At least it would have given her something to do with her hands. She wished he would just get to the point of whatever he wanted to say to her. Did he drink coffee with every new staff member?

"We normally have cake for new staff members." He smiled as if reading her thoughts. "Maybe that's what threw me and why I didn't realize you had just come here. But Sheryll said you asked her not to do anything special."

In reality, Elia hated being in the spotlight. Her family already knew not to signal waiters when it was her birthday. The thought of a group of strangers gathering around her table and singing "Happy Birthday" to her wasn't her idea of fun, although Tomás loved it. Her mom had once told her that she'd wanted a big family with lots of children, but that it hadn't been in the cards, since she'd ended up having a hysterectomy in her early thirties due to endometrial cancer. It had been caught early, though, and her mom had been cancer free ever since, thank God.

She shrugged. "I figured I could get to know people on my own terms." Feeling she needed to add something more, she said, "I'm really happy to be at Westlake."

"And we're happy you're here." His smile grew. "And you really saved my bacon when you helped me understand what our patient was saying."

Okay, so by context she understood what he meant by saving his bacon, but she'd always thought it funny how different languages had expressions that made little or no sense. Like *falar pelos cotovelos* in Portuguese. It meant to talk too much, but translated literally it meant your elbows were doing the talking.

"I remember what it felt like not to be understood. But I'm truly sorry if I spoke up where I shouldn't have." She was doing her best not to notice how his smile softened the hard lines of his face. How it was the tiniest bit crooked, the right side tilting slightly higher than the left, or how it made little crinkles radiate out from the corners of his eyes. It was damned attractive.

"No, you should have. I like to think our unit is a team. We help each other out as needed. So if you ever think I'm not seeing a situation like I should, please bring it to my attention."

"Okay, thank you. Anything else I should know about the burn unit?"

"I want input. If you've heard about a new treatment that has some pretty solid studies behind it…that you think we should try on a more difficult case, feel free to speak up. We all have our own little groups where we talk about work and interesting articles or information gets passed around. I want our team to stay cutting-edge. To excel, for the benefit of our patients."

So he wasn't just looking to be on top. She could respect that. In fact, she did respect it as long as they didn't just turn out to be empty words. Time would tell. But she really did hope he was telling the truth.

"I will." And she would. Even though she didn't like being in the spotlight, she did want what was best for her patients, so if she thought another technique would work better, she wouldn't hesitate to say so. Well…she might hesitate, but she would speak up.

But what she wouldn't do was get too attached to that smile or do her best to make it reappear whenever she was around him. Because to do that was to head down a dangerous path. And she'd already seen where those roads led time and time again. They led to heartache and the fear of loss.

No, Jakob Callin's smile was best saved for those who would appreciate it for what it was. The simple movement of muscles over a scaffold of bone. It might transform his face, but in the scheme of things it meant very little. And she would do well to remember that.

CHAPTER TWO

POSTERS WERE PLASTERED all over the hospital. The annual biking event to raise money for the hospital's different departments was happening in just a couple of weeks. Jake sighed. The announcements had been up for a while, but he'd kind of looked past them until he'd received a memo in his mailbox reminding him to talk the event up in his own department. He was sure every other department chair had received the same notice.

This in combination with the influx of new students they would get in the spring and fall did great things for the hospital, but it increased his workload, sometimes to the breaking point.

It wasn't that he didn't like to ride bicycles. In fact, it was his exercise of choice. He went out at least a couple of times a week to relieve built-up stress. He'd just put new tires on his bike actually, and not for the biking event. Just because the treads had grown thin from use. And once a week he chose to ride his bike the ten miles to work and back. It helped get his blood pumping and got his mind ready for the day at hand. And on the trek back home, he rode at a leisurely pace where he paid attention to the world around him, the way he couldn't do when driving his SUV.

Maybe Sheryll would have some new ideas on how to encourage people to get involved. They normally hung a sign-up sheet behind the nurse's station for staff, but they were encouraged to let the patients know it was open to anyone who wanted to attend. Families with kids often made it an outing for all ages. It wasn't unusual to see a bike towing a baby trailer.

There was nothing cutthroat about the event. Yes, the first one to cross the finish line did get their picture put up at the hospital and usually got a write-up in the local paper. But presenting it as a day of fun to the families of patients who were terribly injured was tricky business, and he didn't want to come across as glib or uncaring. Or that all he cared about was the hospital's PR machine. Because his patients were more important to him than any fundraiser. If it were up to him, he would just let the hospital posters speak for themselves, but he understood where the administration was coming from. It was their job to raise the money for some of their pet projects and plan it around times when there were big repairs needed at the hospital.

He got off the elevator at the fourth floor and headed for the desk. Only Sheryll was nowhere in sight. Nor was anyone else. He frowned at the eerie quiet until he glanced at his watch and saw that it was time to dispense meds for those patients who needed them. Then he spotted a huge glass container with a matching lid perched on the desk of the nurse's station. It looked like an oversize apothecary jar. But unlike the ones that held cotton balls or tongue depressors that were set up in the patients' rooms, these held cookies. Cookies with a layer of smooth blue frosting on top and…bikes. Bikes of all different colors, one per cookie. He frowned, looking closer. Not only were there bicycles on the sweet treats, but there were also clouds and some of them contained tiny flowers along a bike path. On a plate next to the jar was a pair of tongs, evidently to use when fishing out the cookies. In front of the jar a note was propped up saying Help Yourself. On the other side of the jar were flyers about the bike festival.

Sheryll came out of one of the patient's rooms and spotted him. "So you found them, did you? I heard through the grapevine yesterday that those wonderful notices were going out yesterday, and we thought we'd get a little jump on things, so you wouldn't have to give your yearly pep talk. I know how much you like those."

He smiled. "Probably as much as the staff like hearing them."

He wasn't sure what he would do without the department's head nurse. She was dedicated to both the patients and their nurses, going to bat for both whenever the need arose. It was why the burn unit had such a small turnover of employees.

But the cookies…

"Did you make these?" he asked.

"Me? Of course not. I like to cook, but not bake, much to my husband's chagrin."

He tilted his head and glanced at the jar again. They

did look professionally made. They even had lettering at the top that said Bike Festival along with the date. But if she'd only heard about the notices yesterday, there wouldn't have been enough time to order these, would there? "Then who?"

"It was Elia. I gathered the nurses around yesterday and asked for ideas. She offered to bake cookies. But I never thought they'd be this fancy. Or this good. Try one."

He took the tongs and pulled a cookie out, glancing at it. With a red bike that sported a basket on the front of it, he was again struck by the detail. These must have taken hours to make. Then he took a bite and his eyes widened.

This wasn't your normal sugar cookie. It was lemony. And light. And so good.

"Was I right?"

"Unfortunately, yes. Because they're really too fancy to eat."

"That hasn't stopped anyone who's come by the desk. We've refilled the jar once already."

He turned to look at her. "You mean she made more than just these?"

"Yes, and she promised to keep them in good supply over the next couple of weeks."

"She didn't mention anything about doing this when I had coffee with her yesterday."

Sheryll's eyes widened. "You took her out for coffee?"

His brain shifted into high gear at her tone.

"No, I happened to see her in the hospital's café, and we chatted for a few minutes. About work," he added in case she might think there was anything more behind it.

"Whew. Good to know. I was starting to think you were developing a soft spot under that tough exterior."

No, he wasn't. At least he hoped not. That was the last thing he wanted. Especially where the newest member of his team was concerned. He'd already noticed far too much about her.

"I think you know me better than that."

She laughed. "I know a couple of women in other departments say that you're a tough nut to crack. Not that they wouldn't mind trying."

"Not happening. Even if I were interested in dating—which I'm not—I wouldn't date anyone at the hospital. Too messy." He wasn't sure anything could be messier than his relationship with Samantha, though. That had been a fiasco and a PR nightmare.

A woman with a child walked by and spotted the cookies and smiled at them. "This is so nice, thank you."

Sheryll smiled. "They're as good as they look. Help yourselves."

The mom took two cookies and napkins to go with them, and then she picked up a flyer.

Once she left, the nurse turned to him. "Better than having to verbally promote it, yes?"

"Yes. Please tell Elia thank you for me."

"You can do that yourself. She's headed this way."

He wasn't sure if Sheryll noticed the way his eyes shut for a second as he gave an inward groan. He'd been hoping not to run into her first thing, and he wasn't sure why. But maybe it was better just to do it now and get it over with.

Turning, he saw she indeed was headed this way with one of the digital devices they used to record patient information on.

Was it his imagination or was her face pink? He realized he was still holding half of the cookie he'd gotten out a few minutes ago. Surely she wasn't embarrassed about them.

"I was just telling Sheryll that I appreciate you providing these. They're delicious. You made them and decorated them all last night?"

She gave a quick shrug. "Portugal is famous for their pastries and bread. My mom actually drove up from Austin and helped since she still loves to bake from scratch. She was a pastry chef when we lived in Europe. You wouldn't believe the bread oven my dad imported from Portugal for her for their twenty-fifth anniversary. It's better than anything you'll find here in the States. I'll have to bring you some sometime."

He paused as he tried to think of what to say. But he must have hesitated too long because she jumped in with, "For everyone here on the floor, I mean."

If anything, the color in her cheeks deepened. He hadn't meant to imply that her words held any hidden message. "I'm looking forward to trying it. But the cookies are a perfect advertisement for the bike festival. Thank you again."

She smiled. "It was fun. I'm so busy that I don't often have time to spend doing something like that with Mom. So it's a great opportunity."

Sheryll propped her elbows on the upper portion of

the desk. "Jake hates having to promote hospital doings. Things like this take a lot of pressure off him."

"Yes, it does," he murmured.

"I'm glad I could help, Dr. Callin."

Had she been using his title ever since she started working at the hospital?

"Call me Jake. Everyone does."

"Oh…um, okay." Elia bit her lip and glanced at him, looking unsure of what else to say. When her teeth released its hold, that part of her mouth was rosy and he was having a hard time not staring at it. At how moist and lush it looked, and how kissable—

Hell! This was why he hadn't wanted to see her right away. For some reason he was having trouble maintaining focus when she was around. He hadn't had that happen in a long time. Not since his ex. He'd been fascinated by her looks, too. But in the end, there hadn't been much underneath that pretty face, and disconnecting from her had brought only relief. He had a feeling with Elia he might discover there was more to her than met the eye.

Judging from that container on the counter there was. And he honestly didn't want to find out what lurked below the surface. Because if he thought it was hard not to notice things about her now, what would it be like in a month? Two months?

Maybe it would all blow over and he'd simply get used to having her around. Get used to seeing her like any other staff member here at Westlake Memorial.

At least he could hope that was the case. He turned away and took the last bite of his cookie and shook his head. For some reason he had his doubts that it would be that easy.

Or that quick.

Watching Jake bite into that cookie had sent goose bumps over her in a way that she wasn't used to. And she didn't like it. She really had just wanted to help. But now she wasn't so sure that had been a good idea. Yes, she and her mom had had a blast making the cookies. But when he'd looked uncomfortable at her offer of bringing him some of her mother's bread, she'd been mortified. Had he thought she'd been hitting on him or something?

God. Every time she saw him now, she was going to wonder if he was thinking about that nurse who'd been desperately seeking his attention in any way that she could get it.

You're overthinking things, Elia.

She knew she was, but it was probably because she'd noticed him more than she should have.

And making the cookies had had nothing to do with him and everything to do with her patients. She also planned to support the event by participating in it. The movements on a bicycle were more comfortable for her than most exercises, since her right leg didn't have to straighten completely, unlike running or power walking. Swimming ran a close second, since the water helped support her injured leg.

Sheryll patted her on the shoulder. "He can be kind of gruff, but he means well."

So maybe she hadn't been overthinking things after all, if the head nurse had noticed something.

"I just hope he didn't think I was being overly friendly."

This time the other woman tilted her head. "Overly friendly?"

"By saying I would bring in some bread that my mom makes."

"No, I don't think that was it. I think he just doesn't know how to say thank you very well."

They moved away from the desk.

A call button went off. "That's Matt's room," Sheryll said.

They both stopped midstride as Matt's mom poked her head out of his room and said, "Please! We need help!"

She and Sheryll rushed over and Veronica moved to let them inside. "He just started shaking and can't stop."

Sure enough, the teen was visibly shuddering, his face red, eyes huge with fear. Elia was the first to the bed and as soon as she touched him realized why. "He's burning up. Can you page Dr. Callin?"

"Yep."

Matt was lucid, although clearly feeling the effects of a fever. And when she got his temp, she saw she was right. He was at 103.6. The biggest fear, besides tissue trauma from an injury like his, was infection. And although they hadn't seen signs of any so far, with burns it wasn't always easy to judge. The burn damage itself caused redness and inflammation that were also markers for infectious processes. And burns caused exudate that could act as a petri dish, the moist environment ideal for growing various microbes.

The teen wanted blankets, but that was the opposite of what he needed, so she stripped off his covers, despite his protests.

"I know it's uncomfortable, Matt, but we need to get you cooled down." It had been almost an hour since she'd given him his meds, and his temperature then had been near normal.

Just as she was getting some cool moist cloths to put on his forehead and wrists, Jake swept into the room. Evidently Sheryll had already briefed him, because he got right to the point. "What's his reading?"

"One hundred and three point six, as of five minutes ago."

"Let's take it again."

She quickly repeated the process and frowned. "One hundred and three point nine..."

"Chart?"

Elia handed over the digital device and Jake perused it for a second. "Let's pull the cephalosporin and see if that brings it down. When's he due for his next dose?"

Although a couple of the medications Matt was on could induce a fever under certain conditions, it was a fairly common side effect with cephalosporin. She could see why Jake wanted to start by changing that up rather than assume that infection was setting in.

"He got his last dose of that one at midnight, so we're looking at noon today."

She'd noticed that Jake didn't wear a traditional lab

coat but opted for street clothes instead. And today he was wearing a burgundy polo shirt and black jeans. With his swept-back hair, the combination was stunning and she had to force herself to remain on task.

He glanced at her. "Okay, good. If that's the cause, the fever should start subsiding almost immediately as the meds clear his system. If that does it, we'll change over to another class of antibiotics."

She nodded. "Anything else you want me to do?"

"The rest of his vitals are good?"

"I was just going to check." Elia measured his blood pressure and other vitals, and although his pulse was a little higher than it had been earlier, that could be caused by shivering and fear. She relayed everything to Jake as she took them.

Matt's mom broke in. "Is he going to be okay?"

"I'm hoping his fever is just a side effect of his antibiotics. We're going to pull those and see if the fever comes down. If not, we'll reevaluate and make a few alterations to his medications. I want to be cautious, but I don't want to throw more antibiotics at it until we've settled on a 'why' for this spike in temp."

He turned back to their patient. "Can I look you over, Matt?"

The boy nodded, and Elia had to admire the way the plastic surgeon peeled back the moist bandages they'd been using over the wounds. He was scheduled for a debridement later this afternoon, and hopefully they could get started on some of the surgeries to repair his shattered jaw, which would be done by one of their orthopedic surgeons. Jake would follow up with the skin grafting.

Once he'd finished his exam, he swiveled the stool back to look at Veronica. "I don't see anything overly concerning at the moment, but I'll put in a call to Dr. Julle and ask him to come in and have a look, as well, okay?"

Elia hadn't yet met Dr. Julle, but then again there were quite a few staff members she didn't know yet. Even if she'd let them get a cake for her, it would have just been for the staff in the burn unit and whatever other doctors happened to wander through on that particular day, so there was no guarantee she would have met him even then.

She walked Jake to the door. "Do you want me to use cool compresses?"

"Yes. If it rises above one hundred and four page me again and we'll use more aggressive measures. We're nearing the twelve-hour mark, so we should start seeing a reversal soon if it's the cephalosporin."

"Okay."

Sheryll had already left the room to go see to other patients, leaving her alone with Jake. Their arms brushed as he reached for the door and Elia had to repress a shudder that was every bit as strong as Matt's had been.

Nossa Senhora! What was wrong with her today?

His voice when it came was low, his head close to her ear. "If you see anything unusual at all, I want you to call me. I hope this is a simple case of drug-induced fever, but if it's not, I want to get in there and figure this thing out. Who knows what was introduced into the wounds when the shrapnel from the exploded firework hit him."

"Are you thinking sepsis?"

He nodded for her to go out of the room with him. She did and let him close the door behind them. "Not yet. But I want to go ahead and draw some blood. His pulse rate is elevated, but that could just be from the fever itself, since his blood pressure is still in the normal range."

"Those were my thoughts, as well."

He smiled. "Were they?"

She might have thought he was poking fun at her, but there was no hint of arrogance in the words. Instead, it was like he appreciated having another voice added to his own. Her face heated. Some doctors didn't really want to hear from the nursing staff, they just wanted their orders carried out, but she sensed Jake wasn't like that. Maybe because of the way he'd been chatting with Sheryll. But it was more than that. It was the way Sheryll had gathered the staff to help ease some of the administrative burden off the plastic surgeon when it came to the bike festival. The head nurse respected Jake. Liked him, even. It was evident in how she spoke about him.

So she gave him a smile of her own. "Yes, but it's good to know that so far Matt is doing okay."

"Any word from his girlfriend?"

This time Elia bit her lip, a bad habit of hers whenever something was concerning. She quickly stopped when she saw Jake's eyes go there.

"No, but she's probably in school right now. Veronica told me they've been, er..." She had to think of the

English term Veronica had used. "Sweet on each other since middle school, so I'm hoping she'll be supportive."

"Me, too. It will help in his recovery."

"Yes. It will." She could think of her teenage years when she'd had some revision surgery on her leg once they moved to the States. They were able to ease some of the contracture, but not all of it, due to her genetic makeup. She'd had one boyfriend in high school, but only one and he'd been uneasy about her burn scars, although she never wore shorts to school and for gym she wore track pants at the request of her parents to make things easier for her. So she'd still felt different back then, but the thought of wearing shorts and exposing the thing that made her feel the most vulnerable was unthinkable. And thankfully her parents had had a pool in their backyard so she could put on a swimsuit without being seen by anyone but her family.

That was another strike against her with her boyfriend—that she wouldn't swim with him when he came to the house, even though he said he didn't care about her scars. In reality, she didn't believe him. She hadn't believed anyone back then. They lasted about six months and then he broke things off with her.

Jake touching her hand not only jerked her out of her thoughts, it made her jerk her hand away.

He frowned. "Sorry. You just looked like you were a thousand miles away, and I was just going to ask you again to let me know if Matt's condition changes, in either direction."

"I will, and you don't have to be sorry. You were right.

You just startled me." She didn't elaborate on what she'd been thinking about, and she certainly didn't want him to think she was that uptight about being casually touched. She wasn't. And what she'd said was true. It had just startled her. Nothing more.

Or was it? She'd had that same startled reaction when their arms had accidentally touched. Like electricity had shot through her system. In a good way.

Which meant it was the opposite of good. And she'd better get ahold of herself. If she jerked every time they came in contact with each other, he was bound to notice. And if she'd been worried about him thinking she was after him before, she'd be doubly nervous of that if she kept having some weird reaction to him.

And the last thing she wanted was to actually develop some kind of crush on the man.

She shook off the thoughts, before he noticed that she was spacing out again. "Well, I'd better get those compresses going. I'll keep you apprised of his condition."

"Appreciated. See you later."

And with that he turned and was gone before she could say anything else. But not before he cast a glance in the direction of her cookie jar. For some reason, that made her smile as she went back in the room to take care of her patient and to pray that Jake was right about the reason for the boy's fever.

CHAPTER THREE

JAKE COASTED ONTO the hospital grounds, using the designated bike path that continued from the road onto the medical center's property. Matt's fever from the other day, as suspected, had been the result of the cephalosporin, and yesterday, he'd had the first surgery on his lower jaw. The damaged teeth on the right side had had to be removed, which he knew the boy had been upset about, but with the advent of dental implants, no one would ever notice. The more worrisome thing was hoping the bone graft taken from the teen's fibula would take. It had been a multi-surgeon effort, with Dr. Julle performing the bone graft in consultation with a dental surgeon who would later do the tooth implants.

Jake had done the skin graft surgery to cover the site on the boy's leg, harvesting tissue from his buttock. Everything had gone according to plan. If all went well, he would have normal function to his jaw.

Heading toward the bike rack the hospital had installed in the grass near one of the main entrances, he saw that someone else had just stopped their bike and was hooking it up.

He slowed further as he came up behind her and called

out to let her know he was there. She turned to look and Jake jerked on the handlebars and nearly toppled his bike. It was Elia. In her Lycra biker pants, tennis shoes and a racing top that bared her shoulders, she looked very different from the nurse who'd sported loose scrubs the other times he'd seen her. She was sexy as hell.

Not that she hadn't been that before, but she was even more stunning.

She smiled at him. "Careful. You might wind up in your own ER. The thing about never forgetting how to ride a bike is we're sometimes a little more wobbly when we get on after not having ridden for a while."

Not having ridden? Hell, he rode here once a week. "You just startled me, that's all."

Funny that those were the same words she'd used when she'd jerked away from him the other day.

"Okay."

She didn't believe him. Why did it matter? But for some reason it did. "I actually ride in to work fairly often."

But he was almost positive he'd never seen her bike here before. It was a sleek red racing-style bike with black handlebars and spokes, which showed that she knew a thing or two about bicycles.

"Ah, got it. I actually haven't tried that before today. But I thought with the festival coming up, riding in would give me a chance to train without having to make a special effort." She finished attaching her chain to the bike stand, then slung a backpack over her arm. "The only pain is having to change clothes when I get here."

And there it was. The flash of an image that he'd done his best to prevent. Of her slowly rolling those tight pants over her hips and down her legs. He gritted his teeth to banish it.

"Yep, I get it. I only live about ten miles out, so mornings are okay. But the afternoon heat definitely takes it out of you on the way back home." And he didn't say that he had an office with his own bathroom to change in because that sounded kind of privileged. And really, it was. It was on the tip of his tongue to offer to let her use his space, but he knew if he did, that image he'd just suppressed would come roaring back whenever he went into his office.

"Where's a good place to ride around here? I'm from Austin, so that's all I know as far as areas to ride."

"It depends on what you're looking for and how far you want to go. Several of the bike shops offer group rides, including one that I'm in that does a longer Saturday ride. It begins and ends at University Park and makes a big loop around the Dallas/Fort Worth Airport. You're welcome to come along if you want to."

He wasn't sure why he'd offered, but he did. And now that he had, he felt he needed to add some more details, just in case. "It's a forty-seven-mile trip."

"Not too bad. I've done longer, but they've normally been in the spring or late fall when it's a little cooler." She paused for a second. "Do you mind my coming along? I promise I'll find my own niche, but it would be nice to see a familiar face the first time."

Something about the hesitant way she said it made him

glad he'd asked. "I don't mind at all. You'll find most of the biking community in Dallas to be pretty welcoming."

"So you do this a lot?"

"It's something I enjoy."

She nodded. "Me, too."

Her eyes searched his face for a long second before turning away. "Well, I'd better head in." Then she turned back. "I was off yesterday. How did Matt's jaw surgery go?"

He locked his own bike and they headed in together. "It went well. And the girlfriend came for it."

She still had that little hitch in her gait. He couldn't tell exactly where it was coming from but seemed to be in her right leg. It was barely noticeable, but it was there just the same. Even so, she had no problem keeping up with him.

"That is so great. Has he agreed to see her yet?"

He nodded. "Finally, when he came out of surgery. But he was pretty bandaged up so maybe he wasn't as worried about what she'd see." He'd seen that in many patients who'd undergone some type of life-altering event, such as a severe burn.

They got on the elevator and Jake pushed the button for the fourth floor. "Did you get to do any of the skin grafts yet?"

"Just the one to cover the donor site, where they harvested the bone. The facial reconstruction grafts will need to be done a little later."

They arrived on the floor and got off. "So you're on for Saturday?"

"I am. What time?"

"The ride starts at eight. Come with a water bottle and any snacks you might need."

She smiled, and those areas below her cheeks hollowed out again, showing off her beautiful bone structure. "Yep. I'll come prepared. Thanks again for the invitation."

"You're welcome. See you on the floor."

"See you."

As he passed the cookie jar, he noted that they were almost gone. She'd said she was off yesterday. But he also didn't want her to feel like she needed to keep supplying the floor with free snacks, especially since they took so much effort. He made a mental note to mention it when he saw her next. And he also put Saturday's ride in his calendar. There was no need to register, it was just a "show up" kind of thing. Sometimes there was a leader from the shop, sometimes it was self-guided. There were folks who did this every week and could kind of let newcomers in on what to expect and where the places were to wait for help, if needed. They also liked to know if you opted to quit early so they didn't worry about something having happened and send a rider out to try to find you. Just normal trip etiquette types of things.

But for now, he wanted to review patient charts and plan his day. He had two surgeries today that had nothing to do with burns. One was the repair of a cleft palate. And the other was a revision surgery for someone who'd had an earlier surgery for skin cancer at another hospital that had healed badly and left a larger scar than necessary. He felt with an hour's worth of work he could coax the skin to give a little more and to lie a little flatter across her cheek.

As he changed his own clothes, he wondered again about Elia's leg and if her limp had to do with muscle weakness. If so, was a long ride going to be taxing for her? She said she rode regularly, so he assumed she'd done this before. But maybe he should ask.

No. She was an adult who could make her own choices. If she felt she could do the ride, then who was he to second-guess that? He certainly wouldn't want to have it done for him.

He chuckled. Of course she'd thought he was just starting to ride a bike again. That's what he got for letting her get under his skin.

And she was doing it. No matter how much he might try to deny it. Would Saturday make it even worse?

He could only hope not. Again, he wondered if being around her might be a good thing, almost like a desensitization process that made him notice her less.

It might work. But then again, he never really noticed when other women wore biking shorts and cool tops. But at least it wouldn't be a surprise on Saturday when she came.

And this next time, he'd keep hold of his composure and show her that he really did know his stuff when it came to cycling.

She arrived at Walter's Bike Shop on Saturday morning and parked her car. There were several people already here, but there was no sign of Jake, yet. Maybe he wasn't coming. No, he'd seen her again at work yesterday toward the end of the day and said he'd see her here. She'd almost backed out. But then she felt like she'd have to explain why she didn't want to go, and she really *didn't* have a good explanation other than he still made her uneasy. Every time she'd seen him over the last day or two, he'd still had the power to make her face heat up and her nipples tighten. That was the worst thing of all. She'd had to choose a specific sports bra today, one that did a good job keeping that kind of thing under wraps. It wasn't the most comfortable contraption to wear or the easiest to get into. But at least he wouldn't notice if her stupid body decided to betray her.

She unhooked her bike from the back of her car, tucked her ID card and a debit card into the little pack she had for the handlebars and then slid her water bottle into a holder on the frame of the bike.

Jake pulled in beside her just as she was pulling her hair up into a high ponytail that would keep it out of her face and off her neck.

"Hi," she said as he got out of his car.

"Hello, yourself. I see you made it."

Sporting the ubiquitous biker shorts and a nylon T-shirt, he looked totally as at home in this world as he did at the hospital. She couldn't believe she'd thought he was just starting out the other day when he arrived at the hospital. His helmet hung from the handlebars of his bike. Hmm... She'd brought one in her car, but Texas law had made bike helmets optional. This wasn't Austin, where she'd ridden mostly in designated bike areas, though, and she had no idea what the conditions would be. And when she looked around she saw the majority of other folks also had helmets.

That made her decision. She put down her kickstand and unlocked her car, pulling out the helmet. She'd have to readjust her hair to get the thing on, and she hated how hot it could be. But the others knew a thing or two about the road conditions in this part of the state. She would follow their lead. Of course everyone but her was in shorts, too, but that wasn't something she was likely to ever change.

"I did make it." She glanced around. "How many do you normally have ride with you?"

"Around fifteen or so. But for special events there might be forty."

"Wow. The club I was part of in Austin wasn't that large. But it wasn't organized by a bike shop, either, so maybe that's where the difference comes in."

"I think different clubs each have their own feel. This one is pretty laid-back." He nodded at someone who'd moved toward them. "Hi, Randy, how are you?"

He chatted with the other man for a minute before introducing them. "This is Elia. She's new to the area and thought she'd give the club a shot."

He smiled at her. "Well, we'll try not to scare you off, although if Jake hasn't already done that by now, then you should be good. He's the scariest one of all."

She could agree with that. Oh, not about the scary part, but about the scary reaction she had to him. It was kind of like when Matt had had that febrile reaction to his antibiotic. The man somehow made her feel feverish just by being in the vicinity. It was actually a relief to talk to someone else and get her mind off of it.

She decided to play it all off as a joke. "I work with him, so I'm used to him."

Not hardly, but she could pretend, right?

"Does anyone *ever* get used to Jakob Callin?" Randy asked.

Time for another quip. "I don't know. You tell me."

"I think it would take a rare individual."

Jake rolled his eyes, and those in the vicinity all laughed.

A few seconds later, more people gathered around and were chatting. These folks obviously had a good rapport and had done many rides together. It might be easy just to fall in with them, but she wasn't sure that was such a good idea. Maybe it would be better to try out one of the other shops and see what they had to offer. But it was nice to be included, even if it was because of her being Jake's "plus-one." Except she wasn't really. She was just in his orbit for this one ride. And then she would pop right back out of it, if she knew what was good for her.

Glancing at her watch, she saw that it was eight o'clock on the dot.

As if reading her mind, Randy spoke up. "So it looks like Brian—our fearless bike store leader—put me in charge of today's ride, since he's in Florida on vacation. Anyone know if others are coming?"

At the shake of several heads, he rubbed his hands together. "Okay, let's gear up, then."

Elia followed their lead and adjusted her ponytail so it trailed down her back and slid her helmet on, buckling it in place. "How fast do you all ride?"

Randy evidently overheard her and said, "It's pretty much a set your own pace thing. It depends on what you're working toward. Some of us have races coming up. Some are just here for pleasure. If you drop out, though, please let someone know. Speaking of which, can I have your name and phone number?"

Out of the corner of her eye she saw Jake frown. But why? Was he afraid she'd start pushing her way into the group? If that was his worry, he needn't. She wasn't likely to try to stick around longer than this one ride. Maybe she should reassure him.

But that would be awkward.

She gave her name and cell number to Randy, and he put them into his phone. "If we lose each other, I'll text you to make sure all is well."

She glanced around. No one else seemed to think that was something out of the ordinary. Except Jake was still frowning.

How fast were they planning on riding? She leaned toward him. "Are you guys going to run thirty miles an hour or something?"

"No. Don't worry. I won't lose you."

The way he said it made her shiver, even though she knew he didn't mean any more by it than Randy had. And the inference that she might be the only one to fall behind should have irritated her, but it didn't. But it did spur her to make sure she held her own. No leisurely pedaling like she might have done in Austin, where her group was more about scenery than distance traveled.

"How do you know I won't lose you?"

He chuckled. "Is that a challenge?"

That made her gulp. "Actually no. The group I rode with did scenic rides with lots of chatting within the whole group. We pretty much stayed in a clump."

"I see. This group is a little more competitive than that, but it's definitely not a race. For most of us, at least. There are always one or two who like to be in the lead the whole way."

But evidently Jake was not one of those. And yet he led the way in the burn unit, and from what she'd heard he was one of the best reconstructive surgeons in the Dallas area. So he was certainly out in front. But maybe that wasn't about being competitive. She had a feeling he cared much more about his patients than he did about his rankings among other plastic surgeons.

They all got on their bikes and started off in a big group. Within a mile, though, it had spread out a little so they weren't all on top of each other. Jake stayed with her, and she hoped that wasn't just to be nice. She didn't want to hold him back if he wanted to go on ahead. But she liked the fact that he didn't feel the need to show off, either. Randy was definitely up ahead, although he wasn't the leader of the pack.

There were only two people that she saw who weren't wearing helmets. And probably 75 percent of the group were men. If she hadn't had her injury, would she have taken up biking as a competitive sport?

It was kind of a moot question, because she *had* been injured and cycling was one of the most comfortable ways she could think of to keep the range of motion in the leg as close to normal as she could.

"Is this a comfortable pace for you?" Jake's question made her wonder if he'd read her mind.

"This is good. It's a little faster than I normally go, but I'm definitely not having any problems keeping up." And it was true, she didn't even feel winded.

Jake pointed to the right. "We're in the neighborhood of University Park right now."

With its tall trees, manicured landscaping and dappled bike path, it wasn't the concrete jungle she'd always pictured Dallas as. "It's a pretty area."

"It is. It's one of the shadier areas on our route. It'll be a lot warmer around the airport. But we should be done around noonish or a little before, so definitely before the heat of the day sets in."

They started to go down a long hill and Elia stopped pedaling, adding a little brake when her speed picked up. "I guess I should have asked about the topography. Are we in for some steep inclines?"

"Not super steep, but we will start climbing at around the ten-mile mark, where we'll stay until mile twenty-five-ish, where we'll start back down. The rest of the ride will be pretty flat. How were the rides in Austin?"

"Austin is in hill country and most of our rides end up going downhill first—since Austin itself is higher than the surrounding areas—and then climbing to get back to our starting point."

Steep climbs were the only things she found difficult in cycling. For some of it she had to rise out of her seat to pedal, and that required her right leg to straighten to the point that she felt a sharp pull behind her knee from the contracted tissue. She could do it, but normally ended up having to go home and ice the back of her leg. She was wary of using more painkillers than absolutely necessary. She glanced over at him. This was probably the most relaxed she'd ever seen Jake. He definitely liked coming out and riding. And he looked far too good for comfort as he leaned over the handlebars. He had the proportions of a cyclist, the snug athletic shirt showing off the long line of his back to perfection. And the muscles in his calves...

She turned her attention back to the road in a hurry. Time to occupy her thoughts with something else. "Are you the one who came up with the idea for the bike festival?"

"No, actually, it's been around for quite a while. But when I came to the hospital, I was already a cyclist so it fit in with who I am. I haven't missed a year yet."

"It's just a little different. I normally see hospitals doing marathons or the like."

"There's nothing wrong with being a little different."

She would agree with him, although there was a time when she'd felt so different from everyone else that she struggled with anxiety. She'd gotten counseling as a teen that had helped her realize that her burns made her more empathetic to those with challenges. In Austin, she'd helped with the Special Olympics in the area and had loved being a part of something so affirming.

"No. There's not." She said it because it was what was expected of her, but realized she'd actually come to believe it.

"We're coming up to a busier area, so we'll have some traffic lights to contend with. And the path will merge onto the road as part of the far right lane."

Just like he'd said, she saw the first major intersection of the trip was up ahead. Traffic next to the bike path was picking up, as well. And within fifty yards, the path veered onto the street, where a marked-off section identified it with a bike symbol painted on the asphalt.

They stopped for the light, catching up with a big part of their group, the ones who'd lagged behind reappearing and joining them. The light turned green. She put her foot on the pedal and pushed off, only to hear a shout, then Jake's hand reached over and grabbed her handlebars, pulling hard and knocking them both off balance. The pavement came up to meet her, and she heard the squeal of tires. She braced for what she thought was coming, but shockingly nothing hit her or ran over her. But she did hear a scream from someone, and Jake, who was on the ground beside her, leaped to his feet, glancing at her. "You okay?"

"Yes, I think so."

She still didn't understand exactly what had happened until she started to climb to her feet and her eyes caught on the sight of a car who'd hit a nearby tree. And under its tires was a dark blue bike. And the rider… She used her hands to shield her eyes from the sun as Jake and some others ran to an area beside the tree, where a figure lay in the grass, looking far too still.

CHAPTER FOUR

JAKE GOT TO the cyclist's side first and saw it was Randy. Hell! And he wasn't moving. At all.

His helmet was in place but blood was pooled on the ground next to him, looking like it was coming from his nose. Kneeling beside him, he felt for a pulse. It was there, but thready.

If he hadn't jerked on Elia's handlebars, they would have been hit, as well. His knees were stinging as was one of his elbows, but those were the least of his worries.

As if summoned, Elia appeared beside him, squatting in the grass next to him. "God. He's been thrown at least twenty yards. Pulse?"

"Yes. But there's a good chance there's some internal bleeding going on."

One of Randy's arms was bent at the elbow, but the bend went the wrong way. Fracture number one. And there were probably more where that came from. Damn, who in their right mind flew through an intersection like that?

Another of their group came up beside them. "EMTs are on their way. I can't even believe this happened. What was that driver thinking?"

"I have no idea, Serge, but thanks for calling it in. We're not going to move him until the squad gets here." There was no telling if his spine or neck were included in his injuries, but moving Randy could prove catastrophic if there were broken vertebrae involved. "Anyone else hurt?"

Serge shook his head. "No. But if you hadn't purposely crashed your bikes, you undoubtedly would have been hit, too."

He hadn't meant to hurt Elia, but it was either that or chance them both being struck by the car.

When he glanced at her, he noted there was blood on her cheek from a scrape and her bottom lip was also bloody and already swelling. But she seemed okay. "Can you check on the driver?"

"Sure thing."

She got up and disappeared from sight only to come back a few minutes later. "He's out of the car, sitting on the curb. Appears uninjured. But I got a strong whiff of alcohol on his breath, although he denies he's been drinking. And he hasn't asked about whether or not anyone was hurt. He seems totally out of it, so there may be something besides alcohol in his system."

Damn it. The way the guy had come flying down that road, Jake had known he wasn't going to try to stop for the light. And he'd been right. He couldn't believe there weren't more injuries. In the distance he could hear the sound of sirens. Finally!

A police car was the first on the scene. He started to

get up, but Elia shook her head. "You stay with Randy, and I'll go talk to him."

Just then, the man groaned and his eyes opened. But when he went to move his injured arm, Jake stopped him. "Just lay still for a minute, buddy, until they can get you checked out." Jake didn't want to upset the man who prided himself on how healthy he was and how infrequently he visited his family doctor—whom he thought might even be retired. But there was no way healthy living was going to fix this. Not without some help.

He was vaguely aware of the police ushering the driver of the car into the back of their cruiser. Thank God. At least he wouldn't be behind the wheel again today to hurt or kill someone else. The other people of their party were asking about Randy and more onlookers were gathering, so he told those from the bike club what he could but suggested they all either continue on with the ride or head home. He would let them know what he could, if Randy said it was okay. He was still pretty sure the man had more going on than a broken arm. His belly felt taut in a way that was more than just muscle. He needed to be transported and soon.

The band of riders headed off, and the other sirens got increasingly louder. This time they were who he was looking for. At that moment Elia came back over. "How's he doing now?"

"I'll feel a hell of a lot better when he's en route to the hospital. I think he's got some bleeding going on in his belly, and his arm is a mess. He'll need surgery for sure. And there's no telling about his neck or back."

Randy was in and out of it, coherent one minute and unconscious the next. But maybe that was better.

Jake glanced at Elia and saw it wasn't just her cheek and her lip that were injured. She had holes torn in both of the knees of her Lycra pants, and they were covered in congealed blood from where they'd skidded on the pavement. And she held her right arm across her belly, something he hadn't noted earlier. "What's going on with you? Are you hurt?" He reached up to move her arm so he could see, and she winced.

"I think I just sprained my wrist. It's fine. What can I do?"

He studied her face for a second before saying, "I think EMTs are almost here. So just help me keep him still if he starts thrashing around."

Thankfully he didn't, and in a few minutes, Randy had been fitted with a cervical collar and was loaded onto a backboard. Westlake was too far, so they were going to take him to an area hospital that was closer. But at least he was stable for the moment.

There was a second squad and Jake tried to get Elia to get herself checked out, but she refused. "I'm fine. Really. I just want to get home so I can get cleaned up."

"I don't think you should ride with that hand." He looked over at where other bike club members had dragged their two bikes from the road once the police had finished taking pictures of the scene. His looked okay, but Elia's… "And I don't think your bike is road-worthy right now."

The gear shifting mechanism was hanging off the handlebars, connected only by a wire.

"Oh, no." Then she chuckled. "Well, at least I know where a good bike repair place is."

He thought for a minute. "I only live a few minutes from here. If you're up to walking we could wheel the bikes there, and you could get cleaned up a little. How bad is your hand?"

"Definitely not broken. Just sore. I should be able to wheel my bike. I could do with some Tylenol, though, so if you have some, I'll take you up on your offer. My house is a lot further away, and our cars are still at the bike shop."

"I have Tylenol."

All the spectators had left the area, and it was eerily quiet. The drunk's car was still where it had crashed, and he assumed the police would impound it as evidence.

He picked up her bike and wheeled it a few paces to make sure it still rolled freely, then handed it to her. "Are you sure you can do it? I could lock my bike up someplace and come back for it later."

"Your bike is a lot fancier than mine. More chances of someone coming along and breaking the chain. Besides, I can do it."

"I'm about a fifteen-minute walk. Are you sure? I could always ride back to the bike shop and drive your car back."

She gave a visible shiver. "If you're okay with it, I think it would be faster just to walk to your place."

How much pain was she in? "Is the Tylenol for your hand?"

She hesitated. "Not specifically. Just sore and achy and I have a slight headache."

Putting her kickstand down, he came over and tipped up her chin, checking her pupils. They were even and he could see them both reacting to light when he turned her toward the sun. His eyes perused her face, skimming over it, his thumb touching the area of the cut on her lip before he could stop himself. "Hurt?"

She pulled away with a slight smile. "No to the brain bleed. And yes to the lip. It stings, but nothing major."

Hell. What was he thinking? He was glad she pulled away, because for a second the impulse to lean over and kiss the bruise on her mouth had stolen over him. That would be a little harder to blow off as simple concern for her well-being. And he hadn't been lying about office romances being messy.

His ex hadn't worked at the hospital, but their breakup had not been fun. She'd gone on a rant on social media about him, tagging him in a post that he'd only seen weeks later, when his mom had called him asking what was going on. He rarely went on those sites, despite having opened a profile. In fact, he'd only done so because his mom had asked him to, saying she wanted to be able to keep up with what was going on in his life. He didn't think seeing him blasted by someone who was in the public eye was quite what she had in mind. His mom had

had to tell him how to take the tag off and unfriend Samantha. But not before he'd noted that there were thousands of comments from her fans lambasting him for something he hadn't done.

"I'll give you some Tylenol, but if your headache gets worse—"

"*Deus!* I'm a nurse, Jake, remember? You don't think I know the signs?" As if realizing how vehement she'd sounded, she quickly added, "I'm sorry. It's just a little embarrassing standing here with my clothes the way they are. Your shirt is ripped, as well."

Was it? He glanced at his shoulder, which had just started to ache, and saw that his shirt was indeed torn at the seam, his sleeve hanging halfway down his arm. "So it is. Okay, are you ready?"

"I am. Which direction?"

"Back the way we came." He picked up his bike and waited for her to join him.

Their helmets were both off by now, so they buckled them around their handlebars. He'd need to remind himself to replace his before his next ride since they'd fallen and there could be unseen damage to the protective gear.

They started walking and Jake quickly saw Elia's limp was more pronounced than it usually was. He'd never asked her about the slight hitch in her step, figuring that if she wanted to tell him she would. She still said nothing, but within five minutes the tense set of her mouth was unmistakable.

"Did you injure your leg?"

"Just strained an old injury. I'll be fine. I just need a painkiller."

He assumed she was talking about the Tylenol. They could try to hail a cab, but in this part of town they weren't as common as they were near the airport itself. "We have about seven more minutes or so to go. Are you sure you want to keep walking?"

"Yes. I can make it. Once I get off it and take something, it'll be as good as new."

He doubted that, but unless he wanted to challenge her or ask exactly what the injury was, he was stuck taking her at her word. But he could at least try. "Anything you want to talk about?"

Her head jerked to look at him before turning back to the road. "Nope. It's not important."

Except he felt like it was. At least to her.

He slowed his pace twice to accommodate her increasing signs of discomfort and the fact that she was now leaning on her bike for support. Thankfully his apartment complex was just on the next block.

Two minutes later they were there. He helped her connect her bike to the stand that was at the front entryway, while opting to take his own upstairs. The look of relief on her face at not having to push it anymore was obvious. He'd made the right choice.

"Do you want to lean on me?"

"No. I've got it, but thanks."

The elevator was oversize, one of the features he'd liked about the place when he'd looked at it several years ago, and he hadn't regretted the decision. Located in a quiet suburb of northwest Dallas, it was both close to his job and within a reasonable distance to the airport, when he wanted to visit his mom who'd chosen to move to Florida a few years after his dad passed away from cancer.

He unlocked his door and ushered her inside. "Why don't you sit on the couch and I'll get you that Tylenol."

When she didn't argue, just headed over to the couch, using her good hand to help lower herself onto it, he knew she was more uncomfortable than she'd been willing to say. And stubborn, for sure.

He hung his bike on a pulley system he'd rigged from the ceiling and hoisted it up out of the way and then went into the kitchen for the painkillers and a glass of water. Handing it to her, she downed both the pills in one gulp. "Thanks."

She reconfigured her ponytail so that it was up off her neck the way it had been when she'd first arrived at the bike shop. "Do you mind if I take off my shoes?"

"No, of course not."

She toed off her tennis shoes and made circles with her right foot. Had she sprained that one, as well? Or maybe that's where her old injury had been, although he didn't think so. It looked to be more around the knee area, although there was no way to know for sure, since she hadn't said anything about it.

"I have some bike shorts that I think might fit you... or at least not fall off of you."

She was quick to shake her head. "But if you have some sweats that I can snug up around my waist, I'll accept that, though."

Sweats would be horribly hot this time of day, but he sensed it was the shorts she had an issue with. She could have a surgical scar or even a port-wine stain that she was self-conscious about. It would explain the longer gear she'd worn today. "I have some running pants that are lighter weight and have a drawstring waist, if that would work."

She looked grateful. "Yes, that would be perfect, thanks. Can I wait until the Tylenol kicks in before moving off the couch? I know I'm imposing—"

"You're not imposing at all. How about some tea or coffee?"

"I'd love some strong coffee if it's not a problem."

"Not at all."

He made a cup and carried it out to her along with some sugar packets and a carton of creamer. She murmured her thanks and took a sip, leaning back with a sigh. "Perfect, thanks so much. As soon as the painkillers hit my system, I'll call a cab and be out of your hair."

"There's no hurry. I had no plans for today other than that ride. Will you be okay if I take a quick shower?" He paused. "Unless you want to go first? Then I'll call and check on Randy."

"No. Take your time. I'm just going to enjoy this coffee and being off my feet."

"Do you want ice or a heating pad?"

"No. I'm good. Go get your shower."

She did seem more relaxed than she'd been moments earlier, so maybe just sitting down had helped ease whatever was hurting. "I won't be long."

Leaving her, he headed back to his bedroom, pulling out clothes for himself and then finding a T-shirt and a pair of his running pants that he used for sleepwear in his bottom drawer. Then, taking them all into the bathroom, he laid hers on a section of counter next to the sink and turned on the water.

Her leg hurt like fire and the neuralgia in her foot had kicked into high gear, the combination making it difficult to walk without gritting her teeth. It felt so much better to be sitting, where she could keep her leg bent at an angle where the inflammation wouldn't kick her butt.

Jake had looked at her funny when she refused his offer of biking shorts. But covering up her scars had become such a way of life that the thought of him seeing them or going out of the apartment complex with them on display made her break out in a cold sweat.

Her cellphone pinged and she glanced at it. It was her mom.

How was the ride today?

Thank God her mom hadn't yet heard the news about the accident, although she was pretty sure it would be on the internet somewhere by now. So how to answer without making her worried sick or having her rush to Dallas to check on her in person?

She composed her words carefully.

We ended up stopping early because of some traffic problems, but the beginning of it was good. Everyone was nice and helpful.

There. It was all true, even if she had definitely played down their reasons for stopping.

She could still hear the water running in the bathroom. It was somehow soothing to know Jake was in there. If she'd been by herself today, she wasn't sure what she would have done. Someone would have probably helped her get home, but it had been nice to have someone actually there while she walked in case she hadn't been able to go any farther.

Her eyes trailed around the room as she waited for her mom to respond. Jake's place was kind of a minimalist's haven. She was pretty sure it wasn't so much due to preference as it was the fact that he lived alone and was at work most days. Like her own apartment, it was probably just a place to sleep before returning to the hospital.

I'm glad. We're thinking of coming up to see you next weekend, if that's okay? I'm planning on making more of your bike cookies to bring with me.

Thank God they weren't on their way now, like they'd often done in the past, just showing up on her doorstep. Elia definitely wouldn't want them to see her like this.

Thank you so much. That sounds perfect! Talk soon. Love you both!

The sound of running water stopped, and Elia took a couple more sips of her coffee, which was still piping hot. Jake hadn't been kidding about being quick.

What else was the man quick about?

Her eyes immediately widened and her face heated. What on earth had made her think of that? Maybe the fact that she was uncomfortably aware that he was naked in that room.

Well, you'd better wipe those thoughts from your head, right now.

Within thirty seconds, he'd rejoined her, his hair wet and slicked back, making a few strands of gray stand out against the thick darker locks. He was dressed in jeans and a muscle shirt that made her swallow and sent her thoughts flying back in the wrong direction. It didn't help that the scents of soap and a clean body followed him into the space, making her want to trap them deep in her lungs.

For what purpose?

She doubted she would ever be in the room with a freshly showered Jake ever again, so why not enjoy a little guilty pleasure. Like the hint of muscle that rippled in his biceps when he picked up her tray and asked if she wanted more coffee.

"No, thanks. I'm good. The Tylenol is already kicking in. Do you mind if I shower, too? I'm a mess and would love to wash some of this gunk from my knees and face before I head home."

"I thought you might want to. I left some clothes in there and there's shampoo and soap in the shower. And

Band-Aids and antibiotic cream in the medicine cabinet on the wall."

"Thanks." Now, if she could just get to her feet without groaning… Although she hadn't been lying. The Tylenol was hitting her system with a relief that let her breathe again.

He reached down his hand, and this time she accepted the offer of help, somehow levering herself to her feet without an audible sound. At least she hoped not, because the warmth of the hand encasing hers sent a shiver through her that she felt with her whole being.

She limped into the bathroom and was once again surrounded by the scent of Jake. The moist humid air was the same air that had washed over him just a few moments earlier. Another shiver went through her, as well as a rush of heat that centered in her belly and traveled lower. She swallowed, trying to lose the sensation.

Failing that, she used her hand to wipe clear a spot in the fogged-up mirror and leaned forward to look at her face.

Wow. She hadn't been kidding. She really was a mess. Her hair was sticking out in all directions and a part of it was matted with what she could only guess was blood from her scraped cheek. Raising her fingers to touch it, she winced. It was raw and red, and by tomorrow would almost surely be a bruise.

And her lip was also swollen. When he had grabbed her bike and she realized she was going to fall, a shard of sheer anger had gone through her. Until she heard the screech of tires and understood why he'd done what he had. He may very well have saved her life. And when his thumb had touched the injury on her mouth…

She'd jerked away out of self-preservation. Because the sensation of his skin sliding against hers was the sort of thing dreams were made of. Just like when he'd touched her hand.

Pulling in a deep breath, she exhaled and told herself to get her act together. She yanked her shirt over her head and rolled her shoulders, trying to slough off the tension she'd carried all the way up to his apartment. Unclasping her bra and letting it drop on the floor with her top, she set about unrolling her Lycra bike pants down her hips and easing them away from her skinned knees. Once they were off, she turned her scarred leg and craned her neck to see the back of it, where the patchy sections of what were once skin grafts had changed to a ropey tight mass of scar tissue that prevented her from straightening her leg completely. Other than her knees, there weren't any visible injuries, but that leg hurt worse than it had in a very long time. She could only assume that in the fall it had straightened past its limits and had torn some of the adhesions on the inside.

In her normal, everyday life, she tried not to look at her leg that much. It got her to where she was going and she convinced herself that that was all that mattered. Except on rare occasions when someone made her feel self-conscious about it, like the man who'd liked to keep the covers pulled up. But that was years ago, and she would have thought she would have gotten over all of that by now. But picturing Jake, with his perfect smooth limbs that rippled with muscle, had brought it all back again. She'd been horrified at the thought of wearing shorts in front of him. And it made her angry.

She'd cared for people who had burns in very visible places. People who were missing parts of their face or who had scars that couldn't be eradicated with surgery. Places they didn't have the luxury of hiding. And here she was moaning to herself about scars that most people didn't even realize existed.

Get over yourself, Elia. Seriously. Start realizing how fortunate you are.

She turned away from the mirror and went over to the shower, which was actually part of a deep soaking tub. She stared at it for a second. The heat of that would really do her muscles some good. Surely he wouldn't mind...

Stepping under the spray of the shower, she let warm water sluice over her face and knees to wash away the blood, wincing as it hit the scraped flesh. Then she washed her hair using his shampoo, giving herself permission to submerge her senses in something he'd chosen. After all, he'd offered it up to her. And he would never know how it made her feel...right?

Then she turned off the shower feature, pushed a button to stop the water from draining and lowered herself into the tub, adjusting the dials so that the water was much warmer than the shower had been. As the silky liquid covered her calves and then her shins, she reached up and squeezed a little of his shampoo beneath the spigot so that it made a scented froth of bubbles before putting the bottle back and leaning against the backrest.

Closing her eyes, she sighed as the water trailed over her thighs and slid between them, reaching sensitive areas that hadn't been touched in quite a while. She bit her lip, before the sting of the injury on it made her release it quickly. But still, she let herself enjoy the sensations of the warm bath flowing over her belly and up her torso. The heat was already easing the neuralgia in her foot while igniting nerve endings in other places that felt a whole lot better than the pins-and-needles prickling she lived with on a daily basis.

It reached the bottom of her breasts and she held her breath as it slowly worked its way higher, like the teasing fingers of a lover. An image flickered between her closed lids, and although she tried to keep the features from sharpening into something recognizable, she failed. And just as the water reached her nipples and surrounded them with moist heat, she gave in to the temptation and let her hands go up and slide over them, moaning softly as they came to instant life.

She leaned forward enough to turn off the water before sinking back into it and continuing her fantasy. The one where Jake's hands were the ones covering her breasts, his palms massaging and coaxing them to pucker against his skin. She swallowed, trying to banish the sensations. Until, in her head, his mouth covered one… She arched toward the imaginary figure, while her other hand touched her belly, slowly moving down to where a growing need was whispering for her to give in. To give it what it wanted. The fantasy. The unreachable reality of what might have been.

The second she reached lower, the pulsing need grew out of control. It couldn't be stopped. Wouldn't be. Her breathing grew ragged as she let herself climb that hill. As she got closer and closer to what her body needed. Something that would obliterate the pain in her leg. At least for a few minutes.

Her fingers quickened in time with the beat of her heart. So close…

So…very…close…

Her brain froze as sheer pleasure washed over her, her hips arching up and seeking something…

Something that wasn't there.

She came down quicker than she expected, sinking back into the water in instant dismay. She couldn't believe she'd done that. In Jake's bathroom, of all places!

And now she was going to have to climb out of his tub and step into his clothes, and then walk out there and face him.

The man she'd just imagined having sex with!

God! If she could pull on her ratty, torn bike pants and shirt without him questioning why she hadn't used his clothes, she would. But of course he would ask. And she wasn't about to tell him the reason.

So she finished washing and quickly drained the tub, rinsing out any evidence of her illicit bubble bath. Suddenly shivering, she wrapped herself in the thick bath towel he'd left for her and patted herself dry, putting her panties and bra back on. She hesitated for a long time over the clothing folded on the countertop before her shoulders slumped and she reached for them, pulling the

T-shirt over her head and letting the fabric fall. It came down to mid-thigh, making her smile for a second before it disappeared again. Then she pulled on the lightweight jogging pants, cinching them around her waist. It felt intimate. Almost as intimate as what she'd done in that tub.

But he was never going to know about that. Not if she could help it.

Gathering her clothes and glancing at her face one last time to make sure there was no sign of guilt—at least no visible sign—she turned the handle and walked out of the bathroom.

CHAPTER FIVE

SHE CAME OUT of the bathroom, her wet hair wonderfully mussed and her face pink with the heat of her shower. And hell if she didn't look sexy as anything in his clothes. The words he'd planned to say when she emerged curled around his tongue and got stuck for a moment before he finally got them out.

"Randy's okay. I called the hospital. A broken rib hit a blood vessel and needed to be cauterized and the ends of the bone wired back together, but no damage to his spleen or other internal organs. His arm is splinted, but he'll probably need another surgery because of where the break occurred, but it could have been much worse."

"Much worse," she echoed in a weird voice.

"Are you okay? Is the pain worse?" He studied her face. The blood was gone, but her cheek was already turning colors. He wouldn't be surprised if she had a black eye by morning.

"No. The water helped actually. Thanks for letting me use your bathroom. And your clothes." She glanced down at herself.

Her face seemed to turn a darker shade of red, which he didn't understand. Unless she was embarrassed about having to borrow his clothes. It wasn't a big deal. Or maybe she was just anxious to be on her way so she could relax in her own space.

"I had a thought. It won't take me terribly long to ride to the bike shop. Maybe a half hour, tops. I could pick up my car, drive home and then drive you and your bike to the shop to get your car."

She seemed to think about it for a minute. "I was going to suggest I just call a taxi service, but then you'd be stuck with my bike until I could come back and pick it up. Are sure you don't mind?"

"I think it's the most logical course of action. And your bike is out of commission. The shop might still be open and you could leave it there for repairs."

"Okay, that sounds like a plan. Thanks for doing that." She gave a wry twist of her mouth. "It seems I have a lot to thank you for. I never thought I'd be thanking someone for knocking me off my bike, but you probably saved me from being hit along with Randy. I had no idea that car was even coming."

"No need for thanks. And I only just happened to look again as we were crossing the street and caught movement out of the corner of my eye." He grinned. "And I never thought I'd be the one who'd cause a fellow biker to fall. On purpose."

"You saved my life." Her voice held a hint of shakiness that took him by surprise.

He went over and tipped up her chin like he had at the scene of the accident. "We might not have ended up in the danger zone even if I hadn't grabbed your handlebars, but I couldn't take that chance. Even if I'd shouted your name, by the time you had a chance to look it would have been too late."

"Well, thank you, anyway."

His eyes went to her lips and the impulse to kiss her was strong. Strong enough that he allowed himself to lean forward, but only to give her a quick peck on the nose. "I'm glad you're okay. Headache gone?"

"Yes. It must have been...er, those pain relievers I took." She took a step back, and he realized he still had his fingers tucked under her chin.

Hell, the fall must have knocked something loose in his head. Something important.

He forced himself to go over and lower his bike from its spot against the ceiling and set the kickstand. "Do you want something to eat before I go? More coffee?"

"No, I'll be okay, thanks."

"All right. I'll be back as soon as I can, barring any problems. And I'll text you if that happens."

She nodded. "Thanks again."

"Make yourself at home while I'm gone. There's stuff in the fridge and a French press coffee maker on the counter." He wheeled his bike to the door and went through, taking the elevator back down to the ground floor.

Getting on, he started pedaling as if his life depended on it. He'd almost kissed her. Really kissed her and not just on the nose. After the accident, when he was trying to assess Randy's injuries, it had gone through his head that it could have been not only Randy, but Elia flung across the road like a rag doll. It could be her with broken limbs…or worse.

But kissing her? Not in the cards. Not for him. He didn't do relationships. At least not right now. He did not want another Samantha-like situation to contend with. He really was pretty happy with living by himself. At thirty-eight, he was pretty much used to being alone and childless. It suited him. He kept terrible hours and was at the hospital most of the time. His apartment was really just a park-for-the-night place that held no real significance for him. It could have been anywhere and it would have been exactly the same.

So no, he didn't want to start something with her, even if she were interested, which he was pretty sure she wasn't. She'd acted a little odd being in his apartment, and it was probably that she was thinking the same thing…that she hoped he wasn't going to hit on her.

And then he had to go and tilt her face up and give her a peck on the nose.

A friend would have done the same, right? Had he ever kissed a friend on the nose before?

No. But he didn't have very many female friends. And he didn't really know her well enough to consider her a friend.

And maybe it was best to keep it that way. She was a colleague and could stay in that category. No jumping lanes. No getting to know her on a more intimate level…even if he was physically attracted to her. And he wouldn't deny that he was, because Jake didn't make it a habit to lie and that would be lying to himself.

So yes, she was a gorgeous, smart, interesting woman who had secrets he'd like to uncover. But he wouldn't pry. Wouldn't probe. Because if he did, he'd be in danger of getting a little deeper than he intended to get.

So as soon as he took her home, he was going to try to not have much contact with her outside of work. And hopefully, she wouldn't be interested in joining his bike club on more rides like the one today.

Even if there were no more accidents. Physical or otherwise. Because if he kept socializing with her on a casual basis, there was every chance that something not so casual might happen. And that might just upset everything in the little "bachelor forever" pep talk he'd just given himself.

Something he didn't want to happen.

Now...or any time in the near future.

Matt's first skin graft was today. Over the last week, they'd completed the bone grafts for his jaw, and those seemed to be taking without a problem. The tooth implant surgery was coming in the near future, but it was time to start building the scaffolding from the skin cells they would harvest from Matt's clavicle area, which was one of the areas that best matched the skin tones of the face. And Jake had chosen to do a sheet graph—using the skin just as it was harvested rather than running it through a mesh machine, which would thin the layer of skin and allow it to cover a larger area. But the meshed skin would also be more likely to scar, something he didn't want to risk on Matt's face. And there'd be enough tissue to do the job without needing to resort to that.

Randy was home from the hospital as of two days ago. Jake had checked on him daily, and when he'd seen Elia over the normal course of the day at the hospital, he'd relayed the news, but he hadn't spoken to her any more than necessary. And she'd assured him that her leg was better and that her bike had already been repaired and all was well.

Her cheek, which had appeared bruised for the first couple of days, now showed no signs of what had happened. Neither did her lip, which was once again smooth and silky looking.

And those bike cookies kept on coming. And the list of people attending the fundraiser kept getting longer. It looked like it was going to be a record turnout, if the statistics were anything to go by.

He headed down the hallway, bypassing the jar of cookies, to Matt's room to see how he was doing mentally before they got him prepped for surgery.

Pushing the door open, he gave an inward groan. Elia was in the room, getting his vitals and chitchatting with the patient and his parents as if she were perfectly at ease, something she didn't display around him. Instead, she still seemed vaguely uptight, although she did a good job hiding it with a cheery greeting and smile.

Should he apologize for what had happened in his apartment?

Except it wasn't like they'd had sex. But she might

not have welcomed that quick display of relief that she was okay.

So yes. An apology might be in order. If she indicated it was no big deal, they could go on about their lives as if nothing had happened. And if not, then at least she would know that he was truly sorry to have done anything to make her uncomfortable.

She turned and saw him and her smile caved in, becoming the very picture of an efficient nurse. Not that she hadn't had that image before. But she seemed determined not to let him see any other side of her.

And he couldn't blame her.

Jake greeted Matt's parents, shaking both of their hands before Elia recited his vitals—everything looked great—then she asked when they were coming to get him ready for surgery.

"Pretty quickly, I would guess. Surgery is scheduled for ten this morning." A little more than an hour away. He would be heading there to make his own preparations soon.

"How long do you expect it to take?"

Okay, so she wasn't just answering him with monosyllabic replies. She was actually inviting a give-and-take of information. But probably for Matt's folks' sakes, since they were hanging on her every word. He decided to address them instead.

"About an hour and a half, although I have the surgical suite reserved for a two-hour block, just in case we run into any snags."

He turned back to Elia. "You're welcome to observe, if you'd like."

Matt's voice came from across the room. "Would you? It would make me feel better to know you're there. Kind of like a guardian angel, since you've helped us so much over these last couple of days, including recommending a counselor. I think Gracie, my parents and I are going to talk to her together. Gracie said you talked to her and helped her understand what it's like to be burned, since it happened to you, too."

Jake's brain seized for a second or two.

Burned? Elia had been burned? He turned to look at her in a hurry.

Her face flushed dark red, and she didn't say anything for a few seconds, then she just murmured, "I'm glad it helped, although it was a long time ago. But yes, I'll observe the procedure if it helps you feel more comfortable."

Matt's mom went over and gave Elia a long hug before releasing her with tears in her eyes. "Thank you so much. For everything. Especially talking to Gracie."

Jake glanced at her leg and suddenly things seemed to fall into place. She'd said she'd aggravated an old injury when asked why she was limping after falling off her bike. But he'd assumed she'd broken a bone or had some other type of injury to the limb. But what if it wasn't?

Maybe her reasons for working in a burn unit were much more personal than he'd imagined. If so, he completely understood that feeling. Wasn't he working here because of what he'd seen? Oh, he hadn't personally been burned. But the pilot who'd been injured had somehow changed his heart, nudging it to go in a different direction than he'd intended to go. He'd always had his heart set on being a plastic surgeon, but that pilot was the reason that he'd specialized in skin grafting and reconstruction.

Regardless of whether she'd received an injury a long time ago or not, that didn't change the fact that he needed to at least offer an apology. Now more than ever.

She looked at him, her chin held slightly higher than it had been before, as if daring him to ask her about what had happened. He wouldn't. At least not here in front of a patient. "Where is the observation area?" she asked.

"We'll be in surgical suite number four. The viewing room just above it was put in for students to observe specific procedures that go along with their curriculum. But there shouldn't be any students at this point in time, since it's summer. Maybe one or two who have some makeup work to do, but otherwise you should pretty much have the space to yourself."

"Okay, thanks for letting me watch."

Matt nodded. "I'm really grateful. Gracie will feel better, too." The teen's speech was a little difficult to understand, since his lower jaw was immobilized at the moment to help the bone grafts heal without putting any stress on them. But he was able to get his point across since he still had the use of his lips and tongue.

"I'm happy to do it. Although I'm sure everything will go just fine. Dr. Callin is a great surgeon. You'll be in good hands."

Even though it was a normal "nurse" thing to say to

a patient, it still warmed him to hear the words. Even if they really weren't sincere.

She threw Matt's family a smile and turned to leave, but Jake stopped her with a touch to her arm. "Do you have a second?"

Her tongue snaked out to touch her lip, moistening it before she answered. "Sure. How about if I meet you outside."

She slid quietly through the door. Jake stayed for a moment or two longer to give some last-minute scheduling information to his patient and his parents about what to expect after Matt came out of surgery. Then he said his goodbyes, as well.

Elia leaned against the wall outside of Matt's room and closed her eyes for a second. It had been bound to get out, but for some reason she'd rather Jake not know about what happened to her. She hated feeling vulnerable, and having him know about her injury put her squarely in that position. She was normally pretty careful about who she gave that information to, figuring it was really no one's business. But on the other hand, she'd gone into this specialty because she thought she might be able to empathize with her patients better, since she knew exactly what it was like to go through painful procedures like debridement and surgeries. Matt was case in point.

Jake obviously wanted to talk about what he'd just learned, and she mentally tried to scale the information down to the size of a sound bite. Raw information with no commentary to go with it. She'd burned her leg as a child. It was now fine.

Unless he'd somehow guessed what she'd done in his bathroom and wanted to talk to her about that, rather than her leg.

No, that wasn't possible, unless he'd stood outside the door and put his ear to it to eavesdrop, and that would be a very creepy thing. Something she instinctively knew Jake wouldn't do.

Was it any creepier than pleasuring herself in his bathtub?

Deus! She still couldn't think about that without feeling mortified by her behavior.

But no…there was no way he knew about that, so it had to be about her leg.

She sensed more than heard the whisper of the door as it opened and shut, felt the slight breeze as the displaced air whispered across her cheek. She opened her eyes and found him looking at her.

"Not here," he said. "Can we walk outside for about five minutes?"

"Yep. I'm due for a break, anyway." Swallowing, she walked over to the nurse's station, where Sheryll was clacking away at the keys of the computer station. She glanced up, then looked at her over the top of her reading glasses.

She took a deep breath. "Can I run on break for a few minutes?"

"Of course." The nurse looked behind her and obviously noticed Jake standing there. Her eyes widened slightly, although she didn't say anything about that, just added, "Take as long as you need."

"Thanks. And actually Matt—our teen who's having surgery today—wants me to observe the operation. It'll probably be a couple of hours long. I'll completely understand if you can't spare me—"

"We'll be fine. You're off in an hour, anyway. Why don't you just go now. Norma should be here any minute."

"Are you sure?"

"Absolutely. I'll see you… Monday? Your folks are coming in tomorrow, aren't they?"

"Yes." She hadn't forgotten. Her mom and dad were both driving up, and while she was looking forward to seeing them, she didn't want them asking a lot of probing questions about the people she worked with. Ugh. Which might happen, despite the fact that her mom said it was about bringing up more cookies for the fundraiser. Things were getting more and more complicated.

The complicated part was on her end, though.

She was probably the one who was making things weird by keeping her old injury kind of a secret. It shouldn't be. Nor should she be self-conscious about it after all of these years.

She smiled at Sheryll. "Thank you again. Have a good weekend."

"I plan to. Hubs and I are headed to Lake Granbury for the weekend."

"Have fun! See you on Monday."

They didn't always get the whole weekend off, since

the department still had to be staffed, but it had been a while since her friend had taken any personal time off.

Taking a deep breath, she turned back to Jake, wishing she'd told him she'd meet him outside rather than having to walk out of the building with him beside her. It made it look like they were fraternizing when they weren't at all.

She followed him out the nearest exit, which dumped them onto one of the hospital courtyards that attached to the Mocha Café by another door.

As soon as they reached a bench, she dropped onto it and waited for him to join her before turning his way. "Before you say anything, it's not something I normally talk about. I fell into a campfire when I was a child and burned my leg and part of my back. It happened so long ago and I've lived with it for so long, that it's not something I really dwell on."

He stared at her for a long moment before saying, "God, Elia, I'm sorry. That's not what I wanted to talk to you about, but I had no idea. It still bothers you after all this time?"

That wasn't why he'd wanted to speak to her? Then what was it?

She swallowed. "I wouldn't say 'bother,' per se. The scarring on my leg contracted across the back of my knee, creating a kind of slingshot effect where I'm about ten degrees from being able to straighten my knee completely before the pull of the contracture becomes too much."

"Revision surgery didn't help?"

"No. My doctor tried twice to redo it. But I have keloid disorder, which complicated my recovery from the burns.

And yes, after the revision surgeries they tried cortisone shots and pressure dressings to try to prevent the scars from going crazy again with the granulation tissue, but it didn't seem to help. I have a scar on my collarbone that also developed a keloid. Not a huge one, but it's still bigger than a simple scar."

He nodded. "Keloid disorder can be difficult to control. I'm sorry that happened to you, Elia. Is that why your leg hurt so much after the accident?"

She nodded. "It stretched the scarring and irritated all of those nerve endings. I tend to have neuralgia in my right foot, anyway, from the burns." She shrugged. "So now you know. I wasn't trying to make it a big secret. It just doesn't usually come up in normal conversation."

"No, I can see that. And really, it's no one's business, anyway."

She stared at him. "I thought that's what you wanted to talk to me about it, so if not that, then what?"

Elia realized she was the one who'd actually assumed that was to be the subject of this conversation and she'd tried to head him off at the pass and, instead, had revealed everything. Only to find out that he wasn't here to grill her about her leg. At all.

He turned a little more to the right so that he faced her directly. "I wanted to talk about what happened at my house."

Her face turned white-hot, and she knew color was pulsing into it at this very minute. Did he know? Had she somehow been louder than she thought she'd been?

"Wh-what do you mean?"

If he knew, she was going to turn in her resignation. No way could she face the man every day knowing that he knew a secret that was much more private than her scars.

Much more horrifying.

"I wanted to apologize for kissing you."

Kissing her? She racked her brain for... Oh! *That* kiss.

Relief swamped her system. Then she laughed. "You want to what? It was on my nose. It wasn't like you—how do you say it?—planted one on me."

His head tilted sideways as if not understanding her reaction at all. "It didn't bother you?"

"Why would it?"

"I don't know, you just seemed to act a little differently after we parted in the parking lot of the bike shop that evening."

Deus do céu. She had. And it had started long before they reached the parking lot. But there was no way she was going to tell him why. That had been a crazy day, and she could only chalk her actions up to shock from the accident combined with feeling vulnerable from how badly her leg hurt. And how sexy he had looked standing there fresh from the shower in bare feet and wet hair. And the tantalizing scent of his soap. And...

"I think maybe it was just shock from the accident."

He blinked like he didn't really believe her. But as long as he didn't challenge her on it, she should be fine. But she definitely didn't want him to think a little kiss on the nose had sent her into some weird head trip where she couldn't look at him straight.

She couldn't. But it had nothing to do with that kiss,

which she had thought was sweet, even if she secretly wished it had landed just a little lower.

Seriously, Elia? Haven't you learned your lesson?

Evidently not. But she'd better send herself back through the program and try again. Because she could not go on the way she was now. Especially since she was now conjuring up scenarios where he was asking her to reveal personal facts about herself—like her burns—when nothing could be further from the truth. She'd spewed all of that information out for no reason. No reason at all.

But even so, there was a small part of her that was relieved to have it out in the open. He was the first one at the hospital to really know about it. Despite that, she certainly wasn't going to make it a habit of baring her soul to him. Because that could become a more dangerous prospect. Like wishing he'd kissed her on the mouth?

She shook the question away without answering it. "Well, I'm sure you need to go get ready for surgery. Good luck, even though you won't need it. I was serious when I said you were one of the best in the area. You are, although I'm sure you've been told that many times."

He paused for a long moment. "Yes. But not by you."

The words went right past her before she retrieved them and replayed them, unsure as to whether or not she'd really heard what she thought she'd heard. She had. She just wasn't sure what he meant. But he made it sound like her opinion mattered. That he might have moments of insecurity just like she did. That fact somehow made her smile.

"Well, you have now. So go do what you were born to do."

"Thanks." He gave her a sideways grin. "See you on the other side."

CHAPTER SIX

HE KNEW SHE was there.

Oh, he hadn't looked up to see if she'd actually gone into the viewing room, but he somehow knew she had. That she was watching even as he used his dermatome to remove a section of skin tissue from Matt's clavicle and carefully place it into the collection tray. Hopefully the autograft would take on the first try so he wouldn't have to harvest any more. There was always the chance of failure with a free skin graft, where there was no transfer of a vascular supply to the new location. To help combat that, he was using a split thickness skin graft rather than a full thickness, since it was a little less persnickety about how quickly those vascular highways were constructed.

As the nurse carried the skin away to prep it, he allowed himself to finally glance up. She was there, sitting in the front row. Her eyes met his for a second and she gave him a quick nod.

A spurt of warmth washed through his system. Her approval mattered a little too much, and it bothered him. He shouldn't have even looked up. But what was wrong with needing a little word of encouragement from time to time? There wasn't anything wrong with it. Not inherently. But caring that the encouragement specifically came from Elia should bother him.

He turned his attention back to his patient and did his best to forget she was there. But it wasn't easy. And he didn't like that he was taking even more care than usual with this particular surgery. As if he wanted to impress her.

He didn't. What he wanted was for this young man to have a successful outcome. To go on with his life despite the trauma he'd experienced. It was good that Elia had recommended the teen and his family undergo counseling. It would help them know how to support him without suffocating him or turning overprotective. And it would teach Matt to absorb what had happened to him and maybe even use his trauma for something positive. Like using his story to help another burn victim in the future.

Like what Elia was doing?

Exactly like that. She seemed to have been able to get past her childhood accident and not only go into nursing in a burn unit, but do more than that. She was helping individual patients like Matt. It was a boon not only for Westlake Memorial as an organization, but also for individual patients. He was sure this wasn't the first time she'd given someone helpful advice. Or supported a fundraising event in a very tangible way.

Maybe instead of apologizing to her, he should be thanking her. But that would involve pulling her aside yet again to talk to her.

And as much as part of him wanted to do exactly that,

another part of him wanted to avoid conversing with her more than necessary. Because he was starting to care too much about different aspects of her life. About what she did or didn't do. About what she thought or didn't think…of him.

The nurse came back with the prepped skin, and he used forceps to pick it up and examine it for defects or other problems. He saw none.

"Okay, let's get this done."

With everyone doing their assigned tasks, the graft was attached. Jake had opted to use fine sutures rather than staples, since this was an area that would be highly visible and he didn't want there to be a thick line of scarring where the graft met the rest of the skin of Matt's face.

He rinsed the area to examine it closely and gave himself mental permission to call the surgery a success. "Okay, I think we've gotten what we came for today. Good work, people."

The donor site was covered in a pressure bandage and would heal by second intentions, in which the wound would grow a new layer of skin. So there was no need for suturing that area at all, like they would have needed to do if they'd harvested a full thickness piece.

They woke Matt up, and when he glanced up at him with groggy, confused eyes, Jake gave him a simple thumbs-up sign. "Everything went well. We're going to get you back to your room. Your parents are waiting there to see you."

The teen put his hand up and lightly touched the bandage. And motioned for something. Maybe a mirror.

"You won't be able to see it for several days, and you need to keep your jaw as still as you can to let the new skin attach and form new blood vessels."

He nodded in answer. Jake would reiterate those instructions to his parents, since it was doubtful that Matt would remember much of what was said right now. When he glanced up at the observation window, he noted that Elia was gone. What had he expected, though? That she would stick around to talk to him later?

He patted Matt on the shoulder and then headed out the door to go find the teen's parents. When he got to the room, he was shocked to see that Elia was there, already talking to the parents. He only caught a portion of it, but the part he did was about how good of a job Jake had done.

"Well, thanks for the vote of confidence, but I have a pretty good team around me that helps make that happen."

"Oh, I didn't mean to—"

He gave her a smile that was meant to reassure her that she'd said nothing wrong. "You didn't. I was simply including you as part of that team. The recovery portion is just as important as the actual surgery."

Her face turned pink, something he still found attractive as all get-out. It made him want to see what else would make her blush, before shutting down that line of thought.

Matt's mom smiled. "Any projections as to how visible the scars will be?"

He shot a quick glance at Elia to see what her reaction

to that was, since her scars had evidently never healed as smoothly as other people's might have. But she didn't look uncomfortable about the question.

"It won't be so much the scars that are visible as the fact that the skin tone may be slightly different, and there will be no beard growth possible in that area since the hair follicles are different than those in other parts of his jaw. But even that can be altered slightly if he chooses to get hair transplants from other areas of his chin and/or jaw. We can get pretty darn close nowadays."

"Matt will be so happy to hear that. When can we see him?"

"They're just letting him wake up a little more and then he'll come back to the room. Maybe a half hour, tops."

"Thank you again. Will he need more skin graft surgeries?"

"If this one takes the way that I hope it will, he should be good to go as far as skin goes. He'll still need the teeth implants done, but the skin is in place, which is a pretty big thing, since it will help prevent infections from settling into open tissue."

"We are so grateful," his mother said. "So very grateful."

He understood what they meant. Part of it was probably referring to the surgery itself, but part of it was probably also talking about how lucky they were that Matt's injuries could be treated. That he would be able to live a fairly normal life. Like Elia did. She was pretty damn lucky, too. Some of those deep-tissue injuries required a lot of work to get to them to a place where they could still be functional, even if the tissue didn't look like most people's.

"I'm glad it's turning out the way it is." He glanced at both of them. "Do you have any more questions for me?"

They both shook their heads no. "But we do want to ask Elia a little more about the counseling service she recommended to us."

"Okay, good. You have my cell number. Don't hesitate to give me a call if you have any concerns or questions."

"We will."

Jake turned to go out of the door and heard the next conversation start with, "He was great when I talked to him about my experience, even though my injury happened many years ago."

The door closed behind him, shutting him out of the conversation completely. But that was okay. He'd been fairly anxious to get away from Elia before he ended up having to talk to her alone.

He went to the desk, and before he could help himself, he took the tongs and selected a cookie…bit into it. It tasted as fresh and good as they had a week ago when she'd first started bringing them. Maybe he needed to ask her about getting reimbursed for at least some of the ingredients. The sign-up sheet beside the jar looked new, and when he picked it up, he saw that there was a staple in it and that there were at least three other sheets of paper stapled together. At least a hundred people were now signed up. Just on this floor. He frowned. He didn't think they even had that many patients. Were people from other departments coming over to get cookies? That could get pretty expensive for Elia if she was having to foot the bill for providing refreshments for the whole hospital.

Yes, he was going to have to catch her and see where they stood. He frowned. Wait. Maybe he had an answer for that, one that would help on more than one level. He went into one of the supply cabinets and found a spare glass jar that was used for tongue depressor dispensers. He grabbed a Sharpie and a piece of paper and wrote in big letters:

Cookie Fund. Take a cookie, leave a donation.

That should get the point across. And then Elia could use the funds to replenish what she'd spent on making all of these.

Except she came out of the room and took one look at the sign and the marker in his hand. "Absolutely not."

"Word has obviously gotten out that there are some pretty good cookies up in the burn unit. I already feel bad that you're having to spend your free time making these. The least that people can do is donate something to the cause." With that, he took out five dollars and dropped it into the jar.

"My mom is actually bringing more cookies up tomorrow. So it's not just me making them."

"Well, then you can give her some of the money, as well. There won't be a lot, I'm sure, but maybe it will at least buy some of the ingredients."

She shook her head but smiled. "Oh, you don't know my mom. She does it because she loves it. And she makes decent money as a pastry chef in the Austin area. People come from miles around to sample what she makes."

This time, though, she didn't say anything about the bread she'd promised her mom would make for them. And he wasn't about to bring it up.

At that moment, the service elevator pinged and the doors opened. Matt's bed was being wheeled toward his hospital room. One of the orderlies was smiling at something the teen evidently said—despite the fact that Jake had just warned the kid to move his lower jaw as little as possible. It had already been immobilized due to the transplanted bone, but even using the muscles of his lips to form words would jar the skin grafts. He started to go over there, only to have Elia place her hand over his arm.

He looked at her in question.

"His parents will remind him. He doesn't need both you and them getting on to him." Her eyes were gentle. "He is still groggy from the anesthesia. Believe me, if anyone wants this graft to take, it's Matt. He won't purposely do anything to sabotage that."

He relaxed. "I guess you're right. I can be a little overbearing at times."

"Who, you?" Although her eyes were wide and innocent, there was laughter behind them that told him she was joking.

"Very funny. You've never gotten on to a patient for doing something that could be detrimental to their health?"

"Yes, of course, if they were willfully flouting doctor's recommendations. But not right after surgery, when people's thought processes can be affected by the anesthesia meds. It does contain an amnesiac."

"I'm quite aware of that. But point taken. If I see him doing a lot of talking tomorrow, though, I can't promise I won't say something to him."

"If he's still doing it tomorrow, then I'll beat you to it. But I doubt that he will be."

"I'll hold you to that, Elia."

She blinked for a second before sucking down a deep breath and leaning her hip against the nurse's desk. "How is Randy? Have you heard anything else?"

"No, but I plan on calling him sometime later today. I know he's home and was doing well as of yesterday."

"Good. Have you done any more training for the festival?"

"No. And the bike group isn't getting together this week in deference to Randy. People chipped in to get him a new ride, since his bike was totaled." Someone had asked him to mention it to Elia, but she'd only been with them once, so he hadn't felt right asking her to contribute.

She opened the jar and took out the five-dollar bill and then went behind the counter to pull out a wallet. Probably hers. She extracted a twenty and handed him both bills. "Can you add this to what everyone contributed?"

"Elia…"

"I want to. I'm happy to be able to at least do something for him."

She pulled his hand toward her and placed the money on his palm and then closed his fingers around it. Her touch was warm and sure, and he wished it had lasted a little longer than it had. "I'll give it to the bike shop. They'll know what to do with it. Maybe they can start a fund to get him a new helmet or other piece of equipment to go with the bike, which has already been bought."

"How long before he can ride again?"

"I would assume at least five more weeks or however long it takes for his elbow to heal."

She frowned. "He was planning on participating in the bike festival next weekend, wasn't he?"

"He was, but there's no way he'll be able to."

"I get it. But it still makes me sad for him."

Sheryll came out of a room and moved toward them. That was Jake's signal to move on, since she'd kind of given them a funny look when they'd gone off together earlier today. The last thing he needed was for a rumor about them to start making its way around the hospital.

"I need to get back to work, and I assume you do, too."

She grinned. "Nope. I'm off as of an hour and a half ago. I just wanted to watch Matt's surgery, so I stuck around."

"I'm sure he appreciated that."

Sheryll glanced at them as she arrived at the desk. "Who appreciated what?"

At least this was a question he could answer without making anyone uncomfortable.

"We were talking about Matt's surgery and the fact that Elia stayed to watch it."

"I was wondering why you were still on the floor." The other nurse glanced at her watch. "Did your mom make it in?"

"That's tomorrow."

"Oh, that's right. It's been a crazy day. But mine is about to end, too, and then I'm taking a long weekend off."

Jake did remember hearing something about that, whether it was an overheard conversation or whether she'd said it when Elia had mentioned going to watch the surgery. He smiled at her and said, "Well, I hope you have a wonderful weekend."

"Thanks. I'm sure we will. It's been a while since my husband and I have gotten away together."

"Enjoy," said Elia. "And I'm going to take off, too. See you on Monday, Sheryll, and I'll see you...?"

"I'm working tomorrow," Jake said. "You?"

"Same. So I guess I'll see you tomorrow."

Was it his imagination or did she not look very happy about the fact that they would be working with each other the next day? Well, it couldn't be helped, so she'd better get used to it, otherwise they were both going to have a big problem. Like the fact that he was finding himself worrying about things like those damned cookies and how much time, energy and money she was spending on the bike festival, when promoting it was something he should be doing.

"See you then."

With that, Jake turned and headed back to his office, leaving the two of them to talk about whatever they wanted to.

And if it was about him?

He couldn't imagine anything they might have to say about him. And really, he didn't care. Or at least he shouldn't. That didn't mean that part of him didn't wonder, though. But as long as they weren't making plans to match him up with anyone, he wasn't going to worry about it. Just to be sure, he went to his office and dug down to the bottom of one of his desk drawers. He pulled out last year's copy of *Daily Gossip* and stared at the headline for a minute. There was a huge picture of Samantha on the cover with a distressed look on her face. Above it were the words Plastic Surgeon Abandons Model on French Riviera. A second, smaller photo was of him with an angry look on his face, but the anger wasn't directed at Sam. It was at the photographers who'd always dogged their every step back when they'd been an item.

He'd met Sam while at a conference in Dallas, where she had a second home. They'd hit it off and had started seeing each other. They'd been able to keep their relationship a secret for a while at his request, but once it got out, the press had a field day with it and speculated whether or not she'd been one of his patients. Then, when things went sour, there was the tabloid article along with her angry social media post, and even more speculation had happened. So much so that his hospital asked some hard questions that he'd answered truthfully. Things had blown over, but it had been a cautionary tale about rumors and gossip. One he wasn't likely to forget. So when Sheryll had looked at him and Elia with speculation in her eyes, he'd been only too happy to leave the scene, before that speculation grew into something else. He could only hope that Elia wasn't the type to fuel those kinds of rumors, although he didn't get that vibe from her.

But the less the head nurse saw them doing things together, the better. So he would make it a point to treat Elia just like any other nurse. Because that's what she was, right? She was nothing special to him.

A quick twinge in his midsection made him wonder if that was absolutely the truth. But even if it wasn't, he was somehow going to need to get back to a place where it would become the truth. No matter how hard that might prove to be. It was either that or face the possibility of something like this—he tossed the paper to the side of his desk—happening all over again.

Sheryll leaned closer. "Is there something I should know?"

"Know?" Elia tilted her head and looked at the other woman.

"You guys have been hanging out a little bit, haven't you? First the group bike ride and now Matt's surgery?"

She frowned. "Uh, that wasn't exactly hanging out. We were in two separate rooms, for one thing. And *Matt* asked me to stay, and I did as a favor to him...the patient, not Jake."

"Okay, I get that."

"And he was here at the desk because he had the dumb idea that he should take up donations for the cookies I've been making."

Sheryll nodded. "I think that's a great idea. There have been a lot of people eating them, Elia. It has to be costing a fortune."

"No, it's not. Besides, I really like baking and haven't had the chance to do as much of it as I used to. Before

I became a nurse. And now, I'm too exhausted by the time I get home."

Sheryll nodded. "The job does take such a lot of emotional energy out of you. I'm the same way when I get home in the evenings. I don't have much motivation to do much of anything. So I don't know how you can bake cookies. It's like you're still working for Westlake even in your off hours, since it is their event."

"I guess I don't see it that way. I'm doing something besides nursing, so that has to count for something, right?"

"I guess. But I am still going to leave this donation jar up. Because I think it's the right thing to do."

Elia rolled her eyes and said, "Fine. Do whatever you want to do."

"Believe me, I will, so leave this here."

"Fine." She pretended to flounce off in a huff but knew her friend would see right through her. In reality, though, her and Jake's concern warmed her heart and made her feel like she'd made the right decision when she'd moved to Dallas to take this job. It felt right. And right now that was the only thing she was going to dwell on.

CHAPTER SEVEN

ELIA'S MOM SWEPT into the hospital with all of the subtlety of a freight train, and it made her cringe, even though she knew her parents meant well. She'd already been scheduled to work, and she'd asked them to make themselves at home in her small apartment, but of course her mom had wanted to see where her new job was and must have had her dad drive her over to Westlake Memorial.

It was understandable, but she also knew that Jake was somewhere on the floor, and for some reason she didn't want her mom meeting him. She was always going on about how Elia should meet some nice guy and settle down. She'd met plenty of nice guys. They just never seemed to want long-term relationships. More like the friends-with-benefits type of agreements, and she was no longer interested in doing that. Because she got emotionally attached, even when the man in question didn't seem to. She'd asked a friend if there was something she was doing…if she was too clingy, too needy, and they said no. That the men were jerks. But apart from the guy who'd pulled the covers up over them, could they really *all* be jerks? Or was she just attracted to shallow, jerkish types?

Regardless, the last thing she wanted was for her mom

to swoop in and start taking notes on the men at the hospital and ask embarrassing questions. Questions that she wasn't about to answer. Not that she knew too many of the men yet…besides Jake. And she didn't even really know him, right?

Except he'd been willing to save her life on the bike ride that day. And she'd fantasized about him in his bathtub afterward.

Oh, Lord. She definitely didn't want her mom meeting him.

Her mom gave her a big hug and motioned for her dad to put the three boxes he was carrying on the desk. *"Biscoitos."* She looked at the jar holding the current batch and added, "It looks like they are just in time, too. Are you sure you don't want something other than bicycles on some of them? Maybe some with just flowers?"

Her mom spoke in Portuguese, even though her English was really good. It used to embarrass her when she did that in public, but she'd come to understand that it was her mom's heart language and that it made the conversation more intimate to speak to her daughter in "their" language. Her dad, however, had long switched over. So Elia had learned to talk to them in two different languages.

She laughed. "It's for the bike festival, Mom, so no, I don't think flowers or ballerinas or fairies would get that message across."

"Just asking. Hopefully next year the fundraiser will be something different. Something more…interesting."

"They've been doing this for quite a few years and

it's successful, so I don't think they're going to change it anytime soon."

Her dad patted her arm and leaned over to kiss her on the cheek. "Don't let her fool you. She's been trying to make every cookie different and has been looking up countless ideas on that Pinterest site."

The thought of her mom scrolling through endless pictures on social media made her laugh again. Especially when she swatted her husband's arm. "I have not. I do have an imagination, you know."

"Whatever you say, dear." Her dad did respond to his wife in Portuguese.

Time to send them both on their way before they got into one of their little heated discussions about this or that and someone came along. It was all in love, but sometimes it sure didn't sound that way.

"I gave you the keys to the apartment. Why don't you guys get some lunch and then head over there. I should be home in an hour or two." She still needed to check Matt's bandages and make sure the graft was doing okay, and she had a few other patients she needed to see.

Just then the elevator doors opened, and when she saw who got off, she closed her eyes for a second and sent up a silent prayer. Great. Just what she needed, although it was inevitable that they would meet. She'd just rather it happen later rather than sooner and on Elia's terms.

He spotted her, and of course he came over to get updates on some of the patients. She tried to edge away from the desk, but her mom's eyes followed her every move. "Hi, Dr. Callin, I was just getting ready to check on Matt."

Jake's head tilted. "It hasn't been Dr. Callin in a while. Is something wrong?"

"And who is this, *filhinha*?"

The plastic surgeon's eyes changed as soon as he heard her mother speak and gave her an apologetic look. He definitely understood now. Now that it was too late.

"This is Dr. Jakob Callin. He's head of Westlake's burn unit. Jake, this is my mom and dad."

Her mother stood on tiptoe and kissed his cheek in Portuguese fashion, which made Elia wince. Jake didn't seem shocked by it, though. He just smiled at her.

"Tersia and Nelson. Nice to meet you." She glanced at her daughter. "Of course Elia hasn't mentioned anyone from her work yet, and we've been very curious."

Oh, Mom, please don't do this. Not with Jake, of all people.

"She's very good at her job," Jake said. "And of course we're so grateful to you and Elia for providing cookies to advertise the fundraiser. They've been very popular. She also mentioned you make wonderful bread."

He sent a glint Elia's way, and she crinkled her nose, instinctively knowing that he was teasing her. But he had no idea what he was about to unleash. No idea at all. She started a mental countdown and waited for it.

"Yes, I do. You must come over to Elia's apartment tomorrow. I will fix you a traditional Portuguese meal, although the bread won't be as good without my bread oven."

And there it was. Just like she knew it would be.

"Oh, I didn't mean for you to…" Jake sounded startled by the invitation.

This time it was Elia who sent him a raised brow. He'd asked for it. And now there was nothing she could do about it. It would be up to him to say he had other plans, which she hoped to hell that he would. For both their sakes.

"But I insist. If you have no plans." Her mom pushed forward with the invitation.

Evidently her father was not going to step in and intervene, which was probably for the best, because it might make her mom dig in her heels even further.

"I don't. If Elia is okay with me coming over, that is."

"But of course she is. Aren't you, *filha*?" Her mom was now looking at her as if surprised that Jake would even think that might be the case.

"Of course I am." Her delivery was a little wooden, but there was no way she was going to act overjoyed. She really didn't want him *or* her mom getting the wrong idea.

"Let me know the time, then, and I'll see that I'm there. But please don't go to a lot of work."

He obviously didn't know her mom. Or their culture. Of course she would go to a lot of work. She loved to entertain. It was ingrained in her ancestral DNA.

"I won't," her mom said. "How about seven in the evening? That is about the time we normally eat."

"Seven is perfect. I'll see you there."

Her mom's eyes widened. "So you know where my daughter lives?"

"No, but I was going to have her text me the address."

This time, his response was a little more cautious, as if finally realizing what could happen if he wasn't careful.

"I see. Okay, well, we'll let you both get back to… work. And we'll see you tomorrow."

"Thanks again for the invitation."

Her parents headed for the elevator and got on, her mom waving all the way up until the doors swallowed them from view.

Elia plopped onto one of the tall stools and looked at him. "I am so sorry, Jake. You don't have to go. I can tell her you realized you have another commitment."

"Do you not want me to come?"

Was that a trick question? Why would he even want to? "It's not that. I just don't want you to feel bamboozled into a dinner you don't want."

"I haven't heard that term in a while." He smiled. "And I have to say, 'bamboozled' sounds so much more sophisticated when said with your accent."

Her face heated, but this time it was a good warmth. One that was a whole lot better than the embarrassment that she'd felt over her mom's antics. But that was common with her mother, who seemed to know just how to maneuver people to do what she wanted them to do. And she'd done an expert job with Jake. She'd gotten him to do exactly what she wanted. And the only thing was, Elia was a little afraid that dinner might not be the end of it. So she needed to at least put their relationship at the hospital back on professional footing. To do that, she decided to act as if that invitation to dinner had never happened.

So when he suggested they go and see Matt together,

she jumped at it. "I was actually just going in to see how his graft was doing."

"And I was actually headed there when I got off that elevator a few moments ago." He motioned for her to precede him. "Shall we?"

Probably accepting that dinner invitation hadn't been one of Jake's smartest moves, but it had been so unexpected that he hadn't been able to think quickly enough to get out of it. Then again, he was the one who'd brought it on himself by mentioning homemade bread.

And hell, if the word "bamboozled" hadn't been the sexiest thing Jake had ever heard. It sent heat spiraling through him and made him think he wouldn't have minded being bamboozled by Elia in any number of ways.

By the time they got into Matt's room, though, he'd regained his senses and was able to concentrate on the teen. His parents were there, as they'd been every step of this journey. He shook their hands. Gracie was nowhere to be seen, but it was likely that she was working somewhere over the summer. They did a quick check of the pressure bandage covering the site and it was intact. "You're being careful to not move your jaw much, right?"

The teen nodded and wrote something on a whiteboard. "Not talking more than necessary."

Jake nodded. "And you understand why that's so important. Movement of the graft is not your friend right now. The tissue needs to make its own vascular field to grow and thrive—and those new blood vessels are extremely fragile in the beginning."

Matt moved his closed fist up and down in what Jake recognized as the signed word for yes. Then he wrote, "How long before the bandage comes off?"

"About eight days, although it's not going to look perfect when it comes off. The final result will take time and patience."

The teen's face didn't change and Jake wasn't sure what he was thinking. But he didn't want to lie and then take the bandages off and have Matt have a meltdown.

Veronica spoke up for the first time. "Matt also wanted to know how long he'll need to stay in the hospital."

That was also a common question. One with a complicated answer. "We're looking at about two weeks to make sure the graft and the donor site both heal well, especially since we'll be dealing with other surgeries. Your tooth implants won't be able to be done until your jaw and your skin graft are both healed enough."

This time Matt did frown, and Elia, who'd been scurrying around getting vitals and checking supplies, stopped what she was doing and moved back to the bed, putting her hand on the teen's arm. "I know it seems like a long time, and I was impatient, too, when I had my surgeries, but if you rush it and things don't look the way you'd hoped they would, you'll always wonder if it was something you did or simply the way your body heals."

Was that what she'd done? Tried to rush her healing process and then wondered if that was why she had contractures or why her body developed keloids? She acted like she knew it was her body's genetic makeup that was at fault, but was there something more going on below the surface?

Matt seemed to relax into the pillows with a slight nod. Elia pulled Veronica to the side and said something to her, to which the teen's mom gripped both her hands before giving her a long hug.

Elia was good at empathizing. He'd never had anyone complain about his bedside manner, but he also knew himself well enough to know that he tended to be more matter-of-fact and wasn't wired to say things that met people's emotional needs.

It was one of Samantha's complaints about him. Although she'd had a long laundry list of faults that she supposedly hadn't been able to deal with. That along with the request she'd made at the very end of their relationship had done them in as a couple. She'd been really unhappy about his refusal, although she hadn't wanted to talk about it later. But Sam had also had "people" who specialized in smoothing the way for her. The funny thing was, it was one of her staff members who'd communicated with him while she was in France on a job that, while Sam would "always love him and cherish the time they'd spent together," she wanted to break things off. She hadn't even had the nerve to tell him herself. And though he'd been more relieved than angry, almost immediately afterward those tabloids had exploded with the news that he'd abandoned her while they'd been on holiday. It was almost as if she'd planned things right down to the headline.

A few weeks later, she was dating an actor. Someone

much better suited to her. He was happy for her. And extremely happy for himself. He understood they had a child now.

He didn't want to go through that again. Ever. Did he think he might find someone he'd want to settle down with? He didn't see it happening anytime soon. He was happy with his life the way it was.

Glancing at Elia, he saw she was watching him, and he realized he'd been lost in his own world for several minutes. So he shook off his thoughts and went over to where she was still standing. In a low voice, she said, "Would it be okay if I contacted the counseling center to see if they could do their first couple of sessions here in Matt's hospital room? I really think he could benefit from it."

"I think that's a great idea." He had been worried a little over Matt's demeanor. It was hard to be a teenager with a girlfriend and have to not talk or move more than necessary. Who had to sit in a hospital room for more than two weeks while the world went on without him. "Is Gracie still in the picture?" He kept his voice as low as Elia's had been.

"She is. She's been really great. But I can tell Matt is worried about how long she'll stick around. I remember being that age and scared that anything I did would make people look at me weird. I think the thing he's worried most about is being disfigured for life. That he'll look like a monster or something. For someone who's always been popular, it's a hard blow."

Out of the corner of his eye, he saw Elia shift her weight onto her bad leg. Had she been worried about that, even though her burns had not been in a visible place? Just then Matt started waving his arms at them and held up his whiteboard. "What are you guys talking about?" it read.

They moved back over to the bed and Elia spoke up. "Would you like to start meeting with your counselor here at the hospital, since you'll be here a little longer because of your grafts? You could ask Gracie if she wants to join you, if that's something you'd be interested in."

He nodded emphatically and scribbled on his board. "Would they do that? Meet here?"

"I can go call them right after I leave here. If Dr. Callin writes up an order for it, it's more likely to be covered by insurance."

All eyes in the room shifted to him. There was a fine balance in his line of work to order treatments that were necessary while not incurring unnecessary costs to the patient or insurance companies. But he did think if the center that Elia had talked to would consider coming to the hospital, then that would be a good thing. A necessary thing. "I'll be happy to write it up as necessary, if it helps with insurance coverage."

Matt erased what was on his board and simply wrote, "Thank you."

He nodded. "Thank Elia. She's the one who thought of it."

Just then one of the nurses stuck her head in. "You're needed in the ER, Dr. Callin."

Elia turned to Matt and said, "I'll call the counseling center and let you know when they can come."

Not *if* they could come. But when. He had never seen her truly angry, but he knew from experience on that first day that she would move heaven and earth to see that her patients got what they needed.

She left the room when he did and waited as Brittany filled them in. "The squad just brought in a three-year-old who pulled a pot of boiling water onto herself. Scald burns down the front of her."

"Headed that way." He turned to Elia. "Let me know how that call goes."

"I will. Let me know how the child is."

He nodded. "Will do."

Some medical staff had adopted a thick skin—a kind of defense mechanism—to deal with the traumas that came into hospitals day in and day out. To have a tender heart was to be in danger of burning out emotionally.

So he'd been surprised by Elia's request to let her know how the kid was, especially since she'd been injured as a child herself. Brittany walked away to do other things, and Jake found himself touching Elia's hand. "Are you okay?"

She didn't ask what he was talking about, just looked him in the eye. "Little kids are always harder, for some reason."

Gripping her fingers, he gently squeezed. "I'll let you know. Promise."

"Thanks, Jake. Really."

"Not a problem." Then he let go of her and headed toward the elevator and whatever awaited him on the ground floor.

* * *

Elia didn't have to wait a super long time before learning how Jake's little patient was doing. She'd been able to call the counseling center, who promised someone would be out tomorrow morning, despite it being Sunday. She'd sagged in relief. All it would take was for Matt to reach rock bottom and impulsively do something that would damage everything Jake had worked so hard to do for the teen and his family.

The service elevator opened, and the first thing she heard was a child crying, even as the plastic surgeon exited the car and waited while two hospital staff members wheeled the bed into the room. Elia hurried over to them. The little girl seemed so tiny on the huge hospital bed. Her heart cramped. "Let's put her in Room Four for now."

She pushed through the door first, mentally taking stock of the supplies in the room that Jake might need. Once they got to the room, Jake actually slid his hands beneath the girl's back, carefully avoiding the front. Elia could see angry red skin already beginning to blister across the tiny girl's chest and legs, where the clothing had been cut away.

Second-degree burns at least. And probably areas where the damage went deeper. The girl screamed louder when Jake moved her over to the bed in the room, even though he was being extremely gentle. "Her parents?"

He glanced at her. "They're talking to social workers and the police right now, but they'll be up in a few minutes."

"*Deus.* It wasn't on purpose, was it?"

"No. From all accounts, they had company and the mom was fixing a large lunch and went to talk to her guests while pasta water was heating up." He pulled in a visible breath, stroking the child's face, which thankfully looked devoid of burns. "Carly evidently pulled a little stool over that she used to help her mom do the dishes and they heard screaming and found the pot on the floor and the toddler covered with water. They did the right thing and put her under a cold shower, but her clothes held the heat against her skin until they got her cooled off."

"And the police?"

"It's routine to ask questions whenever a child has scalds like this, but they are pretty distraught."

She could imagine. Snatches of her own mom's face as she'd held her in her arms after she was burned were etched in her memory. The fear. The horror. The self-condemnation for not noticing that Elia was getting so close to the fire.

She moved over to the girl. She bent over to talk soothingly to her before remembering that she'd seen a Binky on the gurney she'd been brought in on. "Wait here with her for a minute."

She went outside, glad to find that the orderlies were still waiting for the elevator to arrive on the floor. Just then the doors opened. "Can you hold that for a minute?"

Quickly walking over to them, she glanced at the bed and didn't see anything for a second. Then she lifted the pillow and found a pink pacifier. She normally wouldn't have given it to the child without permission, but right now she'd do anything she could to comfort the little girl.

She returned to the room, and when she offered it to the crying toddler, she opened her mouth and took it. Her little lashes were wet with tears, and Elia couldn't imagine how much pain she was in. Burn injuries hurt. A lot. And for a child who didn't understand what was going on...

"Good thinking. I just got a text that her parents are on their way up," Jake said.

"Okay. What do you want me to do first?" Was he asking her to intercept the parents so he could finish assessing the child?

"Let's get an IV started."

Starting an IV on a child who was in pain or scared was always a tricky process. But fortunately her parents came into the room and were there for the procedure, soothing Carly and holding her arm while Elia placed the catheter. In less than thirty seconds it was in and taped in place. Fortunately that hand was free of burns. Then they were in treatment mode, assessing which of the burns were the deepest and needed immediate attention. It was then that they were able to give some meds for pain. Once that was done, Carly was much less agitated and was able to sleep through some of the procedures, while her mom sat next to the bed and stroked her head, silent tears streaming down her face.

Elia had treated plenty of children since she'd gone through her specialty training, but it was still hard to see them in pain. Especially when the wounds needed to be debrided.

As if reading her mind, Jake pulled the parents aside

while Carly slept. "The burns are serious, don't get me wrong, but from what I can see the worst of them are second-degree rather than third."

"Does that mean no scarring?" her mom asked.

"The deeper ones still can in some instances, but we'll work hard to give her the best outcome possible. If the area was small, we could probably send her home with some care instructions, but because this affects a large area of her torso, we want to keep her for a bit. She already has blistering, which will spread, and in some places individual blisters will join together and she'll lose the top layer of skin. What's underneath will be raw and very tender. That's when the danger of infection sets in."

Carly's dad had been really quiet but finally spoke up. "Do what you need to do. One of us will be here around the clock, if possible."

"I think that can be arranged. The recliner next to the bed folds flat, but we'll want to limit visitors to her room, just to reduce the chance of microbes being brought into her room."

"How long before she'll be released?"

"Give us a couple of days to make that decision. It depends on what her skin does or doesn't do."

"We have three other children. Carly is our youngest. Can they see her? They're all scared and upset. My mom is with them right now."

Elia ached for them. Even though the other kids needed the reassurance that Carly would be okay, Jake was absolutely right that the chance of infection would start soon.

As soon as her skin began peeling to reveal the deeper layers, the danger of that happening increased.

"We can set something up like a Zoom meeting or a virtual hospital visit like they did during the pandemic. But we really don't want any more people in here than necessary."

Carly whimpered in her sleep and her mom immediately went over to try to console her. She lifted her hand, as if trying to figure out where she could touch and where she couldn't. Elia leaned down. "Just stroke her forehead and talk to her. She just wants to know that someone she loves is here."

As Carly's mom did her best to reassure her child, Elia slid from the room to try to give her some privacy. Jake had evidently stepped outside to talk to Carly's dad. It was probably for the best, since as soon as he walked back into that room, it would be to start treating her burns. All she could pray was that, since Carly was young and healthy, she would heal quickly and she would experience as little pain as possible.

Wasn't that what every human being wanted? To experience as little pain as possible? Yes. And it was a good reminder that pain wasn't always physical. It was sometimes emotional. And that pain might not leave physical scars, but she knew from experience that it could leave invisible wounds that lasted long after the causative agent was removed. Like being with someone who didn't want to look at your scars while making love to you.

Heading over to the nurses' desk, she worked on updating their patient information. And in doing so, she tried to forget that tiny touch to the hand that Jake had given her earlier. Because it had been sweet and warming and far too welcome. She was starting to like his presence too much, and for Elia, that could be a very dangerous proposition. One she would do well to avoid, unless she was willing to risk being hurt. Again.

CHAPTER EIGHT

JAKE CLUTCHED THE bottle of red wine that he'd brought as a thank-you for Tersia and Nelson. He'd thrown his bike onto the carrier on the back of his SUV just in case. In case of what? It wasn't likely that Elia was going to want to leave her mom and dad in order to go bike riding with him. He wasn't sure what had possessed him to do it. But with the bike festival next week, he needed to get some training time in while he could. If worse came to worst, he could leave the bike on the back of his vehicle and take a ride during his lunch hour tomorrow or something.

Knocking on the door, he was surprised when less than fifteen seconds went by before someone opened it. It was Elia. She motioned him inside.

"I brought this for your mom and dad for inviting me. But since it's your house, I'm not sure who I should give it to."

"My parents. They'll appreciate the gesture. Wine is actually a customary hostess gift in Portugal. And since she's made a traditional pork dish, it'll pair perfectly with it."

She smiled, and he couldn't hold back his own grin. It

felt homey and comfortable to be standing here talking with her like this. Like he really was meeting her parents for the first time.

Except this wasn't that kind of occasion at all.

"Good to know, since I guessed."

"You guessed correctly." She again motioned him inside. "Come in, please."

Her apartment was just as comfortable as their conversation had been, and he could definitely see the Portuguese influence here. Clay plates with blue and white glaze were hung on the walls in the dining room. Almost every free surface had some sort of representation of Portuguese pottery. It was beautiful and fit who Elia was to a tee.

Despite the heat of the day, she still wasn't wearing shorts or even a sundress. Instead she was dressed in a long, loose skirt that looked both comfortable and safe as far as her leg went. He still hadn't seen the scars, but for there to be contractures the damage had to be pretty rough.

And he wasn't likely to see them, although the surgeon in him wondered if there was anything that could still be done to ease the pull. He'd dissected various surgical procedures in his head, knowing that he would never suggest them. It was Elia's body and her choice as far as what she allowed to be done to it.

It was unlikely even if he did offer to examine her that she would go through with surgery. She'd lived with her leg like it was for a long time. She was comfortable with how it functioned and he needed to let her be.

At that moment, Tersia came out of the kitchen with Nelson following close behind.

"Ah, Jakob. It's so good for you to come." Elia's mom's accent was much more pronounced than that of her daughter, and she gave more weight to the last syllable of his name than she had the first. He wondered if Elia would do the same. He thought she might have said his full name before but couldn't remember. He had to admit he loved to hear the nurse talk. Her words rolled through his senses like fine scotch, and he sometimes found himself paying more attention to her cadence than the phrases themselves. Although if he concentrated hard enough...

Which he did. Because he didn't want to embarrass himself by having to ask her to repeat herself. Although it was damned tempting at times.

Cut it out, Callin.

He would assume Tersia and Elia spoke Portuguese when in each other's company, and so while Elia worked in an English-speaking job, there wouldn't be as much need for Tersia to speak the language. Except, hadn't Elia told him that she worked in a bakery, cooking traditional pastries? Yes, but they also probably had a good-sized Portuguese or Brazilian clientele, if that's what their business catered to.

"*Mãe*, Jake brought wine for dinner."

Okay, even without saying his whole name, it had still come out warm and slightly accented. And having his name whispered against his skin in the heat of passion... how would it sound then?

He shut off those thoughts in a hurry, when he realized both women were now looking at him. "I'm sorry, did you say something?"

"I simply said thank you, Jakob." Tersia's expression was a little sharper than it had been, and her eyes were scouring across his face as if searching for something.

Something she wouldn't find, if he had his way. The last thing he wanted was for some woman's mother to try to play matchmaker. Not that that's what she'd been doing. He knew he was acting kind of strange and that's probably why she'd looked at him sideways. He'd better get his head on straight or there would be a lot more than sideways glances. She'd be asking some hard questions. Ones he really didn't want to answer.

Just then Nelson came in and walked over to give his hand a firm clasp. "Good to see you again. Sorry I was late getting to the door. Tersia had me in the kitchen waiting on the bread to finish cooking. I think you'll like it."

Nelson's speech was reminiscent of Elia's. His English, like hers, was excellent, but there remained a tiny bit of an accent. Enough of one to give their way of speaking an exotic flavor that made you want to sit and listen to them.

"I'm sure I'll like all of it, if that wonderful aroma is anything to go by."

"You must come in and sit, while I uncork the wine. Dinner is almost ready." Elia's mom led the way into the living room as if the space were hers rather than her daughter's. Elia threw him a pained smile and mouthed "sorry."

He shook his head and touched her arm as a way of telling her not to worry about it. Her answering smile was much more at ease. "Why don't you sit on the couch and I'll help Mom with whatever else needs to be done. I hope you're hungry. She always makes enough for an army. Seriously. You don't have twenty friends joining us, do you?"

"Sorry, no." He chuckled and everything seemed okay again. He liked being able to joke about things with her in a way he rarely did with other colleagues. There just wasn't much time or the opportunity, since so much revolved around their work.

Well, tonight didn't involve work, and he might as well just settle in and enjoy that fact. He might even be able to unwind. Really unwind. Something he'd wondered if he'd even be able to do when he'd left his apartment an hour ago. Maybe he could after all.

Suddenly, he was looking forward to spending time with them and getting to know Elia and her folks a little better. It was rare that he enjoyed a meal with friends or anyone else, so he would just sit back and allow himself to eat and laugh and give himself permission not to dwell on work or the cases he was currently working on. Those would all still be there tomorrow. And so would he.

The pork with clams in its rich, flavorful sauce proved to be every bit as good as Nelson had said it would be. Even better, actually. And he was enjoying the stories of Elia and her brother when they were kids.

"And then Elia lifted up her hand to throw the seeds toward the pigeons, but they decided she was being too slow about it and one landed right on top of her head.

On top of the cute little white beret she had insisted on wearing to the National Bird Park. And that beret…" Tersia smothered a laugh with the back of her hand. "That *puro branco* beret—soon wasn't pure white anymore. And what the bird had dripped down onto her nose." She clapped her hands. "If you could have seen Eliana's expression…"

Jake could picture the pure look of surprise that must have been on a young Elia's face. He laughed again, as he'd been doing for the last half hour.

She chuckled. "I did not invite that pigeon to use me as a perch, nor did I invite it to…" She swirled her hand in the air to get the point across.

"And what did you do once it did both of those things?"

She leaned her shoulder in to bump against his. "Well, I can tell you what I didn't do. I didn't wear that beret ever again. I'm not sure what even happened to it."

"Oh, I still have it," Tersia said. "It's been professionally cleaned, but it holds a special memory. Her grandmother made it for her."

Elia's eyes widened. "She did? I didn't remember that. I feel badly about never wearing it again, then."

Tersia came over and kissed her on the cheek. "I had enough pictures of you in it that day to make her think it was your favorite garment. I certainly never told her about what the bird did to it. She might have burned the thing until it was nothing but ashes."

As soon as the words came out, her mom stopped talking and covered her mouth with her palm, a look of horror crossing her face. Then she wrapped her arms around her daughter's shoulders. "Forgive me. That did not come out the way I intended it to."

"*Mamãe*, it is fine. You don't need to worry every time you mention something burning."

Tersia didn't look convinced. If anything, her distress seemed to grow. "If only I hadn't been paying as much attention to Tomás that day."

Elia gave him a helpless look, as if this subject had been repeated ad infinitum. "So was I, *Mãe*. So was I. You were not to blame."

Tomás must be a relative. Or a close friend.

As if she felt like he needed an explanation, Tersia said, "Elia was burned as a child while helping her brother learn how to walk. She backed into a fire and fell on it."

He nodded, understanding that Elia was feeling pretty uncomfortable about this subject appearing on the radar. "She told me about her accident. And although I know it was hard for all of you to go through, it has given Elia a wonderful way of empathizing with her patients, something she might not be able to do if she didn't intimately understand what it felt like to go through all of the pain and treatments that our patients have to endure."

Nelson, who was still sitting at the table, tossed him a grateful look. "I've said this very thing to Elia, and she agrees that it helps her do her job, don't you, *filha*?"

"Yes. Absolutely. I love my job. And it does help me understand them, even though no one has had the exact same experience that I had." Under the table, her knee touched his as if thanking him for saying what he had. Or maybe she'd just accidentally touched him and it meant nothing at all. Except, she didn't remove the pressure like she might have otherwise, so he nudged her back.

And when she turned toward him and smiled...

He was transfixed, unable to move for several seconds before finally shaking himself free and including the rest of her family in his return smile. He shared a little about Matt without revealing his name or any identifying information and said what a help Elia had been the first time he actually met her.

"You actually met me before that. You just don't remember."

Tersia murmured, "But you remember her now, don't you."

There was something about the way she said the words that made her daughter say, *"Mamãe..."* as if her mom had said something wrong.

But she hadn't. Elia was pretty damned memorable. "I do, for sure."

She threw a look at Jake. And he couldn't for the life of him understand what it meant. But all she said was, "Mom, are we ready for dessert?"

"We are. I hope you like," she said to Jake. "We call them *filhós de abobora*. At the bakery, we call them fried pumpkin cakes, but they're not like your traditional American cake. They are Elia's favorite thing. I'll go get them."

There was something about trying something that was Elia's "favorite" that made him anticipate whatever this dessert was that much more.

When Tersia brought in a plate of what looked like

misshapen donut holes, he was immediately intrigued. These were golden brown and sprinkled with sugar. And the smell was wonderful.

"Cinnamon?"

"Yes," Tersia said. "They do have cinnamon and sugar sprinkled on them, and I mix a little cinnamon in with the pumpkin. At Christmas time, *filhoses* are sometimes made with decorative iron molds that are heated in hot oil, dipped into a pumpkin batter and then plunged back in the oil to fry until they come free of the mold."

"They are *sooo* good." The way Elia drew out the word made him take a quick breath.

Anything that got that kind of reaction out of her had to be heaven on earth. And damn if it didn't have him salivating for the dessert. But it wasn't just that. He wanted her. To feed her those desserts and hear her make little sounds as she savored them.

Jake swallowed, suddenly feeling like he was in over his head and wanting things he damned well shouldn't want. And yet he did.

Elia's mom set the tray of pumpkin cakes on the table and then went over to a small sideboard and picked up some blue and white dessert plates that matched the set they had used for dinner. They kind of reminded him of the Wedgwood dinnerware they had in the States, but these were heavier, with a more pottery-type feel. He liked them. They fit with who Elia was. She was delicate looking, but there was something solid beneath that veneer. Something that was more than just a pretty face. It made him glad, for some reason.

He accepted the plate with the small cakes Tersia had placed on it, waiting to see if they used forks to eat them or just their fingers.

Nelson seemed to sense his hesitation, because he glanced at him and then picked one up with his fingers and popped it into his mouth whole. Jake followed suit and a second later saw what the fuss was all about and why these were Elia's favorite dessert. Light and incredibly fluffy, it was like a cross between a donut and a sweet bread. And it melted in his mouth, making him want to repeat the experience.

Elia was watching him as she chewed her own cake, eyes closing for a second as she savored it before looking at him again and saying, "Good?"

"Very." And not only the cake. There was a sensual quality to the way she enjoyed the morsel that seemed to go beyond it as a simple food. And he'd enjoyed the sight a little too much, feeling a little like a voyeur who was watching something he shouldn't. Maybe because he was equating the food with sex. He could admit it, although he hoped to hell no one in this room guessed that little secret. To try to shake it from his thoughts, he popped another cake into his mouth. Except this time it was as if his perceptions had been altered, because he was letting it linger on his tongue just a little longer, trying to keep the sensation from ending.

Shit. He needed to get out of here.

His cell phone buzzed in his pocket, as if the universe had heard him. Taking it out to quickly glance at the screen in case it was an emergency, he saw it was indeed the hospital. "Sorry, I need to take this."

"Go ahead," Nelson said. "There's a balcony right through there, if you need some privacy."

"Thanks." As he walked toward the sliding glass doors, he was vaguely aware of someone else's phone ringing behind him. Glancing back, he saw Elia take her phone from her purse and glance down.

In the second that he went through the door that led to the balcony, he knew his escape wasn't going to be as easy as he'd hoped. He answered it and heard a panicked voice on the other end. "Jake. Can you come back to the hospital?"

"Sure." It was Sheryll calling. "What's up?"

"We've just had someone brought in who, according to a relative, had some kind of lye solution thrown on her by an ex-boyfriend. She's in bad shape."

"I'm on my way. Start lavaging the area immediately, but make sure you keep the water out of her eyes, in case there's any lye around them."

"Will do. I think one eye may already be compromised. Mary is trying to reach Elia to see if she can come, too. Do you know where she is? We're shorthanded and… Wait." She said something to someone in the background before coming back. "Never mind. We reached her. She's on her way in, too."

Elia evidently hadn't said anything about them eating together, so he decided to follow her lead. "Okay, I'll see you in about twenty minutes."

"Thanks." With that she hung up without saying goodbye. But Jake didn't need goodbyes. From what it sounded like, they needed a miracle. A big one.

Elia couldn't believe what she'd heard. She'd never dealt with a chemical burn that was on purpose before, although there were all kinds of ways that people hurt others. But to throw some type of caustic substance onto another human being… It was unfathomable.

Also unfathomable was the fact that she'd gone from laughing with Jake one minute to riding in his car as they each silently prepared for what they were about to find.

They burst through the emergency room doors, and as soon as the staff saw them they directed them to the burn unit.

"They've already transferred her since you guys have more of the needed equipment on hand to deal with serious burns," one of the residents said.

Jake kept moving, throwing back the words, "Nothing internal?"

"Not that we could assess. But the lye… It's caused quite a bit of damage."

Lye burns could be some of the worst, because you didn't immediately feel pain where the chemicals touched the skin. It was a case where the length of contact helped determine how much damage it caused to the skin and mucus membranes. It could literally dissolve tissue, turning it to jelly.

They caught the elevator just as the doors were opening. Jake didn't attempt to talk to Elia, but she couldn't blame him. He was probably running treatment options through his head, the same way she was. But even so, the silence wasn't an uncomfortable one and she didn't feel the need to try to break it.

Her mom and dad sometimes embarrassed her with their enthusiasm toward their guests when entertaining, but Jake hadn't seemed bothered. He'd seemed charmed by them, if anything.

As soon as the doors let them off on the floor, she glanced to the right where the empty nurses' station stood as a testament to the battle that was happening in one of the rooms, the one that people were going in and out of.

Jake nodded to one of the doctors who came out, an ophthalmic surgeon from the ground floor. "How's it looking?"

"She's almost certainly going to lose the right eye. The cornea is gone, and it's reached some of the deeper structures."

"Hell, how does something like this even happen?" the plastic surgeon asked.

"Breakups can bring out the 'mean' in some people. They feel like they have to hurt the other person back in some way. You know how *that* works."

Jake had a weird reaction to the words. He flinched, his head going back an inch or two. The other man didn't seem to notice, or if he did he didn't place much importance on it. "At least skin can be grafted, although her face is going to need some major work."

"Was it straight lye?"

"She evidently has a small business endeavor making

homemade soap products. She was just adding lye to a wet solution when an ex-boyfriend came in and upended the folding table she was working on. She had eyeglasses on, but not safety goggles. He'd evidently made some threats, but nothing she'd taken seriously."

Elia started to edge past the two men so she could go in and help the team, when Jake put an end to the conversation. "Thanks. I'll get in there and see what I can do."

"Let me know. I'll be back in about a half hour. I have a procedure I've rescheduled three times already, and there's nothing more I can do for this patient right now."

With that, the young doctor strode toward the elevator they'd just exited.

They went through the door and found it was strewn with medical wrappers and containers. Two nurses stood next to a patient who was on a special table specifically made for lavaging large areas of the body. With raised sides that kept water and liquids contained, the head of the bed was slightly elevated so that everything flowed toward the base, where tubing was connected to a drain in the floor.

Sheryll came over to her. "Thank God, you're here. It's been just me and Mary, and she's not feeling well… Just went to the bathroom. Again."

As much as they were encouraged not to come in to work when ill, there were times when you just couldn't help it. At least when there was no fever, just a crappy sensation that you could sometimes work through. "Just tell me what you need."

"Patient's name is Dorothy White. We think we've lavaged long enough. But Timmons wants to get Jake's input."

Jeremy Timmons was a newer resident who was working under Jake's mentorship program. From what she understood, more and more cases were being shunted from a nearby hospital, which had just shut down their trauma department. It used to be that only the worst of the worst cases were sent to Westlake's burn unit for treatment after lifesaving triage—like this patient's lavaging—had already been done. But that meant some of them now had a longer ride in an ambulance to get to Westlake, which meant a longer time until they could get that treatment. She didn't know if that was the case for this particular patient, but when you were at home and unsure what to do for someone, it was hard. Westlake had hired Dr. Timmons right out of med school before another hospital could scoop him up.

"What needs to be done right now?"

"Let's see what Jake says. Can you stay here, so I can see to my other patients? It's been mass chaos up here for the last half hour."

"Go. I'm good."

Sheryll squeezed her arm. "Thanks."

With that the other nurse headed out of the room. Elia scrubbed up in a nearby sink and donned her PPE and then offered to help Jake as he did his. Two of the biggest dangers of large areas of tissue damage from burns were fluid loss and infections. Fluids could be replaced, but without the protective layer of the dermis, opportunistic bacteria were just waiting to move in. It was a continuous battle. And she'd seen one case where a patient with 90 percent burns was told he had little chance of survival. He was advised to say his goodbyes. It was one of the hardest cases she'd ever worked on. And true to what the doctors said, he died of sepsis two weeks after being burned, despite aggressive treatment with IV antibiotics.

Jake had instructed her to start treating the less serious burns with antibiotic cream, while he and Jeremy went over the patient with a fine-tooth comb and devised a treatment strategy that the two of them would carry out. Thankfully Dorothy, their patient, had received some sedation medication due to the extreme pain she'd been in.

"Are there any relatives here?"

"Her parents are out in the waiting room. They're pretty heartbroken, as you can imagine. We wanted to get her treated and in a room before we let them in. Dr. Perkins said to go ahead and tape gauze over the damaged eye before they see her."

Right now the patient's eyes were both closed, but the right lid was swollen and inflamed. She could only imagine the damage that lay below.

"The boyfriend is in custody, I hope?"

The last thing anyone wanted to deal with was an angry ex coming in and harming even more people. It was always a risk, but if you knew ahead of time, security could be increased.

"He was arrested at his home after fleeing the scene." Timmons looked up. "The guy had fixed himself a sandwich."

A wave of nausea washed over her. How could one

human treat another like this and then go on as if it were nothing of importance?

She forced back the sensation and concentrated on what she was doing. This patient deserved her thoughts, not the man who'd done this to her.

Timmons came over to stand beside her. "How's it coming?"

"Just about finished with what I can see. Is there anything on her back?"

"Not much. Thankfully her clothing kept it from running down her back, although a little did get on her shoulder."

Looking at the right side of the patient's body, she could clearly see the swath of destruction where the caustic substance had either landed or had splashed as it hit. The damage ran from her eyebrow down to her right hip. Large blistered areas had already formed.

She and Jeremy discussed meds for a few more seconds before Jake came over, a slight frown on his face. Had he found something unexpected in his exam? She tilted her head. "Everything okay?"

"Yes, I just wanted to ask Jeremy if he'd go check on the parents and then make sure there's a room available so we can get her in and start debriding. Sooner rather than later."

Jeremy blinked at the man for a second before nodding. "Sure thing."

When he left the room, Elia said, "I could have done that."

"Her parents would expect one of her doctors to come out and talk to them."

Yes, she'd forgotten about that part of it, and his explanation was perfectly plausible, but there'd been something in his face she hadn't quite been able to read. But it didn't matter. What did matter was getting Dorothy treated and stabilized. And as Jake had said, it needed to happen sooner rather than later.

CHAPTER NINE

FOUR HOURS LATER, Jake was finally satisfied with how the patient was doing. She was stable and all of her deep wounds had been debrided and covered with moist dressings. Dr. Perkins had seen to the right eye and declared it a complete loss.

Fortunately, or unfortunately, depending on how you looked at it, that was the worst of her facial wounds, although the lye had eaten down to the fat layer on one of her cheeks and was certainly going to need some grafting and plastic surgery.

He wasn't sure why he'd inserted himself between Jeremy and Elia earlier, other than the fact that he'd had an uneasy feeling about how close the man was to her and had reacted before he'd had a chance to think. Because really, Elia was right. She could have certainly gone to check on the scheduling at least.

But other than that, she hadn't seemed to notice his gaffe. And he still wasn't sure what that had been about. What he'd said about the parents had certainly been true enough. It didn't matter. It was over and done, and Elia had done a great job in there. She hadn't had a single bobble or paused at anything he'd asked her to do during the procedures. It was as if they'd seamlessly worked together for years rather than just a few weeks. The hospital had certainly uncovered a treasure when they found her.

"Thanks for everything," he said. "I'm headed to my office to get some coffee. Can I interest you in some?"

She stretched, hands massaging the back of her neck for a second or two. "Yes. If I can sit down. I just want to get off my feet for a few minutes."

"My thoughts exactly. Right now even the thought of getting in my car is too much. These cases are hard. Damned hard."

As much as they'd tried to cover the worst of the burns to help ease the transition of her parents seeing her for the first time, they were certainly aware that the amount of bandaging was directly related to the amount of damage their daughter's skin had sustained. They were understandably upset by how she looked. And with the amount of painkillers she'd been given, Dorothy was only semiconscious. She was able to nod, but certainly not aware enough to carry on a whole conversation. And talking prognoses was another hard topic, but one that needed to be discussed.

"Yes they are. You handled the parents well, though."

"So I get a better rating than I did with Matt?" He could still vividly remember the first time he became aware of who she was. She'd been a fierce advocate of her patient and hadn't given a flying flip who Jake was or wasn't. He couldn't stop the slight smile that appeared.

She smiled back. "I'd give you a B."

"Not an A?" He was curious as to what her judging

standards were. They reached his office and he unlocked the door, ushering her inside.

She seemed to think about the question for a minute. "My As are reserved for exemplary work. Which you may or may not have achieved. But I don't want you to get a big head."

That made him laugh. The horrors of what had happened to Dorothy weren't banished, but talking provided the means to transition back to their personal lives after the hard things they saw and did each and every day. Jake had seen excellent medical personnel burn out or their family lives destroyed from taking their work home with them one too many times. He'd learned to actively combat it.

She helped him fix the coffee as effortlessly as she'd worked beside him while treating their patient. He took a deep breath and allowed himself to relax. "Did you let your folks know you'd be late?"

"I did. My mom called halfway through the debridement procedure, so I stepped out and Sheryll covered for me."

He hadn't even noticed. But then again, his attention had been fixed on cutting open blisters and removing skin that was no longer viable. "Did you tell her not to wait up?"

She looked at him for a second before answering. "She already knows not to. In fact, she and my dad headed home right after she called since I have to work tomorrow."

"Hell, I'd forgotten that. And I drove us up here. Do you want me to just take you home?"

"No. Coffee sounds good. As long as you don't mind if I curl up on your couch to drink it. I need some time to decompress."

"Me, too."

She fixed her cup and then handed him the creamer. He glanced at the shelf where his mugs were. "Sorry I don't have espresso cups."

"It's okay. As long as your coffee is strong."

"It is." He followed her over to the sofa and sat next to her. And true to her word, she kicked off her Crocs and curled her legs up underneath her. It was cute and informal, and he found he liked it. A lot. "Not afraid the caffeine will keep you awake tonight?"

"It doesn't usually, and I'm so keyed up that it will actually help bring me down a little. And yes, I know that that doesn't make any sense."

"It does. Because I'm that way, too." He stretched his legs out in front of him and leaned back into the cushions like he normally did after he worked late. But he was always alone at those times. And he could pretty much count on himself to just fall asleep on the sofa. It was why he kept a clean change of clothes in his office. Fortunately his office had a bathroom connected to it. And the sofa actually pulled out into a bed. Although he couldn't remember ever using it. He normally just kicked his shoes off and pulled the large crocheted throw one of his patients had made him over himself and laid flat out on the couch.

They sat there for a few minutes before he said, "How's the leg?" As if worried about her reaction, he added,

"Don't get upset. I just saw you massaging your neck and it made me wonder if it was bothering you. There's a blanket right beside you. You can use it if you're cold."

She frowned and glanced quickly down at her legs before tugging the fabric from her skirt to further cover her right ankle. Then she looked back up at him again as if trying to figure something out. She finally took a deep breath and blew it out. "No. I'm not cold, but thanks. And my leg is a little achy but not terribly. It's used to me being on it for long periods. But being able to bend them when I'm resting takes the strain off the scar contractures and makes it feel better. Are you sure it doesn't bother you? Some people don't like people putting their feet on their furniture."

"It doesn't bother me. I kind of like seeing you do it." The last sentence came out before he realized what he was saying.

But if she found it an odd thing for him to say, she didn't comment on it. Instead she tipped her head so that her cheek was lying against the back of the leather couch. "It's comfy. You should try it sometime."

"I'm not even sure my legs would bend into that position without breaking in half."

She smiled and, as always, it made something shift sideways in his gut. "Exaggerating at all?"

"Let's not try it and find out, is all I'm saying."

They sat there for a few seconds in silence. And he found he liked the quiet after the chaos in Dorothy's room. Then he said something he'd wanted to say ever since he'd thanked her outside of the treatment room.

"You were a great asset in that room tonight. It was like you anticipated my every request. Not everyone has that ability."

"I think nurses overall do. But I also think because I didn't know much English when I came to the States, I had to learn to read body language to understand if what people were saying was something good, bad or of little importance."

That made sense. "Well, your English is excellent now, and I'm glad you haven't lost the ability to read people."

"I still have an accent that I can't quite shake. *R*s are hard for me because they're pronounced so differently in Portuguese. 'Rural route' and 'squirrel' are superhard. I always want to put a *w* after the first *r* in squirrel. And rural route has three of those suckers." Her laughter tickled his insides and made his smile widen.

He could definitely hear what she was talking about when she said the word squirrel, and she overpronounced the second *r* in rural route, but he still found it attractive. And he really liked that she could admit that it was hard. Not everyone would.

"I hope you never lose that accent."

Her head was still resting against the sofa and she reached out to touch his arm. "That was an incredibly nice thing to say."

"Was it?"

She got very still. "It was. And I hope you never lose the ability to be as caring and nice as you are to your patients. As you are to me."

The world seemed to pause as he digested those

words…as they found their way to a place inside that he hadn't opened to anyone in a long time.

He stared at her for a second and then leaned forward and kissed her. Only, unlike the last time, this one was on her mouth. And when he lingered a little longer, her mouth clung to his, her head coming off the back cushions to make better contact.

His hand slid behind her neck to support her when he changed the angle.

God, her mouth was sweet. Much sweeter than he'd imagined in the dark places of his mind, when he let himself think about it. Places he hadn't let surface entirely. Until now.

If she would have hesitated even the slightest bit, he would have stopped immediately and apologized, letting the chips fall where they may. But she evidently didn't mind. At all. Had she been thinking about him the way he'd been thinking about her when they'd been eating dinner with her folks?

He remembered her knee pressing against his and his reaction to it. If that call hadn't come in about an emergency, would the night have ended with a kiss the way it was now?

Too many what-ifs and not enough answers. But maybe that was a good thing. Because when she shifted her body so that she was facing him, she went onto her knees in order to do so, while his left arm went behind her back to pull her closer.

So much closer. Only it wasn't close enough for the impulses that were starting to gather around him, each one part of a long line of wants that were waiting for their chance to be heard. To be felt.

When he shifted Elia again, so that they were front to front, it seemed only natural that one of her knees should come across his thighs and land beside it on the couch. He saw her eyes go to the door before they came back to meet his.

"Do you want me to lock it?" The words seemed to gather in the center of the room as he waited for her reply. Her answer would say it all. Either she would shake her head no and get off his lap, probably beating a hasty retreat from his office. Or she would say yes and...

God, he hoped she said yes.

"No."

His hopes plummeted for a second before she added, "*I'll* do it."

Everything in him stood at attention as she did just that, climbing from his lap and going over to the door and turning the dead bolt above the handle.

He stood and went over to her, pulling her back against him, and then leaning over to kiss the nape of her neck. Her breath released in a whisper of sound that made his arms tighten around her midsection. All of a sudden he didn't care that she'd be able to feel his clear reaction to her nearness. That she would know exactly where he was hoping this would lead. And he was hoping.

Because if she changed her mind now, he was going to have a hard time explaining to his body why it couldn't have what it wanted. But he would. If she pulled away.

But she didn't. Instead, one of her arms came up to curl

around the back of his neck and eased his head against her cheek. And when she turned her head…

His mouth covered hers, and this time there was no pretense. He let her know in no uncertain terms that he was okay with the locked door and everything that went along with it.

There would be no one to interrupt them. Sheryll had gone home and the staff that replaced her would assume he and Elia had followed suit and left the hospital, as well. If anyone needed them, they would call.

And he hoped to hell they didn't. At least not for a while. A very long while, if he got his wish.

When they parted, Elia turned toward him and he took a step back, using his index finger to signal for her to wait as he reached into his back pocket for his wallet, hoping he still had at least one of the packets he used to carry when he and Samantha were dating. He banished her name with a frown. He knew he had some at home, but to ask Elia to leave with him would spoil the mood and give him time to think about his actions, which he wasn't super anxious to do right now.

He flipped his wallet open and sure enough, tucked deep into one of the credit card holders was cellophane-wrapped protection. More than one. He pulled a single one out and then tossed his wallet onto his desk, not really caring where it landed.

Elia licked her lips, making him shudder with all he wanted to do with her. The pleasure he wanted to give her. The pleasure he wanted to take for himself.

He walked toward her with slow deliberation, twirling the packet between his fingers. His ex had started talking about children right about the time he'd started to have doubts about whether or not their futures were entwined together. Except she'd wanted those children to be carried by a surrogate, and that made him even more unsure, although he completely understood her reasons, since she was at the height of her career. But he remembered his mom talking about how excited she and his dad had been when they'd learned they were expecting him. How they'd gone through it all together and how it had drawn them even closer together.

And why was he thinking about all of this now?

He reached Elia and palmed both of her hips, loving the feel of her as he drew her a step closer and then two, until she was pressed tight to him, reigniting his senses and driving everything else away, like he'd hoped it would.

She surprised him by taking the packet from him and placing it on the desk beside him. But when he frowned, she shushed him, pressing her fingers to his lips. "When the time is right."

He swallowed. She was evidently all in but had some ideas of her own about how this was going to go down.

Her fingers trailed down either side of his face, starting at his temples, going over his cheeks, brushing over the stubble that wasn't quite a beard on his face, before reaching his neck. This time she softly raked her nails down his skin, the light pressure hitting all erogenous zones he didn't even know existed. He gave a low groan of approval and buried his fingers in the silky strands of hair beside her face, needing to touch her but not wanting her to stop what she was doing.

But she did stop. Long enough to reach for the bottom of his shirt and haul it up. He raised his arms and helped her take it the rest of the way off. Together they dropped it beside them. She cozied up to him, reaching up to place her lips on one of his shoulders in a warm, wet kiss that made him harden before nibbling her way down the front of his chest. And when she reached his nipple...

Heaven help him. Sensation rocketed out from where her teeth scraped over him and hit every nerve ending on his body. This time his groan was drawn somewhere from the pit of his gut, and he suddenly needed to touch more of her than was exposed. Needed something hot and intimate. She was still wearing the long gauzy skirt she'd had on for dinner, and he bunched it in his fist, moving his way down the fabric until he reached the hemline. Then he was at the skin of her left thigh and trailed up it, her mouth stopping its ministrations for a second before going back to what she was doing, her tongue licking over him like a cat.

A sexy siren of a cat who pushed all the right buttons and made him wish for more. So he gave it to himself, reaching the bottom of her panties. Without hesitation, he slid beneath them and found her wet and warm. So very warm. The urge to unzip and bury himself in that warmth came, and he waited until it passed before doing anything else. Because if he did what he wanted to, it was all going to be over much too soon. And he didn't want it to be over. He wanted to draw this out and experience every single thing he could.

He couldn't bury what he wanted to, but he could do other things. Like touch her. Slide into her with his fingers and use his mind to transfer the sensations to his own body as they happened. His thumb touched her lightly and she went stock-still. Then her hips inched toward him as if they couldn't control themselves.

Hell, yes. Just like that, baby.

His free arm went around the back of her butt, pulling her into his touch just as his fingers entered her. She shuddered, her head coming up to look at him, teeth digging into her bottom lip as he pushed deeper.

"Jakob." His whispered name came off her lips with a shaky tone that he loved. That contained that sexy little accent. That little stress happening on the last syllable, just like he thought it would.

He put his ear to her lips. "I love it when you say my name."

Her breath hissed out when his thumb became a little more insistent.

"I love it when you do that…just like that."

"Do you?"

"You know I do." She rocked against him. "But I want more. *Deus,* I want you. Not just your hand."

That did it. He was done fighting what he wanted to do. He withdrew and yanked her panties over her hips, going to his knees to let his hands trail the backs of her thighs as he carried them down. She tensed and reached for his arms, and he realized why when one of his palms crossed over a thick, uneven section of skin on her right leg and he realized it was her scar tissue.

"Shh...it's okay." His fingers stroked over the area with light wispy motions meant to soothe her.

He felt her muscles relax as she stepped out of her undergarment, only to stiffen up when he reached for the elastic waistline of her skirt. "No. Don't. Please."

His heart ached at the tone of her voice. Had someone said something about her leg? He remembered her wearing the long biker pants that covered everything up. And the skirt that came down to her ankles. He understood it, yet he wanted her to know she didn't need to worry. Not with him. But he needed to be careful. He wouldn't go against her wishes if she was set on staying covered up.

He looked up at her until he caught her eye. "Let me, Elia. Please."

Her teeth worried her lip again before she gave a hard nod, giving him permission. When he reached for the top of her skirt again, she didn't say anything, but her eyes closed tight, as if she couldn't bear to watch him take it off.

God, Elia. She had no idea how beautiful she was, with or without her scars.

He slowly peeled her skirt down over her hips, pushing it past her thigh, her knees...her ankles. And yes, her scars were deep and knotted and uneven, but they also told a story. One of overcoming a pain that went deep. Deeper than her physical injuries.

She lifted her feet one at a time and let him ease the fabric past them. He gingerly set the garment on top of his shirt. His palms massaged their way up both of her calves, giving no more attention to one than he did the other one. He went up her thighs, resisted doing what he really wanted to do. This was about acceptance and letting her know that she was perfect exactly the way she was. He planted a kiss on her right thigh where it joined her body.

"You are gorgeous, do you know that? So beautiful that you take my breath away." He climbed to his feet and used her hips to pull her back against him. "I want to do so much. So many things. But I don't think I'm going to be able to hold on long enough to do them all."

Her eyes reopened and the brown irises were warm, moist with what was maybe emotion. But he'd told the truth.

"You don't need to hold on." With that, she reached down and unzipped his trousers and unbuttoned them. He shoved them down and off his legs along with his briefs. Before he could reach for the condom, she beat him to it.

"Let me…please." She repeated the words he'd used earlier, her fingers brushing over his erection and making it jump as electricity seemed to sizzle across his skin. Only unlike him, she didn't wait for a response. Instead she tore open the packet and reached for him, palming him in her hand before her fingers closed over him, wrapping him in a tight band of warmth and stroking him.

"Hell… Elia. You need to stop." He reached down and physically halted her movements before she drove him over the edge.

She gave a warm laugh and took a step back until her

backside was pressed against the wood of his desk, avoiding the papers he had stacked on one side. Then she put her hands on either side of her thighs and hopped up until she was sitting on top of it.

He'd had fantasies of that desk, but in it she'd been leaning over it and he'd been behind her. But this...this was even better.

She held the condom up in one hand and motioned to him with the other. "Come here, Jake."

He took a step forward, and she opened her thighs to let him come between them. Then she held him again, but not to torture him this time. Instead she rolled the condom over him until it reached the end of him. He wanted to be buried in her the same way...until he reached the very end.

He was so hard it hurt *not* to do anything.

But he didn't have to worry. She finished what she was doing and then hooked her legs around him, evidently no longer self-conscious about her scars. Or maybe she was past the point of being worried about anything.

So was he, because she hauled him against her until there was nowhere to go but in. So he reached down and found her, his arms going around her ass and pressing home. The sensation was beyond anything he could describe, and he stood there wrapped tight in her heat for a few seconds before his mouth founds hers for a long searing kiss. His hands slid to her back, frowning slightly when they encountered fabric rather than bare skin. He leaned back so he could unbutton her blouse and let it fall open.

A pink bra met his gaze. It seemed so "Elia" that he let himself drink in the sight of those two perfect breasts cupped in lace. He pulled out slightly and thrust into her, watching them dance in time with his body.

Hell yeah. He loved the feel of her. The sight of her. He almost didn't want to take the bra off. Wanted to pump to completion as he watched them move. But like she'd said earlier, he needed more. More than just an animalistic act. He stripped off her shirt and then reached behind her for the hooks.

"It's in front."

Her fingers found the clasp and rotated it. Then the pink gave way and released her breasts. He wasn't sure why something that was made to feed babies created such an elemental reaction in him, but they did. He didn't need to rationalize it or explain it. He just loved the beauty of the female body. Each and every curve of it.

And then Elia did the unthinkable. She leaned back until she was lying across his desk, her body wide open to him.

Elia's eyes closed when his fingers curled around her hip bones and pulled her even more tightly against him.

Her nerve endings were singing, and between that and the way his body filled hers, stretching her, she felt things she'd never felt before, even though he wasn't her first lover.

But he was the first to make her feel like she was more than enough. The first one to actually ask her to let him uncover her legs to his eyes. The first one who made her want to say yes. And never once had he reached for that blanket on his sofa. It had taken a second, but she believed his offer had been sincere and had been precipitated out of concern for her comfort, not because of her scars.

He leaned over her, thrusting into her in a way that made her back slide over the cool smooth wood of his desk with each stroke. It was erotic and naughty in a way that was new to her. She'd always made love in beds. And once in a car. But never in a colleague's office.

She skipped over the boss part. He wasn't really. He didn't have the power to fire her. But he did have the power to light her on fire.

And he had. She was slowly being consumed by his heat. His eyes. The intensity of his body as he drew from her power, leaving her weak in the knees.

One of his hands left her hips and went up to cup her breast while still pumping inside of her. He didn't stroke it or squeeze it. And yet there was something so sensuous about it, as if he were feeling for something. Something that was only for him.

She couldn't stop the moan as her nipple went hard against his palm, as if trying to pleasure itself against his skin. She arched into his touch, her legs contracting against his butt, relishing the feel of the muscles in them as they tensed and released with each stroke of his body.

Keeping his one hand where it was, his other moved to where they were joined together and found that tiny little pleasure center and touched, pressing deep enough that her nerve endings were a ball of sudden need and heat. Jake leaned over her, his tempo changing.

Even though neither of his hands were moving in and of themselves, it was as if they were. As if they were stroking in time with his body, driving her higher and higher with each push and pull.

"Yes, Jake. *Deus. Quero te. Agora, quero...*"

He suddenly moved at a speed that caught up with her request and in a split second, he pushed her over the edge and into oblivion, where colors exploded behind her closed lids and her body contracted against his over and over again. Until his movements slowed. Still there was pleasure. Pleasure in the slow letdown that happened as his body came to a halt and rested against her. In the slow aftershocks that jarred her system and reminded her that she'd just been on top of a mountain.

One she needed to leave. In a minute. Maybe two.

Her hands fell to the sides and somehow managed to knock the stack of papers to her right off the side of his desk.

That had her plummeting back to earth. She sat up in a rush. "Sorry."

"It's okay. Don't worry about it." He glanced to the side, then gave a slight frown.

He pulled free more quickly than she anticipated, and her body gave a twinge of protest even as he was bending down to where the neat stack had become a scattered mess. The shiny cover of an entertainment paper came into view with the picture of a supermodel she'd seen on ads in various places. Bold headlines declared something about a renowned surgeon who'd abandoned her in France. Jake hurriedly scraped together other papers and piled them on top of what could only be a tabloid.

Why was it in his office? Maybe it had been left by a patient with whom he'd consulted in his office.

The way he'd just consulted with her?

The ugly thought floored her and she quickly suppressed it. She had not been unwilling or even hesitant. She'd beckoned him over with every intention of this ending exactly the way it had.

Well, maybe not with her knocking stuff over and kind of ruining her slow slide back to reality.

She hopped off the desk, but when she went to help him pick stuff up, he waved her away. "It's fine, really. There's nothing important."

And yet the way he was acting made her wonder.

Deus, she hoped things were not going to get weird.

Really? They were already weird. Really weird.

She bent down and grabbed her clothes, but when she made a move to yank them on in a hurry, he stopped her. Hauling her toward him and leaning close to kiss her, he murmured, "Everything okay between us?"

A second ago she would have said no, but the way he kissed her quieted those doubts. Her eyes skated over his desk, but the news article was nowhere in sight.

It wasn't important. He'd said it himself.

Her glance met his again and she let his warm smile lull her back to solid ground. He wasn't acting like things were awkward at all. But he also wasn't pressing her for anything more.

Which was a good thing. Right?

What had happened had to have been a simple release of adrenaline after their chaotic night. After fighting to help save someone's skin and possibly life, if the next few weeks were kind to her.

"Yes. Everything's good. But I really should get home and at least try to get a few hours of sleep. Unless you want to just crash on your couch. I can call a friend to come and get me."

She didn't say which friend, because she couldn't really see herself calling anyone at two in the morning. But she could call a taxi or an Uber.

"No, I'll take you home. It's not a problem. Can I have five minutes? Unless you want to shower before we leave. There's probably room for two in there."

It was said with a wolfish charm that melted her heart. Okay, so it wasn't really like the proverbial "wham bam" scenario she'd just played in her head. Maybe he really would ease them back to more neutral territory. Like a one-night stand where acquaintances came together and then parted amicably, going back to whatever their previous relationship had been. People did it all the time.

Well, not her. Normally her exes disappeared into the mist never to be heard from again. Or she did. But there was almost never any contact between them again. She glanced at the undisturbed blanket on his sofa and a few of her muscles relaxed. This was a little more complicated because they worked together. But it didn't have to be.

And she could always put it off for a little while. Especially after the offer he'd just made.

She sent him a smile. "Well, as long as there's room for two…"

"If there's not, we'll make it work."

With one last glance at his desk, she followed him into the bathroom, her body already starting to hum with anticipation.

CHAPTER TEN

HE'D ENDED UP spending the night at Elia's apartment. In her bed. And they'd both definitely gotten less sleep than they'd anticipated.

But it had been worth it. And despite the horror he'd felt when that tabloid paper had fallen onto the ground in full view, she'd evidently not read the headline. Or at least she hadn't realized it was talking about him and Samantha.

But he'd left her apartment with a soft kiss and said he'd see her back at the hospital. And he had. And somehow, things had gone back to normal. For the last week they'd worked side by side, but neither mentioned the night they'd spent together.

Dorothy, their chemical burn victim, was doing better than anyone had hoped. She had lost her eye, but still had perfect vision in her left one and the ophthalmic surgeon had assured her that her eye socket was still in good shape and they could fit her with a prosthetic that no one would know was not her own eye, unless they looked closely. Her eyelid would have some scarring. And she would still need some grafts to cover her damaged cheek, but Jake was hopeful he could get it close enough to natural that she wouldn't feel self-conscious. He wanted to work hard to make that happen.

Because of Elia and how she'd balked at exposing her leg?

Maybe. But it was more than that. He wanted his patient to have the best possible outcome. He would say like any other patient, but he had to admit this one was special. Because of the night he'd spent with Elia?

Probably. But he was going to try his damnedest. For Dorothy. The same way he had for Matt, who'd done so well that he'd been released yesterday. The rest of his treatments and teeth implants could be done on an outpatient basis.

The world hadn't imploded after their night together. It had gone on spinning and patients had gone on recovering the way he'd hoped. And he and Elia had fallen back into an easy relationship with no talk about what had happened. It was the best possible scenario.

Although somewhere inside of him there was a little tick of dissatisfaction. And he had no idea what it was about. They really couldn't have an actual relationship. Like he'd told Sheryll, work romances normally turned messy. And for some reason he didn't want to lose the camaraderie he had with Eliana.

They were even planning to meet up at the bike festival tomorrow before the start. They hadn't made plans to necessarily ride side by side, but his bike club crew had decided to at least begin the race together, although they all knew they would eventually separate with the faster riders going out in front, just like they did with all their rides. Randy wouldn't be there for this one, since he was still healing from the injuries he'd sustained in the accident.

And man, that terrible event seemed like ages ago. So much had happened since then.

Originally he hadn't wanted Elia to continue riding with his club, but now he kind of hoped she did. The truth was, he liked being around her. Liked so much about her. He liked working with her and he loved how much she cared about their patients. In fact he loved…

Her.

He loved *her*.

Just then he saw her walking toward him and swallowed all of his thoughts in a big gulp that actually made a sound.

Don't make this awkward, Callin.

He'd probably been wrong. Yes. He had to have been mistaken. Then she smiled at him, and his system went haywire. He forced himself to smile back, but it was awkward.

Just like he was making everything all of a sudden. Awkward.

Even more awkward than when that tabloid paper had fallen on the ground right in front of her.

Well, he'd better figure out how to "unawkward" things right now, if he wanted things to stay the way they were.

And with all his heart he did. Because the idea of their relationship suddenly going sideways left a bad taste in his mouth. So it was up to him to figure out how to bury his feelings so deep that no one would ever find them. Even if he wanted them to.

The flare went off, signaling for the cyclists to start pedaling. There were over a thousand people gathered at the starting line. So many that it had taken Elia a while to locate Jake and his group. But they'd texted back and forth until she found them. The group stayed together for about a minute and a half before the leaders separated out. She was surprised Jake didn't go with them, but he hung back with her.

"Feel free to go on ahead. I don't expect you to stay here and babysit me."

His brows went up. "Do you *need* babysitting? Last I knew, you were all grown-up and able to decide things for yourself."

He probably hadn't meant anything by it, but her face turned hot as she remembered the last thing she'd decided for herself in the bedroom of her apartment. It involved her bathtub and acting out some of the fantasies she'd dreamed about the day of the accident in his tub. They were white-hot, and afterward he'd told her so. What she hadn't done that night was tell him where those ideas had come from.

"I am. But I know your club normally moves at a higher speed than my old one did."

He shrugged. "It's not really a race. It's a fundraiser. I'd rather sit back and enjoy myself."

Implying that he was enjoying himself by riding with her. This time the warmth that washed over her wasn't embarrassment, but pleasure. She was enjoying herself, too. And it had nothing to do with sex, but simply being in his company, something she'd missed in some of her other relationships.

Except this wasn't a relationship, unless they were doing things backward and letting the sex come before the friendship.

Would that really be so bad? Maybe not. But she had no idea if that was something Jake would want or if it was just her. Only she'd not even thought about it in those terms until this very second. And it would be better if she didn't until she could sit down by herself and think things through.

One thing she was thankful for, though, was the fact that the bike festival didn't take the same route as the bike club had on the day of that accident. She didn't know how she'd feel about passing that area and remembering the horror of it. She did wish Randy could ride this time, though. Jake said their club participated in the bike festival every year. The owner of the shop was here this time. And they all wore bracelets with Randy's name on them. She hadn't realized they were doing it until Jake had held one out and asked if she wanted to wear it. Of course she did. Made of leather and etched with his name, it was their way of saying he was missed and that they were riding in his honor.

This ride was only twenty kilometers, so it wouldn't take a huge amount of time, and there would be a cookout held at the park where the finish line was. Whoever wanted to stay could. Jake said it was fun, and there'd been a couple hundred cookies left that would be passed out on a first-come-first-served basis. It was kind of neat.

She glanced to the side just as he did, and they caught each other's eye and laughed. As if there was some kind of private joke. Of course there was. And it was very, very private. She'd told no one, not even her closest friends. Or her mom. This was for her and her alone. Well…her and Jake, since he obviously knew about it, too.

They chatted about Dorothy and Carly and Matt, and she asked what his hardest case was.

"Actually it was a case early on in my career. A Formula 1 driver's car caught on fire during a test run, and due to what they thought was a glitch, they had trouble getting the driver out. When they finally did, he'd been badly burned. He died hours after arriving at Westlake. It was a blow, since most of us knew who he was. Later on, it turned out his vehicle had been sabotaged by someone he'd fired from his pit crew."

"How terrible. Kind of like Dorothy's scorned ex. I'll never understand how someone can hurt someone they supposedly love."

"People sometimes do things you'd never think them capable of doing." There was a hard set to his jaw as he said it.

"The most shocking thing is when there's no remorse afterward."

He glanced at her. "I agree."

They rode in silence for several more miles, but it seemed a little less relaxed than it was before. Because she'd brought up a memory that Jake would rather forget?

She couldn't imagine how horrifying it would be to treat someone like the patient he'd had. Someone who was well known and whose case was probably reexamined countless times to see if anything had been missed. To see if something more could have been done. No doubt, Jake had already rehashed the timeline over and over.

She looked for a way to change the subject. "Does the bike festival ride the same route year after year?"

"They do. It's become a pretty big thing in the community. So much so that there will be people cheering us on as well as press at the finish line, so don't be surprised if one of them pulls you aside to do an impromptu interview."

"Yikes. With how sweaty I'm getting, that's the last thing I need."

He sent her a smile. "You look beautiful. No matter what."

Her face warmed. "I wasn't fishing for a compliment."

"And I wasn't dishing out fake praise."

"Okay, well, thank you."

He nodded toward the curve ahead as air horns sounded in the distance. "The finish line is just around that bend. Get ready to stop. It'll be pretty congested with folks getting off bikes and greeting family members."

It was then that she noticed more people standing on the sidelines waving flags with Westlake Memorial's logo on them. Wow, the ride had gone by really fast. She glanced at her watch, eyes widening. It had been two hours! It sure hadn't seemed that long. And she was kind of sad that it was over. At work, she and Jake saw each other in passing or while working on a case, but there wasn't much time for chitchat. Not like there was now.

She coasted as she neared the bend in the road, following Jake's lead, and as soon as they turned the corner, she saw he was right. Even though riders were being ushered off the course, people on bikes were standing around talking with pedestrians and other riders. Elia put on her brakes, and as soon as she slowed enough, she hopped off her bike. Jake did the same. It was mass chaos, and she wasn't sure where to go to get out of the path of those who were coming behind her.

"Come this way," he said. She followed him toward the edge of the pavement, where there was still a crush of people. But it was either that or risk being hit by another bicycle.

Suddenly there was someone with a microphone hurrying toward them. There was a photographer following close behind. Oh, no! She'd been serious about not wanting her picture taken looking like this.

"Dr. Callin!" the man called. "Dr. Callin! Excuse me, sir. How was the ride?"

Jake smiled. "It was great. Just like it is every year." He glanced back at her and made a move to go around the reporter only to have him step in front of him. "Just one more question. Any regrets since leaving Samantha Naughton behind in France a couple of years ago? I interviewed her a few months back, and she said she didn't understand what happened or why you left, but wished that you had stuck around. She said you were good together. She misses you."

A mental image of that tabloid article that had been lying on the floor appeared in her brain. It had said that a doctor had abandoned the famous model in France...or something like that. Her head swiveled to look at Jake, who still had the same pleasant smile on his face, but a muscle was now ticking in his jaw.

Nossa Senhora, the article had been about Jake! He'd been the one to abandon Samantha. Why? How? And how could he not have mentioned that he'd been involved with the woman?

Why would he? She hadn't mentioned any of her exes to Jake. But she certainly hadn't left someone in a foreign country. Not that she'd traveled anywhere with any of her boyfriends. Except to maybe a local restaurant.

And Samantha Naughton? The woman was drop-dead gorgeous. And a great philanthropist, if the articles about her were to be believed. A huge wave of insecurity crashed over her. Jake had surely slept with the woman. Wouldn't you naturally make comparisons? Elia was not super experienced, and her embarrassment about her scars... Had she looked pitiful to him? He hadn't acted like it, but... He'd left his last girlfriend behind without saying a word about why, if the reporter was to be believed. But even the tabloids got some of the story right, didn't they? Otherwise they wouldn't sell so many copies.

Suddenly she was looking for a way to escape. She'd just headed toward an opening in the crowd when the reporter repeated the question again, this time asking if he was now dating "her" and pointing at Elia. Jake's smile disappeared and he gave the man an ugly glare before simply saying "no comment" in sharp tones. Then he sidestepped the cameraman and smoothly avoided the microphone and stalked away. He glanced back, as if trying to make sure that Elia was following him, but she wasn't. And she wouldn't. Her insides seemed to shrivel up into a tight ball. She couldn't get away fast enough from that look that had seemed to say, "Are you kidding me? *Her?*"

There was no way she could compete with someone like Jake's ex, nor did she want to. Even the thought made her close her eyes in horror.

Once past the crowd, she reached down to ease the strain on her right leg, giving her tight calf a quick squeeze. When she sat back up, Jake was there. "Sorry about that. Are you going to the cookout?"

Sorry about that? Was that all he had to say? He had to know she had a million questions going through her mind. "Um...no. Sorry." As she looked at him, her eyes started watering. *Deus.* There was no way she wanted him to see her break down, so she got on her bike and pedaled away from him—away from the event—as fast as she could without another word.

She knew they were expected to stay if they could, but if she tried, she didn't trust herself not to put on a huge show of waterworks. She just couldn't face Jake again, because somewhere in her heart, she had wanted him to tell that reporter that, yes, they were an item. Had maybe even believed that in her own heart or hoped it might someday be true. And yet that look on Jake's face... She just couldn't shake it. Just couldn't fathom why he'd wanted to sleep with her in the first place. Or why she ever could have thought they might one day be together. How big of a fool was she?

He had walked away from someone like Samantha Naughton. How much easier would it be to walk away from naive Elia Pessoa, who believed the best of people until proven wrong?

Well, it looked like she'd just been proven wrong. Big time. And she had only herself to blame for some baseless romantic notions she'd allowed herself to harbor. Thank heaven someone had burst her bubble before she'd made a complete fool of herself. Time to find a dark corner in her house and sit and lick her wounds for a while. Thank God she didn't work tomorrow because she was not ready to face the man again. Not today. Not tomorrow. But she'd better figure things out before Monday. Because he was going to be at the hospital. And so was she.

After a week of trying to corner her long enough to talk to her, Jake realized Elia was actively avoiding him. Ever since the bike festival when he tried to talk to her at the end. Because the reporter had asked him if they were a couple?

He could only take that to mean that she didn't want them to be a couple. Ever. Especially since she couldn't even stand being in the same room with him, even at the hospital.

Just when he'd started thinking he might have it in him to give love another go. Would she send her people over to tell him no way, no how? Hell, he didn't even know who Elia's "people" were.

Yesterday he had gone to the hospital administrator and told him he needed a break. That he trusted Jeremy Timmons to handle his cases while he was gone. The only good thing was that Jake had not seen anything in the tabloids about the reporter's comments. He guessed the hospital had been right in their recommendation about not engaging when asked a stupid question. And how about Samantha saying what she had. Or had the reporter simply been fishing for a story? Who the hell knew? Or even cared?

He had a little place in Ensenada, Mexico, right on the Baja California peninsula that had been left to him by his father. It was a place filled with wonderful memories of childhood vacations. Maybe it would serve as a good place to clear his head. To reset his future. He'd already booked his flight for tomorrow, and the plan was to stay for two weeks, although he hadn't given the administrator a fixed date. He hoped to hell that was long enough. And honestly, it didn't matter. Because long enough or not, he was going to have to figure out how to go back to working with Elia. Or he was going to have to quit his job and go somewhere else.

Jake was gone? He wasn't at work today and no one seemed to know where he was or when he'd be back.

Elia had come into work after making a decision. She was going to have to have it out with him. Her work was suffering, and she knew Sheryll had given her several inscrutable looks, like when she'd caught her ducking around a corner in the middle of rounds, when she'd spied

Jake heading out onto the floor. Sheryll hadn't come right out and asked her, but she knew the questions were coming if she kept it up.

She really didn't want to get fired. Jake didn't have to tell her anything about what had happened with Samantha, but she needed to tell him that she wasn't looking for a relationship of any kind with him. Physical or romantic. Because it turned out—for her, anyway—that she didn't have it in her to be a friend-with-benefits kind of girl. If the physical didn't at least have the possibility of romance attached to it, it wasn't sustainable on her end. And she didn't want to always wonder if comparisons were being made. So it was better just to come out and make things as plain as she could make them.

Except he wasn't here. And no one could give her a straight answer as to how long he'd be away. Dr. Timmons was taking over his cases. Which meant whatever was wrong had to be kind of serious, didn't it?

An ugly thought slithered into her head and coiled there, waiting to strike. What if the reporter had been right about Samantha missing him? What if Jake had called her and even now they were rekindling their romance?

Her insides squelched, her lunch sloshing around as if seeking an exit. The way she had looked for an exit at the bike festival? She'd heard they'd raised a record number of funds that would go directly to the burn unit this year. A picture of one of her mom's cookies had even made the local papers. Sheryll showed her the picture that morning. As soon as she got home that afternoon, she called her mom, who answered on the first ring.

"Hi, sweetheart. How are you?"

Elia mentally switched over to Portuguese, knowing her mom preferred it. "Doing okay..." Her voice faded away and the next thing she knew she was crying, sobbing into the phone like her heart was breaking. Because it was.

"Elia! Elia! *O que é?*"

Her mom asked over and over what was wrong, but Elia just couldn't get the words out. She tried, but nothing came out except these wrenching cries of pain.

"Is it that Jake?"

She cried even harder.

"Elia, *filha*, I am on my way."

"No..." She still couldn't talk. And she realized she wanted her to come, needed her mom to hold her and tell her she hadn't been a complete fool, whether it was true or not.

As soon as her mom hung up, a text pinged on her phone.

Do I need to call an ambulance for you?

She scrubbed the tears from her eyes with balled fists.

No. Sorry. Just dealing with some stuff.

Stuff. Jake stuff?

Elia hesitated for a long time with her answer. She didn't want her mom to have to drive three hours just to hear some nonsense about Jake. But her fingers seemed to type of their own volition.

Yes, it's about Jake. And I sure could use some advice.

Good. Because I'm already in the car with a packed bag.

Three hours later, her mom came through the door and Elia fell into her arms. She was past the point of crying, having gotten most of that out hours ago. Now she was just numb.

They sat on the couch, and Elia spilled the beans about all of it. How they had worked on a case and had gotten caught up in the emotions of it all and spent the night together. About how they'd ridden in the bike festival together and the part about the reporter and his questions.

"Did he actually respond to the question about whether you were his current girlfriend?"

"No. But the look on his face…"

Her mom tilted her head. "What about it?"

"It was filled with such…disgust." The tears she thought were long gone surfaced all over again.

Her mom scooted over and put her arm around her. "Look at me."

Pulling in a deep breath, she turned to face her.

"*Filha*, I am only going to say this one time. No one who ever looks at you could be filled with disgust. A man doesn't sleep with someone who makes him feel that way. His…er…*coisa*, shall we say, would not stand at attention for someone who disgusts him."

"Mamãe!"

"Well, it is true. Did you ask the man why he looked the way he did?"

"No. I just couldn't bring myself to."

Her mom sighed. "Could it not be that the disgust was aimed at the reporter? Not at whether or not the statement was true?"

"I don't know. I never stopped to think about that."

"Go talk to him. Ask him. If he doesn't care about you, that will be his chance to say so, but if he does..."

Oh, Lord. Not only had she not talked to him when she'd had the chance, she'd rebuffed every attempt that he'd made to talk to her. She assumed he was going to try to let her down easy. But she realized her mind had concocted such a crazy jumble of possibilities that it was very likely none of them were true.

And what about Samantha?

Well, she would never know unless she asked him.

"He tried to talk to me, I think, but I assumed the worst and avoided him, and now..."

"And now what?"

"He left the hospital, and I'm not exactly sure where he went or how long he'll be gone. Maybe he'll never be back."

Her mom squeezed her tight for a second. "Could it be that Jake is struggling with some of the same things you are?"

"But what if he's not? What if he just doesn't want to see me?"

"But what if he does and is afraid, just like you are?

What if after trying to talk to you he assumed the worst, that you didn't want him?"

Why did her mom have to make her see things with such glaring clarity? "And if it's him who doesn't want me?"

"Then you'll know. Life is not without risks, Elia. The doctors told us you might not keep your leg, that the vascular system was badly damaged and it could die. They wanted to amputate. I kept saying to wait...wait...wait, that I would know when the time was right. It never was. That you can walk is a miracle in itself."

"I didn't know that about my leg."

She shrugged. "Just like with the doctors, I felt something was telling me to wait to tell you. That I would know when the time was right. That time is now. Don't cut out part of your heart without at least giving it a chance to heal...without giving it a chance to know the truth."

"But he's gone. I'll need to wait until he—"

"No. You need to decide what it is you want out of life. If you want Jake, you shouldn't wait for him to come to you. He tried. It is now time for you to go to him."

"But how? I don't even know where he is."

"Ask. Ask those who might know. And keep asking until someone can give you the answer you are looking for."

Jake was packing his bags. This was the most ridiculous idea he'd ever had. Had he really thought the answers would magically appear the second he stepped over the threshold of the little two-bedroom bungalow?

They hadn't. And he found he missed Elia like he'd never missed anyone in his life. It was crazy. And terrible.

She wouldn't talk to him, but somehow he had to know one way or the other without looking like some kind of crazed stalker. He'd thought about texting her, but this needed to be a face-to-face conversation. Maybe once that happened, no matter which way that discussion went, he'd finally have a peace about the situation.

Yes. In his soul of souls he somehow knew that was the right way to go. He couldn't text her with the question, but he could text a request for a meeting. He could say they needed to clear the air about a few things. And if she still said no? Then maybe he'd have his answer. He'd never actually gotten that far. She always ducked out the second he appeared. Maybe she was horrified that he'd supposedly abandoned Samantha. Then he could explain he hadn't.

He sucked down a breath and let it hiss back out. That was it. He was going to send that text and then he was going to catch his flight.

He looked up her phone number. When he went to compose the message, he found their back-and-forth texts about where the bike crew was. They were witty little comebacks with a couple of barely hidden innuendos. How had that gone from warm and fun to her wanting to be as far away from him as she could possibly get?

It was after that reporter's questions. He tried to recall exactly what had been said. There'd been the questions about Samantha. Those had surprised him, but they hadn't been totally out of the blue. What had embarrassed him, though, was how it made him sound. He couldn't get out of there fast enough. And then the reporter had asked about Elia and their relationship. And Jake's reply? "No comment."

He shut his eyes. "Oh, Callin, you really are a fool." No wonder she didn't want to talk to him. He could imagine how it might have sounded to her.

He composed his text carefully.

Hey, beautiful…

Nope. He erased the last word. Too forward.

Hey, Elia… Is there a time we could talk? I would like to explain something I said to the reporter that I think you might have misunderstood. I'd like to clear the air and tell you what I would have liked to have told him.

Yes. That was okay. If he was right about why she was upset, then hopefully she would want to hear the truth. Holding his breath, he pressed Send.

Then, picking his bag up, he opened the door only to hear his phone ping from his pocket. Frowning, he fished it out again and looked at the screen.

Can you give me your address? I'm hopelessly lost.

What in the…?

He looked at the top of the screen and saw the series of earlier texts. Yep, it was from Elia.

I'm not in the States at the moment, so I'm not home.

Wait, why was she trying to find him, anyway?

I know. I'm in Ensenada. But, strangely enough, the taxi driver doesn't know who you are or how to find you. I thought everyone knew who the great Jakob Callin was.

He mentally heard her saying the words in that accent of hers, right down to his name. He swallowed, loving so much about the woman.

It finally sank in. She was in Ensenada! She was here in town. But how?

Where are you, exactly?

Her text came through almost immediately.

Some grocery store called Mi Corazon.

Stay there.

No, just give me your address. I'm in the taxi now.

He typed the address and waited for her reply.
Nothing came through.
Two minutes passed before he texted her again.

Elia?

Give me a minute…

What the hell was going on? That grocery store was just around the corner from his house. Just as he got ready to text her again, there was a knock at the door.

When he opened it, there stood Elia. Just beyond her was a taxi.

"Does he need to be paid?"

"No, I just… I just wanted him to wait in case it wasn't really you."

The tremor in her voice cut him to the quick, and he folded her into his arms, waving away the taxi and closing the door. Easing her away from him, he looked into her face. "I won't ask how in the hell you found me. Instead, I'll simply ask you why you're here."

"I'm here because my mom suggested I come."

"Your mom." He was lost. What did Tersia have to do with any of this? "She told you to come to Mexico?"

"No. She told me to come find you before it was too late. She told me about risks and that I'd almost lost my leg as a child, but she'd insisted they wait… Oh, too many things to explain." She took a deep breath. "I love you. And in my heart, I needed to know if you were here with Samantha."

"Samantha? I haven't talked to her since we broke up. Nor do I plan to. She and I were a mistake. One that I don't plan on making again."

She seemed to straighten slightly. "You said I misunderstood something about your conversation with that reporter. What was it?"

He drew her inside and sat with her on the long leather sofa in the main room. "When Samantha and I broke up, she told a tabloid reporter that I had 'abandoned her' in France. It wasn't true. I wasn't even there at the time, but it caused some problems for me at the hospital. Their suggestion if a reporter ever brought it up again was to say 'no comment' and leave it at that." His mind rewound to a previous comment she'd made. "Wait. What did you say a minute ago?"

"About Samantha?"

"No. Right before that."

She smiled. "Oh, that. I love you."

He sat there, stunned. "Why didn't you tell me this when I tried to talk to you?"

"Because…" She bit her lip before continuing. "When the reporter asked about me, you had this terrible look on your face. Like you were stunned that he would even ask that."

"I was stunned. And very, very angry." He tried to find the words. "I'd realized something right before the race. That I wanted to continue seeing you. And not just because of the sex. Because of you. But I wanted to move slowly and see if you were even interested in me. And then that guy comes right out and asks if you were my new girlfriend. I just lost it. I really wanted to do some damage to him, and so I walked away before I acted on that impulse. I think that's what you maybe misunderstood."

She nodded. "The look on your face… It was as if the

very thought disgusted you. My mom assured me that if that were the case, your—she used the word equipment, for lack of a better translation—wouldn't work properly."

Jake laughed. It was the first time he'd done that in a while. "Can you tell your mom that I love her? And you?"

"Really?"

"Yes." He bent down to kiss her. "And your mom is right. My 'equipment' is very...*very*...active whenever you're around."

"But Samantha is just so beautiful."

"Do you seriously think you're not?"

She stumbled, as if not sure what to say.

"Elia, there is so much about you that fascinates me. I can't get my fill of looking at you. Of touching you... like this." He trailed the back of his hand from her cheek to the spot just behind her ear.

"I can't think when you do that."

He smiled. "Do you need to think?"

"Just for a few minutes. Just long enough to know for sure. You really love me?"

"Yes. I really do." He turned her so that he could look into her beautiful eyes. "Do you love me?"

"Yes."

His lips touched the side of her temple. "Anything else?" They trailed across her cheek on a slow journey back to her mouth and paused there, waiting for anything else that she needed him to clarify. "Elia?"

"Hmm...just one more thing."

He kissed her mouth with slow brushing strokes that only made him want more. "What is it?"

"Are you coming back to Dallas?"

"Yes, my bags are packed and I was on my way out the door when your text came through. My flight is in an hour. We can just make it, unless…"

"Unless what?"

"Unless you'd like to spend a few days here instead."

Her eyes widened. "Seriously?"

"Yup."

When her smile came, it was like the sun itself had stepped into the room. "Yes. Let's stay."

His arms wrapped around her, gripping her tightly. "This place has two bedrooms if you'd rather—"

"Yes." When his heart dropped, she added with a smile, "We'll spend one night in one of them and the next… Well, let's see if we even make it out of that first one before it's time to leave."

His equipment rose, right on cue. "Is that a challenge, Elia?"

"Only if you want it to be, *querida*. Only if you want it to be."

And then she was kissing him in a way that said all other questions could wait until they were back in the States. Until then, he would show her exactly how much he loved her. How much he wanted her. And he'd keep on showing her all the days of his life.

EPILOGUE

THE BIKE SHOP was full of bicycles, as would be expected. What wasn't quite so expected were the twirls of white streamers that covered the ceiling. Or the satin kneeling bench that sat at the front of the shop.

But Elia had never seen a more beautiful sight in all her life. The owner of the bike shop, where she and Jake had ridden for the last six months, knew someone who knew someone who was a licensed minister. He'd been willing to come and marry them. In the bike shop. And she couldn't think of a more perfect setting, since it was one of the things that had brought them together.

Randy was all healed up from that terrible accident and stood beside Jake as his best man. And Sheryll was there for Elia, who had chosen a white silk gown that hugged all her curves. It was simple, but evidently met with Jake's approval—he hadn't taken his eyes off her since she'd emerged from the door of the shop's office a minute or two ago.

He came to her and took her hands, leaning down to give her a soft kiss on the mouth that drew some noise from the dozen or so friends and family that were seated in folding chairs behind them. She smiled at her mom and dad and Tomás, who sat in front, along with Jake's mom. There were so many other people in attendance who had become important in her life since she'd come to work at Westlake Memorial.

Gracie and Matt had made it to their prom. Jake had a picture of the couple taped to his refrigerator. Gracie had worn a purple gown for the event, and Matt had a tie that matched her dress exactly. And she'd looked so proud as she huddled close to Matt, her hand pressed tight against his abdomen, as if warning other girls away. And like Jake, Gracie hadn't balked even for a second at embracing who Matt still was. Yes, there were some scars, but if anything, their young relationship had blossomed as they'd gone through therapy and his treatments together. Gracie waved at her, and Elia's smile widened as she waved back.

Carly and her parents weren't in attendance, but they'd kept in touch after leaving the hospital and had sent news that their daughter had just started preschool and was doing wonderfully. It was another photo on their refrigerator. They hadn't been able to be there due to a scheduling conflict, but someone who *was* there was Dorothy. Elia's heart had ached so much for the young woman, but Dorothy had shared that rather than letting her injuries defeat her, they'd given her a sense of control that she hadn't felt in a long time. *She* would decide her own next steps. Her cheek was red from a second skin graft surgery, but she'd done remarkably well through it all.

Elia wouldn't wish what had happened in her childhood on anyone, but that terrible occurrence had been the catalyst that had set her life on a course that ended right where it was now: getting ready to marry the love of her life. Correction. That wasn't an ending. It was a beginning. The perfect one with the perfect person.

Someone who loved every inch of her and wasn't afraid to show it. Someone who shared things with her that no one else knew. That let her take some of his pain when a case rocked him to his core. And he did the same for her.

When one was weak or sad or afraid, the other was strong and supportive. Everything a partner should be. And Elia wouldn't have it any other way.

As they turned to face the minister, she glanced up at her husband-to-be and whispered, "I love you."

He swept a stray tendril from her cheek. "Love you, too."

With that, the reverend opened the service. "Dearly beloved, we are gathered here today..."

She threaded her arm through Jake's and pressed close to his side, needing nothing else in these next moments than the joy of being here with him. Of being with those they both loved. And agreeing together that they would take the love that bound them to each other and do great things with it. Not just for each other, but for those they came in contact with each and every day.

And Elia could think of no better person to do that with than Jake. Her strong, handsome, kind and so very sexy man. The one she intended to spend her whole life with. The one she wanted to live with, love with and have children with. Including the one they were expecting in the next six months.

Life was perfect. *He* was perfect. And she was going to make sure she told him so each and every day. Starting today.

* * * * *

THE DOCTOR'S BILLION-DOLLAR BRIDE

MARION LENNOX

MILLS & BOON

To Sheila, my editor and my friend.

With thanks for so many years of friendship,
of guidance, of skill, of empathy and of travel stories.

On opposite sides of the globe,
it's always felt like the best of teams.

Warmest of warm wishes for always,

Marion

CHAPTER ONE

'I'M SORRY, BUT we have no space in today's class. Maybe we can arrange a private lesson tomorrow?'

Dr Jodie Tavish's surfing classes were almost always full, and she loved teaching the island's kids. As one of Kirra Island's three doctors, Jodie's workload wasn't huge, and her Saturday morning classes were a way of passing on the skills she loved.

But the man demanding a lesson—right now!—wasn't a kid. He looked well into his eighties.

It might be fun to try and teach him though, Jodie thought, but unless he'd surfed before he'd need to accept his limits. He was wearing board shorts, and she surreptitiously checked out his legs—skinny and a bit shaky. If she got him to his knees she'd be lucky, and she'd need to run him through a medical checklist first, even if it did offend him.

From the way he was behaving, though, she suspected it would offend him, but she'd have to do it.

But it might never happen. Right now, she had kids waiting, and this angry man was blocking her path.

'I can pay more than any of these kids put together,' he barked. 'Someone else can teach them. The woman at the resort says you're the best, and I want you.'

'I'm afraid you can't have me,' she said, still mildly. 'These kids have paid up front, and I can't take more than six. It's not safe.'

'Then give me a private lesson straight after.'

'I can't do that either. I'm a doctor and I have other commitments...'

'You're a doctor?'

'Yes, so I only do this part-time. If you'd like to put your name down for a private lesson tomorrow...'

'I'm going home tomorrow. I want a lesson now.'

'No. I'm sorry.'

And the man's anger seemed to escalate. 'Do you have any idea who you're turning down?' he demanded. 'I'm Arthur Cantrell, head of the biggest mining conglomerate in Australia. Tell these girls I'll pay them off—just get rid of them.'

Whoa.

'These girls have limited time too,' she told him, managing, with an effort, to keep her voice mild. 'They booked weeks ago. If you have so much money, I suggest you prebook and visit the island again.'

Enough. His colour was mounting but she turned away and headed for the group of teenage girls at the water's edge. The guy stood glaring after her, his anger palpable.

Kirra Island was becoming a popular destination for the wealthy since the opening of a health resort at the south end of the island. This guy must be at the upper echelons of the wealthy guest list, she thought. His face and upper neck were tanned, but the rest of him looked like it hadn't seen the sun for decades. Short and wiry, he had silvery hair and thick, bushy eyebrows. His voice had been crisp, authoritative, commanding. Aged or not, he'd look distinguished in a business setting.

There was a taxi sitting in the car park. Mack Henderson ran the only taxi on the island. It must have cost the guy heaps to hire Mack to wait, she thought, and idly wondered how much he had been prepared to pay.

But who cared? Normally, on a Saturday afternoon she could have squeezed in a private lesson, but not today. Today's date felt like a leaden weight in her heart—as this date had for the last fifteen years. After this lesson, unless medical imperatives intervened, she intended to surf by herself, surf until she was exhausted.

And right now her students were bouncing, eager to be in the water, desperate to learn. Teenage girls...

Hali would be fifteen today, she thought. Hali. The name meant *the sea*. Hali, her own precious daughter.

Probably she wasn't even named Hali any more.

No! Now wasn't for thinking of the past, nor was it for thinking of obnoxious businessmen waving wads of money. This morning was for teaching the next generation the joy of surfing, the joy of the sea.

She just had to hope, to believe, that somewhere, somehow, someone was doing the same for Hali.

'He's on Kirra Island.'

'What on earth is he doing there?'

It had taken Dr Sebastian Cantrell's receptionist three hours to track his great-uncle down. Arthur Cantrell, corporate mogul, one of the richest men in Australia, had a serious heart condition. At eighty-six, after two major heart events, with implanted pacemaker and defibrillator, everyone knew he was living on borrowed time. Fiercely private, he lived alone in his ridiculously opulent mansion and refused to have staff stay over. On weekends there was no one there.

He had, though, as a concession to Seb's 'stupid concerns' as he termed them, agreed to a personal security alarm, as well as the over-the-top security devices he'd fitted to keep his fortune of antiquities safe.

'What's the point of keeping your valuables safe if you don't keep yourself safe?' Seb had asked. Arthur had reacted angrily, as he always did at what he termed Seb's interference, but he had had the personal alarm installed.

He therefore had a disc he was supposed to wear around his neck. There was also a bedside control he was supposed to press every morning. If it wasn't pressed by nine, then the security firm rang to remind him. If Arthur didn't answer, they rang Seb. Which had happened an hour ago.

His uncle, though, had failed to press the control any number of times before, and Seb had six patients with complex problems on his list this morning. So he'd asked his receptionist to phone, and when Arthur still didn't answer she'd asked his housekeeper to check. She'd reported back that Arthur was away, but she didn't know where.

And now Beth had succeeded in tracking him down, though, he gathered, not without difficulty.

'There's a new resort just opened on Kirra Island,' she told him. 'Mr Cantrell's secretary says he's booked in over the weekend. He flew there by helicopter yesterday afternoon and Trevor's due to pick him up tomorrow.'

'Oh, well done,' Seb told her and grinned. 'I bet you didn't think when you took this job that tracking elderly great-uncles would be on your list.'

'He's a worry,' Beth conceded. 'You want to phone him?'

'Not in a million years. His blast would burst my eardrums, but if you would…can you give the resort a ring? Quietly give them my number in case of issues.'

'Of course—but why does he resent you worrying?' she asked curiously, and Seb shrugged.

'He hates anyone worrying.'

But as he headed for the next patient, he thought his great-uncle didn't just resent him worrying. He resented him *being*.

So why did *he* care about the old man? Why did he keep trying?

Because someone had to, he told himself. Arthur was the only family Seb had, and the opposite was true. If Seb didn't care, there was no one else, and what did it matter if the old man couldn't stand him?

For his father and grandfather's sake he'd do the right thing, he told himself. Even though most of the time what he'd most like to do was walk away.

'Jodie, sorry, I have to go.'

Halfway through the lesson, Ellie Cray, the oldest of her would-be surfers, had glanced towards the beach and seen her father. 'Mum and Dad are picking me up early. We're meeting Auntie Hazel from the ferry and going out for lunch. Sorry.'

She sounded sorry too. She'd just succeeded in tottering to a standing position and had caught two waves. With half an hour's class to go, she sounded like it was almost killing her to leave.

'Next Saturday?' she pleaded, and Jodie gave her a thumbs up. She had five more kids to concentrate on, and the surf was building.

'Dump your board past the high tide mark and have a lovely lunch,' she told her, and watched her safely to shore before turning her attention back to the other girls.

It was a great morning and they were doing brilliantly. The waves were long, cresting rollers, curling in nicely along the relatively shallow beach. As long as they stayed clear of the rocks at the end of the cove, where the current ran sideways, she could almost relax.

One of the kids—Maria, a pale-faced kid with a fierce determination to get out to the big waves—was having trouble. She was standing too far forward, nosediving every time. The others were practising knees to feet, knees to feet, in the shallower waves, so she could spend a little time with Maria.

But... 'Jodie!' It was Katie, at twelve one of her youngest, and the alarm in her voice brought Jodie's fast attention. She swivelled. The remaining girls were fine, but Katie was standing in the shallows, staring towards the cove's corner. 'That guy,' she called. 'The one you were talking to. He's taken Ellie's board.'

She looked—and her breath caught in her throat. Katie was right.

The guy—Arthur whoever—was in the water, right out at the back of the breaking waves. He was lying on the board, looking backwards, as if waiting for the right wave.

He must have had some experience to get the board out that far, Jodie thought incredulously. She wouldn't have thought he'd have the strength, but for the last few moments there'd been a period of calm. She and Maria had been waiting for a decent wave as well.

So now what was he doing? Waiting to surf in? She thought of his body, skinny, shaky. She knew lots of older surfers, but this guy had asked for lessons. If he wasn't experienced... surely he couldn't control a board in decent surf?

And he didn't know the dangers waiting for the unwary at that corner of the cove. Where she and her students were, the waves were long and even, foaming gently to the beach. In the corner though, where the cliffs rose to form a headland, the waves rose higher and stronger, and as they neared the shore the current pushed them into a curve. Instead of rolling to the sandy shore, they veered to crash against the rocks under the headland.

There was a sign on the beach path warning of the dangers.

This guy, though, must have stalked straight past the sign on his way to confront her. And finally grabbed the board and headed away from her group.

Into peril.

'Hey!' She didn't know she could shout so loud, but she needed to shout louder. 'Yell at him!' she screamed to the girls when he didn't react. 'And stay together and get to the beach. Beach, now!'

They were great kids. One of the first things she instilled in her students was that if she yelled 'Beach' then that was where they went, as fast as possible. She'd never had to use the command in the two years she'd been on the island, but it was there... In case of accident? In case of shark? Or right now, in case of a geriatric would-be surfer who was obviously trying to kill himself. The girls were in no danger, but they were her responsibility and she wasn't about to risk them to save him.

But they were heading for the shore, yelling as they went. She'd talked to them about the dangers of this beach, in case they came here without her to practise. They knew the dangers of the corner. Five teenage girls could make a fair noise when they tried, and she blessed them for it.

But the guy wasn't hearing—deliberately or not. He was still lying on the board, letting the shallow waves roll under him. It'd feel great, Jodie thought, to lie out there in the sun...

But not there.

She hit the beach and ran.

In her peripheral vision she could see Mack, the taxi driver. He'd have been watching while waiting for his passenger, she thought, and Mack was a local. He knew the dangers even more than she did. He was in his sixties and overweight, but he was running down the track like the athlete he'd been as a teen.

Neither of them could get there fast enough.

The corner was deceptive. Calm, calm, calm—and then

not calm. There'd been a set of maybe a dozen small swells, but further out Jodie could see the next set forming. Big ones. Who knew what caused the differential? She certainly didn't. All she knew was that a wave was surging in, building, cresting, almost breaking—and then finally it reached the man on the board.

Then, while she watched in horror, it picked up man and board as if they were driftwood. It toppled them over and over within a mass of white water, curving in to smash them onto the rocks on the shore.

'He's gone surfing.'

'What?' Seb had been checking a corneal ulcer. Ron Harvey had been hammering nails into roofing iron when a sliver of metal had flown up and pierced his eye. A week on, it was still touch and go as to whether he'd lose the eye, but he wouldn't if Seb could help it.

Ron had fallen from the ladder trying to descend after the accident. He'd suffered a broken leg and lacerations, so it had been a while until it had been realised there was iron still in the eye. The eye had therefore been inflamed and stained from the iron before Seb had seen it. The inflammation itself was a major issue. There was no way Seb could use a steroid until it had healed, but without a steroid it was a case of meticulous care, daily dressings and a whole lot of hope.

Today, though, the size of the ulcer had slightly diminished. This wasn't the sort of work Seb had dreamed of, but it was satisfactory enough, and hope was front and foremost as Seb emerged from Ron's ward.

But now his bubble of hope was displaced by incredulity. He stared at Beth as if she had two heads. His great-uncle had gone surfing? 'You're kidding me, right?'

'That's what the receptionist at the resort told me,' she replied. 'She's obviously young—no rules instilled yet about guest privacy—and was on for a chat. She says your great-uncle's headed off for a surfing lesson.'

'A lesson...' That was slightly better.

Arthur had surfed in his youth, he thought, remembering stories his father had told him of his grandfather and great-uncle. As kids they'd apparently surfed together, before Arthur had taken over the family business and focused on making his squillions.

As far as he knew though, Arthur hadn't surfed...since when? Since he was a kid? According to his grandfather, Arthur hadn't thought of anything but making money for at least fifty years.

So now, surfing with his heart condition, his failing knee joints, and all the rest...

And, for heaven's sake, maybe this was his fault. There'd been a heated exchange—very heated—a couple of weeks back, and surfing had come into the mix. Arthur had spent his life making money and now, in his eighties, was desperate for Seb to take his rightful place as heir to Cantrell Holdings. Or, as a last resort, to provide him with an heir who would.

'Do you think nothing of family?' he'd demanded. 'You're so damned obsessed...'

'I'm obsessed?' Seb had thrown back at him. 'All you think of is money. Show me you're interested in something else—take a holiday, do something besides obsessing about the wealth you never spend. The world you currently inhabit makes my skin crawl and I want no part of it. There must be something else you enjoy.'

So Arthur had gone...*surfing*?

'He'll be okay,' Beth said, seemingly mirroring his thoughts. 'The receptionist said the instructor's a local doctor. Apparently, she teaches surfing part-time, for fun, but she's an extremely competent doctor. I can't imagine she'll let him do anything unsafe.'

'Since when has he let anyone stop him doing what he wanted to do?' Seb growled, but he was reassured. And hell, his great-uncle wasn't a kid. If he wanted to kill himself, who was Seb to try and stop him?

But as he headed off to see his next patient, for some reason Beth's words stayed with him.

'Apparently, she teaches surfing part-time, for fun.'

Was there really a world out there where a doctor had space to…teach surfing for fun?

The sand stopped at the edge of the cove, becoming a rock shelf around the base of the headland. At low tide the shelf was a great place to sit and watch the power of the sea.

It was high tide now though, and there was shallow water over the rocks. Jodie ran, blessing the swim shoes she always wore. They gave her grip so she could head fast towards the edge of the shelf.

Mack paused momentarily at the edge of the shelf, staring down at his shoes, obviously taking a moment to weigh the pros and cons of ruining leather brogues. The fact that he came right on was testament to how scared he was. How scared they both were.

She reached the edge. The guy's wave had surged back but another was driving in. She had to take a couple of fast steps back or she risked being sucked in herself.

Then Mack was beside her, gripping her arm. 'Where?' he said hoarsely. 'Can you see?'

And then they did. They saw the surfboard first, smashing on the rocks as the wave slammed it down. Arthur was behind, a limp figure being tossed forward. Face down in the foam.

For a moment there was nothing they could do. They watched in sick horror as a third wave came through... And receded.

Jodie stared out at the sea. The set was done, the sea stilled, at least a little. Here under the headland, it was never still, but still enough. It looked as if he was being washed into a crevice-like break in the shelf.

This was her only chance. She started forward but Mack gripped her arm. 'You can't...'

'If I'm fast.'

'Geez, Doc, the guy's crazy.'

'Yeah, but he's probably still alive.'

'There's a rope in the cab. I can...'

'You know there's no time. Mack, I can do this.'

She hoped.

What she was thinking went against all lifesaving rules—or medical rules? *Keep yourself safe at all cost.* But she'd surfed since she was a teenager, climbing in and out of places like this to find the best swells. Besides, she had no responsibilities. If anything happened, there'd be a ripple of sadness on the island, but the ripples would settle and life would go on.

Which was the way she liked it.

All that, though, was a flash of self-knowledge, an instant appraisal of risk and consequences, and then she was pulling away from Mack's arm, stepping forward and slipping down into the water.

The place where she entered was a crevice between two outreaching fingers of rock. The whole crevice was currently a mass of foam, swells pushing in, surging out again and crashing back into the incoming waves.

Jodie, though, was good. Blessing her shoes, using them to stall herself from being washed against the rocks herself, she tried as best she could to balance herself against the wash of water, and then set herself to wait.

There was no way she could push out and try to find Arthur—that'd end in injury or worse to herself. She simply braced as best she could, dug her feet into niches in the rock, spread her arms—and hoped like hell that he'd be washed against her. If she could just hold on...

And then she found him—or rather he found her. His limp body crashed against her, shoving her sideways.

The rest was pure reflex. Somehow, she grabbed, and tugged him hard against her. The water was hauling him back but somehow, she held on. She'd got this far. Dammit, she wouldn't let go.

'You got him!' It was a triumphant shout from above. 'I'm here, Doc, hang on.'

And Mack was lying on the rocks above. He'd be lying in the washing water, but his weight must be stopping him from sliding in while the waves were small.

Please, no big ones...

Mack was leaning down, his arms outstretched, hands reaching. 'Can you push him up? Go, Doc, a bit higher. Higher...' And then... 'Got him!'

And somehow, he managed it, grasping the old man by one arm, pulling him higher, then managing to lock his hands under both arms. He pulled, Jodie pushed as best she could, and then the weight lifted from her. Mack had him out of the water.

His hands came down again. 'Doc...'

'Look after him.'

'Not till you're out,' Mack yelled. 'Big 'un coming. Now!'

It was amazing what panic could do. Her feet found leverage as she grabbed his outstretched hands and somehow hauled herself up. And then both of them grabbed the limp old man under his arms, one on each side. There was no time for trained paramedic holds, no time to do anything but grab what they could. And then they were stumbling back over the rocks, out of reach of the next set of breakers that could surely have killed them all.

Saturday was usually light. With work finished for the day, Seb headed home. His townhouse overlooked Brisbane's South Bank, a park surrounding a gorgeous man-made riverside lagoon. He swam there every morning—hard. Pushing himself to the edge of his physical endurance helped keep some of the demons at bay—but not all.

What was happening in Al Delebe? Border problems were flaring again. Were his people safe? More, what was happening in the camps being set up for the displaced? He knew the camps well, dust bowls where the sweeping sands played havoc with eyes.

Why was he here?

He'd finally accepted the reason, but he didn't have to like it, and the voices in his head gave him no relief. His parents' voices, and his grandfather's, had instilled the same mantra since childhood.

'You're on this earth to do good, Seb...'

He could do so much more if he...

No. *If* wasn't possible. What he was doing was useful. Just not as useful as he needed it to be.

So cut it out with the guilt, he told himself, and for some reason he found himself thinking of his great-uncle.

And then, stupidly, he was thinking of the woman Beth had mentioned in passing.

'Apparently, she teaches surfing part-time, for fun, but she's an extremely competent doctor.'

A doctor who practised medicine on a tiny sub-tropical island, he thought, probably attaching herself to a fancy wellness resort for the rich and indulged. A woman who had space in her life to surf in her spare time. What sort of life would that be?

He'd accused his great-uncle of living a life that made him cringe, but in truth Seb's life was also driven.

For a moment he imagined himself in such a life—a little medicine, nothing hard, then surfing in his spare time.

A life where the voices in his head let him off the hook?

It wasn't going to happen, he told himself, and the guilt kicked in even as he thought about it. But just for a moment, the voices faded and an almost primeval urge took over.

It was a great afternoon and a Saturday. Maybe *he* could surf. Or try to surf. His sole experience was as a teenager, staying with a mate from boarding school over the summer break. He had managed to stand, to catch some smallish waves. It was a fleeting memory but it was a good one.

So… It was Saturday afternoon and there was decent surf less than an hour's drive away. Maybe he could leave the mass of paperwork ensuing from his latest fundraising drive, and the preparation for the speech he'd promised at a charity ball next week. There'd surely be a place he could hire a board.

But back they came, the voices.

Surf? How would that help? How many people's vision depended on him? The voices were a hammering at the back of his head.

He sat down at his desk, pulled up his computer files and stared at the screen.

But the thought didn't fade. A doctor who surfed… For some reason the image was messing with his head.

And then he was thinking of Arthur, probably attempting a surfing lesson right now. Ridiculously. With his heart it'd be crazy.

But then he thought, why not? At eighty-six, what did Arthur have to lose? Maybe at eighty-six his great-uncle could finally change?

As if.

He stared at the screen a bit longer but his fingers stayed still. Maybe he was turning into a version of Arthur? Sure, his compulsion was his charity, whereas Arthur's was making money, but for some reason Arthur had taken time off and gone surfing.

'And I'm thirty-six,' Seb said out loud. 'Am I going to wait fifty years for my turn?'

But...

Enough.

'But nothing,' he told the voices. Then he slammed the lid closed on his computer and headed out to find some waves.

CHAPTER TWO

THIS HAD TO happen when Misty and Angus were off the island.

Normally Kirra Island had three doctors, but Misty and Angus were married with kids, and they'd taken this weekend off.

Six weeks back a tropical storm had crashed across the island, causing untold damage. The fishing fleet had been decimated and houses damaged. With so much destruction there'd been an ongoing stream of injuries as islanders fought to clear debris and make repairs. The minor injuries that entailed meant that for weeks the three part-time doctors had become almost full-time.

Now though, with demands easing and with Misty in the first stages of pregnancy, both Angus and Misty were anxious to take a break and spend time with their little family. They were therefore in Brisbane, which meant Jodie was stuck as the only doctor. So now…she was grazed and bruised, and she'd really like to go home to her snug little cottage and whinge for her country. Instead, she was stuck in Kirra's tiny clinic-cum-hospital, making sure an old man didn't die on her watch.

He should have been airlifted to Brisbane.

Once they'd got him out of the water, they'd called for reinforcements. Martin, the island's nurse-cum-paramedic—had brought the island ambulance. Parents had arrived to pick up kids.

Thankfully, the old man had revived without CPR. His most obvious injury, apart from a mass of minor lacerations and bruises, was a broken arm.

That might well have been from where she and Mack had grabbed him, she'd thought as she'd examined him, but there'd been no choice. They'd been lucky not to have fractured his scapula and clavicle—she'd been relieved to see only a minor break to the humerus. She'd started antibiotics to prevent lung infection, she'd stabilised his arm and she had him propped up on pillows. So far, so good.

His heart, though, was a different matter. His blood pressure on admission was over two hundred, and the tell-tale bulge on his shoulder wasn't caused by the break.

It was caused by an implant.

She got answers to her questions in monosyllabic grunts. He had a pacemaker? An implanted defibrillator? 'Yes.' What heart events in the past? 'Two. Minor stuff. They made a damned fuss.'

Right, she'd thought, almost thankfully. This warranted immediate transfer to Brisbane—she'd call a medevac chopper straight away. But when she'd told him what she intended, she got more than grunts. With painkillers on board, he obviously felt strong enough to blast again.

'You can call anyone you like, but I'm not getting into any ambulance. I'll refuse and you can't make me—I'll have you up for assault if you try. Get the taxi to take me back to the resort, woman, and leave me be. Trevor's coming with the chopper tomorrow. He'll take me home.'

Really? What was the likelihood they'd put him to bed and one of the resort's cleaning staff would find him dead in the morning? High enough to make the idea impossible.

'That can't happen,' she'd said briskly. 'The resort won't accept you. You're not going back to Brisbane without accompaniment either. Trevor's the helicopter pilot? If he's at the controls, there's nothing he can do if you have a heart event. You do understand the risk? Mr Cantrell, who can we call? A relative? A friend?'

She'd got a death stare for her pains. 'I'm fine on my own. Take me back to the resort. You don't have to tell them what's happened.'

'That's not an option,' she'd said, because he might be stubborn but she'd dealt with cantankerous patients before. 'And you *will* need help to return to the mainland. This Trevor, I assume he's a commercial pilot? He needs to know the facts and it's our responsibility to give them to him.'

If anything, the death stare had intensified, but she'd gazed blandly back. With effort. The last thing she wanted was to keep this guy here. Medically, she was by herself tonight. With his history he needed to be in ICU, or at least having hourly obs. Her fingers were itching to ring for evacuation. But...

'I won't go,' he said fretfully. 'I refuse.'

'Then give me a name—someone we can call.' Mack had already been through his wallet and found no emergency contact details.

He glared but she glared back.

'Fine,' he said at last. 'Ring my great-nephew. As far as I'm concerned, he's a waste of space but he'll come if I tell him to.'

But he hadn't. She'd rung the number she'd been reluctantly given—for a Sebastian Cantrell—and the phone had rung out. She'd rung three times, left messages each time, and nothing. Arthur had refused to give her another number.

So finally, she'd taken the only option. She'd settled Arthur into one of the two beds in the island's clinic-cum-hospital and settled herself to wait the night out. This Trevor was coming in the morning, so maybe Martin could go with him and take the ferry back. If Arthur refused to go to hospital once he was on the mainland, that was his business, but tonight, bruised, battered and his blood pressure still dangerously high, sending him anywhere without medical support was impossible.

The clinic's two beds were used for islanders with minor needs, an islander with gastro who needed rehydration, or one of the island's elderly, shaken after a fall but not hurt enough to need the stress of transfer to the mainland.

Usually, Martin stayed with them overnight, but tonight Jodie's attendance was the closest thing she could organise to intensive care. But this was a clinic, not a hospital. There were no state-of-the-art monitors to alert her if there was a cardiac falter, so she had to stay close.

Oh, but she was so sore, and oh, she wanted her own bed. And in the background there was still the nagging knowledge of what day this was. To say she was feeling wretched would be an understatement.

And at nine, while she was sitting beside Arthur's bed, growing grumpier by the minute, finally her phone rang.

'Dr Tavish?' The voice sounded smooth, assured, completely unapologetic. 'This is Sebastian Cantrell. I believe I've missed your call.'

'You've missed three.' Dammit, she hadn't meant to sound peevish but she couldn't help herself. She'd wrenched her own shoulder pulling his great-uncle over the rocks, and it had hurt as she'd lifted the phone.

'I apologise.' He didn't sound sorry though. He sounded irritated. 'I've been surfing. Is there a problem with my great-uncle?'

He'd been surfing? Salt in the wound, she thought. Arthur had described him as *'a waste of space'*, and right now she was prepared to accept the descriptor without argument.

'Your uncle tried surfing too,' she told him. 'Unfortunately, he surfed into rocks.' She glanced at Arthur and saw he was awake, so switched her phone to speaker. 'He's beside me now, hearing this conversation. Arthur, do I have your permission to tell your nephew your condition?' She got a hazy nod—painkillers were making the old man drift in and out of sleep. 'Your uncle agrees,' she said into the phone. 'We have him in our small clinic-cum-hospital. He has a fractured arm and lacerations. Plus...'

'Plus his heart condition.' The voice at the end of the line was incredulous. 'Are you the doctor who does the surfing lessons? You let him surf *near rocks*?'

Deep breath. *Don't lose it too*, she told herself, though she was pretty close.

'Your uncle wasn't under my supervision at the time.'

'But he was with you?'

For heaven's sake, what was he implying? A lawsuit?

'Could we leave this discussion for another time? All that matters now is that he needs evacuation to Brisbane, but he's refusing medevac.'

'He needs medevac. Do you know how dicey his heart is?' The incredulity was still there.

'I don't have a full history but I'm assuming...'

'Don't assume,' he snapped. 'Brisbane Private will send you a history.'

'Not without his permission, which I don't have.'

'You have mine. I have medical power of attorney.'

She looked down at Arthur and got a scowl and a fierce shake of his head. 'My medical history is my business,' he hissed, but he'd already told her that.

So... 'Not while he's conscious and mentally fine,' she said into the phone. But even if she got the history, it wouldn't do her any good. She hadn't the equipment or the skills to deal with the complex cardiac conditions this man obviously had.

'Put him on,' Seb snapped. 'He has to agree.'

But once again Arthur was shaking his head. 'Tell him to get stuffed,' he managed. 'Or…you can tell him to come and get me in the morning. My secretary will give him Trevor's number. He can come with the chopper—that'll fix your stupid edict that I need a nursemaid. And you…' he raised his voice, presumably so Sebastian could hear without Arthur having to take the phone '…you might as well make yourself useful. This stupid woman won't let me go back to the mainland without someone holding my hand. I'll see you in the morning.' And then he closed his eyes and refused to say another word.

'Dr Tavish?' The voice on the end of the phone now sounded resigned.

'Yes.' She was so over the pair of them.

'I'll have to organise a few things but I will come and get him.'

'That's big of you.' Whoa, that was hardly a professional response, but weariness and pain were both kicking in— being bashed onto rocks had left her with enough bruises and scratches to make even the second bed in her little clinic look good.

'What time?' the voice snapped, and she thought *like uncle, like nephew.*

'The earlier the better,' she snapped back. 'I'll endeavour to keep him alive until then, but it would be wise to have medical assistance on the chopper.'

'So you accept there's risk?'

'We don't have a cardio unit here. I'd like him gone tonight but he won't accept it. Of course there's risk. I can't call medevac just to have him refuse to board.'

'What about private medical evacuation? There is a service. He can afford it and it's his money down the drain if he refuses.'

Whoa. Private medical evacuation? A chopper full of

trained medical staff? Did he have any idea how much that would cost? And now...the old man was glowering, his anger building. At this rate he'd work himself into a heart event, she thought.

'He won't go,' she said, stepping in before what looked like an imminent explosion, and that created a pause.

'I guess it's his choice,' he said at last. 'And if he dies before morning...'

'I've told him there's a chance, but he's refused. I can only hope he doesn't.'

'Because it'd mess with your surfing, you mean?' he demanded.

What a toerag. He was trying to turn the tables on her, put the guilt on her?

Enough. 'I'm disconnecting,' she said, just as coldly. 'Goodnight.'

'I told you.' As she disconnected, Arthur was almost spitting invective. 'He's not the least bit interested in me or what I care about. Nothing but his own stupid passions. He inherited family money—money earned from *our* company, our *family* company. But there's no sense of family responsibility. It's a wonder he's even in the country. He spends Cantrell money heading off to godforsaken countries, all of it useless...'

'He's coming to get you,' she said mildly.

'Only because you stood up to him. Good for you, girl.'

'Don't soft-soap me,' she retorted. 'All I did was tell him what a pig-headed relative he has in you. Family is family, it seems, and he's coming. But Arthur, honestly, you'd be much better off in Brisbane. I've explained. You know it's not safe to stay here.'

'I'm over being safe,' he told her. 'Eighty-six and a heart that seems twenty years older. I should have died today.'

'Did you want to die?' she asked curiously, and he shook his head.

'Not before I've pulled my fool of a nephew into line. All I wanted was a surfing lesson.'

'So stealing a surfboard—you'll be billed for that, by the way—was a way of punishing me? You'll be pleased to know you succeeded.'

She was wearing a skirt and blouse—the change of clothes she always left at the clinic. Martin had stayed on while she'd had a fast shower, but she wasn't exactly looking her professional best. Now she lifted her leg to show a mass of grazing down her left calf, from being bashed against the rock shelf. 'Take a look at this,' she ordered. 'Yes, yours is worse, but without Mack and me...'

And that caused a pause. He stared down at the mass of scratches and bruises on her leg and his face twisted. Anger faded and suddenly he sounded older. Exhausted. Even guilty?

'You dived in. I thought... Was it *you* who pulled me out?'

'For what it's worth, yes.'

'It's worth a bit,' he said, closing his eyes again. 'I didn't think...but today on the beach, when I was hurtling towards those rocks... It makes a man think.'

'Does it make a man think he ought to go to Brisbane?'

'Maybe tomorrow,' he said wearily. 'I'll sleep now.'

'Good idea,' she said, suddenly gentle. He really had had a close call. 'As long as your heart keeps ticking, then you'll be fine.'

'And you'll stay?'

What choice did she have?

'I'll stay.'

'Good girl,' he said, and he finally gave in to the effects of shock and drugs and plain old age—and slept.

* * *

She borrowed the pillows from the second clinic cubicle, propped them on the wall and tried to doze in the chair.

Which wasn't exactly possible.

Firstly, it wasn't safe for her to sleep deeply. Given her druthers, she'd have taken a bucketload of painkillers herself and curled up on the spare bed, but Arthur did need watching. Specialling, they'd called it during her training—a nurse would sit with high-risk patients all night.

But nurses would watch in shifts. In a hospital setting one person wasn't rostered to watch all night, especially when that one person was as sore as she was.

Maybe she should have called Angus and Misty to come home, she thought. They could have caught the last ferry. But they hadn't had time off for so long, and they'd planned on taking Forrest, their nine-year-old, to the Brisbane Carnival tomorrow.

Which was actually today, Jodie realised, as midnight came and went, but then she thought of Forrest, excited beyond belief at the thought of the carnival. And Misty and Angus—and toddler Lily—Forrest's family…

What had she said to Arthur tonight? *Family is family.* Forrest had had a tough beginning but now he had parents who adored him, a baby sister he loved, a Gran, a dog, family.

And there were those thoughts again. Thoughts of Hali. Her baby. Fifteen today.

No, fifteen yesterday. She'd missed her birthday. Yet again.

And whether it was the culmination of a horrible day, the shock, the pain and the sheer discomfort of what she was doing now, or whether it was those memories flooding back— surely, they should have stopped by now, but maybe they never would—suddenly she found she was grabbing tissues from the bedside cabinet and disappearing behind them.

And when she emerged, Arthur was awake, looking at her in the dim light cast by the night lamp.

'Do you have a cold?' he growled. 'Oh, great. Contagious? That's all I need.'

'I don't have a cold,' she managed, and there was a long silence.

It was the strangest atmosphere, sitting in this silent clinic. Maybe it was getting to him too, for when he spoke again the gruffness had gone from his voice.

'So…crying? Why?'

'I don't cry.'

'Bull,' he growled. 'Men troubles? No, don't tell me, it's always men troubles.'

'It isn't men troubles. My leg hurts.'

He winced at that, and swore, but then his gaze intensified. 'Okay, I'm sorry, but crying? I still don't buy it. Want to tell Uncle Arthur why?'

As if. 'You're my patient, not my uncle,' she told him. 'Do you need more painkillers?'

'Do you?' He glanced down towards her leg.

'I'm on duty. We're talking about you.'

That produced another long look. Assessing? 'I am grateful you saved my life,' he said reluctantly. 'I still have people to annoy, a nephew to bring into line. But I wouldn't mind painkillers.'

Great. She could be a doctor again instead of a confidante. She busied herself, checking his blood pressure—still way too high—organising meds and wishing she had staff to check dosages. She was tired and she hurt, and there were still these emotions…

They had to be ignored. Drugs administered, she settled back in her chair and hoped Arthur would go back to sleep. But he was still watching her.

'So…crying?'

Oh, enough. 'That's none of your business.'

'I know,' he said bluntly. 'But I wouldn't mind knowing. It seems you saved my life so if there's anything I can do… Fix money troubles? Organise a hitman to take out a lowlife causing you grief?'

And at that she even managed a smile. 'Thank you, but honestly, I have no one to hit.' And then curiosity got the better of her. 'Could you really do that?'

'I'd have no idea how,' he admitted. 'But I have contacts and wealth. I dare say I could organise it.'

'So you can organise anything?'

'Not everything,' he said and glowered. 'Blasted family.'

'Your nephew?'

'You got it. Ungrateful brat.'

'He doesn't sound like a brat,' she said cautiously. 'He sounds like a grown man.'

'He's a brat. Do you know how extensive the Cantrell mining group is? How much power's behind it? He's due to inherit, but off he goes, flibbertigibbeting from country to country, getting into trouble, mixing himself up with all these exotic diseases, caring for nothing but himself…'

'Flibbertigibbeting?' she asked faintly.

'Just stuff and nonsense,' he snapped, anger growing again. 'Wasting his inheritance, spending money like water, doing whatever he wants. He's just like you, only at least you have the decency to save the odd life. The boy's the only family I have, and I might as well have none.' He glowered again and then fixed her with a stare. 'So that's me. What about you? Do you have family?'

'I… No,' she said, caught off-guard, and the old man's eyes narrowed. Homing in for the kill?

'So you're crying because?'

And what was there about the night, the pain, the weariness—and the sheer effort she'd have to make to deflect him—that made her say...

'Because I don't have a family. Yesterday was my daughter's birthday, but I lost her fifteen years ago.'

'You lost your daughter? What do you mean? How?'

She caught herself at that. What on earth was she saying? She never talked about Hali. Her daughter was her business.

No, she wasn't. Hali had stopped being her business fifteen years back.

But Arthur was still at it. Maybe he was using her to drive away his own pain and shock. Whatever, he wasn't letting up.

'Fifteen years back,' he muttered, staring at her. 'You must have been a kid yourself.'

'I was fifteen,' she said, and could have bitten her tongue out for saying it. Where was her head?

'Your parents?'

'I haven't seen them for years. Mr Cantrell, please...'

'So you're as alone as me then,' he said, bitterness returning to his voice. 'I bet you'd like a family who cares.'

And that was a gut punch. There was a long silence until finally she spoke again.

'I guess I would,' she told him. 'But you have...what did you call him...a flibbertigibbet nephew, and I have my work and my surfing and my colleagues. Mr Cantrell, I don't know why I said that. What I just told you was private. Could I ask you to respect that?'

'I've got no one to gossip to,' he told her. 'No wife to whinge to. No family to put up with me. So we're two of a kind and I respect that. But it's time you stopped crying.' And then his voice turned bleak. 'Families just let you down, over and over, and the sooner you accept you're better without them, the better you'll be.'

'But you're still trying with your nephew?'

'Fat chance I have of succeeding,' he muttered. 'I'd need a miracle.'

And then, to her relief, he closed his eyes. Conversation done.

CHAPTER THREE

THE NEPHEW FLEW in at nine the next morning, on board Arthur's private chopper. It landed on the stretch of land between the clinic and the sea. Jodie was at the window, watching as it landed. The pilot stayed aboard. The other occupant—the flibbertigibbet?—strode up towards the clinic like a man on a mission.

He was tall and lean—very lean—with dark brown hair and bronzed skin. Wearing fawn-coloured chinos and the sleeves of his open-necked shirt rolled up, he was striding fast, looking like he had no time to waste.

Well, neither did she. As long as nothing else happened on the island, the moment Arthur left she could go home and sleep. It was Sunday and Angus and Misty would be home later this afternoon. Maybe she could sleep for twenty-four hours?

She headed out to Reception to meet him. 'Mr Cantrell?'

'It's Dr Cantrell,' he said, almost a snap, making it obvious he was not here to waste time. His face looked set and grim. 'You can call me Seb.'

But she was still processing the first statement. 'Doctor?' This didn't fit with Arthur's description. 'Um…philosophy?'

'Medicine,' he said curtly, seemingly annoyed. 'I'm an ophthalmologist.'

'Really?' An eye specialist? That was so far away from his uncle's description of him as a wastrel that she could only stare.

'I know,' he said, still grim. 'Arthur will have told you I'm useless, and I am to him. Maybe I am to myself as well, but that's another story. Regardless, I have enough medical knowledge to safely escort him back to Brisbane. I've booked him into South Brisbane Private—that's the only hospital luxurious enough to cater for his whims, and it also has access to emergency cardio if needed. I assume he's stable now? Good, let's get him moved.'

Whoa. A one-minute handover? But if he was a doctor, and if he knew his uncle's history, hooray, they could both go.

But for some reason he'd paused and now he was looking down at her leg.

The skirt she'd changed into the night before was knee-length, slightly flared. It was what she left at the hospital because when she needed it—which was seldom—it was usually at a time when she was stressed and needed something light.

She hated wearing scrubs—in truth, she and Misty and Angus had made the decision not to wear them unless they were dealing with something really messy. *The islanders should see us as normal people, not medical machines,'* Misty had decreed. *'They'll treat us better that way.'*

So now she was wearing a light skirt, a floral blouse and… okay, theatre clogs. Somehow, her beach shoes had disappeared into the surf the day before.

But it wasn't the clogs Seb was looking at. Her left leg was exposed from the knee down. She'd washed it the night before and applied a liberal coating of antiseptic. The brown of the antiseptic had mingled with the weeping abrasions, making her leg look a bloody mess.

'Ouch,' he said, frowning. 'Did you both hit rocks?'

'Yeah,' she muttered. 'I'll take you in to your uncle.'

But he reached out and gripped her shoulder, stopping her

turning away. 'There are things I don't understand. You're hurt? Because of my uncle?'

This was weird. He was holding her in a grip that was strong and sure, searching her face, his eyes creased into concern. As if he...cared? And for some dumb reason the sensation was doing her head in.

Oh, for heaven's sake, this feeling was just because she was tired. She did hurt, and there'd been no one, but there'd always been no one. Why was she suddenly feeling like she wanted to sink into this man's grip and let herself savour the strength of him?

This was dumb. She did not need this.

She did not need anyone.

'I'm fine,' she managed, trying to pull back. 'It's your uncle who needs the care. I've written up as detailed a medical report as I can. Do you have a defibrillator on board? His blood pressure's lowered but it's still of concern.'

'I won't need a defibrillator,' he said but he didn't release her shoulders. 'He has one fitted.'

Damn. How stupid was she? Basic medicine. If Arthur's heart faltered, the implants would do what an external machine would do.

She flushed. 'I know that. Sorry,' she muttered, but he was still reading her face. Questioning.

'You're exhausted.'

'It's been a long night.'

'What else has happened?'

'Nothing,' she snapped, and it was impossible to stop the weariness coming through. 'But I couldn't leave your uncle.'

'You don't have backup? Nursing staff?'

'Not this weekend.'

'So you slept here?' He sounded incredulous.

'If you could call it sleeping. Arthur's through here.'

Once again, she tried to pull back but his hands still held. 'The grazes… How…?'

'I pulled him out of the sea,' she said, goaded. For heaven's sake, what was happening here? Why was she being held? She just wanted to get rid of the pair of them and get some sleep. 'If you want to know, my surf class was full, your uncle was angry I wouldn't take him so he stole one of my surfboards. Then he went into one of the most dangerous places to surf on the island and was immediately washed onto rocks. I had to go in after him. Our local taxi driver helped me haul him out, but for a while it was touch and go.'

'The driver dived in, too?'

'Mack has more sense,' she said. 'All of us in the water? We're not idiots. Anyway, your uncle lost consciousness, but only momentarily. He's broken his arm—I have that strapped. I've started antibiotics and kept him on IV fluids plus intravenous pain meds. His lungs will need to be checked on the mainland, as will the lacerations he's received. We have a transport stretcher—can you and your pilot help move him? I can call our nurse if I must, but on a Sunday morning I won't call Martin in unless it's really necessary.'

That brought a moment's silence, loaded with incredulity. He let go of her shoulders and stood back, staring at her in disbelief.

'He washed onto rocks—yet you dived in?'

'There wasn't a choice,' she said bitterly. 'The punishment for stupidity and arrogance shouldn't be death.'

'He's eighty-six.'

'So you wouldn't have dived in?'

'I probably would, but he's my uncle.'

'So why weren't you there watching? Someone should be looking after him.'

And that brought more silence. He raked his hair, his long

fingers pushing through already unruly deep brown waves. She thought suddenly, his face was almost too thin, too drawn. He looked...as tired as she was?

Or maybe not. A different form of tired?

A tiredness that seemed bone-deep.

'I do my best,' he said at last. 'But he's not...family.'

There was that word again. Family. That sounded like a rabbit hole she had no intention of heading down. It was not her place to care for the two of them.

'Fair enough,' she said. 'Let's get him transferred.' Oh, the thought of them both leaving. She might not even make the effort to walk back to her own little house. She might just sink onto the spare clinic bed and sleep right here.

But then the phone rang. The clinic phone. Her own phone buzzed at the same time.

Work.

Medical calls came through to the clinic, but they were also directed to the private phone of the doctor on call. This synchronised ring meant this was a medical call, and at the weekend the islanders knew only to call in cases of real need. She sighed, glancing longingly through at the spare bed, but she had no choice but to answer.

'Excuse me,' she told Seb and turned away.

Her last call on the desk handset had been to a pharmacy supplier, and she'd been left on hold for fifteen minutes. Therefore, the phone was still on speaker, which meant the man's voice at the other end came through as clearly as if he was in the room.

'Doc?' She heard the immediate anxiety. 'It's Cliff Michaels.'

She knew Cliff—he and his wife ran a surf shop in Kirra's little township. 'Hey, Cliff. What's the problem?'

'It's Ruby. She and her mates decided to build a cubby.

Seems they found a sheet of tin, blown off from somewhere during the storm. They got into my shed and got nails. She's thumped a nail into tin and something's slivered off. Gone into her eye. She's in real trouble, Doc. A lot of pain and there's bleeding. Can I bring her in?'

'Of course,' she told him, and had to suppress the urge to groan. There went her chance of sleep. 'I'm at the clinic now. Bring her right in.'

She disconnected and sighed.

She turned and found Seb was now looking at her with speculation. That impression, that he was somehow reading her thoughts, seemed to intensify.

'So...' he said slowly. 'Lacerated eye?'

'Yeah,' she said wearily. 'Ruby's ten, a tough little kid. If Cliff says she's in trouble, then she really is. If it's serious... I'll do what I can but she'll probably need to go to Brisbane.' She frowned, thinking forward. 'I'd ask you to take her back with you, but I'm not sure yet about her flying. There's a ferry at midday...'

'I can help.'

'*Really?*' She hadn't meant that to sound like it did—as if the thought of him being useful was absurd. His uncle's attitude must have embedded itself, she thought. But then...if he truly was an ophthalmologist...

'Your uncle needs transfer,' she said.

'I understand that' he told her, still watching her face. 'But Arthur's choice was to wait here overnight, so unless things are deteriorating, he might as well wait another hour. Are things deteriorating?'

'I... No.'

'Well, there you go then,' he told her and he smiled. And that smile...

It changed his face. He'd been looking questioning, but before that he'd seemed grim, angry that his weekend had just been interrupted by an idiot uncle. His initial approach, a man in a hurry to get this over with, had left her with a feeling of distaste. But this smile…it changed things. It made him seem…gentle? Kind?

How could one smile do that? And why was it making her feel…like she didn't understand what she was feeling?

'I know what my uncle thinks of me and maybe he's right,' he was saying. 'But just occasionally my qualifications come in handy. It seems I'm in the right place at the right time, and maybe I owe you. Maybe my uncle and I both owe you. So I'll go see him and tell him we need to pay a debt, and if things seem stable then he can wait a bit longer. Then I need to see what equipment you have. Right, Dr Tavish, let's deal with Ruby together.'

Arthur might consider his great-nephew a waste of space, but five minutes after Ruby's arrival Jodie was having a serious rethink.

Ten-year-old Ruby was a wiry, scrappy kid, one of the gang of island kids who travelled as a pack. Her parents' surf-hire business right on the beach made the Michaelses' home a base for most of them.

Jodie had met Ruby a few times before, and it was mostly for trauma, falling out of trees, slicing her leg on the fin of a surfboard, cutting her feet on shells. Normally she arrived blasé—even belligerent—her attitude was that injuries were a nuisance, and her parents had no right to mess with her day by dragging her to the doctor—but today she came in huddled against her dad, holding a cloth to her eye, looking bedraggled and scared.

'Hey,' Seb said, before Jodie could introduce him. He stooped so he was on eye level with the child. 'You're Ruby?

I'm Seb and I'm an eye doctor. It's a fluke that I'm here visiting Dr Jodie when you've hurt your eye. I'm guessing it must be hurting a lot, so the first thing we need to do is give you something to make you feel better. Then we need to fix it. Can we pop you up on the couch so Doc Jodie and I can take a look?'

It was exactly the right approach, direct, reassuring, positive. Cliff lifted his daughter onto the couch and Ruby's tough little persona reacted to Seb's direct approach. Where most kids would cry and cling, Ruby sank onto the pillows and calmly waited for him to follow through.

And he did. The lid of her left eye was lacerated, still sluggishly bleeding, but the deep scratch—and the pain—showed something had gone past the eyelid.

Ruby wasn't the most voluble kid. Jodie had expected to have trouble drawing her out, but Seb did it in minutes.

'So what sort of a cubby are you making?' he asked as he worked. 'I used to make big ones when I was a kid. I spent a lot of time overseas, in a place called Al Delebe. When I was about your age my mates found a hole at the back of our local rubbish dump, and we found all sorts of cool stuff. We never found enough iron for a proper roof, though. We used an old mattress once—it took four of us to drag it home. We propped it up on bricks. It made a great roof until we had a thunderstorm with really heavy rain. The whole thing collapsed and stuffing went everywhere. We had to admit where we'd got it from, and Dad had to hire a trailer and pay to take it back to the dump. We all had to help collect the stuffing. Boy, was I in trouble.'

And he had Ruby fascinated.

He had Jodie fascinated as well.

With Cliff sitting nervously in the background, close enough for Ruby to know her dad was near, Seb was doing a careful examination, with Jodie assisting.

Their little clinic was well equipped, and Seb had done a thorough check of what they had while they'd waited for Ruby to arrive. He'd also incidentally queried Jodie on what she was comfortable with him doing and what she could do herself. Now there was no hesitation.

He was wearing loupes, the specialist magnifying eye glasses they kept in their well-stocked equipment store. In between chatting—and Ruby was relaxing enough to chat— he had her focusing on a particular point in the ceiling. 'Dr Jodie will waggle her fingers above my head. Can you count how many fingers she's holding up? Now I'm just going to ask her to gently, very gently, hold your eyelids apart so you don't blink on me. Patients always blink. Can you try not to?'

And then… 'Yep, I see it. It looks like a tiny sliver of metal. It must have bounced up when you hit the tin. Wow, Ruby, you must have hit that nail really hard. Good arm muscles, huh? But the good news is that it doesn't seem to have gone into the inner eye—the part of your eye that makes you see.'

He looked for a little longer, checking and rechecking until he was sure he'd seen enough. Then he sat back, motioning Jodie to release Ruby's eye. 'Okay, team, we need to talk,' he said, and in those six words he'd pulled Cliff, Ruby and Jodie into a shared consultation.

Most doctors wouldn't do this, Jodie thought. They'd leave the room, take the parent outside, talk to their colleague separately. But Seb…this was some bedside manner.

'The sliver doesn't seem too deep but it's still a bit deep for me to tweezer it out,' he told them, and he was looking at Ruby as he spoke. Treating her like an adult. 'And also, where it is…it's important for us to get it out as fast as we can. It looks sharp and we don't want it working its way in further. Ruby, we could send you to Brisbane but that'll waste time. Luckily, I'm a specialist eye doctor and I can do it here. I've given you a painkiller—you're probably already feeling a bit better—right? That's great but pulling the sliver out might hurt a bit more. If Dr Jodie agrees, what I think should happen is that we use more of the anaesthetic and make you sleepy.'

'Ruby had an anaesthetic six months back when she cut her feet on oyster shells,' Jodie told him. That was an accident that happened often on Kirra—surfers ending up on the oyster beds. The damage to their feet was often extensive and needed rigorous cleaning, so with nervous kids, or even some adults, a light general anaesthetic was often the way to go.

'So you'll know the process,' Seb said cheerfully. 'I give you a pinprick in your arm, the stuff in the needle will let you go to sleep for a few minutes, and I can pull out the sliver without you feeling a thing. Dr Jodie will help me. Is that okay with you, Ruby? Okay with you, Cliff?'

It seemed it was fine. So, twenty minutes later, with Cliff settled beside Arthur with instructions to call if needed—Kirra locals were used to this sort of all-hands approach to medicine—Jodie found herself assisting while Seb did as swift and neat a piece of ocular surgery as she'd seen.

Not that she'd seen much. This was the sort of injury she'd normally send on to Brisbane, and send on fast. Speed was vital here. Even if there was no penetration into the inner eye, foreign bodies moved, they caused infection and the chance of Ruby losing her sight in that eye—or it even causing a sympathetic loss of sight in the other eye—was real.

But because of Seb that risk was minimised. She watched in appreciation of his skill as he mounted a needle on the end of a cotton tip, bending it with sterile forceps. Then, with his hand resting on the sleeping Ruby's cheek, using only the very tips of his long fingers, holding the blade tangentially to the eye surface, he deftly lifted the offending sliver up and away.

The sight of that tiny sliver was such a relief… What a gift, she thought as he irrigated, scrupulously checking and washing out any residual foreign body material, then applying antibiotic ointment and a double eye patch, doubling the inner pad to prevent the eyelid from opening.

'She'll still need to come to Brisbane,' he said. 'I need to repeat fluorescein staining and check vision with the right equipment, but that can wait until tomorrow. As soon as she's awake and the IV's finished, if Cliff can assure us she can be kept quiet for the rest of the day I see no reason why she can't go home now and come across to Brisbane on the ferry tomorrow. A night in hospital might be stressful for the whole family and I think it's avoidable.'

'But it takes weeks—months—to get an appointment with an ophthalmologist,' Jodie said. She knew the drill. Patients who needed urgent care were admitted to hospital. Then the specialist could see them on their morning or evening rounds. It was much more efficient—for the specialist. She also knew ophthalmologists' fee structure. She thought again of Arthur's description of this man as a waste of space—and thought of the doctors whose career plans seemed to be making as much money as possible.

Today this man could be surfing or making money. Donating this morning to his uncle—and now Ruby—must be some sacrifice.

But it seemed he'd made the decision to be generous.

'I'll make time for Ruby,' he told her. 'I'll take details and have my receptionist ring Cliff first thing tomorrow. She'll organise a time after the ferry gets in.'

'That's…kind.'

'Not as kind as saving my uncle.' He smiled again, but this time his smile was rueful. 'Though what you did was kindness to my uncle, not to me. The old man gives me such grief…'

His smile died, but then he gave a decisive nod—moving

on? 'Right, then. You agree? I'll go talk to Cliff. As soon as Ruby's drip's through and she's nicely awake we'll all let you sleep.'

'Thank you,' she managed.

And then he frowned. 'Will you sleep?'

'I guess. As long as nothing else happens.' She caught herself then, aware there was a note of pathos in her voice, and he must have heard it. What was she doing, feeling sorry for herself? 'It shouldn't though,' she told him. 'It's a small island. I'll be back surfing in no time.'

'Because that's the way you like it?'

'Absolutely.'

'But he was still watching her, still frowning. 'So no other commitments? You don't have six kids and two dogs waiting at home for Sunday lunch?'

'Heaven forbid,' she said, trying to lighten her voice. 'I don't even have a goldfish, and Angus and Misty—the island's other two doctors—will be back this afternoon so I can go back to being a part-time doctor.'

'You love surfing more than medicine?' He was watching too closely for her liking. What was with the inquisition?

'You like surfing too,' she said, a bit too tartly. 'And your uncle says you don't do family. I suspect we're birds of a feather.'

'And I suspect that we're not,' he said, and his voice was grim again. 'But moving on...let's go see if Cliff has managed to annoy Arthur yet. It doesn't take much to annoy him. He's done more than annoy you, though, so I suspect the sooner we're gone the better you'll like it.'

Which was very true, she conceded, but as he gave her a rueful smile and headed out to deal with his great-uncle...why was she feeling an inexplicable sense of loss?

CHAPTER FOUR

Five months later

'MARRIAGE! YOU HAVE to be kidding.'

This morning Arthur Cantrell had been buried. Given his way, Seb would have organised a small private ceremony but, as per Arthur's prepaid instructions, a very expensive funeral consortium had conducted an over-the-top ceremony that would have done any of the politicians who'd attended proud.

And there had been politicians. And company directors. And pretty much the entire who's who of Australia's financial world. They'd arrived for the ceremony, shaken Seb's hand— there were no other family hands to shake—and then departed with all possible speed.

None had had any personal affection for Arthur, and at his age his sudden death from a catastrophic heart event had surprised no one. The attending suits had had only one thing in common—they wanted to know who'd now be controlling the massive Cantrell Holdings.

Which could be him. Cue incredulity. Given the animosity between himself and his uncle, he'd never thought of such a possibility.

But now...

He was currently facing a trio of lawyers. With a fortune like this at stake, they'd obviously decided that giving this news was too much responsibility for one man. The law firm's senior partner had just read out his uncle's will, and it had left him stunned.

'Choice?' he managed, struggling to get the word out.

'His original will was firm,' the senior lawyer told him, looking grave. 'But after your great-uncle had that incident on Kirra Island he decided to add a second option.' He shot Seb a nervous glance. 'We have no idea who this Dr Tavish is, but she must have made an impression on him. Given the gravity of the situation, and it is in a sense a bequest to her, we decided to inform her at once. A registered letter should be with her now.'

'But this is ludicrous.'

'We did query the legality as soon as we were made aware of it,' the junior of the trio told him, sounding apologetic. 'Your uncle was elderly, and he'd had major health issues. With such a clause we initially thought that the current board of Cantrell Holdings might be able to argue mental impairment. But your uncle made sure this was watertight. It seems he arranged a consultation with one of Brisbane's top neurologists, and there's now an attached specialist opinion stating he was in sound mind. We don't believe it can be fought.'

'Ludicrous,' he said. Seb had picked up the document and was staring at it as if it might explode.

'Nevertheless, it's what your uncle decreed. You might need time to think about it—maybe consult your own lawyer or lawyers? The current directors of Cantrell certainly will.' The man's severe face twisted into the trace of a bemused smile. 'Is this… Jodie Tavish…someone you might like to marry?'

'You have to be kidding!' For heaven's sake… The thought of marriage, to a woman he'd met once…this was indeed ridiculous. Even marriage itself… There'd never been time in his world and maybe there never would be time. Plus, he hardly remembered her.

But...he did remember her. He fought for images now and found them—Dr Jodie Tavish, battle-worn after a dreadful day and night, injured, weary, but strong. A formidable woman.

But...*marriage*?

'Is she someone you'd object to marrying?' the lawyer was asking. 'The inducements seem...favourable.'

'Favourable? That's surely a joke.'

'I'm afraid it's not a joke.' The senior lawyer was already starting to put papers back in his briefcase. 'As my colleague said, you might like to consult your own lawyers, but the choice seems stark. It's up to you—and this Dr Tavish—to decide.'

It was eleven in the morning and she was off-duty. Misty was doing clinic. Angus was on duty for house calls or emergencies. Jodie had just had a truly excellent surf, she was now free for the rest of the day, and the day was glorious. She came home, showered and then wandered along the beach path into town for coffee—and maybe a croissant?

Or two croissants, she conceded. Surfing made a woman hungry. She collected her mail, swapped island gossip with the postmistress—Dot—then headed to the baker's. There she bought coffee, a croissant *and* a raspberry Danish, and then settled on the trunk of a palm that had crashed during the storm. Most of the debris had been cleared, but this tree trunk had been left as a lovely place for a seat overlooking the bay. Perfect.

Or almost perfect. There was one thing now marring her contentment—the registered letter Dot had just handed her.

For years, every such official envelope had her thinking: was this Hali trying to reach her? Was it information about her daughter? But she'd had enough let-downs over the years to realise no such information would be forthcoming. Whatever she'd signed, or her parents had signed on her behalf, all those years ago, the stipulation of no contact was pretty much binding.

So now... This'd be something to do with her apartment, she told herself, putting the letter aside until she'd coped with her messy pastry. She still owned her small apartment in Melbourne, and occasionally there were things to deal with on it.

So she finished her first pastry, licked her fingers, turned her attention to her coffee and finally opened the letter.

What the...?

Her coffee splashed over the top of the letter. She stood up, shaking coffee off the thick parchment, ignoring the coffee on her shorts, trying to see the words under the coffee stains.

It wasn't about Hali. Or her apartment. This was absurd.

It was a legal notice from a firm called Noah, Bartram and...and coffee splodge? The paper was thick and creamy, expensive. Even under coffee, it looked very, very formal.

Dear Dr Tavish.
We regret to inform you of the death of our client, Mr Arthur George Cantrell.

Her eyes were blurring—or was that coffee? This wasn't making sense.

...the bequest is as follows. The sum of one million dollars to Dr Jodie Catherine Tavish, on absolute condition that she marry my great-nephew, Dr Sebastian Michael Cantrell.
This marriage must take place within one calendar year of my death, and the marriage must be seen to be

*genuine, using the rulings for visa requirements for entry
of foreign nationals as potential Australian citizens as
minimum requirement.*

*Dr Tavish is also required to sign an agreement set-
ting up a trust fund for any future offspring of this marriage, facilitating the Cantrell name continuing and
giving such offspring a controlling interest in the corporation known collectively as Cantrell Holdings...*

Ouch! The spilled coffee had scalded her knee and she
hadn't even noticed. She noticed now and left letter, remaining coffee and remaining croissant on the bench while she
headed for a nearby tap. When she got back the seagulls had
pinched her pastry and knocked over her remaining coffee.
She watched the croissant being held aloft by no less than three
warring seagulls. It was dropped, swooped on by others before it hit the ground and then carried triumphantly out to sea.

'Ridiculous,' she said out loud, staring at the disappearing
croissant—and then she looked again at the coffee-stained letter and she even grinned.

She'd had proposals before—of course she had. Almost
every young—or youngish—health professional she'd ever
met had learned to cope with patients who saw professional
caring as something more. Even on the island, one of the old
fishermen she'd cared for after a stroke had tried to set her
up with his bachelor son. The fact that his son was well over
sixty, had a major drinking problem and smelled of fish was
irrelevant. 'He's got a great boat,' his dad had told Jodie. 'And
so what if he's older than you? That means you have every
chance of eventually inheriting his boat.'

This was the same thing, she thought. She'd treated Arthur
for what, less than twenty-four hours, and she'd met his great-

nephew once. And she didn't even know if his great-nephew normally smelled of fish.

She had looked him up though. She'd had an impressive professional letter from him after he'd followed up with Ruby. She'd been impressed with his skills, and had thought maybe she could continue referring patients to him.

As if. It seemed he was a part-time doctor. A phone call to the Brisbane hospital where he worked had told her he was only there three days a week. He did weekend call work but only for inpatients, and he was booked out months ahead. 'He only takes patients referred within the hospital system,' his receptionist had told her apologetically. 'He has other interests.'

Like surfing?

That'd have to mean he probably didn't smell like fish, she conceded, and a million dollars was probably a better inducement than an ancient fishing boat. But...

'Ridiculous,' she said aloud, and headed back into the post office to buy a postcard and borrow a pen. She might as well get this out of the way fast.

She made her reply formal.

I am in receipt of your letter informing me of the conditional bequest from the estate of Mr Arthur Cantrell. Please take this letter as my definite refusal of such a bequest. Could you also please inform Dr Sebastian Cantrell that my acceptance of this offer is out of the question.

Enough? The letter she'd received appeared to be a valid legal document, so she signed her reply with care, printed her name underneath and asked Dot to co-sign. Then she paid extra for registered post, handed it over to Dot and went to buy another coffee. And, feeling firm, another croissant.

CHAPTER FIVE

HE ARRIVED TWO weeks later. Jodie had just finished work—
she was on clinic duty this week but by three she was done.
Time for a surf? She walked along the beach track home,
rounded the last bend and Dr Seb Cantrell was standing on
her front porch.

He looked out of place on her saggy little veranda, with the
sea a backdrop that defined her cottage as more of a beach
shack. He was dressed casually in chinos and an open-neck
shirt, but he didn't look like any of the tourists who frequented
the island. Even in casual gear he looked...professional. Like
he was here to work?

'Dr Tavish?'

He was wary?

Her wariness went off the charts.

'Dr Cantrell,' she said and waited for more, but he said nothing. What was he doing here?

'I got the lawyer's letter,' she said at last. 'I assume they
received my reply. I also assume your great-uncle must have
been...'

'Not of sound mind?'

The wariness was still there, and by now she'd assessed him
further. He looked exhausted, and maybe even more lean than
he'd looked the last time she'd seen him. There were deep lines
around his eyes. Strained to breaking point?

Had he been fond of Arthur?

'I'm sorry for your loss,' she said, gently, deciding sympathy was the way to go. 'Was it sudden?'

'In his sleep.' His reply sounded grim. 'It was the way he'd have chosen, though too soon for his liking. He'd have liked to be pulling the strings for another decade or six.'

'I'm sorry,' she said again, and that was followed by more silence.

A flock of lorikeets were arguing with gusto in the eucalypts behind her cottage. Their squawking seemed unreal.

Actually, this whole situation seemed unreal. Why was he here? Had her simple refusal caused complications?

And, finally, he spoke. 'Dr Tavish, seriously, I think I need to marry you.'

And there was a conversation-stopper. Was he kidding? She fingered the phone in her pocket. Maybe she should put in an urgent call to Misty and Angus. *Guys, come fast, bring sedatives and a straitjacket. I suspect hallucinogenic drugs are involved.*

'Well, that's not going to happen,' she said, deciding to be brisk. Professionalism was surely the way to go here. 'I made that clear in my letter. Sorry, Dr Cantrell, but I'm not for sale. Now, if you'll excuse me…'

'Not even for a million?'

She had to walk past him to get into her cottage. This was annoying. Maybe she could remember something she needed at the shops? Excuse herself?

Run?

'Not even for a million,' she told him. 'This is ludicrous.'

'I know, that's how it seems and I'm sorry.' He raked his hair, a gesture she found she remembered, and his look of weariness intensified. 'Maybe I'd better explain.'

There was no way such a proposition could be explained,

but the exhaustion on his face had her hesitating. The doctor part of her even had her concerned. Okay, she could give him five minutes.

'Fine,' she told him. 'But I'm not inviting you inside. We stay here on the porch.' There were a couple of families on the beach below the cottage. If she yelled hard enough, she'd get help.

But he didn't seem like the kind of guy who needed a strait-jacket, she conceded. He looked...

Suddenly, she wasn't sure how he looked because, weirdly, her body seemed to be remembering that twinge of...some-thing...she'd felt when he'd held her shoulders. What? She didn't have a clue—*and it wasn't wanted now.*

'Are you okay?' she managed, forcing the professional side of her to kick in. The tiredness she was hearing in his voice seemed to be almost bone-deep. She'd seen this before in pa-tients who'd lost someone they loved with all their hearts. Surely, he couldn't have felt this about his uncle. 'You look like you haven't slept for weeks.'

'I'm okay.' He managed a tired smile. 'I'm just between a rock and a hard place.'

'So explain,' she told him, coming to the decision that she might as well put this on a clinical basis. He was clearly in trouble and she was starting to think...irrationality caused by depression?

Where was a psychiatrist when she needed one? There wasn't one on this island. Was she all he had?

'Okay, sit,' she told him, and she got a look that said, aston-ishingly, that he got it. A tired smile lit his eyes.

'You're going to charge for a consultation?'

'You can give my receptionist your billing details later,' she told him. 'You want me to get you a box of tissues before we start?'

'It's not that bad.'

'Your eyes say it is,' she said gently, continuing in the way she'd decided to play it. 'So sit down and tell me.'

So he sat on one of her old porch chairs and, despite his refusal, she fetched a tissue box and sat it firmly on the rickety table in front of him. His smile emerged again as he saw it. 'As if,' he said.

'Neglecting to place tissues in reach of adult males would be an omission that's both sexist and ageist,' she told him as she sat herself. 'Deal with it.'

'I promise there won't be tears. It's not that bad. Or, rather, it is but I won't...'

'Don't promise anything. Just tell me.'

He cast her a curious look. 'You sound like a professional.'

'That's because I am, though I would have thought you'd have done a serious background check before proposing.'

'It's my great-uncle who's proposing—' he winced '—or commanding.'

'And I'm trying hard not to laugh at the proposal and pack you back on the ferry with instructions to the crew to keep you confined,' she said bluntly.

His smile emerged again—and, stupidly, the smile made her feel less than professional—but her growing conviction that here was a man exhausted to the point of collapse grew.

'Explain,' she said again. 'This is to do with your great-uncle's will, right?'

'Of course it is. I assume...' He raked his hair again. 'The thought of a million dollars wouldn't...'

'Please don't go there. The idea of buying me as a bride is nonsense. Leave me out of the equation for a moment. Tell me why you haven't slept.'

Once again, she got a look that said she'd surprised him. He sat for a while longer and she decided to think of the surf forecast, and the fact that her front garden needed weeding, or that she'd forgotten to buy anything for dinner tonight. Anything. Her personal mantra, set in stone fifteen years back, was not to feel emotion. Not to get involved.

But then...why was the look on this man's face making her feel distress?

'You know my great-uncle is...*was* head of Cantrell Holdings,' he said at last and she hauled her attention away from the possibility of take-away pizza and decided to focus. She'd just told him she was a professional, she told herself. She knew how to keep boundaries in place. Sort of.

'Yes,' she said briefly.

'And you know how big Cantrell is?'

'Huge,' she agreed. She had done a little investigation after Arthur had left, and realised she had heard of it. 'Aren't there big environmental issues though? Mining on the reef, damage from leaching from mines, that sort of thing?'

'There are massive issues,' he agreed. 'But Cantrell has the resources to ride roughshod over any concerns, and the fact that its controlling interests have been privately owned has meant the government has had trouble touching it, or influencing its direction. Now, though, I have the chance to move to the helm of Cantrell.'

'Hooray,' she said, but noncommittally. There was still so much she didn't understand here. 'I assume you're pleased?'

'I'm appalled.' He paused and stared down towards the beach for a while. There were kids playing in the shallows while their mums watched, their squeals drifting up on the warm breeze. The scene looked idyllic. Sebastian's face said this was anything but idyllic.

'Can I explain background?' he said at last.

'You risk taking this from a short to long consultation,' she told him. 'That'll cost you thirty dollars extra.'

'I'll risk it,' he said with another tired smile and then forged on.

'My whole family is wealthy,' he told her. 'But not always. My great-grandfather was born on a farm in outback Queensland but hated farming. He moved away to do engineering. When his father died, he returned—reluctantly—to the farm, and at a time when drought was forcing a lot of farmers off the land, he found high grade coal. He persuaded a couple of friends to help him buy the surrounding land, he quietly bought up mining licenses, then approached small mining companies and offered to share profits. Within a couple of years, he was able to buy his friends out, take control of the mining himself and the rest is history.'

'And the Cantrells have been mining ever since?'

'Not my side of the family,' he said wearily. 'My great-grandfather had two children, sons, Arthur—my great-uncle—and Frank, my grandfather. Frank died just after my father was born, and Arthur never married, so Arthur's been pretty much in control of the company ever since.'

'I'm not seeing…'

'I'm getting there.' He flashed her a look of annoyance—she was obviously interrupting a story he wanted to get over with fast. 'Sorry. I hate this. Anyway, the long and short of it is that when my grandfather died my father ended up owning half the company, but he hated it and sold it to Arthur. Arthur objected—violently—but my father gave him no choice. He did medicine—ophthalmology, like me. He met my mother, another eye specialist, and together they used the funds they'd received from the sale to set up a foundation to provide critical eyecare in Al Delebe.'

The sudden switch had her blinking. 'Al Delebe?'

'You won't have heard of it. Hardly anyone has. It's a tiny African nation wedged between two bigger and much more warlike ones. It's so small and war-torn that few aid agencies are on the ground. Mum and Dad were intrepid travellers. They went there on their honeymoon, but instead of sightseeing they found themselves treating eyes. That care's been ongoing and it's so important. The heat and dust, the poverty, the lack of education... Jodie, for less than most of us pay for a basic meal, we can remove cataracts, restore someone's sight. For a few lessons teaching basic eyecare, we can save kids from glaucoma, from sight-threatening infections, from a lifetime of blindness.'

Whoa. This conversation was getting away from her. She was staring at him in astonishment, hearing the passion in his voice but totally confounded as to where this was heading.

'So?' she said cautiously.

'So,' he repeated, heavily now. 'I now have a choice. My parents' funds have pretty much been spent—setting up a hospital and attracting staff has bitten into what was a massive fortune. They worked for peanuts, but most doctors won't. Within a couple of years, the funding will run out.'

'Are your parents still involved?'

'They were, until they were killed in a border skirmish twelve years ago.'

That made her flinch. 'I'm sorry.'

'Don't be,' he said, though the brusqueness in his voice told her there was still pain. 'They loved the country; they loved what they were doing and they knew the risks. I'm just sorry they didn't have more time.'

'And you?' The situation now had her intrigued.

'I worked there for a while,' he told her. 'Now I run operations from Brisbane.'

Really? She eyed the tissue box with distrust. This wasn't turning out to be the empathic mental health consultation she'd planned.

'So...um...me?' she ventured at last. 'A million dollars. Marriage. I'm not seeing the connection.'

'If you don't marry me, the foundation will fail.'

She stared at him open-mouthed, and then carefully raised her hand and pushed her mouth closed. 'Huh?' she managed. Okay, that wasn't the most intelligent of responses, but it was all she could get out.

He was looking at her now with something that seemed... a lot like sympathy? As if he knew she wouldn't want to hear this messy story.

'For years, Arthur hated that my father insisted on leaving the business,' he told her. 'To be frank, he was gutted when his brother—my grandfather—died. For him, the company was his only remaining family, and my father refusing to be part of it seemed like deciding to chop off part of him. Dad's decision to take his inheritance rather than invest it into more and more mines—well, to Arthur that was yet another gut-wrench. We were all that was left of his family. He couldn't understand us, he was grief-stricken—and his response was to put every waking minute of his life into building the company.'

'But...this doesn't fit,' she said slowly. 'The Arthur I knew... Every waking minute... How does that fit with de-ciding to surf when he was over eighty?'

'That was me,' he said heavily. 'We had a huge row just before he came over to the island. He knew the foundation was running out of money, that it couldn't continue for much longer, and he was pressuring me again to return to the com-pany. He accused me of never thinking of anything but my "do-gooding", as he called it. And I countered that he never thought of anything but how much money he could make out of destroying the planet. I was also worried about his health. He was demanding I spend time with him, learning about the company. He held out the carrot that if I did, he might be persuaded to do something for us—and in desperation I said if he did something outside his office I'd think about it. He had major health issues—he had so little time left to enjoy. To be honest, I never dreamed he'd do it. But he obviously planned to take one weekend away and then come back and throw it in my face.'

'Ouch.'

'As you say. And now I'm dealing with his will.'

'Which is?' She was intrigued, but there were major warnings blaring in her head. Back away! This was surely none of her business.

But she'd asked and now he was forging ahead.

'He's given me…us…two options,' he was saying, looking down towards the kids on the beach—carefully not looking at her? 'And they depend on what I do. Or… I'm sorry, but in part it's what you do. The first is that I do nothing. I inherit nothing. The directors will stay as they are, and profits, plus his personal fortune, will continue to be funnelled into further coal mining, plus huge gas exploration off the coast. Both of which will cause untold environmental damage. All profits will be distributed to shareholders. Many people are about to become seriously rich.'

'But not you?'

'Not me.' His face was bleak. 'I guess… I had hoped that he'd leave at least part of the company to me. I couldn't have influenced the way it was run but I could have sold my shareholding and used it to keep the Al Delebe foundation going for a few more years. If you knew how many people's sight that would have saved…'

He stopped at that, just stayed silent, staring down at the beach. The sounds of the children playing on the sand had faded. Everything seemed to have faded.

'But there's another option?' she said at last, trying to figure this out. 'Which is where I come in?'

'The marriage option.'

'With me? That's so crazy.'

'I agree. It is crazy, but you need to hear what's behind it.' He hesitated again, but she stayed silent. And finally he spoke slowly, heavily, as if forcing every word out.

'Arthur was obsessed with family,' he said. 'And you have no idea how much he pressured me to join the company. The first draft of his will, leaving everything to shareholders— was obviously made in frustration—he'd given up on me. But then he met you.'

'Which shouldn't have made one whit of difference.'

'Do you think I don't know that?' He spread his hands. 'It's senseless, but he was obviously impressed, really impressed— so impressed that he thought of another way to force my hand. Marriage. Marriage to you.'

She was starting to feel like she was surrounded by snakes. Cautious didn't begin to describe it, but anger was now cutting through caution. She was starting to feel trapped and she didn't like it one bit. 'If that's not ridiculous...'

'From his point of view it wasn't so ridiculous,' he told her. 'I don't know what you talked about that night, but somehow, he decided that you're ideal breeding stock.'

'Breeding stock!'

He managed a smile then, but a crooked one. 'Good childbearing hips? A nice fertile woman?'

'What...? Thanks very much!'

He grinned, but then he shrugged and the smile died. 'Sorry. I'm only trying to imagine what Arthur saw. To say he was a misogynist would be an understatement—he had no time for women—but you did save his life. Maybe he wanted to reward you and he thought this was a way to do it. And maybe he thought this might just be a last-ditch plan to bring the company back into the family.'

'But it's crazy.'

'Yes, it is,' he said, in that heavy voice again. 'But in hospital, recovering from a fright, with a battered body and a faltering heart, he wrote a second option into his will. He seriously proposed that we marry, and marry...seriously. For it to work we'd need to live together for at least two years, to satisfy the legal eagles that the marriage is real. But if we agree... His plan seemed to be that you get your million dollars, I inherit his personal fortune and we have children.' He put up a hand as if to ward off her instinctive reaction. 'No. Please, just listen. If that happened, the majority shareholding of the company—all his shares—would be put in a family trust—the Cantrell Family Trust—until the kids he suggested we have come of age. The company can't be sold before they come of age, but I believe he decided that, even if I'm obstinate and keep doing my work abroad, by the time any offspring have grown they'll have come to their senses and Cantrells will once again rule the world.'

She stared at him, growing more and more stunned. This was absurd.

'It's crazy,' she said at last, starting to feel like she was a parrot, repeating the word over and over. *Crazy, crazy, crazy.* 'A trust? *Children?*'

'The lawyers seem to think we wouldn't have to have them,' he said weakly. 'For some reason, Arthur thought it might happen if...if he forced us to live together.'

'In your dreams,' she managed. 'In *his* dreams. And you? Where would that leave you?'

'Well, that's the chink in the armour,' he said, deciding to focus on the beach again, carefully not looking at her. 'This last option was put in just after you'd treated him—it was dictated to his secretary while he was still in hospital in Brisbane. He'd obviously been badly frightened. He wanted the change done in a hurry, so he didn't have lawyers help draft it. A nurse co-signed it, and for some reason he forgot to outline who'd control that trust. It's a big omission because, as he's called it the Cantrell Family Trust, the lawyers believe control would come to me.'

'You...'

'So they say. And even if there are no children, it'll remain with me. It seems I can do anything bar sell the company outright, but the corporation itself can now be redirected, beginning to undo all the damage the company's done. And I can channel his personal fortune to Al Delebe. Jodie...'

Enough. The feeling of being trapped was suddenly overwhelming.

'Stop!'

How did she begin to deal with this? She rose and walked down the steps into the garden, then decided to focus on her breathing for a while. For some reason, breathing seemed really hard. She stared out at the sea; she concentrated on getting her heart rate settled—this seemed incredibly important— and then she took a deep breath and returned to the veranda. It wasn't Seb doing the manipulating, she told herself. It was one scheming old man. She might be angry, but maybe this anger shouldn't be directed at Seb.

He, too, was a puppet.

'So,' she said at last, 'how much money are we talking?'

And he told her. She stood stock-still while he outlined the value of Arthur's personal fortune and how much the company was worth. He told her how much good that personal fortune could do to an impoverished people. He told her how the mining company could be redirected to green energy, to repairing environmental damage. He spoke with passion, with commitment, with emotion, and when finally he paused she felt as if she had nothing left in her. She had nowhere to go.

'But...but you,' she said at last, weakly, fighting to find loopholes. 'This isn't...you. You don't even work full-time. You're like me—you don't commit.'

'How do you know that?'

'Your uncle said. And your receptionist. I rang and tried to get an appointment for one of the islanders who's suffering from what I think is a corneal dystrophy. She said you only worked in the mornings, and you won't take on any patients outside the hospital.'

'I work for the foundation.'

'What, in all your spare time?'

'Yes.'

She frowned. 'So why aren't you in Al Delebe if you care so much?'

That brought more silence, this time seemingly loaded. His face seemed to freeze.

'You're assuming...'

'I'm not assuming,' she flashed back at him. 'I'm asking, and if you want me to take this stupid thing seriously then I need answers. It's you who's assuming that I might even consider this. How do you even know I'm free to marry? There's an assumption.'

'I believe Arthur asked his secretary to find out for him. She told me he believed you were aching to marry.'

'He what?' It was practically a screech.

'Okay.' He held up his hands as if in surrender. 'I apologise.'

'I don't need your apologies,' she snapped. 'How dare he?'

'That's pretty much what I think. He was a scheming, manipulative old man, obsessive about one thing, and he's still pulling strings to continue that obsession from the grave.'

'Oh, this is dumb,' she said, suddenly weary of the whole

discussion. 'We might as well finish this now. I don't do commitment. I don't do family and I surely don't sell myself. You're telling me you can save the world if I agree? That's not a plan, it's blackmail. And tell me how your life would change if you went ahead with this. Would you go back to Al Delebe? Would you expect me to go with you?'

'I expect we'd stay in Brisbane,' he said tentatively. 'You could still work, though you wouldn't need to. Of course, all your expenses would be met. Your inheritance would be on top of that. Jodie, I haven't thought that far but...'

'But don't bother.' She was trying hard to sound calm, maybe even get this back on some sort of professional footing. 'So let me see. You marry me, you send a lot of cash to this charity, you then control a huge corporation and you go happily on with the lifestyle you have now?'

'I have no choice,' he said, goaded.

'What, no choice but to work part-time in Australia, earning your over-the-top specialist salary rather than giving your expertise to a people you care so much about?'

And the look on his face—the anger... But mixed with the anger she also saw distress.

But how was his face so readable? This was weird. It was almost like there was some link...

There was no link. Nothing about this made sense, but when he spoke again, the anger and the distress were still there. 'I can't go back to Al Delebe,' he said, as if goaded.

'Why not? Is it so unsafe? Your parents...'

'It's not unsafe in that sense, at least not at the moment. But I can't...'

'Why not?'

'It's personal.'

'So's marriage,' she snapped. 'Get over it. I need facts if you even want me to think about this.'

He closed his eyes, and once again she got the impression of someone carrying a load that seemed almost too great to bear. And with that came an inexplicable urge to respond. Not with more speech, more questions, but suddenly her instinct was to walk forward and give comfort. To take his hands and hold?

This was surely crazy. Where was her professional detachment when she needed it? What was it about this man that made her want…?

No. She wanted nothing. Somehow, she managed not to move. It cost an effort, but she waited, and finally he spoke again.

'If you must know…'

'It's your decision to tell me. I'm probably going nowhere with this, but I'm definitely going nowhere without facts.'

His gaze locked on hers. There was a long moment where she saw pain. The urge to walk forward and take his hands grew again, and inexplicably she wanted to withdraw her demand. Withdraw from this whole situation?

She should, but she didn't, and finally he responded.

'I spent a lot of time there when I was a kid, with my parents,' he told her, and his voice was now clipped and harsh. 'I was home schooled but, almost as soon as I remember, Mum and Dad had me working in the wards, doing everything I could. But in my teens I caught dengue fever. I was fourteen and fit. It wasn't a bad dose but it was enough to make my parents super-cautious.'

'Transmitted by mosquitos?'

'Of course. I can't tell you how much insect-repellent I went through, but after that my parents sent me back here. I was in boarding school in Brisbane and my parents only let me go over during the dry season. I spent holidays with school friends here during the wet season. But then, when I was almost through university, my parents were killed in a border incursion. I went back to help repatriate their bodies and I caught it again. But it was okay,' he said quickly, maybe responding to concern on her face. How could she help herself feeling it? 'The second dose is supposed to be severe but I somehow got off lightly.'

She nodded, satisfied that at least this explanation made sense. 'So you can't risk it again?'

'I felt… I had to,' he said, his voice again heavy. 'I had to see their work continue, and as soon as I qualified I was over there. I was an adult, I told myself, and I was so damned careful. I was vaccinated. I took every precaution possible, but eighteen months ago it hit again, haemorrhagic dengue, and it nearly killed me. So that's it. I may be idealistic but I'm not suicidal. Tropical countries are out for me for ever. I work as hard as I can from here. I know I could do more over there but…'

'But you're no use to anyone dead.'

'No.'

As excuses went for not heading back to a country like Al Delebe, this was a no-brainer. A second dose of dengue fever often killed. A third time…he'd been extraordinarily lucky to survive.

No wonder he was hunkering down in Brisbane.

'So when your uncle described you as a waste of space…' she said slowly.

'I don't waste time—I don't have enough time. I organise the administration from over here. I do online tutorials to train our staff—I need to keep my skills up because of that—and I fundraise. I give presentations to every fundraising organisation that'll have me.'

'So days off?'

'There's a reason I'm not married—I simply don't have time for it. If you marry me, you'll hardly see me.'

There was a statement to take her breath away. This was starting to feel like a punch to the stomach. Or serial punches.

'Cut it out,' she managed. 'Enough of marriage.'

'You mean you won't consider it?'

'No!' And then she paused and finally she said...slowly, almost fearfully, 'You say...you don't have time for marriage. Have you even thought how this could work?'

And she saw a light in his eyes. She held out her hands instinctively, a gesture that might be seen as warding him off, but he didn't move.

'It might,' he told her, suddenly careful and obviously neutral. 'Believe it or not, I have thought this through. It's important enough to consider.'

'So tell me.'

He nodded, took a deep breath and appeared to dive in. Talking a bit too fast. 'It'd have to look real,' he told her. 'We'd need a decent apartment, or a house where we could have our own space, but we'd need...my lawyers tell me...something like a bathroom set up for two, a bedroom that looks like it's shared. No one's going to break in in the middle of the night to check, but we could be given less than a day's notice. And that might happen. The suits currently controlling the company, the minor shareholders, have a lot to lose. The façade of our marriage would have to continue for a couple of years. But we could be independent. I'm so damned busy and you could keep on with your surfing, your part-time medicine, whatever. I imagine that could happen anywhere. But children...' He hesitated and then forged on. 'I... There was a letter included in the will. My uncle said you're hungry for babies.'

It was like a slap. She stood silently, feeling the colour drain from her face, feeling almost dizzy. *Hungry for babies*, she thought. No.

Hungry for a baby.

For her fifteen-year-old daughter.

'Jodie?' He must have seen her instinctive flinch. She backed away, her hands coming up again.

'No.'

'I'm sorry. Jodie, did I...?'

'Nothing,' she managed. 'Leave it. The last thing I want is babies.'

He was still watching her intently, obviously seeing—well, he couldn't see it, she told herself—a pain that she'd hidden for so long. But obviously he decided to keep going.

'Well, that's a relief, because neither do I,' he said, but he still sounded...puzzled. 'As far as I'm concerned, this would be a business arrangement only, although it'd have to look more from the outside. Maybe we'd need to attend a few fundraisers as a couple, that sort of thing. But Jodie...'

'No buts.' She was starting to feel panic. 'Leave it,' she told him and closed her eyes for a moment, desperately trying to assemble her thoughts. This was a lunatic scheme, not to be thought of, not to be even imagined.

But...

There were buts. She knew it. There was a voice in the back of her head, scrambling to be heard through the panic, that said, *Jodie, honestly, if you calm down then maybe, just maybe, you could do some good here.* Without being involved?

All her life, well, all her life since Hali, she'd fought to stay apart. The pain of that time, the loss of her daughter, her parents' absolute rejection, had scarred her bone-deep, and the fear of letting anyone close had ruled everything she'd done since.

She'd learned to live with it. She'd also managed to put pain aside and have a fun life. She'd made good friends—okay, superficially, but people who were fun to be with. She'd enjoyed her medical training and that was useful and satisfying. She taught surfing now, and that was fun and useful. Her life was pretty much how she liked it.

But the voice in the back of her head was now starting to insist.

If this guy is really serious...if what he says is true...maybe my actions could make a difference to so many people. Maybe I could do some real good.

And at little cost to herself.

She could still hold herself apart—in fact, that was what he seemed to be asking. There were technicalities that'd have to be ironed out—lots of technicalities. Some sort of contract, she thought, a document known to exist only by the two of them.

She'd have to trust.

There was a biggie. She met his gaze and he looked back at her. He was silent, maybe seeing that this was the moment where everything hung in the balance.

Did she believe him? Was this a real thing? It seemed preposterous and yet, looking at him, she was seeing trouble in his eyes, seeing need...

But she was also seeing concern. He was worried about her?

Well, that was crazy. To him, she'd only be a means to an end. If they were to continue down this crazy path, he'd have to be that to her.

And yet...

All her life she'd held back. There'd been dates in the past, flings, fun forays into the world of romance.

Or not really romance because she was only ever in it for a good time, and she'd always made that clear. So...could she do it again? Could she do it for this?

'We *would* be separate,' he told her, and it was as if he was reading her mind.

'Two years...'

'That's what my lawyers say. Jodie, you could consider it

a job offer, and a good one. There're not many jobs that come with a million-dollar bonus paid upfront.'

'I don't care about your money.'

But did she? There were things she could do…

'But will you think about it?' His voice was gentle now, as if sensing she was wavering.

Oh, this was nuts. She was feeling dizzy, as if she was in the middle of some twisted dream and needed to wake up.

But Seb's voice said this was no dream. His gaze said this was deadly serious, and so much was at stake.

'I need facts,' she said, a trifle desperately. 'All the facts. And I need time. I want everything you can throw at me about the foundation, facts from inside and out. I want facts about Cantrell Holdings and I want facts about you. Leave nothing out, and I mean nothing. I need time to gain an independent view.'

'We have a month,' he said cautiously. 'And I'd need to know about you as well.'

'What you see is what you get,' she said bluntly. 'But you probably won't get. Give me two weeks, Seb, and then we'll talk about this again.'

'You mean you will consider it?'

'I… Maybe.'

'There's no one else?' he asked cautiously. 'No partner? No…'

'No,' she snapped. 'Not that it's any of your business.' And then she couldn't help herself. 'You?'

'I've never had time for dating.'

'You're kidding. Are you as obsessed as your uncle?'

'I care about what I do,' he said neutrally. 'Jodie, the million dollars…'

'Will you shut up about the money?'

'It's all about the money.'

'If it was then I'd say leave now,' she snapped. 'But if my research says this might well change people's lives... Well, you implied that a gun was being held to your head. Maybe this is a gun being held to mine.'

'That's nonsensical.' He paused and then said seriously, 'Okay. Jodie, I know this is crazy but the gun isn't being pointed at either of us. It's being pointed at the eyesight of so many of the most vulnerable people in the world.'

'That has to be an overstatement.'

'I'll send you the facts,' he told her. 'All I ask is that you consider them with an open mind.'

He left soon after, catching the ferry back to Brisbane. He'd brought work to do on the boat, but in the end he didn't open his satchel. Instead, he let his mind drift over what had just happened.

In the two weeks since he'd read the will, he'd had time to investigate. What he'd learned was that Jodie Tavish was bright, exceedingly well qualified and out for a good time.

Her university record spoke of brilliance—it seemed she could have gone into any specialty she'd wanted. But instead of more lucrative career paths, she'd gone down the route of family medicine, committing herself to train with some of the best doctors in the field. Her reports from that time were impeccable.

Most doctors though, after that intense training, would have devoted themselves to their career. Family medicine was usually the specialty of those who liked personal involvement, who valued getting to know patients for the long term, treating everyday illnesses but also being there for the birth-to-death dramas that eventually encompassed all.

But not Jodie. From the time she'd finished training she'd moved from job to job, working as a locum, a fill-in for doctors wanting a break, for communities that were temporarily short-staffed. She'd pretty much made a career of it. The only constant in her career choice seemed to be the need to be close to the surf.

His mind had pretty much closed against her when he'd realised that. A doctor who put surfing first.

This last job though, the first time she seemed to have put down roots, was the position on Kirra Island. She'd been there for over two years so maybe she was starting to get involved. He'd been impressed by her actions when Arthur had been injured, and a careful phone call to a colleague he knew on the medical board had confirmed that impression.

'Jodie Tavish? Kirra Island? There's a great medical set-up—I wish we could have that sort of arrangement in all our remote communities. They're three excellent doctors giving an excellent service. Misty's been there long-term—I gather it was her family home. She was overloaded for years until finally she married Angus and they split the load. Then they persuaded Jodie to work there as well. On the surface they look like they treat their careers as a holiday job, but every one of them puts intense effort into keeping their skills current. You know the point system we have each year to make sure our people are up-to-date? The points those three accrue would just about cover every medical practice south of Brisbane. If Jodie's treating your uncle… Well, to answer your question, our only beef is that we could use her full-time in so many other places, but in our view there's no finer doctor.'

So there was no quibble about her skills. It was only her personality.

Her desire to surf when she should be working?

And then he thought…was the word *should* appropriate?

What was there in his head that made him think what she was doing was a cop-out?

He sat on the front deck of the ferry and let his thoughts drift. There were a couple of dolphins surfing on the bow wave of the ferry, enjoying themselves.

'Shouldn't you guys be fishing?' he said, almost to himself, and realised that was exactly what he was thinking about Jodie. What was she doing, wasting her time, when she could be committing…?

She'd made it very clear that she didn't commit. But he wasn't asking her to commit, he told himself. She could continue playing and working as she was doing now. She could spend a couple of years sharing a house with him. She'd have a million dollars in the bank for herself while she lived off the Cantrell profits. Maybe she could cut back on medicine, surf even more?

That was what he'd thought when he'd had time to consider his uncle's preposterous will. It was why he'd decided to try and argue his case today. Jodie was a part-time doctor to whom surfing seemed paramount. She could marry him and keep surfing. If she wanted, she could get another part-time job in Brisbane but there'd be no need. She could live entirely at his expense for two years and her life wouldn't need to change at all.

So, what was there in today's meeting that told him it wouldn't be that easy?

The dolphins surfed on, but as they neared the mainland they veered off—finally to pay attention to their dinner? And Seb's attention was caught by a group of kids on the shoreline, dressed in some sort of scouting uniform, sweeping the shore for litter.

'Yeah, that's reality,' he told himself. 'Some of us need to work to help the world. Surely Jodie will see…'

But then he let himself think of Jodie as he'd last seen her, standing confused in the sunlight, looking at him with a gaze that saw...more than he wanted her to see?

He'd thought this proposition might be simple, but now...

There were depths he couldn't see, he conceded. Things his background check couldn't reveal.

What was in her head? What was driving her?

It couldn't matter. All he knew was that it was imperative she marry him, that she lived with him for two years as his wife.

His wife.

She was beautiful.

Why was he thinking that?

And it wasn't true, he told himself, or not...not beautiful in what was maybe the world's view of what a gorgeous woman *should* look like.

She was tall, almost as tall as he was, and he was six feet. She wasn't thin like the world of fashion seemed to decree was desirable. Her body looked lithe, fit and muscled. Today she'd been wearing scuffed sandals and he'd noticed sand between her toes—sand after a day doing clinical work? It was almost as if the sand was part of who she was. And her hair was...gorgeous?

But then he thought...no, not gorgeous. It was long, blonde and tangled, as if a comb had been pulled through in a hurry but the tangles had been left as too much to bother with. She had freckles under her wide blue eyes, and the lips on her generous mouth seemed permanently twitched upward—as if her permanent state was laughter.

Okay, he conceded. She was beautiful.

How would he feel being married to such a woman?

No. Not married, he told himself. Marriage had never been on his agenda.

He had thought about it, though—of course he had—but

he'd deliberately thought *no*. If he ever married it would need to be to someone as passionate about his work as he was, who wouldn't demand that he back off from the forces that drove him. It'd need to be a marriage such as his parents had, where work was everything.

And the thought of his parents' marriage…where work was everything…where their only child had felt himself an outsider, someone to fit around the edges of their shared passion…it left him cold.

But he'd just proposed to Jodie. If they lived together for two years…if Arthur was right and she did indeed want children…

She'd shrugged off the idea as laughable and that was just as well, he thought. Children…

A wife…

Not a wife, he told himself harshly. He'd be house sharing and he'd be acting, nothing more. And with so much at stake, maybe he could do it. Maybe it wouldn't mess with his life. It wasn't as if he'd have free time to spend sharing.

Sharing Jodie's life.

What was she thinking now?

They were pulling up at the dock. As he headed for the gangplank, he thought he'd done all he could.

He'd asked a woman to marry him. He'd asked Jodie to save lives. He could only hope that the indecision, the concern he'd seen flash through those deep blue eyes meant that she cared.

But part of him was already thinking…if she cared…

For him?

Yeah, right. Shove that thought right out of your mind, he told himself. It was only if she didn't care, if neither of them cared, that this thing could possibly work.

CHAPTER SIX

HE WAS WHO he said he was.

In the hours and days after Seb left, her online searches seemed to spit out information almost faster than she could take it in. There were links to videos of field hospitals in Al Delebe, to online tutorials run by Seb, to fundraising events, to discussion and assessment of his charity in reputable broadsheets and so much more.

It seemed this whole proposal was genuine.

The older online tutorials, those aimed at staff on the ground, were the most illuminating. She approached them with a certain amount of distrust, but soon she felt astounded. She was watching Seb at work in Al Delebe.

She saw a training video following a little girl, surely not more than six, born with congenital cataracts, almost blind from birth. She saw Seb's initial consultation and examination, the reasons for surgery being carefully outlined. Then, in what looked like a field hospital, in a makeshift operating theatre, she saw the child being comforted by her parents until the anaesthetic took effect. She saw Seb's reassurance, both to the child and to her parents, and to her astonishment Seb was speaking seamlessly in their own language. The video was dubbed in English, but even if it wasn't she could see the trust the family had in him.

She watched on as the little girl slipped into sedation, as the well-trained medical team took over. Led by Seb.

The procedure was complex—this was surely something that needed to be done in a major teaching hospital, but there was no doubting his skill. As he worked, he spoke out loud for the camera's sake, or maybe for the sake of a cluster of trainees in the background. He was explaining what he was doing every step of the way.

When he asked for anything, from the senior nurse, from the anaesthetist, even from the elderly man who stood in the background, seemingly as a gofer—he explained what he was asking for, directing whoever was behind the camera to pan to illustrate. And all this time his focus was absolutely on what he was doing.

Finally, as the little girl was wheeled out of the theatre, she saw him turn to the trainees and talk them through what he'd done. He also talked of amblyopia—the problems associated with the child's vision having been restricted from birth—and suggestions as to follow-up advice.

And then she saw the final consultation, a little girl awed and her parents unbelieving—their little girl could see.

This video alone left her feeling winded, humbled by the depth of his skills. She checked the stats online and saw this one clip had been watched so many times it made her head spin. Who by? Surely not just those in Al Delebe. Even though it was in the local language, the subtitles meant this could be a teaching tool the world over.

She also found news clips, incidents where neighbouring fighting had spilled into the country. She saw pictures of Seb, hauled out of his world of saving sight to save bomb victims, to be there for the casualties of war.

She thought of the words Arthur had used to describe his great-nephew.

'*He's a waste of space...*'

As if. He was driven, she thought. Driven as his uncle had been, but for such a cause...

So, finally, she let herself think seriously of what he was proposing—what he had proposed. Surely it had to be ridiculous, but the more she watched, the more a voice in her head was starting to say... *This isn't about me. It's about so much more.*

The thought was almost overwhelming. She desperately wanted to back away, but somehow, she made herself work on, doing her own research as well as following the links Seb had sent her. She worked through reams of information about the Cantrell mines, about the power the company held, about their reputation for riding roughshod over anything and anyone who got in the way of profits.

The voice was growing louder.

But...*marriage?*

Finally, she reached the point where she had to talk to someone—someone who wasn't Seb. So, a week later, she ended up sitting in Misty and Angus's kitchen, spilling everything to her friend and colleague.

This big and messy house had always seemed a haven for Jodie. Angus was out for the evening—island choir, for heaven's sake—and it seemed Misty's grandma was at bingo. Their two kids were asleep. Jodie was on call for any medical need, but the island seemed quiet and the decision she was about to make was doing her head in.

So she set her laptop on the kitchen table, loaded the video of Seb's tutorial and asked Misty to watch it. Then she showed her the website of Cantrell Holdings.

A bemused Misty watched—and then listened incredulously as she outlined Seb's proposal.

To say Misty was thunderstruck would have been an understatement. She stared without saying a word for what surely must have been three or four minutes. 'We need wine,' she managed at last. 'How dare you tell me this when I'm pregnant and you're on call?'

'I'm dizzy already and wine might make me even dizzier,' Jodie told her. 'Best not.'

'So...so what are you going to do?'

'Marry him?' Jodie managed. 'I think I have to.'

'Marry!' Her friend was staring at her as if she was out of her mind. 'This is like something out of fantasy fiction, it can't possibly be real.'

But then she looked again at the image of Seb on the foundation's website—they both looked—and Misty frowned in concentration. 'I've heard of this foundation. What they're doing is stunning. Jodie, the difference...'

'I know.' It was practically a moan.

'And he looks nice too,' Misty said, still sounding dazed. 'In the video...spunky?'

'Spunky?'

'I'm looking at the overall picture here,' her friend said hastily. 'You have to admit he looks hot.'

'Misty...'

'Yeah, not a factor,' Misty agreed, somehow hauling herself together. 'Or...it shouldn't be. But it's not like you're being asked to marry the great-uncle.'

'But...marriage?'

'I know,' Misty said, sounding dazed again, but then she appeared to think it through. 'But it's only for two years. And I've read about arranged marriages. If you take romance out of the equation, you might even be able to make it work. As long as you're emotionally and physically safe, as long as you have and give respect, and as long as you like being in their company, the chances for a decent marriage are predicted to be pretty good.'

'That sounds…clinical.'

'Maybe, but we're talking a house share situation for two years.' She gazed again at the screen. 'I don't know. What do you have to lose?'

'So much.' She closed her eyes.

'This island?' Misty asked, her voice gentling. 'Your work here? We could cope without you.'

'But you're about to have a baby. You'll need time off and that'd mean only one doctor on the island.'

'We'll cope,' Misty said stolidly. 'For something like this… Think of what else is at stake.' And then her voice softened. 'Jodie, what else is scaring you?'

'Him,' she said, before she could stop herself.

'Seb?' Misty looked again at the image on the screen, the front page of the foundation's website. It was a plea for funds, so the image tried to evoke emotion. On the screen was a photograph of Seb, stooping to talk to a young mother. She was holding her little boy in her arms, the child had a patch over one eye and the hope and trust on both their faces was almost tangible.

The gentleness and professional reassurance on Seb's seemed equally real.

'He looks wonderful,' Misty said. 'Is there something I'm not getting? Jodie, would you be afraid to marry him?'

'No. I… Yes.'

'Because?'

'Because I don't want to be… I don't want to be…'

'Drawn into caring?' Misty ventured. 'I get that.' She hesitated. 'Jodie, this is way beyond my ability—or right—to even think about giving advice. I know you've always held yourself apart. Sometimes I've even tried to guess why, but

I won't ask. It's none of my business. Bottom line is that this has to be your decision and your decision alone. If you can't do this then there'll be no judgement from me. We'll forget this whole conversation.'

And then, blessedly, Jodie's phone rang. She answered and rose, with some relief. 'Croup,' she said, and Misty nodded.

'You know you're needed here,' she said softly. 'And you're doing good. We all do what we can. Go and deal with croup, Jodie love.' And then she gave her friend an impulsive hug. 'There's no judgement from anyone if you can't do more. But…'

'But?'

'But, no pressure, love, but if everything else fits…he does look really, really sexy.'

'That can't possibly fit into the equation.'

'I don't see why not!' Misty retorted with a grin. 'There's no rule about life not being fun.'

The call from Jodie a week later was brusque, to say the least.

'We need to talk. Can you come this afternoon? I'll meet you at the ferry.'

Was she about to accept? Seb forced his mind carefully into neutral, trying to suppress panic at the thought that she might refuse. To lose so much…

But there was also fear of what lay ahead if she said yes. Marriage.

No. House sharing, he told himself. Independence. It couldn't work any other way. But when the ferry reached the island and she was outside the terminal waiting for him, the qualms he'd been trying to suppress at the thought of marriage came flooding back.

Why did the sight of her make him feel…as he had no right to feel?

She was wearing shorts and a frayed T-shirt, her sun-bleached hair still looked like it could do with a good comb and her long, tanned legs looked like they went on for ever.

She was leaning against a beach buggy that looked ancient, as did the battered surfboard strapped on its rollbars. But even though she looked scruffy and the vehicle she was driving looked as if it was almost ready for the scrapyard, the way she looked... Weirdly, it made him feel amazing. That this woman was waiting for him... That she was smiling and waving, straight at him...

And she was here to talk marriage?

'Hey,' he said as he met her. And then, because he felt like his entire body was clenched in readiness for a verdict, he asked directly, 'What's the decision?'

'Not here. We need to go somewhere private.' And she refused to speak again, just shook her head and motioned to the passenger seat.

The silence continued as they drove. The need to know was hammering in his head but she seemed intent on her driving. Finally, she turned off the main road onto a sandy track, then pulled up at the entrance to a cove which seemed both secluded and lovely.

'This island has ears everywhere and I don't want us to be disturbed,' she said briefly as she parked. She produced a picnic blanket from the back, spread it out on the sand, then fetched a basket containing coffee and a packet of biscuits. She sat down, opened the biscuits and poured coffee. Then, as he was still standing, feeling bemused, she came right out with it.

'Okay, Seb. Bottom line is that I'll marry you. But with conditions.'

Whoa. To say he was hornswoggled would have been an understatement. He was about to be married. How did that make him feel?

Panicked, he conceded. Very, very panicked.

'Conditions?' he managed, and was surprised that his voice actually worked.

'Arthur threw conditions at us,' she told him. 'We can surely throw a few back.' She held out a coffee. 'Sit.'

He sat and she proffered her biscuits. 'Tim Tams,' she told him, her voice amazingly steady, given the circumstances. 'These are my favourite biscuits, especially through coffee. Are they yours? I suspect that should be one of our marriage conditions. If you don't like Tim Tams we're clearly incompatible.' Then she bit off two diagonally opposite corners of her biscuit, stuck one end in her coffee and proceeded to use it like a straw.

What was happening here? He'd arrived thinking this would be a businesslike discussion—and they were sitting on the beach eating Tim Tams.

And there was the lesser—surely lesser?—fact that this woman was starting to seem…gorgeous. Had she been gorgeous the first time he'd seen her? She'd been battered and weary, he'd hardly taken in what she was wearing, but she *had* made an impression. Or more than an impression.

Had Arthur seen the same thing? Was that why he…?

No. That was too deep. He shook his head, trying to clear confusion, but confusion refused to be cleared.

Marriage?

'Did you really just say yes?' he said faintly, and she looked at him in surprise. She lifted what remained of her Tim Tam out of her coffee, half biscuit, half oozing melted chocolate, and popped it all into her mouth. And focused. Her eyes said bliss.

She had him fascinated.

'I really did say yes,' she managed when it was finally gone. 'I swear these are nectar of the gods. When life gets compli-

cated, Tim Tams and coffee—or Tim Tams and hot chocolate—are the only answer. This scheme seems complicated
enough to warrant all three.'

'Is this a discussion of marriage or an advertisement?' he
asked, still befuddled.

'I just thought…how long since you've done this? Sat on a
beach and eaten whatever you wanted? I've done some major
research on you now, Seb Cantrell, and your lifestyle sounds
appalling. I apologise for implying you were as much a waste
of space as I am.'

'I never implied that you…'

She cut him off. 'Of course you did. What was your proposal? That I come to Brisbane and spend a couple of years
surfing and spending a million dollars? As if I'd be happy
doing that. But to a certain extent I agree. I don't take life seriously.' She shrugged. 'But you…how often do you surf?'

What sort of a question was this when so much was at stake?

'Not often,' he confessed. 'In fact, not for years. But I was
surfing the day my uncle was injured. I accused him of never
enjoying himself, and then…'

'And then you both decided to surf? But before then? Or
since?'

'Um…what's this got to do with marriage?'

She shot him a strange look. 'Hey, am I wasting your time
discussing details? Do you want to go straight to the register office?'

'Jodie…'

'Yeah, I know.' She shrugged again. 'This is serious. The
whole thing's ridiculously serious. But I have done my due
diligence, and you're right, there doesn't seem much choice
but for me to marry you.'

What? Had she just said 'I do'? Was he about to be *married*
to this…beach nymph?

'There's a romantic acceptance,' he managed, feeling winded. Or feeling more than winded. It wouldn't be a real marriage, he told himself a trifle desperately. Not a real commitment. She was agreeing to sign a piece of paper. She wasn't promising to commit long-term.

He wouldn't have to commit either.

She'd gone back to concentrating on the next Tim Tam. He watched her eat in silence until finally she sighed, put down her empty mug and faced him head-on.

'It's not romantic, is it, and that's what I've figured,' she said bluntly, her gaze locked on his. 'So let's get this straight. You're suggesting we marry, I live with you in Brisbane, I get some sort of job over there—not that I'll need to, according to you. You're proposing that I can be as frivolous as I like, while you get on with saving the world.'

'That's an overstatement.'

'But essentially correct?'

'Jodie, I don't see how else it can work,' he told her, fighting back emotions he was struggling to understand. 'I can't go back to Al Delebe, but I'll need to be in Brisbane, to keep up my skills, but also to focus on company matters. You have no idea of the complexities of changing the direction of such an enormous corporation. I still don't know how I'll do it.' He paused and gestured out towards the beach—the beckoning waves, the sunlight glinting through the palms. 'So I can't afford to do this.'

'But my condition is that you'll have to.'

'Have to what?'

'Stay here. On Kirra.'

'How can I do that? My work is in…'

'Brisbane. No, it's not. Not all of it. Seb, I get what you need, but this marriage can't be a one-way deal. I need to focus on me.'

'You'll get a million…'

And that produced silence. He saw her eyes flash with something he didn't understand—but suddenly he did. Her anger was almost tangible.

'You know, if you say one more word about payment I might get back in the buggy and drive away,' she said at last, very, very carefully. 'You can get back to the ferry whatever way you like, but you'll do it alone.'

'It's not payment. It's…'

'Shut up. I'm not kidding. Enough of me being a wastrel, a layabout. Without being insulting, are you prepared to listen to my part of the deal?'

Was she implying the money wasn't important? A million dollars? It surely had to be, but she was moving on.

'I told you, I've been doing some research,' she told him. 'And a lot of thinking. The work you're doing for Al Delebe can surely mostly be done online. You'll need to cut down your public presentations, but for the sake of Al Delebe's future, with your uncle's entire legacy at stake, surely the cost/benefit breakdown will be worth it.'

'But…'

'Shut up and listen,' she told him quite kindly. 'You're also currently doing clinical work three days a week and one weekend in three. I've thought that through, and I see no reason why you can't continue. Lots of islanders use the ferry to commute. You could leave here at seven in the morning, get to Brisbane at eight, leave Brisbane at six at night and get back here by seven. Or there's a company helicopter. Your uncle used it. I don't see why you can't.'

'But the work I do…'

She held up her hands as if to stop him, realised two fingers were covered in chocolate and obviously decided they needed to be licked. She proceeded to lick, then carefully wiped them on a napkin before proceeding.

'I do realise there might be the occasional need to stay,' she admitted. 'Sometimes with surgery you need to be on hand for complications, but Brisbane Central has overnight accommodation for medical staff. I think the marriage boundaries can stretch to the occasional night apart. I assume there'll be meetings with your corporation people too, lots of meetings. You can go back and forth to Brisbane if you must, or hold them online here.'

Whoa. He stared at her, stunned. 'You really have been researching...'

'This is marriage. Why wouldn't I research?'

'But why do we need to stay on the island?'

'Because,' she said slowly, 'contrary to what you think, I do care. I came here as a part-time locum but it's become my home. Misty's about to have a baby, which means the island would essentially be left with one doctor. Besides, I'm not doing this all on your terms. A quick wedding in a register office and then off to live a life of indolence in your fancy apartment? I don't think so. Oh, and speaking of weddings...'

'Weddings?' He was feeling dazed.

'Marriages require weddings,' she said. Her flash of anger had gone and she was now even managing to sound cheerful. 'And if we go through with this, I want a big one. Huge.'

He blinked. 'You're kidding.'

'Nope.'

'But it's not a real marriage.'

'Of course it's not, but I don't see why it can't be a real wedding. We...the islanders...have had a couple of bad fishing seasons, and the recent storm caused major damage. We could use some cheering up.'

She hesitated but then continued. 'Seb, everything I've read in this contract is all about you, and the company, and the good you can do. I acknowledge your work is save-the-world-important. But I only have one little life, and that's important to me, too. So I've decided, if I'm indeed part of this equation then I need to stick with what makes me get up in the morning.'

'Which is?'

'Surfing,' she said tentatively, and then at the look on his face she held up her hands. 'I know, there it is again. You think that's a waste of space, and maybe it is, but it holds my head together. And teaching kids surfing is great too. It gives me joy.'

'You can't just…'

'But that's not all,' she cut in. 'Two years ago I would have said surfing was my passion, medicine was my job and there was little else. But I've been on this island for a while now. I came to help a friend but I ended up staying, and its inhabitants…well, somehow, they've become part of who I am. Seb, as a kid, a teen, even into early adulthood, I felt like a drifter. A loner. You don't need to hear about it and I don't need to tell you, apart from saying moving to this island, growing closer to these people, has made my life seem more… solid. I'm not sure if you can understand that, but if this wedding will give everyone pleasure…'

'Jodie…'

'Don't you dare say saving the sight of so many people should be a bigger reason,' she said. 'I accept how important it is, and if still living here would prevent that then I might even change my mind. But I don't see how it would. You can work yourself into the ground as easily here as in Brisbane. So, what do you think?'

She paused then and waited while he tried to think of how to respond. To move here… To live here properly… To become part of a community, even if only for two years… Why did that seem like some sort of chasm where he couldn't see the bottom?

But now Jodie was frowning, her gaze intensifying.

'Speaking of your work,' she said slowly. 'Your workload seems crazy, and...are you okay? Have you lost weight since I last saw you?'

'Hardly. It's only been a week.'

'No, I meant over the last few months. You look...' she stared at him, obviously concerned '...a bit...drawn?'

'I'm fine. Jodie, I can't live here.'

'Take it or leave it,' she said bluntly, her gaze still intent. 'I guess worrying about what's facing you might put anyone off their food. But you haven't even eaten a Tim Tam.'

'I had sandwiches on the ferry.'

'What sort of excuse is that?' But she gave a small nod, as if telling herself to move on—that his weight was none of her business? 'Seb, I would like you to see just a glimpse of what's important to me. I brought you here to show you this beach, to show you one source of my love for this place, and now, if you'll allow me, I'll show you another.'

'Another beach?'

'A patient,' she told him. 'Mrs Isabelle Grundy. Ninety-four years old. Six kids, more than a dozen grandkids and heaven knows how many great-grandies. I asked if I might bring another doctor when I visit her today and she reacted with delight. If you have enough energy with no Tim Tams on board...'

'Of course I have. Let's go.' He felt as if he was being rail-roaded, and saw her smile return.

'Feeling out of control?' she asked. 'Well, that's how I've been feeling for the last week, and if we're talking marriage then sharing's surely part of it. Welcome to my world.'

* * *

Isabelle Grundy had lived her entire life on the island. Her father had been a fisherman, her husband had been a fisherman and now so were four of her adult children and six of her grandkids. She lived in a tiny cottage overlooking the harbour.

'By herself?' Seb asked as she outlined Isabelle's background and condition.

'Of course by herself. She wouldn't have it any other way.'

'But what you tell me…'

'Yep, advanced pancreatic cancer, crippling arthritis, general debilitation—she should be in a nursing home, right? Her kids and grandkids are in and out, though, and if there's anything she needs…well, her cottage is great. You'll see.'

They were outside the cottage. Jodie knocked and a 'Hooroo…' echoed from above.

'Door's not locked,' an old voice called. 'Did you bring your doc friend?'

'I did,' Jodie called back. 'Are you respectable?'

'I got Maureen to get me a new nightie,' she called back. 'Just in case.'

Bemused, Seb followed Jodie up a narrow flight of stairs. The house was tiny, one room up, one room down.

'She didn't raise her family here?' he asked, and Jodie shook her head.

'They had a bigger place further up the hill, but when the kids left and her husband died she swapped to this one.'

'It's hardly suitable. These stairs…'

And then Jodie pushed open the bedroom door and he changed his mind about what was suitable.

The room was small but his eyes were immediately drawn to its window, which was wide, double-hung and overlooking the harbour below. And not just the harbour. You could almost

see to Brisbane, he thought, awed, and then realised that both
Isabelle and Jodie were looking at him and grinning.

'I told you he'd like it,' Jodie said, and Isabelle chuckled.
It was a weak chuckle—the old lady's eyes, sunk into a gaunt
face, spoke of serious long-term illness, but it was still infectious, even cheerful.

As was her bedroom. The room was simply furnished, most
of it taken up by an old-fashioned double bed, pushed hard
against the window. Isabelle, obviously small to begin with
and now wizened with age, seemed almost dwarfed by her sur-
roundings. A litter of magazines, balls of knitting wool and a
half-finished...scarf?...were scattered across a gaily coloured
patchwork quilt. Three cats, two tabby, one ginger, were re-
garding the newcomers with benevolent caution. They'd been
snoozing in a beam of sunshine and their combined look said,
Disturb us at your peril.

'You like my nightie?' Isabelle, propped up on pillows,
was demanding this of Jodie, but her eyes were blatantly assessing Seb.

'It's great,' Jodie told her, eyeing the pink and lavender,
high-necked and frilled nightwear with appreciation.

'Maureen went to Brisbane yesterday. I gave her instructions, and she went to four places to find it. Pretty, huh? So,
are you going to introduce us?'

'Isabelle, this is Dr Cantrell. Is it okay if he stays?'

'Of course he can stay,' she retorted and turned to Seb. 'Do
you like my nightie?'

'It's fabulous,' he told her honestly, and Jodie grinned.

'So, tell me...' Isabelle started but Jodie cut across her.

'Isabelle, before you start grilling Seb on his life story, could
you tell me what's happening with you. Pain level?'

'Six,' Isabelle said, not taking her eyes from Seb.

Ouch. In a range of one to ten, six was pretty much unbearable.

'Then we need to adjust your syringe driver,' Jodie told her, and that made Seb notice the up-to-date medical apparatus around them.

'You have a syringe driver?' he asked incredulously. 'Do you have in-home nursing care?'

'We have everything we need,' Jodie told him, perching on the bed and lifting Isabelle's wrist. 'And the family's back and forth.'

'But no one stays here?'

'Jacob, Isabelle's son, lives just down the road, Maureen lives around the corner and both the neighbours are friends. These cottages are jammed right against each other and if Isabelle needs help in the night all she needs to do is thump her cane on the wall.'

'But…'

'Oi! No buts!' Isabelle's voice was thin but firm. 'Last time I saw the doc in Brisbane he said I'll die soon, and I'm ready. He wanted me to stay in hospital and he couldn't take responsibility if anything happened to me at home, but I said, "What's the worst that can happen?"'

'And this is surely the best,' Jodie said warmly. 'You and your family are great. But that pain's up. Let's see the cocktail.' She outlined the dosage running through the driver. 'What do you think?' she asked Seb.

He was an ophthalmologist. This wasn't his field—surely a pain specialist was what she needed—but Jodie was looking at him expectantly. And he did know pain—from both sides, doctor and patient.

'You might up the morphine,' he said diffidently, and she shook her head.

'She'll take nothing that'll make her drowsy.'

'Two of my grandkids are at sea,' Isabelle told him, still

watching him with interest. 'Boats are coming in at dusk. I need to check their catch.'

'They'll unload just below the cottage,' Josie said, and Isabelle nodded.

'That's right, and Maureen might bring me a nice bit of snapper for my tea. Fresh off the boat, and what's a bit of pain compared to missing that?'

He had to agree.

And he also saw why Jodie had brought him here. For a woman like this to be able to stay in her own home, to not need to spend the last weeks of her life in a hospital far away from those she loved… Okay, maybe it wasn't a saving-the-world calling, but he couldn't deny its worth.

He couldn't deny what Jodie was giving to this community.

He watched while Jodie asked gentle questions, carefully examined, did everything in her power to make her comfortable. Then, as she made a call to a pain specialist in Brisbane, he sat on the bed and let Isabelle talk. She had him fascinated, but in turn she also seemed intrigued. Within minutes she'd learned about Al Delebe and her questions were intelligent and interested.

'You not going back?' she demanded.

'I can't,' he said regretfully. 'I've had dengue fever.'

And she obviously knew about dengue and its risks too. This seemed one intelligent woman.

'Bugger,' she said and then she brightened. 'But that means you can stay.' She paused for a moment, obviously considering the implications. 'He looks a good 'un,' she told Jodie when she'd finished her call. 'You going to try and keep him here?'

'I'll try,' Jodie said. 'But first there's a couple of things he needs to agree are of value. Like helping you stay here instead of hospital. What do you reckon that's worth, Isabelle?'

'The blasted world,' she said stoutly and then she fixed Seb

with a beady stare. 'So… This is a great place and Doc Jodie…
she's the best. You married?'

'I… No.'

'Then there's a solution. Marry Jodie, settle on the island,
have a few kids and live happily ever after. Sixty or so years
from now I'll tell the kids you can rent this bed for your passing. How good would that be? What do you say?'

What did he say? Both women were watching him, seemingly waiting for a decision.

'I'm not so sure about the bed,' he said cautiously. 'Its
springs might be sagging a bit by then.'

And then he looked at Jodie and discovered her eyes were
dancing. Had she set this up? Of course she had.

So…was this decision time? Was he about to commit to
giving up his life in Brisbane?

But he wouldn't be totally giving it up, he realised, and he
thought about taking Jodie away from this—how could he ask
that of her? Even for a million…

And marriage… He was getting deeper and deeper. He
thought of Arthur and his Machiavellian scheme. Family. Commitment.

To a woman called Jodie. To a woman whose presence alone
seemed enough to unsettle his ordered world.

But there seemed no choice and Jodie and Isabelle were both
waiting for him to answer. So finally…finally he raised an
eyebrow towards Jodie in an unspoken question. She grinned
and nodded. *Go ahead*, her smile said, obviously knowing exactly where his thoughts were headed. And her eyes twinkled
straight at him.

And the way that made him feel…

What a step to take, he thought, but Jodie's look was
warm and teasing and suddenly the step didn't seem so huge.
Even…desirable?

Whoa, he thought, one step at a time. But the first step seemed about to be taken.

Why not?

'I guess you might as well be the first to know,' he told Isabelle. 'I've asked Jodie to marry me.'

The old lady's eyes widened so much they almost enveloped her face, but Seb wasn't looking at her. He was looking at Jodie.

Her eyes were still smiling.

Where was this landing him? He had no idea but right now, standing by this lady's bed, looking at Jodie's smile, all he could do was smile back. And the way it made him feel... The chasm before him suddenly seemed...like a siren song?

'Has she said yes?' Isabelle's delight was palpable.

'Can we stay on the island?' Jodie asked, still smiling.

'Of course.' It was the sensible course, he told himself but the frisson of whatever that siren song contained seemed to be growing.

'Then yes,' Jodie said, and Isabelle gave a whoop of excitement.

'Really? Was that a real proposal? Do you two want to kiss?'

'No,' they said, totally in unison, and Isabelle's eyes danced with approval.

'You want to do it in private? I can close my eyes, but it's done and accepted and that's all that matters. Can I come to your wedding?'

'Of course,' he said, feeling as if he was acting on automatic pilot. Marriage. A wedding. But there was no choice.

And Jodie was still smiling. 'If you can stay alive long enough, why on earth not? No promises, but let's see if we can make that happen.'

'Ooh.' Weakness forgotten, Isabelle was all excitement. 'Will the wedding be big? Can all the islanders come, like at

Angus and Misty's? And oh, I have a cute little pattern for bride and groom knitted rabbits. I made them for Maureen's wedding and we put them on top of their wedding cake. Two white rabbits, one with a veil, the other with a top hat. She and Geoff still have them on their mantelpiece. They have brown feet now, though,' she said with a hint of disapproval. 'I never knew the cake was going to be chocolate and they can't get the stains out. What colour's your cake going to be?'

'I have no idea,' Jodie said faintly.

'Well, there's lots of ideas,' Isabelle told them, moving on. 'I'll get Dot to order in bridal magazines and we'll have a look. Dot's a pretty good cook, too. It'll have to be big, but she could bake it and you could get Lionel to ice it. You know he did Maureen's? And Misty and Angus's. But no chocolate.'

'No chocolate,' she promised faintly.

'And what do you reckon my chances are of living long enough to make you some baby clothes?' she asked.

Baby clothes? *What?* No!

'No baby clothes,' he decreed, and Isabelle pouted.

'What, not ever?'

Not ever? He thought of his uncle's will, and then he looked at Jodie and there was a flash of something he didn't understand.

She'd been smiling, caught up in Isabelle's excitement, but now the laughter had gone. Was that fear?

'Enough,' she said, almost roughly, and bent over her bag— to put equipment away or to disguise emotion? When she lifted her face again the fear was gone, her smile was back, but it seemed forced. 'One step at a time,' she told Isabelle firmly. 'For now...'

'Let's just concentrate on rabbits?' Isabelle asked cheekily.

And Jodie said, 'Why not?' Then she kissed her on the cheek and ushered her now-fiancé out of the room.

* * *

Then there were details to be sorted, and for a while emotion took a back step. They drove back to Jodie's, they sat on the veranda and went through what needed to happen, point by point.

They were both strained, both unsure of where to go from here, so all they could do was be businesslike.

'If we need to be together for two years, we may as well get it over with as fast as possible,' Jodie told him and he agreed.

The minimum time it took to register their intention to marry with the authorities—and for Isabelle to knit rabbits— seemed a good idea to them both. One month.

Then the details.

He asked—very tentatively—how many islanders would like to come. She thought maybe a couple of hundred. He nodded, as if this was totally normal. He figured his list was about ten—including lawyers. She smiled perfunctorily and her reply was clipped.

'The weather should still be great, and it'll be outside,' she said stiffly. 'The islanders should enjoy it.'

'Will you?' he asked, and she stared into the middle distance and seemed to consider.

'Maybe I will,' she said at last, with a tension behind her words that he didn't understand. Or maybe he did—maybe he was feeling the same.

'I'll try,' she said at last. 'When I was a little girl, I used to dream about a fairy tale wedding—a princess dress, a tiara, a floaty veil, flowers, flowers and more flowers. I pretty much gave up that dream but…well, why not?'

'Why did you give it up?' he asked curiously, and her face closed.

'I grew up,' she said shortly. 'Don't we all? But maybe…'

'Maybe the princess dress might be fun?' he ventured,

thinking why not? 'The estate will cover it. You won't need to cut into your million.'

'As if that's a factor,' she said, suddenly grim. 'Screw your million, Seb Cantrell.'

He looked at her oddly. 'Jodie, you need to know, no matter what the cost, at the end of this marriage you will walk away with...'

'I said shut up,' she snapped, really angry now. 'I refuse to go into this thinking I'm being bought.'

'You mean you don't want...'

'Okay, maybe I do,' she admitted, but grudgingly. 'But I hate that I want. I can surely use a million but I'd have accepted without. It's not a deal breaker.' She closed her eyes for a moment and then visibly moved on. 'Okay. Flower girls, pageboys, a fairy tale wedding—that should silence your lawyers. What I want won't come into it.'

But then she managed a rueful smile. 'But okay, maybe I *would* love the excuse, for once in my life, to shop for a fairy tale wedding dress. Misty and I will have fun. So next... Living arrangements? Here's good.'

'Here?' He looked around him at the worn little beach shack and thought...really?

'Let me show you.'

And as she led him through her home, he thought why not? There were two bedrooms, one big enough to hold a decent desk.

'This can be yours,' she told him. 'I can do any desk work at the clinic.' A light-filled living-room-cum-kitchen looked over the bay. There was a serviceable bathroom, a veranda, a washing machine on the deck and that was it. 'What else do we need?' she asked, and she looked at him almost defiantly.

He thought of his luxurious unit in Brisbane and then

he thought of the rough hut he'd used as living quarters in Al Delebe.

'This is great,' he said, and she shot him a disbelieving glance but nodded.

'It should work. Short of having a team of lawyers watching on our wedding night—and if you say that's required then I'm out of here—we're doing everything we can.'

'It's not required,' he said faintly. 'At least, I don't think so.'

'Then check,' she said firmly. 'Two bedrooms, Seb Cantrell, and that's that. Your room's big. You can ship over a decent desk, maybe an armchair, a telly. We can share meals...'

'You don't think we can watch telly together?'

'Maybe,' she conceded, still stiffly. 'Tell me what you like and we'll discuss it. But Scandi Noir's off the table, as is every single show that involves body parts.'

He managed a smile but he felt dazed and that feeling continued as they proceeded to discuss dates, times and details. Finally, she dropped him off at the ferry, deal done.

Finished?

But as they pulled into the car park they realised the news had already spread. Obviously, Isabelle had sent out carrier pigeons. They were met by surely more islanders than would normally use the ferry. Word was obviously out that this man was a doctor, that he was about to marry *their* Doc Jodie, and he was coming to the island to live. So, what was there not to like? They were surrounded by well-wishers.

Once aboard though, he was left alone. He sat in the bow and thought...*what's there not to like?*

He thought of Jodie, standing stiffly among the ferry passengers as she'd said farewell, the congratulations around them obviously messing with her head.

He should have kissed her, he thought, and as he'd said goodbye there'd been an urge to do just that. But somehow he'd sensed that if he had, she'd have backed right off. Maybe even pulled out of the deal?

What had gone on in her background? He'd researched the basics but he needed to know more. He had a sudden urge to demand the ferry turned around, for him to take time, to figure out what was making her tick. To see if he could remove the shadows that caused those intermittent flashes of fear.

But the ferry wouldn't turn, and even if it could he didn't have time. He had to get back, see the lawyers, start the mind-blowing legal process that'd mean he could take charge of the Cantrell mines.

The thought was doing his head in. The thought of everything was doing his head in.

What he wanted, he thought desperately as the island disappeared in the distance, was to be back in Al Delebe, in the operating theatre, making a difference. But there was also a part of him admitting what he'd really like was to stay on the island tonight, to get to know this woman he was about to marry.

But there'll be two years, a voice in the back of his head murmured, thinking again of her stiffness, of her fear.

This is business only, he reminded himself.

It had to be only business.

He was suddenly thinking of his parents, consumed by their passion to save sight, impressing him over and over with their mantra.

'You're on this earth to do good, Seb. Nothing should get in the way of that. Nothing.'

Jodie shouldn't get in the way.

But still there were whispers of something growing louder. Jodie. Two years.

Two years to do good—in all sorts of ways?

* * *

And Jodie? She watched the ferry disappear into the distance and thought, what have I done?

Promised to marry.

Promised to share her home.

Promised to share her life?

The thought left her scared witless. Since she'd been fifteen she'd been alone—or maybe even before that. She'd fought her own fights; she'd dealt with life on her own terms and she'd depended on no one.

'This doesn't mean I'll depend on him,' she told herself. 'He'll be living here on my terms. I can treat him like a boarder, nothing more. And hey, I can buy a dress.'

The thought almost distracted her. She was a jeans and T-shirt woman, or shorts and T-shirt, or skirt and dead plain shirt for work. She used the hairdresser once every six months to cope with split ends. She had a toilet bag that contained toothbrush, hairbrush, a huge tub of sunscreen and not much else. So why had the fantasy of a fairy tale dress suddenly slipped into her head?

Her parents would love it, she thought, and for a moment she let herself play with the idea of phoning them, which would be the first time she'd done such a thing in over fifteen years.

'Hey, parents, I'm respectable again and next month I'm marrying one of the richest men in Australia. You want to come to the wedding?'

They might even come, she thought. They might even decide their 'filthy little tart' of a daughter had redeemed herself. She could be their daughter again.

'But I haven't redeemed myself,' she said out loud, regardless of the guys setting up their fishing rods on the jetty now the ferry had left. 'Somewhere there's my daughter, and wherever she is I'm proud of her.'

Hali.

Oh, God, would she ever forget?

'I've just agreed to marry one of the richest, and surely one of the most gorgeous, males in this country,' she told herself angrily as she turned and headed back to the beach buggy, fighting back stupid, useless tears. 'Why can't I stop thinking of Hali?'

Because...

Because this seemed a betrayal?

'And that makes no sort of sense,' she told herself. 'You're not moving on. You're not planning on babies, of replacing...'

Yeah, that was dumb.

'Business only,' she told herself. And that million?

It would make a difference.

'So Seb's saving one part of the world and I'll be saving a little bit,' she said, still out loud, as she climbed into her beach buggy. 'Nothing else matters—but I will buy a dress, and damn them all.'

CHAPTER SEVEN

Four weeks later

SEB STOOD ON the headland and waited for his bride.

This wedding had become almost bigger than the cast of *Ben-Hur*. A colossus.

The islanders had reacted to the news with incredulous delight. When Jodie had confirmed, almost sheepishly, that she was about to marry someone who was bound to become one of the country's richest men, and he was intending to live here, they'd assumed the wedding would be an invitation-only, celebrity-heavy affair. When Jodie had said no, the wedding was to be on the headland, everyone was welcome, and who wanted to be a flower girl or pageboy? they'd been mind-blown.

'Because why shouldn't everyone enjoy it?' Jodie had asked the dumbfounded Misty. 'It's not as if I'm doing this for me. Let's open it right up.'

And why not? There'd been no way they could keep it quiet, and if Seb was to use this as a means to take control of one of Australia's largest corporations it had to be public knowledge.

So the islanders had come on board. When Seb had arrived the night before the wedding, Jodie had taken him on a tour of the venue—a gorgeous swathe of grassland on the bluff overlooking the sea, edged on three sides by gumtrees filled with noisy lorikeets settling down for the night. The locals had set up what must have been every spare chair on the island. They'd set up an arch with a backdrop of sweeping ocean and they'd covered it with flowers, flowers and more flowers. The entire setting was spectacular.

'Gorgeous, huh?' Jodie had told him and, to his astonishment, she didn't sound nervous—she sounded as if she was enjoying herself. 'But I can't believe you won't have anyone with you other than Angus.'

He hadn't wanted anyone. His life had been so intense until now that no one was close enough to expect to be part of the ceremony.

He had met Angus, though. Misty's husband, the other island doctor, had come across to Brisbane especially to meet him and, to Seb's bemusement, the meeting had turned out to be pretty much a grilling on his 'intentions'. It seemed Jodie was to be protected. The questioning had been intense, but in the end Angus had relaxed. Seb had taken time off to have a beer with the guy and they figured they had the beginnings of a tentative friendship. So as best man...

'He's all I need,' he'd declared. 'Why do we need attendants anyway?'

'Because it's fun,' Jodie had replied. 'Though I guess any attendant you choose wouldn't exactly be heading to the internet to find pink tulle and glitter.'

'Is that what your attendants will be wearing?' he'd asked faintly, and she'd grinned.

'You'd better believe it.'

So now...

He was standing under the arch, Angus by his side, wondering how on earth he'd ever got himself into this...fantasy?

For that was what it was, he told himself as the music swelled, as hundreds of islanders rose to their feet, as the bridal procession finally arrived.

And what a bridal procession.

She hadn't been kidding when she'd said that any child could be part of this. Here they came, what, twenty or thirty kids?

When Jodie had told him her plan, he'd expected a bevy of little girls, but she'd put it out there—any child who'd like to be part of her procession was welcome to come, dressed as anything they liked, but the theme was fantasy. So there was a mass of pink tulle but there were also... Space Invaders? Supermen? Superwomen? Medieval knights? The only stipulation—decreed by Misty rather than Jodie, he gathered—was that every participating kid should carry flowers, any shape, any way they wanted.

So now they filed along the flower-strewn aisle, in rows of three, intent on carrying this out with all solemnity, walking in time with Handel's Water Music, played by the local string quartet. A mass of kids and fantasy and flowers, reaching the arch, smiling beatifically and then laying their flowers down to further mark the makeshift aisle for Jodie to walk along.

Then they scattered to sit beside their parents, and Jodie was standing alone.

He'd thought she'd have Misty beside her but no. Misty had been there, behind the kids, but she too had edged back. She was now sitting in the front row beside Isabelle Grundy, who was in her wheelchair, beaming as if she'd organised this whole wedding herself.

So Jodie walked the flower-strewn aisle by herself.

And she took his breath away.

This wasn't the Jodie he knew—or sort of knew. This, too, was fantasy. Her dress was all gold and glitter. The bodice seemed sculpted to her breasts and waist. The scooped neck was edged with gold embroidery, diamonds—surely fake! Three-quarter-length sleeves seemed also moulded as if she was sewn into the garment, and at the waist the dress flared out in a glorious circle of white and gold, with a train stretching out behind.

Her sun-blonde hair was coifed and curled, and a glinting diamanté tiara nestled in her locks. Wide blue eyes smiled out at the world and he thought, surely those have to be fake lashes? And surely this was professional make-up? He'd only ever seen her in work clothes or the simple gear she used as casual but now she seemed almost ethereal. A fairy princess. Every little girl in the gathered crowd was beaming with delight.

A fairy princess. His fairy princess? Certainly his bride. She walked steadily towards him and she was smiling. He caught that smile and smiled back. But why was his overwhelming impression suddenly that of loneliness?

And suddenly, inexplicably, he knew that what was happening here was a form of protection.

This was a mock ceremony. This wasn't real, so why not make it something out of a fairy story? Cinderella with her prince? Sleeping Beauty? A story where the fantasy wedding ended with the words 'They lived happily ever after' and then the book was closed.

So this book would be closed after today, he thought. He'd be a boarder in her cottage, and she'd stay as the solitary woman she'd always been.

Always?

What was behind that mask? Who was this woman—this ethereal princess bride who smiled and smiled, but whose smile couldn't quite disguise fear?

She reached his side and he held out his hand to take hers. There was a moment's pause and he glanced at her and thought, Is this why the make-up? To disguise a white face? To hide terror?

'This is okay,' he said softly, holding her gaze. 'I won't intrude on your space, I promise. You're still your own woman, Jodie Tavish.'

She blinked and he saw astonishment. There was a long moment while their eyes held.

'We'll do good,' he said, so softly that no one but them could hear. 'But we'll do it apart. This is pretend, to save the world, so we might as well get on with it. What do you say?'

'I… Yes.'

'And it might even be fun,' he said, his smile encouraging her to smile back. 'That's some gown. You should have told me; I would have come as a medieval knight. Maybe without the armour though.' And then he hesitated. 'But I'm thinking… Jodie, I trust you and I hope I don't need armour. Will you trust me as well?'

And there was a long pause while almost the entire island seemed to hold its breath. And finally the look of fear eased off.

'I do,' she whispered, and somehow she managed to smile back—and then they turned to make 'I do' official.

What followed was the party to end all parties, and Jodie even found herself enjoying it.

When she'd first suggested this idea to Misty it had boggled her mind—and then she'd been overwhelmingly enthusiastic. Together they'd taken their tentative plan to the island's community leaders. The recent storm that had battered the island so badly had cast a pall. Every gathering since seemed to have been a fundraiser to help those most badly affected.

'This is just what we need to cheer everyone up,' Misty had declared. 'We'll have it out on the headland where there's little damage and we'll have fun!'

And they did have fun. A feast to end all feasts—contributions from almost everyone. Jumping castles, jugglers, acrobats—everyone who could do anything was invited to do their bit. There was even a fortune-teller, for heaven's sake, and laughingly the islanders insisted the bride and groom be first to have theirs told.

So in a rainbow-covered tent, full of crystals and incense and make-believe, they sat hand in hand while a gloriously gowned Mystic Marigold—alias Dot Hemming, postmistress—predicted a hundred-year marriage blessed with twelve children and a dog.

Jodie even found herself relaxing enough to giggle. If this whole two years could be treated as fantasy she could get through it, she told herself. She wasn't losing her independence. She wasn't!

'You'd think if she can predict twelve kids she might have predicted twelve dogs,' Seb grumbled as they left the tent. 'One dog's never going to last the distance.'

'Why not a unicorn or two as well?' she asked. 'Honestly, I'm feeling short-changed.'

He chuckled and the tension eased. This might even be okay. They could be business partners. Friends. She could do friends.

But then, as the sun's shadows lengthened, as the local band decreed it was time for the bridal waltz, as Seb took his princess bride into his arms and whirled her round the makeshift dance floor—who would ever have guessed he could dance like this?—she found herself...melting?

Melting? No. What was the word?

Once upon a time one of her aunts had run a ballroom dance studio in the small outback town where she'd been raised. She remembered her uncle coaching her to move with him, schooling her to dance as one, so as Seb held her and led her into the waltz, her feet moved with almost muscle memory.

He was surely a better dancer than her uncle—and he definitely felt better.

He looked gorgeous—or was gorgeous too small a word?—in a deep black dinner suit, crisp linen shirt and a black tie flecked with tiny gold specks. Misty must have given it to him, she thought. Misty had helped choose her dress and she might have organised his tie to match. But now, held in his arms, twirling across the floor, matching his every move with instinctive sureness, feeling his strength and skill, she thought, no, this man would have chosen his own tie.

It was an odd thing to think, but strangely it brought back the fear. She must have faltered because he pulled back a little so he could see her face.

'Jodie?'

It was a question. He knew all wasn't right with her and the question disturbed her still more.

'It's okay,' she managed. 'More…more than okay.'

'I think it can be,' he told her and then he smiled, that heart-stopping smile that did something to her insides she had no hope of controlling. 'And right now I'm thinking it might be more than okay. Let's just relax, my bride, and go with the music.'

And what was there in that to make her even more panicked?

They headed back to her cottage…*their* cottage?…at midnight, clattering back in her beach buggy, the clattering caused by the mass of old boots and tin cans tied to the bumper bar.

Jodie drove, somehow bunching up her bridal dress and squashing it into the footwell. Seb sat silently beside her. After the clamour of the crowd shouting their farewells there seemed nothing to say. The vastness of what had happened seemed to be overwhelming.

The cottage seemed strangely still in the moonlight, far away from the music, laughter and chaos of the day. They sat for a moment as she cut the engine, staring out at the scene before them. The moon was hanging low in the sky over the sea. They could hear the faint hush hush of the surf. Otherwise, the silence was absolute. Not even an owl or a scrambling bush turkey disturbed the stillness.

'I'm going in to take off this dress,' Jodie said at last. 'It weighs a ton. I can't wait to get it off.'

'Fairy tale ended?' he asked, turning to face her in the moonlight. He hadn't come close to figuring her out yet. She was obviously a beloved member of this community, a skilled and caring doctor, and yet all this day he'd thought she seemed so alone.

Why was his sense of her isolation deepening rather than weakening? Even during the waltz… At times he'd felt her body melt against his and then, almost in a panicked reaction, there'd been stiffening, until somehow she'd forced herself to relax again.

What was behind the fear? He'd told her his background, yet he knew almost nothing about her.

Oh, he knew the basics. The moment he'd read his great-uncle's will he'd done a search—of course he had.

Jodie Tavish. Born in Conburrawong, a small town some two hundred kilometres west of Brisbane. Parents, Brian and Evelyn, Brian a pharmacist, Evelyn a librarian. Stalwarts of the local church. Part-time scout leaders, full time leaders of the Conburrawong Tidy Towns committee. Jodie was an only child. She'd gone to school at Conburrawong, before completing her final two years at boarding school in Brisbane.

That all seemed standard. If she'd decided she wanted to study medicine, moving to the city would have been sensible, and the elite boarding school she'd attended would have almost assured her a place in Brisbane's medical school.

While she was at university there'd been a series of part-time jobs, cleaning, washing dishes, standard student stuff which told him money had been short—maybe her parents had spent everything sending her to boarding school? But he'd seen nothing unusual. A brilliant undergraduate course, further training as a family doctor, then a series of placements.

It was only the placements that gave rise to questions. Until she'd moved to Kirra there'd been nothing longer than a year, and all of those had been part-time.

As was her present job. She was a part-time doctor, a part-time surf instructor. Also, he noted, there'd been no mention of her parents coming to the wedding.

Was she a loner like he was?

Why?

He glanced at her now and saw her face was set. Was she afraid? Of what? The terms of the next two years had been spelt out clearly between them. This was a business contract, the only difference between this and any other contract being that it couldn't be put down on paper.

Was she afraid of him moving in with her? Afraid he'd intrude into her solitude?

'Jodie, you do know I'm not about to seduce you,' he ventured, and she swivelled to stare at him.

'What…?'

'You look afraid.'

'I'm not.' She took a deep breath. 'Of course I'm not. Besides, I know karate—and three other Japanese words.'

It was an attempt at a joke and it made him smile, but the tension was still there. She looked so wary.

How to break this moment? Give her space?

How? Go inside, head to separate bedrooms, close the doors and start their separate lives?

That was what they should do. In truth, the weariness that had followed since his last dose of dengue was weighing hard, but after such a day he knew sleep would be impossible.

So...

'So, given I'm dead scared of a karate-wielding woman— do you wield karate?—knowing you're absolutely safe, if I tell you I'm thinking I might head down to the beach for a swim, would you like to join me?'

'What, now?' she said, startled.

'Why not?'

She looked dubiously down towards the beach. The moonlight was glinting on the water, ripples of silver playing over the gentle surf. Surf? This wasn't a surf beach, it was more a wallow and paddle beach.

'Night feeders,' Jodie said.

'Night feeders?'

'I... Stingrays and stuff.'

'Really?'

'But...the water's so clear,' she murmured, and it was as if she was talking to herself. 'In this moonlight we could see everything.'

'And you know karate.'

And she smiled. It was a real smile too, tension easing. For a moment he let himself feel smug, but he had to keep going. He had to make her feel...safe?

Why would she not? It didn't make sense, but instinctively he knew to reinforce what he'd gained.

'Sadly, I don't know any karate,' he confessed. 'But I do want a swim so, if needs must, I'll go alone, with or without my warrior woman.' Then, 'Sorry. *A* warrior woman,' he amended, and to his relief she grinned.

'Okay then,' she told him. 'Let's go.'

CHAPTER EIGHT

THIS WAS THE strangest of nights, though surely no stranger than the day.

As Jodie struggled out of her dress she could hear Seb in the other room—his bedroom. Ditching his suit? He obviously didn't need to struggle with forty tiny buttons. Oh, the cost of being a fairy princess. But Seb's idea of a swim seemed a siren song. All she wanted right now was to be in her swimmers, for things to get back to normal.

But what was normal? Living with Seb?

Seb had moved his belongings into the cottage the night before, but he'd stayed at the resort until the ceremony. 'Because the islanders will expect it,' she'd told him. 'If we're going to do this, we need to do it right.'

But what would the islanders think of her resolution to not sleep with Seb at all? They'd think she was nuts, she acknowledged, or at least the island's women would. Seb was gorgeous any way you looked at it. Or looked at *him*. Why would she not want to sleep with him? What did the islanders really think of this strange wedding, of the publicity surrounding them?

Who cared? She certainly didn't—hadn't she gone through a lifetime of judgement and come out the other side? This arrangement made some sort of sense. Seb was to be a housemate and that was that. Except, right now, the bedroom wall seemed pretty thin.

And the noise next door had ceased. He was waiting for her.

A midnight swim. Was this crazy?

Oh, for heaven's sake, how many shared houses had she lived in, how many friends had she gone swimming with, at any time of the day?

The last button undone, her dress fell to the floor and she stepped out of it. She'd sell it online, she told herself. What a waste. Fancy pretending…

But she knew that she'd never have made it through this day without pretending. If she'd gone to a registry office, worn normal clothes, been who she really was, to make those vows would have been impossible.

So now I need to stop pretending, she told herself. *Now the reality is that I have a new housemate and we're going for a swim and then we're getting on with our lives.*

And that's all.

The fairy princess was gone. In her place was Jodie. His new housemate.

His wife.

Officially, the second title had to be front and centre, but personally, Jodie needed to be simply the woman who shared his house.

No. The woman who shared *her* house. This needed to be on her terms, he told himself. So much depended on her holding it together.

Why did he think there was a risk that she couldn't?

Because he could sense her fear.

She emerged from the cottage, bridal gown and accessories gone, swimmers and towel in their place. She'd let her hair down and scraped off her make-up. She managed a smile, but he could tell it was forced.

'You lead the way,' he said gently, thinking she knew the

path to the beach but there were so many other paths they'd need to negotiate.

Part of him wanted to reach out, to take her hand, to walk together in the moonlight, but he sensed enough not to even try. The silence between them seemed a tangible barrier, one they were almost afraid to break. So they walked in silence, reached the sand, dropped their towels and walked straight in.

The water was cool, deliciously so after the heat and tension of the day. They waded through the shallows without hesitation, then Seb dived into an oncoming wave. When he surfaced, Jodie was gone.

For a moment he was confused. He stood and looked—and found her surfacing further out. This woman was a seal, he thought, to stay under like that...

Did she want to swim alone? But surely she was too far out, and at this time of night...

Should he let her be?

She was treading water beyond the shallow breakers and she seemed almost to be waiting.

Was that wishful thinking? Regardless, the urge was suddenly overwhelming, to be in contact, to somehow make this night normal, to be...friends?

He dived under another wave, but this time he stayed under. He wasn't bad at swimming—he'd learned as a kid in the river near where his parents worked. He'd last swum on the day his great-uncle had had the accident, but his body knew what to do, even if physically that last dose of dengue had left its mark. He wasn't sure if his weakened lungs could manage to reach her, but he aimed at the place where Jodie was and stroked his body forward underwater until he ran out of air.

And when he surfaced, he was right before her. A metre, maybe even less.

He'd startled her. Even as he surfaced, he saw the shock,

and he almost expected her to dive again. Instead, he saw the almost conscious decision to stay put.

'Scare a girl, why don't you?' she managed.

'Did you think I was a shark?'

'This beach is too shallow for sharks.'

'So what do you think I am?' he asked, and there was a question.

'My husband,' she said at last, flatly, without inflexion, and something in her voice made him wince.

'Is that so bad?'

'I… No.'

'Jodie, has someone hurt you?' It was shallow enough here for them to be able to stand—just. They could relax enough to talk, but there was nothing relaxed about the way she was looking at him. He was starting to think…abusive relationship in the past? Violence? It fitted with the fear.

'No,' she said flatly.

He didn't believe her. Somewhere in her past, someone had hurt this woman, badly.

'I will never do anything you don't like,' he said, but thought: *That sounds weak…there must be a better way of saying it. How do you reassure a woman who's experienced…what?*

'You'd better not,' she muttered.

'Because of karate?' He smiled and hoped she'd smile back. Their eyes locked. There was a moment's stillness—and then finally she did smile. And there was even a trace of relief.

'Because of karate,' she agreed. 'Seb, believe it or not, I do trust you.'

'That's a relief,' he said, wondering if he did believe it. He thought about probing more but the tension had lessened and he wanted to keep it that way. 'Okay, how about we race to the end of the cove?'

'I'd beat you.'

'I'd like to see you try!'

She did beat him and she felt a bit astonished.

She was a strong swimmer but speed wasn't her strength. She could surf for hours, she could fight her way through breakers twice her height, but she'd learned long ago that when it came to sprints most decent male swimmers could beat her.

And Seb did, for half the distance, but then, just as she was feeling as if she was falling back, she sensed rather than saw him slacken.

A bit puzzled, she slowed her own pace, hopefully not so much that he'd notice, but honestly, did she really want to beat the pants off him on her wedding night? Guys have pride, she thought, maybe a bit condescendingly, but most women would understand the instinct to nobly grant him a win. It was dumb, but did it matter?

And practically, he should win. His almost naked body in the moonlight had looked lean and muscled. Seeing him dressed only in boardshorts, she'd felt…well, possibly not what it was wise to feel, given her vow to stay apart. But when he'd dropped the towel he'd had draped around his shoulders, she'd been aware of a jolt that was purely primeval.

Down, girl, she'd told herself. That sort of hormonal urge meant trouble and she wasn't going there. But she had been expecting him to beat her. Hoping that he'd at least match her? Why was it important to her that he was strong?

Well, that's primeval too, she'd told herself as she slowed. *Human, animal, whatever, as in nature, the fastest, fittest, strongest gets the girl.*

'Except this girl isn't to be got,' she muttered under her

breath, and as they neared the rocks that bordered the cove's end she put on a spurt of speed that meant she did beat him.

She reached the edge of the cove and surfaced by the rock ledge, then watched him come in behind her. He finished, found his feet and waited for a moment, breathing heavily.

'Okay, I'm out of practice,' he managed. 'So I now have two years to get fit.'

But he looked spent, she thought, and suddenly the medical side of her kicked in. She let him recover for a moment and then ventured, 'Seb, you copped dengue three times?'

'Yeah, the last knocked the stuffing out of me,' he admitted, obviously realising what she was on about.

'And the third bout was eighteen months ago?'

'Hey, isn't this our wedding night? Can I make an appointment to see you professionally in the morning?' Then he sighed and relented. 'Okay. Yes, it was eighteen months ago and I still have some fatigue.'

'And yet you're challenging me to race when you've already had a huge day.'

'Moving on,' he said firmly. 'I'm fine.'

'Except puffed. Physician heal thyself?' she quoted.

'There's nothing any other physician can do. I just need time.'

Okay, she conceded. He was probably right. Ongoing fatigue could be a long-term side-effect of dengue, and tonight was hardly the time to talk medicine.

'We'll get you fit,' she told him. 'Two years on the island… A swim every day… A bit of surfing…'

'There'll hardly be time. I still need to work.'

'Of course you do. But you also need to relax.'

'Yes, Mum,' he said, and she raised her hand and splashed him. It was a practised move and a wall of water hit him full-on. He gasped and choked, and when his eyes cleared, she saw disbelief—and then challenge.

'Haven't we talked about expectations within this marriage?' he demanded, and she blinked.

'What?'

'Surely we should have included this. Love, honour and obey—and don't splash!'

'There was *not* an obey.'

'Really? There must have been respect at least. I was too discombobulated by the princess bride bit. Which was gorgeous, by the way. But did we get a copy of our vows? What the hell have we signed?'

'You signed a pledge to give me a million dollars. I remember that.'

'That was the legal bit, not included in the wedding vows. And even if it was…a million doesn't include splashing your husband.'

And, for answer, she raised her hand and splashed again.

'Pooh,' she said.

It was like a battle cry. Pooh? How was a man to ignore such a taunt. Almost instinctively, he raised his own hand and splashed back.

And kept right on splashing.

They'd been concerned—a little—about night feeders. There was no such worry now. No matter what sea creatures were lurking in the depths, the furious splashing that ensued would surely have sent any self-respecting critter to the depths. For it didn't stop. Suddenly, it felt like all the tension of the day, maybe all the tension of the last month, found itself a way to explode. A man and a woman, standing breast deep in the surf, splashing like their lives depended on it.

It was almost as if the spray of water was holding each of

them at a distance that seemed vital. It was ridiculous, child-like, starting almost as a joke but somehow turning to something serious. Was there anger there, frustration, fear?

Or was that just her? Jodie thought. What was she doing, splashing this man as if her life depended on somehow holding him at bay? She splashed and splashed and then, when finally he ceased, she hardly noticed.

Until his hand came out and caught her arm.

'Jodie,' he said very softly as she tried to splash again with her free arm. 'Jodie, I've promised I won't hurt you. I've promised I'll respect your independence. What's wrong?'

'I... Nothing's wrong.'

'Then why are you so scared?'

'And why are you so tired?' she countered. It didn't make sense as a retort but it was all she had. She tugged back against his hold but he didn't release it.

'I told you. I'm still recovering from dengue,' he replied, softly though, as if gentleness could reassure her. Really? Gentleness was the way to get under her defences. She didn't need it. She didn't! 'So will you tell me what you're recovering from?'

'I'm not.'

'No?'

'It's none of your business.'

'I know it's not.' They stood silently for a moment, both of them looking down at the link, his hand on her arm. And then slowly, carefully, he released it, but instead of stepping away he lifted his hand. He touched her cheek and then, so lightly, he traced her cheekbone. Almost as if he was searching for tears, which was crazy, seeing as her face was dripping with seawater.

But did he know how close to tears she was? Why on earth? What was she doing, wanting to cry?

It was the day, she told herself frantically. The emotion. The build-up and the tension.

The fear.

What did she have to be afraid of? she asked herself with something akin to desperation. This was a contract only. It meant nothing. How could it mean anything?

He let his fingers drop but he didn't move back. 'You're safe, Jodie,' he said softly. 'I swear.'

And, as if on cue, something brushed her leg.

What was it? Seaweed? No, something solid. Moving!

To say she levitated would not be an understatement. Somehow, some way, she was in the air—and when she descended, she was in Seb's arms. And he had her and he was lifting her away, striding back out of the waves into the shallows.

Chuckling?

Chuckling!

'What…? What…?' The shock of something brushing her leg wasn't as great as being in this man's arms.

'It looked like a groper,' he told her. 'A big 'un. I saw its shadow in the moonlight. It bumped right into you. I've never seen a woman levitate before.'

'A groper…' She caught her breath. Of course. She'd seen one here before, a big, beautiful creature that moseyed around in the shallows.

Gropers were a lot more wary of humans than humans were of them, and given noise and splashing, they'd flee. It had probably been hiding under the rock ledge, and then, when the splashing got too close, decided the safest course was to get out and bolt.

They were harmless. There'd been no reason at all for her to end up in this guy's arms, and for him to be carrying her out of the water.

'I… Put me down,' she said shakily.

'When I reach the sand,' he promised. 'Chivalry demands no less.'

'Seb…'

'You can't expect to do the fairy princess bit and not have a gallant knight do his thing in return,' he said severely. 'Where's my sword when I need it? Or my pet dragon?'

And then, to her own astonishment, she heard herself giggle. Giggle! She was being carried, whether she liked it or not. She was in this guy's arms and…

And why not enjoy it?

She was being carried by her husband. The thought should have been overwhelming, it should have been enough for her to fight to be put down, to retreat to the place where she always retreated, her own head, her only place of refuge.

But oh, the way she was starting to feel. This was crazy, but somehow a tiny betraying sliver of her brain was saying, *You've dated before. You've had fun before. Why is this any different? You can surely enjoy this man, enjoy his body, take pleasure and walk away, as you've walked away in the past?*

The logical part of her brain was trying to yell a response— *No! You can't walk away. You'll be living with this guy for two years, like it or not. Don't be so stupid. What you need are barriers, so put them up now!*

But that betraying sliver was growing louder. *You've walked away before, no problems. You can do it again. Just for tonight… Just for now…*

He'd reached the shore but, instead of putting her down, he carried her further up the beach, to where they'd dumped their towels.

'There'll be crabs,' he told her before she'd even protested. 'I've already saved you from a groper, and I'm on a roll. A knight in shining armour. If I've saved you this far, I'm not about to let you get nibbled by sand crabs.'

And astonishingly she heard herself giggle again, and that betraying voice turned into a betraying clamour that was almost enveloping her whole brain. A knight in shining armour... How crazy was that, but this night...this man...this moment...

What was happening? She had no idea. All she knew was that something weird was taking over. This whole fantasy, this night, the moonlight on the water, this man's arms...

And when finally he reached the pile of towels and set her back on her feet, the fantasy held. She found she'd lost all capacity to step back, to move away.

And he didn't move back either. His hands were still resting lightly on her waist. He was smiling down at her, his gaze gentle and a little quizzical.

'Safe, Jodie love?' he said softly.

'I... Yes. Thank you for saving me from...a groper.'

'It's my very great pleasure,' he told her, and she looked up at him and saw his smile—and something inside her simply melted.

This wasn't what was supposed to happen. She wasn't allowed to feel like this. No!

But why not? What was she scared of?

Was she scared?

Somewhere, under the woman fighting an inner battle right now, was the Jodie who lived life on her terms. Who'd made decisions years back to call the shots. Who'd had the stuffing kicked out of her at fifteen—or even earlier, if she was honest—who'd had to live with the anger and emptiness caused by the decisions of others and had resolved never again to do... what was expected. What was demanded.

What was demanded, right now, was that she keep her distance.

The sensible voice in her head—the one she'd trained for

years—was shouting, *Stay away from this guy, don't let him near, keep your distance.* But this night, this fantasy, this man, they were all conspiring to allow another voice to build. The voice that said, *You know you want to. Who's to say you can't?*

No one.

Be sensible, the first voice whispered, but it was struggling to be heard. The second was drowning it out. Because of this night? Because of this man? Because of the way he'd carried her out of the surf, because of the way he was looking at her, smiling at her…respecting her wishes?

So many sensations had been building over these past weeks. The images of him in Al Delebe, doing such good. Seb, a man of such power, looking at her shabby little cottage and not raising any doubts. Yes, he'd live here, yes, he'd do what he could, but she knew it wasn't just for him. There was so much at stake, so much he could do for so many.

He was so…so Seb? Her mind couldn't find the right descriptors, but she must. She was fighting for logic but it was nowhere. After all the logic she'd used to agree to this arrangement, was her body suddenly deciding to capitulate?

Capitulate? It was no such thing, her inner voice was saying. She was taking power back, because right now she wanted him.

She'd had lovers before, of course she had—that disastrous adolescent fumble hadn't put her off for ever. Boyfriends had been transient, no strings attached. She'd enjoyed them. Sometimes she'd even fancied she'd loved them, but she'd always moved on. So why not this man?

Why not take this night, this time, even these two years and milk it for all it was worth? Why not…?

He was looking down at her, still smiling, but the smile was gently questioning. Seb. This man.

And in the face of that smile, the inner voices faded to nothing. The arguments were a muddled mess, to be kicked aside in the face of something far, far more important.

Before she knew what her betraying self intended, she raised herself on her toes, she looped her hands around his neck—and she kissed him.

And as her mouth met his, as his arms strengthened their hold, as her tentative kiss was met with a desire that said he felt the same, the last of her qualms dissolved.

She was being held close, cradled, skin against skin, wet, warm, filled with adrenaline, high from the day...

Wanting.

The voices could go fight among themselves, she thought with the last sliver of consciousness available for such awareness. This man, this night, this moment—this was all that mattered.

The fear could take itself right out to sea and disappear for ever.

One moment he was swimming with a woman who seemed almost afraid to look at him. A woman—*his wife*—who'd seemed nothing but clinical and businesslike as she'd organised a wedding that was pure fantasy, and then who'd stepped out of her fantasy clothes and moved on. She was a bride under contract for two years, a paid arrangement, a million dollars for a make-believe bride.

And then there'd been one groper, brushing a leg, causing her to jump, causing him to catch her in his arms, causing him to feel the warmth, the strength of her body, causing...desire.

But maybe there'd always been desire. He had to admit it. The first time he'd seen her, working professionally, a competent, brisk doctor, tired and frustrated with both him and his arrogant great-uncle, there'd been a frisson of something he'd struggled to understand.

Or maybe he did understand it. Maybe it was a feeling as old as time itself.

This was a no-frills woman, normally in shorts and T-shirt, now in a sliver of a bikini, with nothing to hide her essential essence. A woman who said what she thought. A woman who...

Who...what? He didn't know. He hardly knew her at all, he conceded, but he knew her enough to realise there were barriers that meant she kept herself to herself—that this wedding was purely business.

And this day, this wedding, had cemented that. Yes, they'd made vows, but he had enough intuition to sense that it wasn't Jodie making the vows. It was a front, a carefully orchestrated defence, a way of keeping herself apart.

But now... One sea creature brushing her leg...

No. It was more than that, much more. The culmination of what?

The straw that broke the camel's back? The analogy drifted across his thoughts. Was that what it was? A slow build of desire that culminated in this?

It was surely like that for him—only this was no straw. He too had built barriers—he'd had to. All his life, there'd been so much need. Even as a kid he'd had it instilled into him. *You can do good, Seb. We can do good.* But most of that good had been done by holding himself apart. Not needing his parents. Taking a back seat to their desire to do good.

He remembered getting appendicitis as a child, when his parents were about to leave on field work. He'd been handed over to another doctor on the team. 'Aaden will look after you, mate. We'll radio in tonight to see how you are, but you'll be fine.'

There'd been weird Christmases, carefully orchestrated, always in Al Delebe, where he'd been showered with gifts from his parents, so many gifts. And then, after a morning playing feverishly because he knew what would happen, there'd always been a serious talk with his parents. They'd used his over-the-top Christmas as a teaching tool.

'Seb, you have so much, and there are so many kids in the camp here, sitting with nothing while their parents wait for treatment. But it's your decision...'

Was it really his decision? Maybe it had been, but in the process, he'd learned about things being taken away.

Even his parents. He remembered one of the doctors in Al Delebe talking to him after his parents' death. 'You must be proud, Seb. They gave their all.'

So he got it, Jodie's barriers. They were rational, expected, to be encouraged. This fantasy wedding had been sensible. The plans for living with her, the organisation of his life, they too made sense.

This swim, though, had been a bad idea, fatigue, the emotions of the day leaving them open to...

Open to his bride being in his arms, him carrying her out of the water, feeling the warmth, the delicious curving of her body against his wet chest, the way she'd shuddered and then clung. The way he'd set her down and she'd looked up at him. The straw that broke the camel's back? The chink in both of their armour.

But, armour or not, it no longer mattered—it could no longer matter. For now, their defences had dissolved. She'd looked at him for that long, considering moment—and then she'd smiled and raised herself to meet his kiss.

And then there was only this night. This moment. This woman.

The kiss... Its power...

He was lost.

Or maybe he wasn't lost. Maybe this was where he was

meant to be. This perfect place, this wonderful woman.
His bride.

And for a moment he let himself think, he let himself believe...

Had he learned nothing? All those Christmases...

But they were in the past, gone. Here, there was only Jodie,
the feel of her, the taste, the way she was moulding to his body,
her breasts against his chest, her arms holding him, claim-
ing...her man?

His bride.

This was no fantasy bride, he thought as he held her close,
as he savoured the feel and taste of her, as the last of those
damned defences crumbled to nothing. The glorious golden
vision of a bride who'd made vows beside him this day had
been unreal and of no account. This was the real Jodie in his
arms right now.

This was...his true bride?

CHAPTER NINE

THEY WOKE SPOONED against each other in Jodie's big bed. There'd been no choice between rooms. Seb had furnished his with a single bed so he could fit a desk and filing cabinets into the room, setting it up so he could continue life as he knew it.

Only somehow life had changed.

It had been a real wedding night. Somehow, they'd made it home, laughing, stumbling, holding each other, but each sure of what lay ahead.

'Jodie, do you really…?' he remembered asking. He'd had to ask, but as they'd reached the house she'd turned within his hold and kissed him again, long, languorous, the heat within building to unbearable limits.

'I'm no virgin bride, Seb Cantrell,' she'd breathed. 'Rational or not, right now, I want you and I know what I'm doing. So…you?'

There'd been no need for him to answer, and now he lay with Jodie spooned against his chest, skin against skin. He could feel her heartbeat. He could almost taste the salt of her. Wisps of her hair were lying across his shoulders and he felt…

She stirred and suddenly he was remembering those Christmases. The memories were dumb, outdated, something to be forgotten, but instinctively his arm tightened around her.

To have and to hold… That had been in the wedding vows, surely. For two glorious years…to have and to hold.

Her eyes were open. She twisted within his hold and she was gazing at him with an expression he couldn't hope to understand.

'You look like the cat that got the cream,' she whispered, and he smiled and she smiled back.

'So do you,' he told her. 'Mutual bliss?'

'Yep.' She stirred and stretched, a movement so sensual that he had to fight to stop himself pulling her back in to him. There were things that needed to be said. Surely there were.

Oh, but he wanted her.

'Jodie...'

'Yeah, I know,' she whispered. 'Barriers. This wasn't supposed to happen, but there's no law against it, is there? To have fun?'

'Every night for the next two years?' he managed, and she raised herself on one elbow and gazed down at him.

'One night at a time,' she murmured and then seemed to force herself back to reality. He could see her face tighten.

'Seb, it can't be a real marriage.'

'Yeah, we're playing with fire,' he managed. 'An affair where we're held together for two years... What about things like...well, snoring?'

'Did I snore?' She sat up promptly and gazed down at him in shock. 'Did I?'

'No, but you might have. And so might I. Or we might discover we have different toothpaste-squeezing techniques. I've heard that's driven thousands of couples apart.'

'Seb, we're not a couple.'

'No,' he agreed cautiously. Where was this going? He had no idea. Married and yet not? Where was the rulebook? But then he said, almost before he could help himself, 'Jodie, is there any reason we can't be?'

'No. No!'

'Because?'

'Because I don't know you.'

'Fair enough.' He lifted his hand and traced her cheekbone with his finger—and saw her shudder. There was trouble in her eyes, but he also saw the flash of desire. All he wanted right now was to take her in his arms again, to sink back into the wonders of the night before, but there were boundaries that obviously needed to be adjusted.

'I'm a loner,' Jodie said, and he nodded.

'I can see that. So am I. We have no need to share tooth-paste. But can two loners manage to have fun as well as get on with their lone lives? Lone when we need to be, together when we don't.'

'How can that possibly work?'

'I have no idea,' he told her. 'But maybe we could try. And if it did end up that we wanted...'

'Seb, I won't have kids.'

There was a bald statement, seemingly coming from no-where, and it shocked them both. The silence stretched on. Jodie lay down again, but this time she wasn't touching him. They lay looking upward, thinking...what?

'Jodie, if we wanted to have kids, I'd need to ask you to marry me,' he said at last.

'You already have.' It was a whisper and she sounded... scared.

'No. My great-uncle did. He coerced both of us into this situation.' He took a breath, trying to think it through. 'He was trying to change both our lives, and maybe he's done it. But it was coercion, blackmail if you like, and we don't have to agree to blackmail.'

She hesitated and then said, almost reluctantly, 'I guess it was blackmail.'

'So we don't need to play his game. Yes, we've married,

sort of. Yes, we've ended up in bed, which is probably what he intended. But the rest...'

'He wants us to have kids.'

'Wanted. Past tense.' Her body was still touching him, but only just. A sliver of skin against his hip. Warm to touch. Enough to make a man want...'

But he had to take this slowly. Last night had been a time out of frame—part of the fantasy. Right now, he was in bed with a woman he sensed wanted to run.

'Where we go from here has nothing to do with my uncle,' he said at last, feeling his way with care. 'He doesn't control us. Last night...this...it felt...it feels like something we both want, not something he orchestrated. Is that right? You don't feel coerced?'

'Um...no,' she conceded, and he even heard the trace of a smile in her voice. 'Or, if I'm honest, maybe I even did the coercing.'

'Mutual coercing,' he said and grinned, and he felt himself relax a little. 'And that's the way it needs to be. Checking along the way to see if we're pushing boundaries. Honestly, one day I might want kids.' Did he? He'd never imagined himself with children. Why was he thinking of them now? 'But that's a whole future consideration,' he said hastily. 'With you or someone else. That's not part of our deal.'

'It had better not be.'

He frowned then and it was his turn to prop himself on one elbow and look down at her. The tone of her voice... 'Jodie, what is there in that to make you afraid? As if you think somehow I could persuade...'

'You couldn't.'

'I know I couldn't.' He didn't get this. Here was a vibrant, strong woman, accepting this situation on her own terms, and yet reacting with what seemed like panic. 'Jodie, is it the idea of kids that makes you frightened?'

'I'm not frightened.'

'Maybe that's the wrong word.' He was looking into her eyes and he was still sensing panic. 'But you're alone, and you seem always to be alone. I've asked you before… Has some guy hurt you in the past? Some lowlife?'

'No.'

'Really?'

'Leave it, Seb,' she said. 'My past is my business. If we were really married…'

'Even then I wouldn't push.'

'Good.' She closed her eyes for a moment—and when she opened them he saw the fear had been replaced by determination.

'Okay, moving on.' She rolled sideways and rose, standing for a moment, naked, beautiful, smiling down at him with a wry smile. He noticed a scratch running down the back of her leg but before he could say anything she'd grabbed a robe. 'Enough of the intense discussion, Seb. I'm hungry. Toast and coffee?'

'Let me make them.'

'Nope.' She shook her head, her lovely hair swinging out behind her. 'I need a shower and then I need toast and Vegemite and time sitting on the porch saying good morning to the morning. Separate breakfasts, Dr Cantrell. Separate lives.'

'So what about tonight?'

Dear heaven, she was beautiful. Breathtaking. It was all he could do not to reach out for her again.

'We'll let tonight take care of itself,' she said, her serene and confident façade in place again. 'But what happens under bedclothes stays between bedclothes. Our real lives are different.'

Did that mean…? There was a leap of hope.

But she was backing away, still smiling. 'I might or might not invite you to my bed again,' she said. 'Okay, based on last night's performance, the likelihood of it happening is pretty strong. But that's it.'

'And if I invite you to mine?'

'Every invite will be considered on its merits,' she said demurely, and then she grinned, once again a woman in charge of her world. 'There are no promises, Seb Cantrell, but I don't see why parts of your Uncle Arthur's crazy last will and testament shouldn't turn out to be…fun.'

She showered, standing under cold water, closing her eyes, blocking the noise of the last twenty-four hours from her mind, deliberately putting her mind into neutral. But neutral refused to happen.

She tugged on shorts and T-shirt, she carried her toast and coffee outside, sat on the front steps and considered her day, acutely aware that Seb was still in the cottage behind her.

Still in her bed?

What had just happened?

So much for separate living, she thought ruefully. It would have been fine if her new husband wasn't so gorgeous. If he wasn't so sexy.

If he hadn't made her feel like the most desirable woman he'd ever held.

Maybe he did that with all his women, she thought. With all his wives? The idea made her smile a little, but there was trouble behind the smile.

She hadn't meant this to happen, and to feel like this on the day after her mock wedding… It went against everything she'd ever promised herself.

And kids…

Where had that discussion come from? Why had they even talked about it?

Because she'd brought it up, she conceded, and once aired it had hung. A possibility.

Not a possibility. Oh, the pain…

She was playing with fire here, opening herself up to hurt, betrayal…

She was doing no such thing. She was still in control, she told herself fiercely. She could still call the shots.

But should calling the shots mean allowing Seb to keep holding her as he'd held her last night? Could it mean allowing herself to love him back?

Love? Where had that word come from? She'd meant hold. But even hold… To continue to hold him… It really was playing with fire.

But how could she not? The feel of him, the taste, the touch… The way her body responded to his. The feeling that… here was her home.

Well, that was crazy, she told herself angrily. She was a loner and she intended staying that way.

But, as if on cue, the screen door opened and banged shut again. Seb came out, carrying coffee. The veranda steps were wide and he sat just about as far away from her as he could— but he was still sitting on *her* step.

Go away. That was what she wanted to say, but she couldn't quite form the words. Which was just as well, she told herself. It'd be petty. What was more, it'd smack of fear—and who was afraid?

Why on earth should she be afraid?

And then a car pulled into the drive and Angus and Misty and the kids piled out, smiling and laughing. Their little boy was still wearing his Space Stars costume from the wedding. Forrest had been one of the leading kids in the pageboy procession. There'd probably be island kids wearing crazy costumes for months.

'Good morning,' Misty called, at eight months pregnant struggling to get out of the car. 'Congratulations, newlyweds. We have your gift.'

'Our gift?' Jodie rose, feeling thoroughly discombobulated. This scene was far too domestic. Too…close? And then she forgot about being discombobulated—or maybe discombobulation went up a notch, because Forrest was reaching back into the car and lifting out…a puppy.

'So how was the wedding night?' Angus, the island's senior doctor, was grinning broadly as he looked at the two of them. 'You want to tell us about it?' And then he shook his head. 'Okay, don't answer that, we don't want to know.'

'Yes, we do,' his wife retorted. 'Any details you want to share, Jodie, love, we're all ears.'

'In front of the children?' Angus grinned as he tried to frown her down, but by then all attention was on the puppy.

He—she?—was beautiful. Adorable. Chocolate-box cute.

A golden retriever? Maybe not, because there was a hint of something else, maybe a collie? The island wasn't known for pedigree dogs. Regardless, the pup was fluffy and golden, with huge brown eyes that were gazing out at the world with awe, and a tail that was rotating like a helicopter blade. Forrest was struggling to contain the bundle of wriggling excitement.

'Seb, this is Forrest,' Jodie said, introducing Seb to the kid holding the pup. She added, very, very cautiously, 'And who's this? I didn't know you guys were getting a puppy.'

'We're not,' Forrest said happily. 'This is yours.'

'Ours?' Why did something inside her feel as if it was freezing?

But Misty's smile was pure mischief. 'I know, you don't want commitment, but this is our wedding gift.' Then, as Jodie stared in stunned silence, she continued, almost as if this was no big deal, 'Well, we had to give you something. Our best friend and colleague getting married is a really big deal. When we got our Biggles you said you still didn't know how long you were staying, and you couldn't commit to a puppy. That meant you missed out on Biggles's sister or brother, which made us sad because we know how much you love him. Every time you come to our place, he's all over you. But now...'

She paused, grinning, looking from Jodie to Seb and back again. 'Well, you've told us the terms of your marriage. We understand it's a fixed term contract. We get it.' There was another pause then, while she seemed to focus attention on Seb's hand—still on Jodie's arm—but she forged on. 'So okay, it's only for two years, but why should you miss out on so much because your time's limited? We think Biggles and Freya... this is Freya, by the way...are bound to get on. Therefore...'

She paused again, as if gathering her words, but then continued on a note of triumph, 'So, at the end of two years, if you really both decide to walk away, if you haven't fallen in love—with Freya, I mean,' she added hastily, 'no pressure on you two, then we'll take her back. But she's from a Craig Mc-Conachie litter, which means there's a queue if you really don't want her. So, say so now and we'll give you, I don't know, a frying pan or a set of towels instead.' She paused and looked hopefully from Jodie to Seb and then back again. 'So, what do you say?'

A dog. Commitment. Emotion. No. Her heart screamed it. *No!*

But Seb had dropped her arm and was already moving forward. Forrest lifted the pup to meet him and Seb gathered the pup into his arms. And as he cradled the fluffy golden package Jodie felt...lost.

What had Misty said? *'If you haven't fallen in love...'*

She'd meant with the dog.

She didn't do love. She didn't love…anything.

But Seb was holding the pup—Freya. Freya was trying her best to lick every part of Seb's face she could possibly reach, and Jodie's friends were laughing and the look on Seb's face…

He was standing in the early morning sunlight, wearing faded jeans and T-shirt and nothing else. His dark hair was wet from the shower, his feet were bare, he stood wrangling his armful of ecstatic pup—and his face said… Love?

And with a moment's flash of intuition, she knew this was the perfect gift. She knew he'd fallen in love.

How could he fall like this? How could he?

Why could she not?

Because…

'You're not allergic, are you?' It was Forrest, nine years old and obviously worried about the way she was reacting. 'Miriam at school is allergic. She wanted a dog and she had to get a poodle.'

'She can't be allergic,' Misty told him. 'Have you seen the way she cuddles Biggles, and Biggles is an allergenic dog. Very allergenic,' she added darkly. 'You should see our sofa.'

'But do you want her?' Forrest asked, still looking worried.

And then, suddenly, all eyes were on her.

Everyone present knew that Seb was sold. He was still holding the pup, still trying to calm her down, but now he was watching her as well, his dark eyes questioning.

'Jodie, if you don't want her…' he said, suddenly talking only to her. 'She'll be a lot of work, Jodie, love, and I'll be in Brisbane three days a week. I think it needs to be up to you.'

And he got it, she thought. It was unspoken but it was in his voice, in his look. There was an understanding…

Or maybe not an understanding. He didn't know—how

could he—the pain that was always in her heart. None of these people knew the pain of loss.

This was a dog. Not a child. A dog!

Why did it feel so terrifying? As if she was facing a chasm and if she took one step forward...

And he'd called her 'Jodie, love'...

'Jodie?' Seb asked gently. He stepped towards her, still carrying the pup. For a moment she thought he was going to put it into her arms and she took an instinctive step back.

Everyone else was silent, not understanding but somehow... surely sensing how big a deal this was.

And then Seb put the pup down. 'Jodie, I won't do anything you don't want,' he reiterated. 'None of us will. I would love the pup—I can't disguise it. If at the end of two years you don't want her to stay here, then she can come with me back to the mainland. I think... Well, for some reason, things seem to be changing for me, all sorts of things, and maybe I need to make room for...other things in my life. And it seems Freya is one of them. So, once again, no commitment after two years, but if you want her for now...'

'I'll fall for her,' she whispered.

'I already have,' Seb said, speaking to her only. 'It's a leap into the unknown, but what's life if not a succession of leaps?'

And...he got it, she thought. He understood her fear.

How?

There was no way of knowing. All she knew was that she had a choice: back away...or leap.

And the pup was sniffing and waddling forward, finding her bare toes, giving them an investigative lick. Then she looked up, her big eyes seeming to implore, her tail wagging with hope.

Oh, for heaven's sake, what was there to fear in one pup? What?

And while her friends watched on, while Seb smiled his

smile, questioning but somehow understanding, finally, she reached down and scooped her up.

And as her arms closed on the warm, wriggling mass she thought—*Why does this seem more real—why does this seem more terrifying—than the vows I made last night?*

The feeling he'd had when he'd lifted the pup into his arms was almost indescribable.

All his life he'd been a loner. He'd been loved, though—of course he had—but… His parents had been passionate about their work, so passionate that his arrival had been a mistake. Once his mother had even said, 'We couldn't justify bringing someone else into the world when there's so much to be done.'

Once he was there though, they'd loved him to the best of their ability, but he'd had to fit into their world. He was minded by others as they'd worked. As he'd grown into someone who could be useful he'd been trained to help, but he'd been sent back to Australia to boarding school as soon as his health had interfered with their work.

For his parents, the idea of stopping, of spending time, what, smelling the roses, was anathema to them. As was the thought of doing something so useless as owning a dog.

Or loving a woman who couldn't advance his work?

Where had that thought come from? But it was there as he watched Jodie lift the puppy into her arms, as he watched the fear on her face, as he watched her expression almost crumple as Freya's wriggles seemed to transform into ecstasy.

This woman…

He didn't know her. She was a woman his parents would have castigated as wasting her time, not using her talents, not committing herself to the greater good. Part-time medicine. Surfing. Lying in the sun and almost aggressively batting away connection.

But there were reasons. He knew it.

He thought of the night that had just gone, the passion, the fierceness of her lovemaking. The aching desire…

What was driving her? What?

He had two years to find out.

What was he thinking? Of making this…permanent?

Why not? If he could persuade her to commit to his passions? If he could persuade her to care?

To care for him—or to care for the whole world?

Maybe she couldn't do one without the other. But if she was onside… He had a sudden flash of his parents, facing down obstacle after obstacle, fighting together for what they both believed in. With Jodie by his side…

It was too soon. Somehow, he'd need to expose the shadows in her past, somehow get past the rigid control that seemed to be holding her in thrall.

To make her part of his world?

It was far too soon, he told himself firmly, but as he watched her hold the pup—were there tears tracking down her face?— he thought, *Why not?*

And then he thought of all those Christmases past, gifts given and then taken away.

Was this something that would be taken away? Were his fears somehow shared by Jodie?

He didn't understand, but this pup was theirs, he thought. It was a shared gift, and maybe together they could fight for it. Even when this time on the island was over, they could surely fit a dog into a life of doing good. Maybe there was some way this could work.

His conscience needn't even bother him. These two years were set aside to build for the future.

And in two years, maybe he might even persuade Jodie to be part of that future.

CHAPTER TEN

HE WORKED TOO HARD.

They'd been married for three months and in all that time she'd persuaded him to take three whole days off.

One had been for Isabelle Grundy's funeral—an all-island affair, seeing the old lady out in style. One had been when Misty and Angus had introduced their newest addition to the island, a tiny girl named Alice. That had involved a naming ceremony and then a party—music, laughter and far too much food.

In the face of such joy, Seb and Jodie had danced into the night, inhibitions, cares forgotten, but that had led to the third day off. Seb's stomach had cramped during the night, he'd woken whey-faced, and Jodie had almost had to barricade him into the room to keep him in bed.

He wasn't well. There was nothing specific, but living in the same house with him, sharing meals, sensing his slight withdrawal and the way his face sometimes seemed to close... If he was her patient, she'd have packed him off to Brisbane to see a specialist physician, but he wasn't her patient.

If he'd simply been a patient she might not have seen any signs to worry her, but sharing her house—okay, sharing her bed—she was aware that things weren't right.

He'd been extraordinarily lucky to survive three bouts of dengue fever. She knew that, and she also accepted that long-term fatigue was almost to be expected. But at times he seemed…ill. He was careful with what he ate, almost to the point of hunger. There were times when he hurt. In a patient she might not have picked up the subtle signs. She might have accepted fatigue as a reason, but living with him, holding him…

Worrying about him?

'I've pretty much taken care of myself for over thirty years now,' he growled when she tried to voice her niggles. And then he'd added, as he'd seen her real concern, 'Jodie, the last bout of dengue hit me hard and I was warned recovery could take years. So, this is normal. It can be a nuisance—symptoms come and go, usually when they're least wanted. The way I see it, though, is that I can ignore it and get on with my life, or I can treat myself as an invalid until such time as my body decides to cooperate. Which, Professor Martin, head of tropical diseases at the North Queensland Institute, tells me would do more harm than good. I have regular blood tests, I'm monitored and I'm as good as can be expected.'

'So you have seen him,' she said, worry backing off a little.

'I'm all grown up,' he told her, and then, seeing the cloud of concern in her eyes, he'd taken her face in his hands and kissed her. 'I don't take risks with my health. But I love you for worrying.'

And that word—love—it did make her back off. She didn't know what to do with it.

They were now solidly established in the routine they'd set themselves. Seb worked three days a week in Brisbane but he took the ferry home each night. Jodie was working as she normally did, in the clinic on the island, doing house calls, surfing when she could, playing with Freya. Trying not to feel like she was constantly waiting for Seb to come home. Trying to tell herself she wasn't doing any such thing.

But even when he was home he was working, at his desk, on the phone, constantly driving himself. Sometimes he had to take extra days in Brisbane, spending time at Cantrell Holdings, struggling to understand a business he wanted to change.

He worked and worked—and stayed apart.

Except at night. At night they shared her bed and she loved it.

And that was fine, she told herself, trying to justify her pleasure in lovemaking that was possibly more than a little stupid in what was little more than a short-term arrangement. But the temptation was irresistible—to enjoy each other's bodies under the sheets, and during the daylight hours to be apart.

But, more and more, it seemed boundaries were being crossed.

But what boundaries? They were hazy, she conceded. Ill-defined. The two-year boundary was the only thing that had persuaded her into this situation, but Seb always seemed to be overstepping her admittedly indistinct limits. Like when she'd worried out loud about his health. He'd reassured her and then he'd kissed her, in broad daylight, in the kitchen, which was supposed to be neutral territory. And then he'd scooped up Freya—already a lanky juvenile—and hugged the pup. Like he wanted to hug her?

He'd used the word *love*.

It was worrying because he seemed to be savouring this situation. When he arrived back after being in Brisbane, he'd hug Freya, and increasingly he hugged her. Until she backed off. Which was probably stupid, but she was struggling with boundaries she hardly knew herself.

More and more, she thought Seb was acting like…he was hungry for family? It was a family, though, that only existed in the fragments of time he had left in his crazy schedule. He didn't want more.

He seemed to want a family, but only on his terms.

Well, maybe that was like her own family, she told herself. That construct had been on her parents' terms, a family to be wiped as soon as the rules were broken.

This one was to be wiped at the end of two years.

But still, as the months rolled on, as their lives settled into a routine she could deal with, she found herself relaxing a little. Housemates with benefits? That seemed okay. If she could keep her boundaries almost intact, well, the benefits were obvious. The way he made her body feel… The way he smiled at her and kissed her as they woke… The way he went out onto the veranda and stretched and seemed to soak in the sounds of the dawn chorus before another frantic day… The way he frowned over his laptop over breakfast and swore and sometimes admitted her into the overwhelming complexities of his life…

Then he'd head back into his bedroom/study or race to catch the ferry to Brisbane and she'd get on with her day, so there was no reason at all for her to feel different. Like there was a part of her that was starting to feel…grounded?

Like she had a home?

That was a crazy thought. It'd be gone in two years, she told herself, but still, the settled feeling persisted. And it grew, until she started to feel that something was changing, deep within. Something about the way he held her… Something about the way he made her feel…

And then, with this feeling growing stronger, one morning, when Angus was on call but things were quiet, when Seb had stayed overnight in Brisbane, when Freya was asleep at her feet after she'd taken her for an early morning swim…finally, finally, she sat down and started a letter.

Fifteen years ago, she'd given up her daughter for adoption. After an appalling birth, a time she only dimly remembered as a black hole of pain and terror, she'd held her baby for a whole ten minutes. Ten minutes and then she was gone.

She remembered feeling dazed, lost, helpless, and her aunt sitting by her bedside, spelling out the terms which had been negotiated by adults, her parents, the social workers, adults she didn't know.

'This adoption's through an intermediary agency, Jodie. The adoptive parents are required to report to the agency every six months, updating progress, but those updates stay with them. Because you're underage, your parents can access those updates for you, and you can access them yourself when you're of age, but there's to be no contact. However, when the child's eighteen, if she wishes, then she can approach you via the same agency. You might like to meet her then, if she wants to meet you.'

So why put out a tentative hope for contact now?

Why was Seb's arrival making her feel...as if she might have the strength to...just ask? To question her aunt's decree?

At fifteen, she hadn't had the courage to ask questions. She'd accepted what her aunt told her because she didn't have the strength to fight for what she couldn't cope with anyway. She'd had no resources. She'd had nothing.

And more, what she was left with, as Hali had disappeared into the unknown, was a shame so deep she could scarcely bear it. It wasn't her parents' shame she was left with though; it was her own. To bring a child into the world and then simply to discard her... How could she ever hope for contact? What if Hali looked at her with the contempt she deserved? What if she damaged the relationship with her now parents? Surely she had no right to try.

And so she'd built barriers, and she'd built them so carefully she'd thought they were impenetrable. But now... What was it about the way Seb held her, the way Seb hugged her before he left for Brisbane, that made her barriers feel like they were crumbling? All her barriers.

She didn't understand. All she knew was that for some reason she felt compelled to write—to the adoptive parents, via the agency.

I know this will seem out of the blue, and I understand if you and/or your daughter...

Her pen faltered over the words *your daughter*, but she made herself continue.

I understand if you and/or your daughter don't wish this, but if you could find it in your hearts to allow me to meet...

This was so hard. She crumpled the paper and tried again. And again.

Five attempts later, she had something that didn't make her cringe.

'Just do it,' she told herself, and Freya looked worriedly up at her and then nuzzled her hand. Like... 'We're in this together?'

'Yeah, you and me and Seb,' she whispered, and wondered why it seemed important—vital even—that Seb be part of this request.

Seb is not part of my life long-term, she told herself hastily. *But when he's holding me, within this makeshift marriage, I seem exposed anyway. So why not send the letter? And maybe, even if it's a blunt refusal, Seb will hold me in the night and make everything more bearable.*

Was that such a scary thought? Was she leaving herself far too exposed?

'You can do this,' she told herself out loud, but as she walked Freya along the beach track to the post office, she wondered whether she could try. In her relationship with her daughter?

In her relationship with Seb.

His gut hurt and it was getting worse.

Irritable bowel syndrome. That was what the physician he'd seen had told him more than once.

'Three bouts of dengue, Seb. I've never treated such a patient. Have you seen the list of drugs they used when you were fighting for life, in Al Delebe as well as here? It's enough to make your eyes water. I suspect the combination saved your life, but I imagine your gut's reacted exactly as it has. You know how long it takes for the gut flora to re-establish after even a short dose of antibiotics. Just give it time, Seb. And rest. Have you heard of rest?'

Yeah, right, as if he could rest. But he was sensible. He ate right, he took probiotics, he followed instructions…

Except rest. The legal complexities of taking control of Cantrell Holdings were enough to do his head in. Once the initial transfer had been sorted, he'd started transitioning to a leadership team to take the company in the direction he intended, but right now he felt responsible for everything.

He'd cut back on his media work as the face of the Al Delebe foundation. There was more than one reason for this. He seemed only to get voyeuristic questions about his marriage when he fronted the press, and he now had the funds to employ an excellent media team. But there were still mountains of foundation work to do behind the scenes, and he was damned if he'd give up his hands-on medicine.

His body was stretched to the limit.

The obvious thing to do would be to sleep solidly at night,

he told himself, but there was the rub. At night, Jodie let him close, and how could a man resist that?

He wanted her, as simple as that. The more time he spent with her, the more he knew that, though the marriage might have started as fake, he wanted it to be real.

Why? She was lovely, desirable, tender, funny, strong. Unbelievably, his great-uncle seemed to have chosen him the perfect bride.

But as well as her reservations—and he still didn't understand them—in his driven mind he had to accept that she was an indulgence. Time out from what really mattered. There was so much to do in the world, so many things he could change, and Jodie wasn't helping any of them.

That wasn't totally fair, he conceded. Without her agreeing to marry him he could have done nothing. Cantrell Holdings would have continued its path of ecological destruction. There'd have been no funds to continue the work in Al Delebe. Jodie had given him this.

But she hadn't…given. Not really. She'd accepted a cheque for a million dollars—heaven knew what she intended to do with it and it wasn't his business to ask. Maybe at the end of two years she'd leave medicine entirely and surf full-time.

He wouldn't be surprised. He was aware that she held herself distant, from her patients, from the islanders—and from himself.

Only at night did the rigid boundaries seem to crumble, but oh, the nights…

The nights where he sensed her longing to let go, to sink into him, to be…truly married.

How could he let that go in order to get the sleep his physician demanded?

He couldn't, but hell, his gut hurt.

CHAPTER ELEVEN

JODIE'S PHONE RANG at midnight.

She wasn't on call. She was, in fact, where she wanted to be more than anywhere else in the world. She was in Seb's arms, warm, safe, sated with loving. She was not on call, she told herself again, but Seb was already stirring, the ringing was continuous and she had to tug away.

Seb flicked on the bedside light as she answered, then lay back on the pillows, watching her.

He'd know this was trouble. Doctors' phones didn't ring at this hour except in need. Tonight, the after-hours calls should be directed to Angus's phone—he was officially on call—but the ID on the phone was… Angus?

This was definitely trouble.

'Jodie?'

'Yep.' She was sitting up now, the last vestiges of sated wonder falling away.

'A minibus has crashed.' Angus sounded distracted, and she could imagine him tugging on clothes as he spoke. 'Kids, camping at the end of the island. Overseas uni students. Seems they've been to the pub. I don't know who was driving—one of the kids? Surely not, but Les Irvine went home at the same time—he was at the pub too and saw them there. He was driving behind them and said the bus was weaving all over the road. He was already on the phone to Sergeant Cody when they went round the headland at Needle Bluff—and went straight over. Cody's on his way. Les is heading down the cliff now. He reckons there were maybe a dozen or more kids on the bus. It's fifteen, twenty feet down onto rocks. Can you come? And Seb? We're going to need everyone we can get.'

Seb was already swinging out of bed. Angus's voice had been loud and urgent, easily audible in the quiet of the bedroom.

A dozen kids. And she knew Needle Bluff. *Dear God...*

'We're on our way.'

The minibus had smashed its way down the rockface, landing on its side. By the time Jodie and Seb arrived, Les was already down the cliff. He must have seen their car lights and he shouted up to them, struggling to make his voice heard above the sounds of the surf.

'Track down twenty metres that-a-way. Jodie, you know it.'

Jodie obviously did. She turned to go left, holding one of the big torches they'd grabbed on the way out, but Seb gripped her hand, taking a moment to look down. To assess.

His work in Al Delebe had been mostly in the hospital, treating eye conditions, but medical facilities, medical help had been scarce. Often the team had been called to assist after accidents, or outbreaks of conflict, or any of the myriad disasters of a war-torn country. He'd therefore undertaken extra training in emergency medicine. He'd often had to deal with injuries far different to his specialist ophthalmology training, and some of those injuries had been dreadful.

And with that extra training, the DRABC code had been instilled almost as an instinct. Danger, Response, Airway, Breathing, Circulation.

Danger first. The moon was almost full. He could see, but he needed to know more.

'Tide?' he snapped. The minibus was on a rock ledge, and waves were washing up and over, already reaching the up-turned bus.

And Jodie, who'd been tugging away from his hand, took a moment to think.

'It's coming in.'

'How fast?'

Jodie knew these waters, and how fast the tide was rising was vital knowledge in how much time they had to get the kids out. As they watched, they could see a kid struggling out through the smashed front window. Les was helping. There were already four kids out of the bus, sitting dazedly on the rocks.

'Maybe half an hour before it's in the bus,' she managed, and then caught herself and focused. 'No. The wind's from the south and it's building. Maybe less. And it'll take half an hour at least to get help from the mainland.'

'Then we get 'em out regardless,' he said grimly, feeling sick. If kids were trapped inside, knowing the tide was rising limited their options.

'Misty's rounding up locals,' Jodie told him. Angus had barked information to her before they'd ended the call. With a newborn and two other kids, Misty could hardly help, but she'd know the right islanders to call, the right emergency services on the mainland to contact. Angus had told her he was grabbing equipment from the clinic on his way, but for now Seb and Jodie were on their own.

Seb took one last glance down at the bus, using this higher vantage point to get a clearer idea of what they were facing. His hand tightened on Jodie's—but suddenly the hold became a hug. Fast but fierce. And then he moved on.

'We can do this,' he said simply. 'But the way the bus is lying... Why aren't more kids out? We might need to smash our way in to free them.' He took a swift glance around the area where they'd parked and grabbed a couple of thick pieces of timber from the undergrowth. He handed one to Jodie. 'Grab your bag,' he told her. 'Let's go.'

What followed was a nightmare. Sobbing, wounded—drunk?—kids seemed to have packed the minibus to capacity. By the time they reached the rock ledge, Les had six of them out through the smashed front windscreen. They seemed to be almost incapable of getting out themselves, with some, maybe the most wounded, blocking the way of others. But as Jodie stared in consternation at the scene before her, trying to figure where to start, Seb was suddenly in charge.

He'd held her up before they'd started down the track, and her instincts had screamed that they were wasting time. But as soon as they reached the bus he did a fast walk around, and now it seemed he had a plan. His voice reached out, not a yell, more like a sonic boom, sounding over the sobbing, the cries from inside the bus, the surf.

'Listen up. This is Dr Cantrell, Emergency Rescue.' That sounded official, Jodie thought, but she knew why he'd said it. These kids needed assurance that there were people in charge, people who knew what they were doing.

'We're coming in to get you out, but we need to break the rear window,' his booming voice continued. 'There's damage blocking it from opening so we need to smash it.'

He was playing his torch around the bus as he called, checking there was no one trapped underneath. Jodie did the same. Les had been helping kids out through one of the front windows, the only one that seemed both smashed and accessible, but now Seb's torch focused on the rear.

'We're about to break open the rear window,' he called, still in that amazing voice. Where had he learned to do this—it seemed loud enough to be heard from one end of the island to the other! But there was no panic behind it. 'Those still in the bus, turn away from the rear, and if anyone's trapped, I want them protected. I want faces covered from any debris coming in. Use your bodies if you must, to protect yourself and others. Right, everyone keep absolutely still. Now!'

Then he grabbed the stick Jodie was holding and handed it to Les. 'Sorry, love, but Les is stronger. You change to front window duty, helping anyone who can still access there.' His voice rang out again. 'Back window clear?'

'C-clear.' It was a quavering voice from within the bus, full of terror.

'Then hold still, everyone, and we'll clear a way to have you all free.'

There'd been thirteen kids on the bus. They got twelve of them out and, thankfully, among the kids being helped out of the wreckage, there seemed no critical injuries. There were lacerations, many of them deep. There were fractures. All these kids would need to be checked for internal damage, but for now there were no fatalities, and hopefully no injuries that meant death was likely.

By the time the twelfth kid was freed, Angus, Martin and as many capable islanders as Misty had been able to contact had joined them on the ledge. Floodlights were being set up and there were enough helpers to make the ledge crowded. It was growing even more crowded because the water was washing in.

Angus, Jodie and Martin were working as swiftly as they could, checking airways, stemming bleeding, trying to keep injured kids still, trying to calm rising hysteria. The least injured kids were being helped up the cliff, out of the range of the water. The tide was coming in at such a rate now, though, that the more seriously injured would need to be moved.

They needed choppers, stretchers, airlifts. They needed an army.

But in the minibus Seb needed a miracle. Someone other than him. There was one kid still in the van. One kid still trapped and the water was rising.

A girl. Eighteen? Nineteen? Trapped by the arm.

Cody was in the bus with him, the local cop, big, burly seemingly unflappable, following Seb's directions. Both of them were trying to ignore the rising water as they tried to shift crushed seats, struggling against whatever was holding the girl trapped. She seemed to be drifting in and out of consciousness, moaning for her mum, crying with pain and fear in her moments of consciousness.

Finally, the mangled seat that had been blocking their ability to figure what was holding her came away in Cody's hands. And Seb saw why they hadn't been able to tug her free.

Somehow, her arm was through the window. Trapped under the crushed side of the bus? *Dear God...*

Another wave washed through, two inches deep, maybe more. Another.

The girl's face was lying on metal. They couldn't lift her. They couldn't...

'We gotta lift the bus.' Cody's voice was grim as death, but Seb wasn't listening. He was lying full length on the metal frame of the bus, playing his torch over the trapped arm.

And what he saw... He felt sick. He pulled back, just a little but far enough so he could speak, softly but urgently, to the cop.

'Mate, it's half amputated already, and trying to move the bus—a team out there trying to lift, rocking it, the mess, the broken glass—if it slams back we'll kill her. We need airbags to slowly lift the whole bus, but there's no time, and all to save an arm that looks crushed beyond repair.' He took a deep breath, faced the inevitable—and then he moved on.

'Right. I need Jodie in here. Angus won't fit where I need him to be—Jodie's smaller.' He gave a mirthless laugh. 'Also, the last thing Jodie's scared of is a bit of seawater. I suspect even if we're submerged she'll just hold her breath and keep going. I'll need her for the anaesthetic. Tell her what's happening—between them, Angus and Jodie'll figure what I need.' And then, as another wave washed in, he said, 'Tell 'em fast.'

She wasn't an anaesthetist. She wasn't trained for this sort of crisis. Was anyone?

It seemed Seb was.

Anaesthetising a severely injured patient while lying in a wash of water among the chaos of a smashed bus was the stuff of nightmares, but Seb gave Jodie no time to indulge in fear.

'I've worked in a war-torn country for most of my life,' he told her simply. 'I'm no surgeon but I've faced this before.'

Part of her was horrified, but she didn't have time to ask more. From the moment she crawled through the chaos of twisted metal to reach him, he acted as though they were in Theatre already, scrubbed, ready to go. His calm voice implied this was normal, nothing out of the ordinary. His instructions were crisp, imbued with authority—infinitely reassuring in a situation that was anything but.

Before she'd crawled into the bus, she and Angus had done a fast think-through of what they'd need. There'd been no directions from Seb apart from that one passed-on order: 'Tell Jodie I need her as an anaesthetist for an amputation. Tell her I need everything.' Then Seb had simply assumed their competence, assumed the tools, the drugs he'd need would be there. And as she manoeuvred herself into the tiny space she needed to be in if she was to be of any use, as she tugged the bag of gear in after her, she thought he was assuming she was simply part of a team skilled in this sort of crisis.

Had he slipped back into war-torn Al Delebe?

But thank God for that, she thought, as she organised lights, a place to store the instruments they'd need out of reach of the water, as they talked fast and quietly of anaesthetic and risk. Of all the people to have...

She had a sudden flash of Seb as a kid. Living in a country where this sort of thing happened all the time.

They were working in a wash of seawater. Outside were the sounds of continuing chaos—the surf, the shouts of rescuers, the sobs of frightened kids. She could hear a helicopter above, maybe circling, trying to find a place to land.

Maybe a chopper would hold someone more qualified than her to help, she thought as the anaesthetic took hold, but then Seb's voice cut through.

'Ready? Block everything out, love, there's only this.'

And there was.

There was only Seb, and oh, thank God for him. The operation was appalling but they were fighting to save a life and there was no choice.

She couldn't have done it. She wouldn't have the skills, she wouldn't have the courage. But the alternative was to let the girl die.

And it seemed she did have the skills, or enough of the skills to support Seb's surgery. He simply assumed she was up for it—and maybe that was because he had no choice. She was all he had.

I'm all he has...

And at some time during that dreadful interlude, the phrase started echoing in her head.

She was all he had.

Right now, it was true, but it wasn't just now. He'd used her to prevent Cantrell Holdings continuing its path of ecological destruction. He'd used her to keep the team in Al Delebe functioning.

And more.

He'd used her body to comfort him, to warm him, to give him strength when so many depended on him, when the weight of responsibility must seem almost impossible.

And now...the way he was working, the skill, the assurance, told her that horror had been part of his life. For ever?

And then she thought, what a privilege to be part of it. What a gift to be a partner to this man. To be a...helpmeet.

Helpmeet. The word was old-fashioned, used in the past in an almost derogatory sense. A man and his helpmeet.

This was her turf, though. Her island. This bus crash was her responsibility.

So, right now, she was a woman with a helpmeet.

She was working swiftly, handing implements, swabbing, making sure the lights were in the right place, adjusting her head lamp, the torches, to make sure his focus was where it needed to be. Working as hard as he was, doing the work of a team of theatre staff.

But no, she thought. She wasn't working as hard as he was. She didn't have the skills to save this girl. He had the skills— and the opportunity, she conceded—to save so many.

And when finally he pulled back, using his strength to pull the girl free, leaving the mangled arm where it lay, but finally able to hold her head above the rising water, when he said, in a voice that was curiously detached, 'Right, let's get her out of here,' she felt a wave of something so powerful she almost forgot to breathe.

He'd done this thing, but he'd done so much more besides. So much before.

And with that thought came more. She'd held herself back because she was afraid to commit. She'd held herself apart. Why?

She thought of the solitude of his life and she thought solitude had been her god. Was she utterly, totally selfish? Was she crazy?

She wanted to reach for him now, to hold him, to take the strained look from his face, to take as much of his burden as she could from his shoulders.

She couldn't—of course she couldn't. All she could do was back out of her crawl space, clamber out of the wreckage, leaving him holding his patient out of the water.

Outside there was chaos but it seemed the chaos was organised. There were paramedics from the chopper—they must finally have found a place to land. There were so many more. They were treating injured kids, but as she emerged, they all stilled. They'd been waiting for Seb—to save a life?

'He's done it,' she croaked, and her voice didn't come out right. There were so many emotions. 'She's free. If you could get the stretcher in there...'

And then Angus stepped forward and gave her a fierce hug—and she took it with relief and hugged back. She needed a hug.

She was a loner. She'd always been a loner. But right now the concept of being a loner seemed ridiculous. Seb was still in the bus, still working, still intent on saving a life. All around her were islanders, paramedics, a team of people all intent on doing just that.

No man is an island...

It was a quote from a poem. Donne, she thought, almost hysterically, and she remembered learning it in school as a fourteen-year-old, just before...just before Hali.

And then, after the drama, the pain, the fear surrounding

the birth of her little girl, she remembered thinking of the same quote and deciding the poet was wrong.

No man is an island...

So now...she hugged Angus back and she thought, *Maybe Donne had it right all along?*

CHAPTER TWELVE

WHO KNEW WHAT the time was?

Who cared? She woke and sunbeams were streaming over the bed. It must be late, she thought dreamily, but it was more than late when she'd finally slept. The first rays of dawn had been creeping over the island as the last of the kids had been loaded onto the third medevac chopper and sent on their way to Brisbane.

There'd been no fatalities. There'd been broken bones, lacerations, things that would heal.

Or things that wouldn't. One lass would be facing a future without her left arm. Months of rehabilitation. A life that was changed for ever.

As was hers.

Instinctively, she reached out for Seb. Her bed had become their bed, a shared space where their precious independence had been put aside. What independence? It had been an illusion, she thought as the emotions, the self-knowledge of the night before flooded back.

'Seb,' she whispered and turned to touch him.

He wasn't there.

Blearily, she opened one eye and checked out the bedside clock. Eleven. Eleven?

Yikes.

Monday. It was Monday, she told herself. Monday was one

of Seb's Brisbane days. Seriously, would he have risen at six and caught the ferry to the mainland? Was he so driven?

And once again the thought of his overwhelming responsibilities swept over her. How could one man keep on with such a load? And be alone.

Right now, she felt alone. She wanted him…here.

She just wanted him.

What was happening in the outside world? It felt surreal that she was lying in bed, soaking in the sunbeams washing over the bed, while Seb was somewhere in Brisbane—what, operating? Did he have a surgical list today? Or at one of his interminable company meetings as he struggled to get the control he needed?

Meanwhile, his wife lay in bed and thought, *Angus is rostered on for clinic this morning, and Misty will still be able to back him up if there's trouble. I can lie here for a while longer. Maybe I can go catch a wave?*

No. It felt deeply wrong.

Her whole life felt out of kilter.

Confused, she flung back the covers and headed out to the kitchen. And paused.

Usually, Seb had a fast breakfast before he headed out. This little house didn't run to a dishwasher, so he'd rinse his dishes and leave them on the sink. Also, he'd feed Freya and let her out.

But there were no dishes on the sink and Freya was still on her bed by the stove. She wriggled her welcome as Jodie appeared, and then headed for the door. Fast. It seemed she'd been holding on. How early had Seb left? He must have been running for the ferry.

Jodie let her out. A letter lay on the veranda. Mail. Every islander would be doing what they could this morning, she thought, picking it up. Dot must have delivered this, thinking to spare her the walk down to the post office to collect it.

One letter. Formal. Buff envelope, almost the type a legal firm might send.

She double-checked the address, thinking legal letters were surely Seb's domain, but it was definitely hers. She sat on the back step, gave Freya a hug as she raced up for a pat and then slit the envelope.

Dear Ms Tavish
We're writing on behalf of the child you gave up for
adoption on the…

Her heart seemed to just…stop. Her eyes were already starting to blur. She swiped unwanted, surely unnecessary, tears away with the back of her hand, and forced herself to read on.

It appears that Hali is eager to meet you, and her parents have signified their willingness to get in touch. If you're agreeable they've suggested a possible meeting.
There's no compulsion for you to agree to this, and if this raises concerns for you we suggest you get in touch with our counsellor on…

For long, long minutes she stared down at the parchment, almost as if she was afraid it might disintegrate in her hand.

Hali. Her Hali.

Oddly, the joy that suffused her first and foremost was that they hadn't changed her name. She was still…her Hali?

Freya was now turning mad puppy circles in front of her, anxious to share her morning ritual—a piece of toast? But that was Seb's job, or rather Seb's pleasure. A vet would have frowned him down—dogs shouldn't eat human food—but

Seb had just laughed. 'Aren't we lucky there's no vet on the island, hey, Freya?'

Seb. She rose and went inside to put bread in the toaster, but her mind was in overdrive. This letter. She wanted—no, she *needed* to show Seb. She wanted to share.

Maybe she could go to Brisbane. Find him.

She had a sudden vision of seeing Hali…together? She'd need courage and Seb could…would…give her courage.

Why would she need him?

Why *did* she need him?

She turned back to read the letter again, and there was such a jumble in her mind that she could hardly take it in. The emotions of the night before. The way Seb had held her when they'd finally showered and fallen into bed—they'd been exhausted beyond belief but still he'd held her. She'd gone to sleep in his arms, the nightmares of the night receding.

But she was a loner. Wasn't she?

What a lie.

And suddenly she found herself kneeling and hugging the big puppy tight, holding her as if her life depended on it. Confused but game, Freya did her canine best to hug back.

She'd never let anyone close. She'd never even let her dog close.

But why?

'Stupid, thy name is Jodie,' she whispered, thinking of the exhaustion on Seb's face, thinking of all he was facing, thinking of…her helpmeet.

Her lover.

Her husband.

'I need to find him,' she told Freya and rose but, to Freya's disapproval, she didn't move across to the bench to fetch the toast. Instead, she headed for the bathroom. She needed to dress. If she had to go to Brisbane to find him then so be it.

'Toast'll have to wait,' she called back over her shoulder. 'Sorry, Freya, love, I need to find…my other love.'

And then she tugged open the bathroom door—and there he was.

Seb.

He was slumped on the bathroom floor. Unconscious. Lying in a pool of blood.

Dear God…dead?

He wasn't dead. Those first frantic seconds as she knelt, as she fought to find a pulse, as panic almost overwhelmed her, would live with her for ever.

What…? How…?

Think. As she found his pulse, thready but racing, as she realised life was still there, she had to fight with everything she possessed to put herself in doctor mode. What she wanted to do was to tug him into her arms and wail. Somehow, she managed to sit back, force back panic and assess.

Blood. He'd been vomiting blood? Bright blood, fresh. He hadn't been here for long then. But so much blood.

Dear God, what?

Instinctively, she was clearing his airway, tugging him into recovery position, her mind racing.

What? What?

Vomiting blood. Stomach ulcer? Malignancy? Oh, God, the fear of that.

Don't go down that path, she told herself, panic surging again.

He looked ashen. Grey. How much blood had he lost?

Far too much.

She needed help. Now. Angus. Misty.

It took every shred of strength she had to get off the floor and run.

Freya met her at the door—she'd been promised toast and she wasn't a dog to forget. Get her outside. She grabbed the toast, opened the back door and hurled it into the backyard. Two slices—more than a dog could possibly hope for—but as Freya bounded after the toast she paused, just for a second, to look back. Almost as if she was figuring there was something else a dog should do. Something was wrong?

And Jodie gave an almost hysterical laugh. She had her phone and was already waiting for Angus to answer.

'Jodie?'

'It's Seb.' She wasted no words. 'Possible gastric bleed. Massive blood loss. Unconscious. I need help. Medevac but blood. Do we have plasma expander?'

There was a sharp intake of breath. 'We used it all last night,' he told her. She could hear Misty in the background, her voice sharp with concern.

'I guess… IV saline…' Her mind was refusing to work. With this much blood loss, if they didn't restore pressure… No, that was unthinkable.

And then Misty was on the line. 'Jodie, Angus is grabbing gear and he's on his way. I'll ring Brisbane and organise medevac. Ben Roberts and Sylvia and Donna Marchant are O negative and Martin'll dredge up records to see if we have more. Universal donors—I know they'll help and we can do it faster than it'll take medevac to arrive. We'll call them in now. Go back to him and hold on.'

What followed was the worst few hours of Jodie's life.

What followed was the realisation of just how deeply, how completely, how absolutely she loved him.

When she thought she might lose him.

The IV lines weren't enough. Mere fluid wasn't enough to increase blood pressure for long, and for a few appalling minutes it became almost unrecordable. For those awful minutes she expected the worst at any minute—that Seb's heart would simply fail.

How long had he been there? Why hadn't he called her? He must have felt appalling, must have had the strength to get to the bathroom.

He hadn't woken her because...

Because he was a loner? Or because she was. Because she'd made it absolutely clear they didn't depend on each other, that they stayed apart.

Oh, God, how long would help take to arrive?

She and Angus were fighting with everything they had. How long before the medevac chopper could arrive with life-saving blood expander? How long before they could get him to Brisbane? How long before skills were needed that neither she nor Angus possessed?

But then, before she thought it possible, Dot, the postmistress, was calling from the kitchen, 'Blood—Misty and Martin have a queue at the clinic lined up to donate. This is the first but they'll have more. We're bringing it in as it comes.'

Jodie went into the kitchen to receive it—it seemed more important to her that Angus stayed, because surely he was more skilled than she was. Surely someone had to be.

And as Dot handed her the bag she looked at Jodie, blood-stained, white-faced and grim, and she reached out and gave her a hug.

'He'll be fine, love,' she said in a voice that was none too steady. 'Seb has the whole island behind him, and so do you. Every single islander's wishing they were O negative now. You're not alone, girl, and if people power means anything, then he'll be just fine.'

CHAPTER THIRTEEN

Seb woke and he was surrounded by tubes, by lights, by beeping machines, by glowing screens. Where?

He'd been in enough hospitals to figure it out, though it took him a few moments. Intensive Care. ICUs the world over were terrifying places. There was no way they could be made cosy and personal. They were set up to save lives.

His eyes had flicked open for just long enough to take it in, but now he closed them again, trying to recall… Trying to figure…

Pain. Fear. Blood.

Nothing.

Someone was holding his hand.

'Seb?' It was a whisper.

Jodie. That was enough for him to force his eyes open again, fighting a fog that seemed to be trying to envelop him. 'J…' His mouth wouldn't work. His head wouldn't work.

'I'm here,' she whispered, and her face was on his cheek, her hair a faint whisper brushing his skin. And then the lightest of kisses—and a quiet sob.

Jodie was crying. What? He had to surface; this was important. Nothing was more important than Jodie crying.

But her hand was on his face, lightly cradling, her fingers on his lips.

'Don't try and talk, love. You're safe. Duodenal ulcer, a

bleed, a big one. But we…we got you here, to Brisbane Central. You've been in surgery. You're all patched up.' Here her voice broke again and he heard tears behind the words. 'You tried…you must have woken and tried…to cope alone. That's never going to happen again, I swear. Never. I'll cling like a limpet. Seb, I love you so much. I'll love you…for ever.'

It was too much. No, it wasn't too much. His eyes closed again because it seemed he had no choice, but somehow his hand groped and found hers. Fingers intertwined and clung. The feel of her…the strength of her…

For some reason, the years of bleakness were washing through him. A childhood where his parents had loved him but were so caught up in their careers, their passion for caring for others, that he had to be an outsider. Then the years of joining them in their care, of considering every other moment was wasted. The work, the passion, the time…

But now…this. Maybe for this moment he could just…

'For ever, Seb,' Jodie whispered, and her lips brushed his. 'I've made a vow and I've realised…if you want me to break that vow, I'll fight you every inch of the way. I love you, Seb Cantrell, and whatever it takes, I'll love you for ever.'

Doctors look after their own. Seb was a Brisbane Central specialist and Jodie was a referring doctor. She was therefore shown to a tiny apartment used for doctors on call. That meant that if anything happened—the merest hiccup—she could be with Seb in minutes.

But his body was so debilitated. For those first days, as complication after complication set in, even though he was barely conscious, even though there was nothing she could do, she hardly left his side.

For four long days his life seemed to hang in the balance. For days the haematologists, the gastroenterologists, the cardiologists were in and out, adjusting, working, doing their damnedest to pull him out of the woods.

Seb's normal treating doctor, the tropical diseases specialist, was there as well, efficient, clinical, but deeply concerned. And on day four, when blood counts finally started to stabilise, when his heart rate finally settled, when finally, finally the treating team was starting to relax, the man even apologised to Jodie.

'It's a trap,' he said grimly. 'The dengue fever was such a big flag. Polyarthralgia, myalgia, joint and muscle pain, plus ongoing fatigue, they're known long-term after-effects of dengue. Seb and I both know that, and we haven't looked any further. But the duodenal ulcer…after the treatments he's undergone, the effects on every part of his body, hell, we should have looked further.'

'And I'm betting he didn't ask you to look,' she told him, and fought to keep the quaver from a voice she needed to imbue with steel. 'He's been too busy. So, so busy. Well, that's about to change.'

'Really?' He eyed her curiously. 'You know how important his work is?'

'It's not important at all if he's dead,' she retorted. 'So that's my priority. To keep him alive.'

And the doctor's face softened. 'You must have been terrified. I'm so sorry.' He hesitated and then added, 'The doctors here have told me you've hardly slept yourself. You must love him very much.'

'Not nearly as much as I'm going to love him,' she said fiercely—and then she burst into tears.

And then, ten days after he was admitted, he was finally discharged. Into her care.

Misty and Angus came over from the island to help Jodie

take him home. 'That'll leave the island without doctors,' he'd
protested when they'd told him, but Misty had dismissed his
protests out of hand.

'Martin's there, but I think the islanders are too busy getting things ready to worry about getting sick.'

Getting things ready? He didn't understand but then, he
was still feeling dazed. The surgery, the ongoing treatment,
had knocked the stuffing out of him—or maybe the stuffing
had been knocked out of him a long time ago. It was only now,
when Jodie was watching every move he made, when he was
surrounded by a medical team that was not only skilled but
also deeply concerned about him as a person, that he'd decided
to let things go. To let other people worry.

To take the care and be grateful.

To take Jodie's love?

There was so much he still didn't understand. Jodie, who'd
stood apart from him for the whole time he'd known her, who'd
sworn she needed no one, was suddenly fiercely with him.

His wife.

She'd decided she loved him? In truth, he hardly knew how
to accept such a gift. All he knew for now was that it seemed
a gift without price. Unconditional. Absolute.

He'd figure it out in time, he decided when the daze of illness receded, when the effects of shock and drugs wore off—
when he got home.

Home to the island. Home to Freya.

Home with Jodie.

Leaving the hospital turned out to be almost a ceremony in
itself. He hadn't realised how many of the staff knew him, and
many of the team members managed to be in the corridors, in
the foyer, out on the entrance ramp as he left. He'd been offered a wheelchair, which he'd scorned, but he was grateful
for Jodie's arm. Very grateful.

He couldn't manage this alone.

And Misty and Angus were right behind.

'I've read your history,' Misty told him when he protested. 'How many things have you had wrong with you, Seb Cantrell? Angus and Jodie and I have decided to split your rehab. I'm in charge of exercise. At post-partum, our exercise regime should pretty much match. As of tomorrow, you and I both get to tie each other's shoelaces. How about that for a plan?'

He grinned and subsided, and now, as Jodie held him, as Angus and Misty followed, as the medics of Brisbane Central cheered his farewell, he felt...

That these were his people. This was his place.

His life.

The ferry felt the same. A place had been reserved for him in the front of the boat. The crew offered cushions, blankets and enough care to make a man revolt—but their eagerness to help couldn't be rejected. He allowed himself to savour it, and the emotions within grew and grew.

When he arrived, there were islanders at the terminal, hugging Jodie, not hugging him but clearly wanting to, hugging Angus and Misty instead. Hugging each other.

And then finally they were home. There were people at their front gate. Someone had been holding Freya. She was released and surged forward to greet them. Angus caught her before she jumped, but Jodie was on her knees, hugging the dog, eyes misty with tears.

'She's been staying with us,' Misty told them. 'You want her to stay with us for another few days?'

'She stays here,' Seb growled, struggling against tears himself. 'Home.'

Misty smiled and hugged the dog herself. Then she and Angus escorted them to the door, gestured them in, dropped their bags in the porch and closed the door behind them.

Home.

He stood for a moment, still holding Jodie's hand, trying to come to terms with a mass of emotion so huge he could hardly take it in.

'Home, love,' Jodie whispered, and he tugged her around and kissed her, a kiss that was long, deep, sure. There were things he didn't understand, things he needed to figure, but all he knew now was that she was here. His Jodie. His wife.

When they finally surfaced, he saw she'd lost the struggle with tears. She swiped them away and turned, seemingly overwhelmed.

'Oh, for heaven's sake,' she managed. 'The islanders have been here.'

He turned and looked. The little cottage looked super clean, super bright. Freya was sniffing round, obviously checking out new smells. There were containers on the bench—he could see cakes, biscuits in clear plastic containers. A massive bunch of flowers took centre stage on the table.

'Oh, my heaven!' Jodie walked forward and opened the fridge, and its contents almost fell out at her. So much love was being shown by so much food. 'There's enough for an army here. Seb, look!'

But Seb was distracted. There were a couple of notes on the table. One, a card, had obviously come with the flowers.

To Drs Seb and Jodie,
Please accept these as a tiny token of our gratitude for your role in saving our daughter's life.

Beth's recovering well. It'll take time to come to terms with the loss of her arm, but she accepts how appalling the alternative was. The doctors here have spelt out that alternative—and they've also described the skills needed to amputate in such circumstances.

Dr Jodie's already visited and made an offer of surfing lessons as soon as Beth's up for it. She says who needs two arms for surfing? And for some reason that's given Beth more hope than we can convey.

So, to both of you... There are simply no words to express our thanks.

'You've been in touch with Beth?' he said wonderingly.

'She was in the same hospital,' she retorted, her head still in the fridge. 'You kept sleeping. What else was a woman to do? Wow, beef bourguignon. That's dinner settled.'

Her voice was rough, almost embarrassed, and he thought, *Is she retiring into her shell again? Jodie?* There was so much he didn't understand.

And then he picked up the second letter. It was formal, typed. And before he'd realised it was addressed to Jodie, he'd scanned the first couple of lines.

Dear Ms Tavish
We're writing on behalf of the child you gave up for adoption on the...

It wasn't his letter. This was none of his business. He pushed the letter aside as if it burned, and looked at Jodie.

Who was looking at him.

And on her face...fear?

'I'm sorry.' She reached forward and snatched the letter, crumpling it. 'I didn't... It's just... Oh, the islanders will have seen it.'

'I'm sorry.' He hesitated and then said softly, 'Jodie, it's your letter, but I can't unsee it.'

'I didn't want...'

'Anyone to know you have a child?'

'I don't have a child.'

'But you...*had* a child?' His voice softened still further, sounding each syllable with care. 'A girl? A boy?'

'A daughter.' The distress on her face was obvious, a warring of emotion. 'My daughter. My Hali.'

'Hali?'

'It means the sea. Greek mythology. I was really into mythology when I was fifteen.'

'Fifteen.' He felt as if all the air had been sucked out of him. He was watching her face, seeing her distress, and feeling as if some giant jigsaw puzzle was suddenly assembling before his eyes. 'You had Hali when you were fifteen?'

'I don't want to talk about it.'

'Why not?' he asked gently and she shook her head.

'I don't know. I... Tea? Cake? There seems to be enough.'

'Tea and cake would be great,' he said gravely and sat and watched her as she collected mugs and boiled the kettle and then seemed to take a great deal of time choosing which of the cakes to bring to the table.

Sponge cake with what looked like raspberry filling and icing? Great choice. He sat and watched her slice and serve, but then hesitate. He had the feeling she wanted to run, but of course there was no choice. This was where they lived. This was their life.

And finally, she sat. And stared at the table.

The letter was still in her hand. Crumpled. She'd made tea, she'd served cake without letting it go.

'I suspect your letter's precious,' he said, feeling as if he was making his way through a minefield. 'You might like to put it away before you get raspberry cream on it.'

'I... Everyone's seen it.' Her words were flat, dull, filled with pain. 'I just... I'd just opened it when you...'

'When you found me.' The cake, the tea, lay untouched in

front of them. 'Jodie…a daughter. That's huge. Could you find it…could you find it in you to tell me?'

She closed her eyes, took a deep breath and then handed the letter over to him.

'You want me to read it?'

'I… Yes.'

He hesitated for a long moment, and then read and reread. When he looked up, Jodie's eyes were fixed on him, her expression unreadable.

'Have you had no contact?'

'I couldn't… I couldn't bear to. I had no right.'

There was so much behind that statement it took his breath away.

'Do you want to know about her now?' he asked tentatively, but he didn't have to finish the question. Her eyes blazed with such intensity that he knew. In that look…longing, hurt, need, the ache of a loss past bearing…

'Tell me,' he said, his eyes not leaving her face. 'If you can.'

She winced and stared down at the crumpled letter. 'Nothing to tell,' she muttered. 'Sordid little story. Kids on the beach late at night, a fumble in the dark that got out of hand, a teenage pregnancy.'

'At fifteen?' He closed his eyes. 'I can't imagine. Your parents?'

She gave a hollow laugh. 'I wasn't their daughter. I never had been, not really. They tried really hard to have a baby and then they had their daughter, Joy. She died at birth. So they adopted me but I was never… Joy. I was their duty. Everything I did…well, I just wasn't Joy.'

'Oh, love…'

She shrugged. 'Enough. They did their duty by me but we weren't close. Anyway, I was dumb. I didn't even realise I was pregnant—or maybe I did, I just blocked it out until I was six months gone when my gym teacher guessed and phoned my mother. And then…' She closed her eyes. 'I remember… I came home from school and she hauled me to the doctor and then there was this interminable weekend where they wouldn't even talk to me. They were…well, they were committed to a religion that pretty much told them I was a whore. So, on the Monday, instead of school they packed me into the car and drove me to Melbourne. To my aunt's.'

'Your aunt.' He hesitated, trying to think this through. Trying to imagine himself in her place. 'Hell. Was she good to you?'

'You're kidding. She was as puritanical as my parents. I was the fallen woman and I gather… I learned later that they paid her.'

'Oh, love…'

She shook her head. 'It didn't matter. I coped. I buried myself in my books and my…unreality. My parents didn't even come when…when Hali was born. A thirty-six-hour labour and then a Caesarean. And then, while I was still so fuzzy, there was talk and talk and talk, my aunt talking at me, about what was best for the baby, about what was the only course, talking about the disgrace I'd brought to my parents, and I knew I had no support, no way to keep her. I guess…there was just no one. So she was adopted and I was enrolled in boarding school. I never went home—my parents couldn't bear the shame. From then on, I spent my holidays with my aunt. There was nothing left for me but…but study. Oh, and surfing. I could catch a bus from my aunt's—an hour to the nearest surf but it was worth it. I was a loner but that was okay. No one judged me while I surfed.'

'Jodie!' This was like something out of a nightmare. Did parents really react like this? How could they?

Jodie's face said it was all too real.

'Afterwards, I tried to ask for contact,' she whispered, speaking almost to herself. 'But of course I was too young to push past barriers I didn't understand, too young to even know how to go about it, and the things I apparently signed...' She shrugged. 'By the time I realised I could fight it, I wondered what right I had to mess with a life I didn't deserve. But then... somehow...' She hesitated and for the first time she looked directly at him. 'A few weeks back it suddenly seemed like I might try again.'

And there was something in her face...

'Because of us?' It was hardly a whisper.

And her eyes filled with tears. 'Maybe,' she managed. 'Maybe I realised I didn't want to be a loner any more. Maybe...maybe I found the courage not to be?'

And then he was out of the chair, around the table, kneeling before her. Hell, he hadn't realised he could kneel. Probably it hurt—who cared, who even noticed? But he was cupping her face in his hands, searching her eyes, seeing...truth.

'Because of us?' he asked again, because it was so important.

'Seb, I don't want... I never thought... I don't need you.'

'Really?' he murmured and there was something in his heart that said this was right, this was true. And with that thought so much fell away. Priorities that had been instilled since birth.

Surely love needed to come first. Surely everything else could follow. This was Jodie.

His love.

'Then that's a shame,' he said softly, 'because I sure as hell need you.' He was looking into her eyes, seeing what he must have known all along. That this woman was strong, true, wonderful. This woman was a woman in a million. This was the woman he wanted to spend his life getting to know.

'Jodie.' It was all he could do to get his voice to work but this was important. So important. 'Why did you agree to marry me?'

'Because of your work,' she murmured. 'I knew how much it meant.'

'So the million…'

'It's already given away.'

'What…?'

'There's an organisation, set up in rural Queensland, supporting young mums, helping them keep their babies if they want. Giving them mothering skills. Helping with their continued education.' She took a deep breath. 'With my million… Okay, it's a drop in the ocean, but it's not only you who'd like to save the world, Seb Cantrell. But we can't keep on. *You* can't keep on. You'll kill yourself. Surfing saved me. What's going to save you?' She took a deep breath, swiped more tears away and took a deep breath.

'Seb, I love you. I've figured that out and it's…it's changed my world. But I can't watch you kill yourself with what you're trying to achieve. I've spent fifteen years not needing anyone. I'm damned if I'll…'

'Jodie,' he said, very softly now. 'Shut up.'

She tugged back a little, her expression changing. 'What?'

'I love you too.'

'You…' She shook her head. 'You can't. There'll be someone…more worthy…'

'You're kidding me, right? A woman better than you? A woman who's had a baby when you were too young to cope, but who's managed just fine. Who's faced down her parents' cruel judgements. Who's coped with love and loss, who's built a career, who's become a surfer with skills so extraordinary she even teaches. A woman who dives into rocky surf to save a geriatric megalomaniac without even thinking. A woman who crawls into smashed buses and helps me save lives. You're a…

what? You're a woman in a million.' He paused and frowned. 'Jodie, have you answered that letter?'

'I... No.' She was thrown off-kilter. 'I...'

'You received it ten days ago and it's lain on the table ever since. You ignored it...'

'I didn't ignore it. At least...' She shook her head, almost wonderingly. 'I forgot about it,' she confessed.

'You forgot the most important thing?'

'I... It wasn't the most important thing. You were dying.'

'I didn't die.' He grinned then, and everything was suddenly in its right place. He was kneeling before the woman he loved with all his heart. Everything else—his medicine, Al Delebe, Cantrell Holdings—they needed to fit around this, he thought, and it was suddenly a vow. It would take more delegating, more trust, more determination, but if he didn't have Jodie... if he didn't share her life as well as asking her to share his...

And with that knowledge came the certainty that he'd have to step back. Changing the world was all very well, but Jodie was part of that world.

No. Right now, it seemed that Jodie *was* his world.

'Jodie, will you marry me?' It was a simple request, said humbly, said with such love, such conviction that even Freya, nosing around under the table—she could smell cake—paused and raised her head to listen. It seemed the whole world was hanging on these next few moments.

'Seb...'

'Really marry, I mean,' he said, and there was urgency in his voice. 'You married me the first time so my world could continue. Now, I'm asking if I can be part of your world. Yes, the work I do is important, but surely it can be delegated. Part of that will mean sharing my life with you. And me sharing your life. Living on this island, meeting your daughter, training Freya, learning to surf—because hell, there's no way you can keep that to yourself, I want—no, I *need* to share that as well. It's going to be tricky. There'll be so much we need to work out, but if we can…for now, please, Jodie, will you marry me?'

There was a long, long silence. His hands were cupping her face. She was looking into his eyes and there were so many questions, so many answers, silently spoken in that gaze.

And finally, blessedly, wonderfully, she smiled, her eyes brimming with unshed tears.

'Yes,' she said, but her voice was muffled with emotion.

It didn't matter, for after that there was no need for words for a very long time.

A wedding. A man, a woman and two witnesses, or three if you counted a dog—Misty and Angus and Freya—but no one else. A simple ceremony in the island chapel, because it seemed that this time the vows needed to be made in a place where such vows felt sacrosanct. But these were simple vows, made to each other, with no need for priest or celebrant.

There were no costumes this time. No finery. The bride wore shorts and a simple white blouse. Her legs were bare, her hair free and flowing. The groom wore chinos and a casual shirt. The bride carried a tiny bouquet of wattle, picked that morning from their cottage garden. The groom had attached a sprig to his shirt.

'I, Jodie, take thee, Seb, to love and to honour, from this day forward…'

'I, Seb, take thee, Jodie, to love and to honour, from this day forward…'

These were vows meant only for each other. These were vows that would last a lifetime.And then, as Angus and Misty beamed mistily and held tightly to Freya, who was threatening to surge forward and show her own appreciation, as the flautist Misty had sneaked into the church vestry piped a simple, perfect version of Ed Sheeran's *Perfect*, as the vows they made echoed and faded into the walls of the sunlit chapel, Seb Cantrell and Jodie Tavish smiled at each other and then walked hand in hand out into the sunshine. To begin the rest of their lives.

EPILOGUE

IT WAS DONE. She'd arranged to meet her daughter.

After that first letter Jodie had written back, offering to go to her, to meet wherever they suggested. But, amazingly, Miriam and Bob Holt had replied saying they lived in one of Brisbane's outer suburbs and would love an excuse to take the ferry across to Kirra Island.

'Let's make it informal,' Miriam had suggested. 'We could bring a picnic, go the beach? Hali's very tense, but if she could tie in a swim it might help break the ice. She has a little brother, adopted four years after Hali, and they both love the sea. If they could play in the surf, make it mostly about fun, meeting you might not feel so nerve-racking?'

It was a good idea, but for Jodie there was no way the day could be anything but nerve-racking. But Seb was beside her and so was Freya. They'd checked to make sure there were no family allergies, but it seemed no one was allergic to dogs. No one was allergic to anything.

So on a gorgeous Saturday afternoon, a month after their true wedding, Seb and Jodie headed to one of Kirra's most beautiful beaches and settled down to wait.

They had offered to meet the ferry, but there was no way six people and a dog could fit in the beach buggy—maybe one day they'd need to do something about that? So Jodie and Seb had driven to the beach alone, and Mack was under instructions to collect and deliver…whoever came.

The taxi pulled up right on time. Jodie walked up the track to meet it—and came face to face with her daughter.

Hali. Fifteen years old. Blonde, skinny, freckled. Tall for her age. Trying to smile through nerves. Behind her were her parents and a kid brother, smiling nervously as well.

'I guess…you must be my birth mum,' the girl managed, because Jodie was clearly unable to say anything at all. And then she gave her a shy smile. 'I've wanted to meet you. We've all wanted to, for a long time.' She waved across to her brother, a gangly kid, all arms and legs. 'Josh met his birth mum when he was eight. She wasn't much interested though. Why didn't you want to meet me until now?'

Trust a teenager to get right to the point. This was such a huge question.

In her imagination, Jodie had thought this could take many meetings, maybe with a counsellor present, someone professional to unpack the emotional baggage threatening to overwhelm her. But she had Seb and Freya. Seb was by her side and his hand was gripping hers, warm and strong, and Freya was nosing forward, sniffing Hali, and Hali was stooping to pat her.

Miriam and Bob were standing back, letting their…their daughter…take the lead. Both of them were smiling.

And finally, Jodie found her voice. 'I didn't know how to,' she managed. 'Hali, I was so scared. I had you three days after I turned fifteen—that's younger than you are now—and I didn't know what to do. I… I didn't have parents who loved me. I felt alone and frightened and all I knew was that… I wanted you to have parents who loved you. Parents who wouldn't let you be alone and frightened. And Hali…until now I didn't feel… I didn't feel old enough or brave enough to follow through. I was so ashamed that I couldn't keep you.

That I couldn't care for you. I didn't even feel like I had the right to have a daughter.'

What followed was a long silence, where Hali seemed to take this on board and consider. Everyone seemed to hold their breath as Hali surveyed Jodie from head to foot—until finally she seemed to come to a decision. And, teenager-like, her decision was blunt.

'That's cool,' she said, and then she said tentatively, 'And my...birth father?'

'He was a kid too. I haven't kept in touch, but he knows about you. If you want, maybe we can figure out a way...'

'You didn't love him?'

'I was a kid, Hali. I didn't...' Deep breath. 'I didn't know what love was.'

'But you know now?'

That was easy. Seb was right here—and she was here for Seb.

'I do,' she said, and it was a vow all on its own.

But Hali was losing interest. 'Fair enough,' she said, but she was now looking around the cove. She saw the sea glistening through the palms, she saw the golden sand—and she saw Seb and Jodie's surfboards, which were permanently on the roof of their buggy.

'Do you surf?' she demanded.

'I do,' Jodie said again.

'I never have,' Hali said wistfully. 'And you?' She turned to Seb. 'Do you both surf?'

'I don't surf very well,' Seb admitted, and Jodie felt him tug her close. 'But Jodie's teaching me.' He hesitated, looking from Jodie to Hali and back again, then seemed to come to a decision. 'Jodie's the best teacher. If we can organise it, maybe she can teach you?'

'And me?' Josh piped up eagerly from the background.

'We're family. If you're going to teach Hali, then you have to teach me.'

'Fair enough,' Seb said, grinning, as Jodie's insides seemed to turn to mush. Was this what it meant for a heart to melt? And then, as Seb kissed her lightly, then released her to untie the boards from the buggy, her heart melted even more.

'I guess it's just the way things are,' he was saying. 'Family... Isn't it where we find it? And how lucky are we that we have?'

* * * * *

MILLS & BOON MODERN IS
HAVING A MAKEOVER!

The same great stories you love,
a stylish new look!

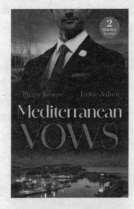

Look out for our brand new look
COMING JUNE 2024

MILLS & BOON

COMING SOON!

We really hope you enjoyed reading this book.
If you're looking for more romance
be sure to head to the shops when
new books are available on

Thursday 23rd May

To see which titles are coming soon, please visit
millsandboon.co.uk/nextmonth

MILLS & BOON

MILLS & BOON®

Coming next month

UNBUTTONING THE BACHELOR DOC
Deanna Anders

'Dance with me,' Sky said, her blue eyes dancing with a
fevered excitement that flowed over onto him.

He knew he shouldn't. This wasn't a date. They were
there purely as professional colleagues. Nothing more.

But as her arms wrapped around his neck, his own arms
found their way around her waist, pulling her closer. And
when she laid her head against him, he let himself relax
against her. What could it hurt to share one dance?

It only took a minute for his body to answer that question.
It was as if a fire had been lit inside him as his body reacted
to the feel of Sky against him. His muscles tightened and
he went stone hard. He tried to keep his breathing as even
as possible as they swayed to the music, her body rubbing
against him with each movement. He glanced down and
their eyes met. As she drew in a breath that appeared as
labored as his, his eyes went to her lips, the same lips that
had teased him for months. For a moment he considered
tasting them. Would they be soft and supple? Or would they
be firm and needy? He had just started to lean down when
the couple next to them bumped into him, breaking whatever
spell he'd been under.

What could one dance hurt? It could destroy his whole
reputation if he let himself lose control on the dance floor.

He pulled himself back from the brink of doing something that would scandalize the whole room with a willpower he hadn't known he possessed. But when the song ended and she stepped away from him, his arms felt empty. It had only been one dance. The fact that her body had molded so perfectly to his didn't mean a thing. But he'd danced with many women before Sky and he'd never felt anything like this before.

'We should go,' he said, though his traitorous feet refused to take a step away from her.

'Why? Do we have plans?' she asked, her voice soft and breathy. His body responded as once more she stepped toward him.

He wanted to pull her back into his arms, to kiss that mouth that had teased him for the last six months. Only he couldn't kiss her now any more than he could have kissed her all those other times. He had to step away from her now just like he'd done over and over when she had tempted him. He needed to put things back to the way they'd been before that dance. Before he'd felt how right her body felt against his.

It should be simple. One step. Just take one step and walk away. But this was Sky. Nothing about the woman was simple.

Continue reading
UNBUTTONING THE BACHELOR DOC
Deanne Anders

Available next month
millsandboon.co.uk

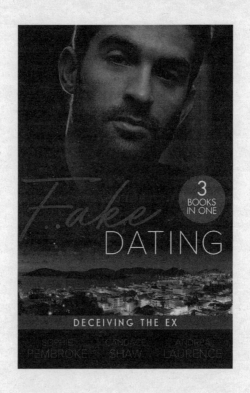

OUT NOW!

Available at
millsandboon.co.uk

MILLS & BOON